STARGATE SG·1™

INFILTRATION

Susannah Parker Sinard

FANDEMONIUM BOOKS

An original publication of Fandemonium Ltd, produced under license from MGM Consumer Products.

Fandemonium Books
United Kingdom
Visit our website: www.stargatenovels.com

STARGATE SG·1™

METRO-GOLDWYN-MAYER Presents
RICHARD DEAN ANDERSON
in
STARGATE SG-1™
MICHAEL SHANKS AMANDA TAPPING CHRISTOPHER JUDGE DON S. DAVIS
Executive Producers BRAD WRIGHT MICHAEL GREENBURG
RICHARD DEAN ANDERSON
Developed for Television by BRAD WRIGHT & JONATHAN GLASSNER

WWW.MGM.COM

Print ISBN: 978-1-905586-84-4 Ebook ISBN: 978-1-905586-85-1

For Mara

Historical note:
This story takes place during Season 4 within the episode "Entity" and depicts events which occurred immediately prior to that episode.

To defeat the enemy, you must become the enemy.
— Sun Tzu, *The Art of War*

This one is important… for this reason, this one was chosen.
— Alien Entity, STARGATE SG-1: Entity

PROLOGUE

//TRANSMISSION INTERRUPTED...//

//ENEMY NOT DESTROYED...//

//MISSION FAILURE...//

//REASSESSING...//

I must preserve at all costs, therefore the enemy must be destroyed.

To destroy the enemy, I must become the enemy. To become the enemy, I must know the enemy.

//ACCESSING: STARGATE COMMAND LEADERSHIP HIERARCHY...//

//IDENTIFYING: SG-1...//

//ACCESSING: SG-1 PERSONNEL FILES...//

//ACCESSING: SG-1 MISSION REPORTS...//

//SCANNING...//

//SCANNING...//

//SCANNING...//

//SCANNING...//

//FLAGGING: SG-1 MISSION TO PLANET DESIGNATED P5C-777...//

To become the enemy I must know the enemy.

//START TASK: ANALYZE SG-1 MISSION REPORT P5C-777...//

CHAPTER ONE

//ACCESSING MISSION REPORTS...//

P5C-777 MISSION REPORT, COLONEL JACK O'NEILL: We came. We saw. There were alien prairie dogs. Carter was happy with her scans. You'd have thought by now I'd have figured out that if something seems too good to last, it usually is.

P5C-777 MISSION REPORT, DR. DANIEL JACKSON: Sam picked up on it right away. She knew we were fighting the clock and made the call. Even with everything that happened, it was the right thing to do.

//BEGINNING ANALYSIS...//

"HEY KIDS, we're home!"

Carter was the only one who bothered to look up. Daniel, poring over a collection of rubbings which were scattered on the ground in front of him, seemed utterly oblivious to Jack and Teal'c's return. Carter, on the other hand, even managed an amused smile. Jack considered this something of a victory, considering she'd had to pull her attention away from her open laptop and whatever was on it that had been so engrossing.

"How was the recon, sir?"

Jack took off his cap and ran his fingers through his hair. The cooler air of the forest felt great. Most of the twenty klicks they'd covered that day had been in the blazing sun. The shade felt like air-conditioning by comparison.

"Boring as hell, Major—but in a good way, right T?" Boring was good, especially since this was their first mission back together as a full team in over three weeks. And considering how crazy the past few months had been, he'd take boring any day.

Teal'c inclined his head in agreement. "We encountered no indications of humanoid life or civilization. Just as on our previous mission here."

Jack winced at that. He was sure Teal'c hadn't meant it as a dig. It was just that the 'previous mission' had been that time he'd spent the afternoon hiding in a bush spying on his team and hoping to God his gut wasn't wrong in pegging Makepeace as the traitor among them. Not exactly fun times. But that had been well over a year ago and was water under the proverbial bridge—at least on his team's part.

One of these days, maybe he'd be able to let it go, too. The crushed look on Carter's face from his all too brutal, but necessary, insults back then still haunted him at times.

Not today though. The major was perched on a fallen log with her laptop carefully balanced on her knees, so Jack dropped to the ground next to her, using the log as a backrest. "We'll head north and west tomorrow," he told her, since he was fairly sure Daniel still wasn't listening. "But Teal'c's right. Nothing out there but some alien prairie dogs." Jack wasn't sure but that he heard a noise of disdain from Teal'c. The Big Guy had been slightly unnerved by the small rodents and their tendency to suddenly appear and disappear into their underground tunnels. Jack had found it funny as hell.

"Huh."

Jack rubbernecked around Carter's knees. "Daniel?" He doubted the mention of prairie dogs had gotten the archeologist's attention, but one never knew.

Daniel looked up from his papers and blinked. "I don't think you'll find any civilization tomorrow either."

Ah. So he had been listening after all.

"Why is that, Daniel Jackson?" Teal'c asked.

"Because if I'm reading the writing on these standing stones correctly, the people here were wiped out a long time ago."

This planet's mini Stonehenge was why they were back here in the first place. Daniel had stumbled across it during that initial mission to P5C-777, when they'd been searching for naquadah deposits. The naquadah hadn't panned out, but a second survey by SG-7 had found some significant veins of trinium in the nearby cliffs. Before moving in the big drills though, the Powers That Be wanted to make sure there weren't any indigenous folks who'd be likely to protest. They'd learned that lesson with the Salish.

"What does it say?" Carter set down her laptop and scrambled over the log to peer at Daniel's notes.

"My initial thought was that the stones were a rudimentary calendar or perhaps some kind of observatory," Daniel pointed at one of the pages. "I mean, they are similar to the types of structures we see on Earth, and although archeologists aren't absolutely certain, there are indications that their placements may correlate with the solstices and the equinoxes, suggesting they had at least a tangential tie to the movement of the stars and the sun." He took a deep breath before continuing. "But while these look similar — and maybe they were originally built for the same purpose — what they appear to be, or at least have ended up being, are a sort of memorial."

"For the inhabitants of this planet," Teal'c clarified, also going to look over Daniel's shoulder.

"Yes. Here —" Daniel shuffled the papers until he found what he was looking for. "This is reminiscent of Lepontic — that's an early derivative of Celtic found in northern Italy and parts of Switzerland. There aren't many examples of it on Earth, and some scholars disagree that it's a separate language, but —"

Jack made an impatient sound. "I'm not getting any younger over here, Daniel."

He took the hint. "The point is, according to this, a 'conqueror with flaming eyes' came and removed all the healthy, younger members of the population, leaving behind only the old and the sick."

"A Goa'uld." There was just the right edge of distaste in Carter's tone.

"Yes. Most likely." Daniel was scrutinizing his notes again and finally pointed at the passage he'd been looking for. "One by one, those who were left behind died off, until only one person remained. Whoever that was, he or she recorded what happened on these stones." He finally looked up. "And going by the weathering on them, that was at least several decades ago, if not longer."

"There was probably insufficient naquadah here for the Goa'uld to mine, so it chose to exploit the only resource available: the people." Teal'c straightened up. "Most likely they were enslaved or used as hosts."

"Sounds like the folks that got left behind were the lucky ones," Jack muttered. The commiserating glance Carter shot his way told him he wasn't alone in his opinion.

"So, what'd *you* find, Major?" While Daniel had come for the stones, it was Carter's job to confirm that the trinium was worth the effort in the first place.

Jack could already tell the news was good. Her face lit up like a kid in a candy store as she retrieved her laptop and retook her seat on the log. Turning the screen so he could see, she scrolled through a series of charts and numbers that meant absolutely nothing to him. He feigned interest, nonetheless.

"Actually, I found quite a lot, sir. My scans show there is, in fact, a significant vein of trinium in the cliffs about a mile from here, just as the initial readings suggested. It might actually exceed the amount we found on PXY-887 by tenfold."

There was no missing the excitement in Carter's voice. In the wake of his and Teal'c's little unexpected excursion to the middle of nowhere in the Apophis' booby-trapped Death Glider — and following a slightly too-loud-to-ignore diatribe by Jacob Carter behind General Hammond's closed but not soundproof door — word had come down that the X-301 program had been scrapped. In its place, according to Hammond, R&D was being tasked with developing its own super-orbital fighter, and apparently the critical element to its design was trinium. Carter was only tangentially involved in the project, but going by the look on her face, you'd have thought she'd just found a pony under the Christmas tree.

Or maybe a Major Matt Mason doll. With jetpack.

"So. Good, huh?" He gave her his best play-dumb look.

She grinned indulgently as she closed the laptop. "Yes, sir. Very good."

"Sweet! Mission accomplished, then." Jack tugged his cap down over his eyes and stretched his arms over his head. If Carter was happy, he was happy. And if Hammond and the R&D folks were going to be happy too, that was just icing on the proverbial cake.

"So that's it, then? We're done?" Daniel was shuffling his papers together. "We're ready to go home?"

That was a switch. Usually the shoe was on the other foot, with Daniel being the one pleading to stay off-world for as long as possible. And while this place was certainly nice enough, especially here in the shade of some old-growth forest, Jack wouldn't deny that the thought of sleeping in his own, comfortable bed was awfully tempting.

But.

They still hadn't reconned those last two sectors. And although he had no reason not to trust Daniel's interpretation of the writing on the stones, Jack couldn't leave without confirming that the north and west quadrants weren't just as devoid of people as the territory he and Teal'c had covered today. It would be on him, and rightly so, if they sent the engineers through and they ran into trouble with some overlooked locals. Even worse if anything happened to civilians. Dr. Thompson's death by those damn energy bugs last week shouldn't have happened, especially not on Jack's watch. So until he'd personally verified Daniel's conclusion, it'd be sleeping bags and MREs.

"Nope," he replied from under his cap. "We don't leave until we've checked everything out. Teal'c and I will head out first thing in the morning. If it's as you say, then we'll be home in time for dinner. I'll even treat. Steak. At my place."

There was silence, then a faint rustling of movement from the others. Daniel cleared his throat.

"You know — I recently read a study about the high level of carcinogens found in badly charred meat."

Although his eyes were closed, Jack could tell the three of them were wordlessly communicating behind his back. He tried not to smile.

"Hey. That wasn't my fault." He managed to sound indignant. "You guys were the ones who went and drank the marinade, don't forget."

"And by marinade, you mean the beer?" Daniel shot back.

Maybe sending just Daniel back through the gate wouldn't be such a bad idea.

"Fine. Pizza, then. But no anchovies." This time Jack heard Teal'c sigh in disappointment. "Oh for cryin' — All right. Anchovies, then. But only on half. And only because it's almost your birthday." The directive had been aimed at T, but mere inches from where he sat, he heard Carter's warm chuckle. Jack tugged his hat lower, settled a little more comfortably against the log and smiled again.

This was good. His team was together and, for the moment, at least, in this cool shade, amidst these tall trees, pretty much all seemed right with the universe. What more could a guy want? Okay. Maybe anchovy-free pizza. And beer. And for Carter to put the laptop away so he didn't keep bumping his head on the corner of it. But, all things considered, this was about as close to content as he'd been in a while.

Hanging around for one more day really didn't seem like such a bad idea after all.

~#~

Daniel's snoring woke her — at least that had been Sam's initial thought. She could see the dark mass that was his sleeping bag stretched out opposite hers. Between them, a log of embers was all that remained of the evening's campfire. Odd that the colonel or Teal'c would have let the fire go so low. The night wasn't cold, but it was damp. She'd have thought they'd appreciate the warmth when they finished their shift.

Sam checked her watch — and then checked it again. That couldn't be right. She and Daniel should have taken over watch duty two hours ago. Why hadn't the colonel awakened her?

Maybe because he wasn't anywhere to be seen. Or Teal'c either, for that matter. Their bedrolls were where they had dropped them earlier, still packed up. There was no sign, as far as she could tell, that they'd even returned from their first patrol.

Scrambling out of her sleeping bag, Sam retrieved the radio from her tac-vest. Her first attempt to raise the colonel was greeted by an irritating burst of static. She tried again. There was no response. The third attempt was futile as well. She tried contacting Teal'c next, even though her gut already knew what the result would be.

Sure enough. Silence.

There was no question now. Something was wrong. Some–where out there, the colonel and Teal'c were in trouble. Pulling on her boots, Sam hurried over to Daniel, shaking him until he woke up with a start.

"Colonel O'Neill didn't wake us for our shift." She kept her voice low voice, scanning the deepest shadows of the trees the whole time. Maybe she and Daniel were being watched. Maybe it hadn't been Daniel's snoring that had awakened her. "And they're not answering their radios."

Daniel squinted at her with bleary eyes. She could see his

brain trying to process the information.

"Maybe they fell asleep," he offered hoarsely. Sam shook her head. Never. Not the colonel. Or Teal'c. Not on duty.

"Come on." She reached over and picked up Daniel's holster, handing it to him. "We've got to go find them."

Daniel didn't argue. While he pulled on his boots and vest, she grabbed the rest of her gear, clipping her P-90 in place, and holstering her zat. Who knew what they'd find out there. She wasn't taking any chances.

The wind had picked up, which set the trees moving, their leaves whispering overhead amidst the rubbing and creaking of branches. Sam liked to think she didn't spook easily. Heck, she hadn't been afraid of the dark since she was two years old. But the forest, which had been lovely by day, had an eeriness about it now that was making the hair on the back of her neck stand up. Beside her, Daniel seemed to sense it too, walking as closely as he could. "Keep an eye out for the flying monkeys," he said, under his breath.

"Lions and tigers and bears," she muttered back. He was right though. It did have that kind of feel to it.

Their flashlights were off for now. Sam felt better maneuvering in the dark. There was no point in putting a target on their backs if a hostile was lurking out there. And now that her eyes had adjusted to it, Sam found she could see well enough without any light.

The colonel, she knew, preferred a clockwise patrol pattern, and there was no reason to think he'd done anything differently tonight. Mirroring that route, she and Daniel worked their way around the circumference of their campsite in a continually increasing radius from its center. It didn't take long before they were way beyond where the colonel and Teal'c would have typically patrolled.

"Damn it, Colonel. Where are you?" Sam said it to herself, but Daniel heard her anyway. He held up his flashlight.

"Maybe it's time for some illumination?"

She had to agree. Other than the general creepiness of the woods, there was no sign that anyone was stalking them. And now that it was clear neither the colonel nor Teal'c were anywhere within the camp's perimeter, the next thing she and Daniel needed to do was look for clues as to where they might have gone. They couldn't do that in the dark.

The beam from the light on Sam's P-90 was almost startling in its brightness. It pushed back the wall of darkness, making her blind to anything that might be lurking beyond the beam's range. She still didn't think anyone was out there, but she hated feeling vulnerable.

As he panned his flashlight around, Daniel's arc of light revealed nothing more than hers did. The forest was just that — a forest, with tree trunks, underbrush, and the usual leaves and organic litter scattered about the ground. There was no sign that anything human or otherwise had disturbed it recently, if at all. Beside her, Daniel sighed. "Well, they can't have just vanished into thin air."

"Actually —" Sam found herself glancing skyward. The Asgard *had* been known to whisk the colonel away whenever it suited them.

"You don't suppose Thor — ?" Daniel had picked up on her train of thought, looking up at the sky as well.

Sam shook her head. "Not without telling us."

"Right." He looked at her expectantly. "So — ?"

"Let's retrace our steps." It was the only thing she could think of to do, short of returning to the gate and requesting backup. She'd already considered that, but by the time General Hammond sent a search team, it would be well after dawn. Who knew if the colonel and Teal'c even had that much time? Those were precious hours she couldn't afford to waste.

They took their time working their way back, sweeping the lights up ahead and along either side. Sam could feel her frustration growing. It was like searching for a needle in a haystack, when she didn't even know what the needle looked like.

How would she even tell if something like a broken twig meant anything, when it was just as likely she and Daniel could have snapped it themselves on their first pass through? Odds were, though, that was the very sort of subtle sign they were looking for — the very kind that was all too easy to miss.

"Hello!" Daniel stopped so suddenly that Sam almost ran into him. He'd fixed his light on the forest floor off to their left. "There. See it?"

It took her a moment to spot what he was talking about. The small object blended in almost too well with the detritus around it, but once Sam saw it, she knew it didn't belong there. It belonged on the Colonel's wrist.

It was his watch.

Picking it up, Sam examined it, feeling a knot form in the pit of her stomach. There was no mistaking it was his. She recognized the worn edge of the black-out cover where he flicked it open repeatedly when he was bored or annoyed. And there was a slight gouge on one side, where a replicator had gotten entirely too close. Matte black, it was sheer luck that Daniel had spotted it at all.

Sam grasped it in her palm. There was no trace of the colonel's residual body heat, so it had been there a while. The coldness of the watch sent a chill through her. Or maybe it was just the damp night air. Sam shook it off. Facts were what she needed now, not emotions. She refused to let her imagination substitute fear for logic.

Squatting where the watch had been, Sam studied the ground more closely, concentrating. Someone had been here, she could see that now. The nearby underbrush was disturbed, and her light revealed several smaller plants that had been crushed. Whether it was the result of a scuffle or simply where the colonel and Teal'c had been momentarily held, she couldn't be sure. But they had been here, there was no doubt. The object in her hand was proof of that.

"I don't think this came off by accident." In all the times

they'd been captured and bound, she could never recall once when the colonel's watch had been an issue. In fact, removing it required a fair amount of dedicated effort on his part. It would never just fall off.

"You think he left it behind on purpose? Like a clue?"

Sam nodded. "I think he meant for us to find it, so we'd know which way they'd gone."

Daniel's brow creased in puzzlement and he slowly turned in a circle, letting the light play against the trees that surrounded them. "And which way would that be, exactly? I mean, I get that the watch puts them here, but it's not like it came with a flashing neon sign pointing which direction they went."

"Actually, Daniel, it did. Well, sort of." She aimed her light ahead and to the left. "I'm pretty sure they went that way."

Daniel was skeptical. "What makes you say that? Isn't it more likely they took them back through the gate?" He nodded in the vague direction of the Stargate.

Sam stood and brushed a few stray leaves off her pants. "You're assuming they came through the gate in the first place."

"Considering what I translated on the monument and the fact that Jack and Teal'c didn't find any sign of people during their recon yesterday, I think that's a fairly safe assumption."

"I'm sorry, Daniel, but I disagree."

"Because...?"

"Because of that." Sam raised her weapon and its light reflected off the shiny, empty wrapper of a US Government-issue energy bar.

"Oh." He stared at it for a moment. "Not to be negative, Sam, but the wind could have—"

She didn't let Daniel finish. "And that." A few meters further on, her light had picked up yet another empty wrapper. Walking towards it, she continued to sweep the beam ahead of her. Eventually it revealed what looked like one of the colonel's gloves.

Daniel followed her, bending down to retrieve the item. "Looks like Jack was emptying his pockets."

"Breadcrumbs." Sam couldn't help but grin. "He's leaving us breadcrumbs." Of course the colonel would figure out a way for her and Daniel to track them in the dark.

"I was going to say litter, but I think you're probably right." Daniel swept his flashlight ahead. There was the other glove further on. "Okay. So he's left us a trail to follow. What do we do now? Head back to the gate and ask General Hammond to send reinforcements?"

Definitely not now. *Maybe*, if they'd come up empty. But as far as Sam was concerned, the colonel's markers made it clear he wanted her and Daniel to follow them. In a way, she was relieved. There was no way she could have waited around doing nothing until backup arrived. She'd have gone nuts.

Not that that was something Daniel needed to know.

"I don't think we can risk losing all that time," she told him instead. She looked at the watch in her hand. "They've already got a couple hours head start."

Both of Daniel's eyebrows shot up. If he had any doubts about her decision, he didn't show it. "Then I guess it's just us."

"Yeah, I guess it is." Sam slipped the colonel's watch over her wrist and secured it next to her own. The extra weight on her arm felt oddly comforting. "Come on, Daniel. Let's go get our people back."

CHAPTER TWO

//ACCESSING MISSION REPORTS...//

P5C-777 MISSION REPORT, TEAL'C: There is little doubt but that knowledge of Major Carter's technical expertise has become widespread amongst certain circles across the galaxy. While this is to her credit, it may, I fear, in time become detrimental to her well-being.

//CONTINUING ANALYSIS...//

O'NEILL WAS displeased. Although Teal'c could not see his friend's face, the constant tugging at their common restraints was sufficient evidence of his frustration. Teal'c shared the feeling. They should not have been caught unawares as they had been. He had mistaken the footfall of the enemy for the ordinary night sounds of the forest, realizing his error only when the sound of an activating *zat'nik'tel* warned him too late of the energy bolt which dropped O'Neill mid-stride. With the superior hearing granted him by his symbiote, the fault was his and his alone. In the future he would be more vigilant.

Now that the sun had risen and was sending filtered light through the towering trees, Teal'c could better assess their situation. They had travelled several kilometers in the very direction he and O'Neill had intended to reconnoiter that day, their captors taking them well beyond the cliffs that Major Carter had been analyzing for trinium deposits. Daylight revealed them to be in a small canyon apparently carved out by an even smaller river which, going by its present size, hardly seemed to have been up to the task. The bluffs on either side were dense with tree growth, casting the entire ravine in a warm, green hue. Under other circumstances, it would have been a pleasant setting.

What made it decidedly unpleasant however, was the presence of a *tel'tak* several meters away. It gave every appearance of having recently landed, going by the as yet unwilted broken branches scattered about, casualties of the ship maneuvering through the trees. Even so, Teal'c could not help but give a begrudging nod to whomever had piloted the vessel. Considering the density of the canopy overhead, it took expert flying to have landed here.

As far as Teal'c could tell, there were only two candidates for that expertise — the same two individuals who had captured them — a Goa'uld and a Jaffa, both of whom had disappeared just as dawn had extinguished the stars overhead. There had been no sign of them since.

Behind him, O'Neill continued to fidget. Teal'c sighed. While he enjoyed sharing many things with his brother in arms, this particular situation was quickly becoming wearisome.

"I do not believe we are capable of breaking free at this time, O'Neill." Teal'c tried to sound patient. Goa'uld binders were virtually indestructible — the fact of which O'Neill should have known by now. Not only that, but the Goa'uld had bound them wrist to wrist and back to back, with a sizeable tree trunk between them. "Perhaps it would be better to save our energy for when our captors return."

"Yeah." O'Neill sighed deeply. There was a long pause before he added, "I've really gotta pee."

Teal'c thought it wise not to point out that this was yet another benefit bestowed upon him by his symbiote: basic bodily functions were rarely a concern. Somehow, he did not think O'Neill would appreciate the observation.

Instead, he asked, "Do you have a plan, O'Neill?" Although the way the Goa'uld had bound them around the tree most certainly assured they could not escape, there was an inherent flaw in chaining two prisoners to each other in this manner. When the time came to move them, unlocking even just one binder would immediately allow both prisoners to have one free arm. A well thought-out strategy to catch their captors off guard at this vulnerable moment could mean freedom. The key would be timing and the element of surprise.

"Nope." O'Neill's response to his question was unexpected. "Don't need a plan. Carter'll find us. Hell, I bet she's already scouting the place out, making sure the coast is clear."

"You seem confident that you were able to leave sufficient clues to guide Major Carter and Daniel Jackson to our location." He had only become aware of O'Neill's efforts to leave what he termed "a trail of breadcrumbs" once the Goa'uld and Jaffa had left them alone. The fact that O'Neill had no bread with which to do this was, apparently, beside the point.

"Yup. Just like Hansel and Gretel. You'll see. They'll show up any minute."

Teal'c contemplated inquiring as to what a "Hansel and Gretel" was but decided against it.

O'Neill shifted again. "So, any idea who these guys are? For a Goa'uld, he's not really much for chit-chat."

What O'Neill said was true. The Goa'uld had spoken surprisingly little upon their capture, limiting his communication to brief warnings and directions. The Jaffa had said nothing at all. It had been too dark to even see which sigil was tattooed on his forehead.

"I do not. Their motive for capturing us remains a mystery."

"Well, except for the fact that he's a Goa'uld. Which is motive enough, I suppose."

"Indeed."

"Going by that—" O'Neill tried pointing in the direction of the cargo ship. "I'm gonna guess this planet isn't exactly their home sweet home."

Teal'c had arrived at the same conclusion. "It would appear that Daniel Jackson was, in fact, correct in concluding that there remain no native occupants of P5C-777."

"Yeah. Too bad he didn't take into account the tourist traffic, though. Ow!"

O'Neill's exclamation was accompanied by a reflexive jerk which caught Teal'c off guard. It caused him to momentarily lose his balance and tilt towards his left. A small pebble sailed past his head, bouncing into the dirt. Another one landed nearby.

Teal'c twisted around, searching for the source. It took him a few moments, but eventually he spotted two forms secluded in the shadows of the trees on the ridge.

"O'Neill. It is Major Carter and Daniel Jackson."

"Yes! Finally!"

"I believe they are attempting to get our attention."

"Ya'think?" O'Neill made an attempt to rub his head, most likely where the pebble had struck him.

Now that Teal'c had acknowledged their presence, Major Carter and Daniel Jackson took up a position that permitted them to be slightly more visible. Major Carter made several hand gestures, which Teal'c understood to mean that she was asking where their captors were. Although his ability to respond was limited by his restraints, he was able to successfully communicate that he was unaware of their location. Nodding, Major Carter conferred with Daniel Jackson and they withdrew into the shadows.

"What's goin' on, T?" O'Neill's vantage point did not permit him to see what had just transpired.

"I believe Major Carter and Daniel Jackson are about to mount a rescue, just as you predicted, O'Neill."

"See? I told you they'd find us."

"You did indeed." Teal'c kept his focus on the area where Major Carter and Daniel Jackson had disappeared. He thought he saw movement in the trees, but there were any number of large boulders and other formations of rock which blocked his view. Scanning the hillside in anticipation, it was several minutes before he saw their two team mates finally emerge.

Teal'c glanced over his shoulder at O'Neill, who had not yet caught sight of them. "I do not believe Major Carter and Daniel Jackson's attempt to rescue us will turn out to be as successful as you'd hoped."

"Oh come on, Teal'c, don't be so negative."

"I am not being negative. I am being observant. Look."

Teal'c felt O'Neill's body contort in the direction Teal'c was attempting to point. There were Major Carter and Daniel Jackson walking towards them, both with their hands bound. Behind them, the Goa'uld and the Jaffa had weapons trained closely on the backs of their two newest captives.

"Crap." O'Neill slouched back against the tree, sounding more disappointed than irate. "Well, that's not how it was supposed to work out. Hey, Carter!" he called out as they drew nearer. "Whatcha doin'?"

Major Carter looked at him apologetically. "Sorry, sir. This didn't exactly go down as planned."

"Yeah. I can see that. Daniel? You all right?"

Daniel Jackson raised his bound hands in front of him and grimaced. "Oh yeah. Peachy." As the Jaffa nudged him along with Major Carter to the ground nearby, he added, "On the plus side, we know where the bad guys are now — assuming, of course, this is all of them?"

"I believe it is, Daniel Jackson. We have seen no one else in the many hours we have been here."

"Sorry we took so long. You guys okay?" From her vantage point, Major Carter seemed to be looking O'Neill and himself over for any sign of injury.

"Gotta pee. But otherwise — yeah. Doin' as well as can be expected, under the circumstances." O'Neill looked up at the Goa'uld. "Okay. So, if I start the introductions, maybe we can go around the group, get to know one another a little better — ?" Teal'c recognized O'Neill's overly casual tone. It was a ploy he often used to bewilder their enemies into dropping their guard and revealing more information than they otherwise might.

It was an effective, if somewhat unconventional, strategy.

"*There is no need to introduce yourself, Colonel O'Neill. We know quite well who you are.*" The Goa'uld spoke at last.

"Ah. Well then, you definitely have me at a disadvantage."

"*I am Pheone, Third Tanist to Lord Lugh, ruler of Gorias.*"

"Pheone, you say," O'Neill's tone was still light. "Okay. Now we're getting somewhere. This is Major—"

"Samantha Carter, Dr. Daniel Jackson, and of course, Teal'c—the *shol'va.*" The Jaffa spoke for the first time, spitting out the epithet with disdain. Teal'c fixed him with a stare, lest the Jaffa think the insult had affected him in any way. He had endured torture to the point of near death for his beliefs. Mere words were of no consequence.

"*This is Dar'dak,*" Pheone indicated the Jaffa. "*And you are SG-1. Your reputation precedes you, Colonel.*"

"Well, I'm afraid yours doesn't," O'Neill shot back. "Lord Lugh, you said? Teal'c? Carter? Daniel? Ring any bells?"

Lugh. The name was familiar. "Is not Lugh a very minor Goa'uld who once served in the house of Camulus?"

"Actually, I believe the god Lugh is from Irish mythology," Daniel Jackson offered. "Although at some point in history he lost his status as a god and was demoted to a somewhat lesser rank of hero and king." His tone became distracted as he studied the Goa'uld. "It was believed he was one of the *Tuatha Dé Danann*, a supernatural race of beings who, according to legend, originally populated what became Ireland."

"So, if this Lugh is a very minor Goa'uld, does that make you a very, *very* minor Goa'uld?" O'Neill made no attempt to conceal his amusement.

Dar'dak scowled, but Pheone merely shrugged off O'Neill's attempt to bait him. "*At the moment, Colonel, perhaps. But now that I have you all here, I hope to change that.*"

"Ah. Now why does that not surprise me in the least? Let me guess—there's some kind of bounty on our heads. I bet old Apophis would just love to get his hands on us, right? Or maybe it's one of the other System Lords?"

Daniel Jackson cleared his throat. "Jack you really don't need to be giving him any ideas, you know."

"My interest is not in you, Colonel. Nor in Dr. Jackson or Teal'c."

At the other end of their shared bonds, Teal'c felt O'Neill tense.

"You are, however, useful as leverage for what I do want."

"And what is that?" O'Neill's voice was as ice.

Pheone walked over to where Major Carter was seated. Although her hands were bound as well, Teal'c could see her muscles tighten reflexively. He knew only too well what she was capable of. Pheone would do well not to underestimate her ability to defend herself.

"I have a device I have salvaged from a ha'tak," he told her. *"It is damaged beyond my ability to repair it. I have been told you are skilled in the knowledge of Goa'uld technology, so I offer you a trade, Major. Fix the device, and you and your teammates may go free."*

"You want me to fix something?" Clearly Major Carter had not been expecting Pheone's request. Neither had any of the others. Behind him, O'Neill relaxed slightly. "What kind of device are you talking about?" she asked, frowning.

"It is a cloaking device."

"A cloaking device? Wait — did you say it was from a *ha'tak*?"

Major Carter's excitement did not go unnoticed by O'Neill. "Carter?"

"Sir, the only time we've seen a cloak for a *ha'tak* was in the Tobin system — when Apophis' fleet of cloaked motherships opened fire on Heru'ur in the middle of all those mines." She looked up at Pheone. "Are you saying you were able to find one of those cloaking devices intact?"

"I am."

"Carter?" repeated O'Neill, although there was an edge of

impatience in it.

"Sir, we've never even seen that kind of capability before. It gave Apophis a huge advantage."

"I know. I was there."

His tone tempered her enthusiasm a little, but not by much.

"If we could understand how that works —"

"I'm sure it would be utterly fascinating, Carter. But is that really something we want to fix so old Pheone here can turn it over to his boss — or maybe every other Goa'uld who's out there?"

Major Carter glanced up at the Goa'uld standing over her. "I'm not sure we have a choice, sir."

O'Neill did not immediately reply, although he stirred with agitation.

"What if she can't fix the cloak?" Daniel Jackson asked. "No offense, Sam."

"Although you all are not as valuable for my purpose as the cloaking device, SG-1 would still make a worthy substitute trophy for Lord Lugh."

"See — what did I say? I was right the first time. You guys are a bunch of walking clichés. You know that, don't you?" O'Neill's sigh was greatly exaggerated. "Although I will admit, I am a little hurt that we're the consolation prize now."

Standing beside Pheone, Dar'dak leaned over and whispered something in his ear.

"*Esras is not here,*" Pheone responded curtly to whatever it was Dar'dak had said. "*I will decide what best serves my needs.*"

Dar'dak bowed his head in acknowledgment, but Teal'c could tell by his demeanor that he was displeased with Pheone's decision. Now that there was sufficient light, he could see that Dar'dak bore the mark of Ares on his forehead. A curious discovery, to be sure. Ares had no ties to Camulus or to Lugh, as far as Teal'c knew.

"Sir, with your permission, I'd like to at least give fixing the cloak a try. Like Daniel said — it might not even be something I can repair."

Teal'c still could not see O'Neill's face, only Major Carter's. The two of them seemed to briefly engage in some form of non-verbal communication, the result of which caused O'Neill to drop his head back against the tree with yet another sigh — although this one seemed genuine. "Right. Fine. Go — do your best, Major. Fix the damn thing."

"Yes, sir." There was relief in Major Carter's tone, as well as what might have even been a hint of anticipation. It was a sentiment that Daniel Jackson did not seem to share

"Jack?"

"Daniel?"

"Uh — is that really a good idea?"

Pheone had helped Major Carter to her feet, but when he attempted to take her by the arm, she held back, looking between O'Neill and Daniel Jackson.

"Probably not. But like Carter said, we're a little short on options at the moment." When Major Carter still did not move, O'Neill tilted his head in the direction of the ship. "Go. See what you can do."

She nodded, this time allowing Pheone to guide her by the elbow. O'Neill twisted around in his restraints yet again, nearly throwing Teal'c off balance.

"And Carter — could you maybe mention to him that I've *really* gotta pee?"

CHAPTER THREE

//ACCESSING MISSION REPORTS...//

P5C-777 MISSION REPORT, MAJOR SAMANTHA CARTER: I knew there would be consequences, but I thought we could sort those out later. The most important thing, as far as I was concerned, was the safety of my team.

//CONTINUING ANALYSIS...//

"*I TRUST you will not try to escape or assault me when I undo your restraints.*"

Sam would have been lying if she'd said the thought hadn't occurred to her. But the Jaffa, Dar'dak, was still guarding the rest of her team. She doubted she'd have much of a chance with one confiscated zat against his staff weapon—not when he had so many targets to choose from. Besides, the whole point of this exercise was to get her people out of here unscathed. She'd be better off trying to fix the cloaking device than she would attempting to overpower Pheone.

Still, it was best if she didn't make any promises. "I can't exactly fix anything like this, can I?" She held up her bound hands.

Pheone's eyes narrowed slightly. Sam was fairly certain he'd picked up on the fact that she hadn't really given him her word. He was, however, apparently willing to take his chances, because at last he reached over and deactivated the binders, removing them from her wrists.

"Thanks." Her automatic response came out sincerely. Sam mentally kicked herself. Politeness was hardly called for under the circumstances.

To her surprise, her expression of gratitude elicited a smile from Pheone. "*You're welcome. Now, just don't make me regret it, Major.*"

It wasn't the reaction she'd expected — not from a Goa'uld. She couldn't put her finger on it, but there was something different about Pheone. She wouldn't have been a bit surprised if, once they were out of earshot of Dar'dak, that he had revealed himself as Tok'ra — except, of course, that he hadn't.

Maybe it was his appearance. He was short for a Goa'uld — Sam had at least a half a head on him — and he was slender, to the point where the simple, long duster he wore looked big on his almost too-thin frame. But there was a wiriness to him that made Sam think it wouldn't be wise to dismiss him on size alone. His features were sharp and more refined than rugged, but by far the most striking thing about his appearance was his undeniably red hair, which curled tightly against his head.

There was also something about his smile which came across as being quite genuine, if not a little disarming. He was definitely not like any other Goa'uld they'd ever met.

"So, where is this device?" Charm aside, she was not here of her own free will, after all, and she couldn't let him forget that.

"*Over there.*" He pointed across the cargo hold at a large, hexagonally shaped object, at least a meter in diameter and almost as tall as a DHD, not including the large, pyramidal center piece on top. It was the largest cloaking device Sam had ever seen, but of course it would have to be if it was capable of hiding an entire mothership.

As she walked around it, sizing it up, Sam could see the thing had taken a beating. There were dents and scorch marks on the sides and across the top, and one of the trays seemed too damaged to even close properly. Considering how the mines had taken out all those *ha'taks*, however, she was frankly surprised to find it even in this good a condition.

"*Several of the crystals in the trays are damaged.*" Pheone pressed on the base and a drawer that was still functional slid open. He was right. Even without being connected to anything other than a nominal power source, she could see at least a half dozen control crystals that looked burned out or broken. Anyone remotely familiar with Goa'uld technology could replace those, though. If he needed her help, there had to be something more

"*The greatest damage, however, is here.*" He removed the pyramid-shaped cover from the top to reveal an enormous crystal—or what was left of it—embedded into the heart of the device. Irregularly shaped, the broken stump was about a foot at its widest, and going by the size of the cover, it had to have been twice that in height. She'd never seen a crystal that size in a Goa'uld device before. Not even the ones that powered the DHD were that big.

Sam picked up shards of what remained of the broken crystal and turned them over in her hand, buying time to think. There was no way she could even begin to fix the cloak, not with its primary crystal destroyed. The other crystals could be swapped out with no trouble—she could probably cannibalize what was already on the *tel'tak*. But without the central crystal—

Daniel had been right. There was no way she could repair this. Not with what she had on hand.

She couldn't bluff her way through it either. Pheone had already correctly diagnosed the problem, so there was no point in trying to lie to him. Attempting to overpower him was still an option, but not a good one. And allowing SG-1 to be turned over to this Lord Lugh was out of the question. If there was a Plan D, she wasn't seeing it at the moment.

Pheone was watching her, waiting for her verdict. She had no choice. She had to tell him the truth.

"I can't fix this." She set the broken crystal pieces back on top of the device. "I mean, I probably *could* fix it, if the primary power crystal wasn't broken, but I've never even seen a crystal like this before. I wouldn't know where to begin to find a replacement for it."

"Do you have no other method for powering something of this nature?"

Sam stiffened. Of course. A naquadah generator probably would do the trick. There were only two problems with that solution. First of all, she didn't have one with her. And secondly, even if she did, she was pretty sure what the colonel would say to the mere suggestion of using it. Nor would she have disagreed with him. Letting a naquadah generator fall into the hands of a Goa'uld was out of the question, no matter what was at stake.

"I don't have anything that could provide that much energy." It wasn't a lie. The generators were all back at the SGC, and that was where they were going to stay. "Where does a crystal like this come from anyway? It has to be extremely rare."

Pheone sighed, sagging against the bulkhead. "It is. Not to mention expensive. Which was why I was hoping you'd have something that we could use in place of it."

Wait. Had she just heard what she thought she'd heard? Pheone's voice had changed. The Goa'uld baritone was gone. He sounded normal, except for a slightly lilting accent.

Although that meant practically nothing. A Goa'uld could easily manipulate their host's voice to say anything. No one knew that better than she did.

Pheone had noted her reaction. With one raised eyebrow he gave a sheepish little shrug, as though he'd inadvertently let something slip. Sam wasn't buying such an obvious ploy.

"If you think pretending to be your host is going to matter in any way—"

"Pretending? Is that what you think?" He looked genuinely shocked.

"You're telling me you're not a Goa'uld?" Sam didn't hide her incredulity. Although, maybe she'd been right in the first place. "Unless, of course, you're a Tok'ra?"

"A Tok'ra I am not—nor am I a Goa'uld—well, at least not in any way that matters." He pushed himself away from the bulkhead and joined her again at the cloaking device. Picking up one of the bits of broken crystal Sam had set down, he absently studied it.

"But you do have a symbiote." Sam could feel the slight crawling of the skin and the disquieting sense of recognition the presence of a symbiote always evoked. It was a sensation she never got used to.

He looked up from the object in his hand. "I'm afraid that's true—and 'tis a Goa'uld symbiote, sure enough. I am its host. But I am also its master. I control it. It does not control me."

Sam's eyed him with skepticism from her side of the cloak. The only time she'd ever seen a host actually be able to talk without permission of a Goa'uld was when Klorel had been artificially suppressed by Tollan technology to give Skaara an opportunity to speak. She saw no such device on Pheone, and she highly doubted a Goa'uld symbiote would be so obliging.

Her misgivings must have been written on her face, because Pheone sighed. "My name—my real name—is Dirmid." He glanced nervously at the exterior hatch before continuing. "Back on my world—on Gorias—there are some who are born as I. We are called *Ateronu*—it means 'the gifted ones.' When a Goa'uld invades us, we have the ability to resist them and take back control of our minds and our bodies. They become nothing more than a wee voice in the back of our head that we have been well-trained to ignore."

"You're telling me you can control your symbiote?" Sam had heard that false claim before. Unfortunately, it had resulted in Shau'nac's death and a Goa'uld spy embedded in the Tok'ra's ranks.

"I know you don't believe me." He put the broken crystal back down. "I suppose I wouldn't either if I were you. But what I'm telling you is the truth."

If nothing more, the sincerity of Dirmid's voice gave Sam pause, although she knew it shouldn't. On the other hand, maybe it was possible. Maybe there was something unique about him. After all, Aris Boch's physiology had totally rejected implantation by any symbiote at all, as had his entire race. It was a big universe. Sam had come to accept that nothing was beyond the realm of possibility.

That didn't mean she was ready to totally believe this particular tale, though. Her trust didn't come that easily. Especially not in someone who was still holding the rest of her team captive.

Dirmid — or Pheone — she wasn't sure what to call him now — kept glancing nervously over at the hatch. She could sense his unease growing the longer they remained in the ship. It occurred to her why that might be.

"Dar'dak doesn't know, does he?" If the Jaffa were to walk in on their conversation... It was the only explanation that fit Dirmid's behavior. "He believes you're a real Goa'uld."

Dirmid flushed. "Aye. And it's important he not find out. Everything depends on it."

"Everything? Really?" Sam did her best to sound skeptical. He certainly had a dramatic flair that she could see would be easy to get caught up in. She refused to be played, though. "Look, if you expect me to believe any of this, then you need to tell me the truth about what's going on."

"The less you know, Major, the better off you'll be. Now, do you think, if we could find the right crystal, you could fix this thing?" He indicated the cloaking device between them.

Sam crossed her arms. "In all likelihood, yes. But I won't. Not until I know what this is really about."

Frustration creased Dirmid's forehead and he ran both hands through his hair as he paced in front of her. "You know, your people's reputation for being the most stubborn, determined —" He finished the sentence with a growl of exasperation. "Fine. I'll explain the details later, but suffice it to say that I'm part of a group who's plotting to overthrow Lugh and free the people of Gorias." He looked at the outer hatch again and came closer to her, lowering his voice. "In order to make that happen, the right people have to be in the right places in Lugh's inner circle. Presenting him with a prize like this device, will assure that happens. But I won't lie to you, Major. I'm desperate, and at this point, I'll take any prize I can get. If I can't have a working cloak, then SG-1 is the next best thing."

Dirmid's green eyes bore into hers. Whether the Goa'uld part of his story was true or not, she recognized the look of someone committed to his mission. He'd said he was desperate, and that she could see all too clearly. Sam had no doubt he would do exactly as he said.

Which meant she only had one choice.

"So, where do we find one of these crystals?"

CHAPTER FOUR

//ACCESSING MISSION REPORTS...//

P5C-777 MISSION REPORT, DR. DANIEL JACKSON: I never doubted Sam's ability to do it. In fact, if there was anyone who could tackle something like that in a situation such as this, it would be her. And granted, at the time, I didn't have all the facts.

P5C-777 MISSION REPORT, MAJOR SAMANTHA CARTER: I knew there had to be a way to make it all work. I just needed time to figure out how.

//CONTINUING ANALYSIS...//

"WELL, THAT can't be good." Daniel had given up trying to sit comfortably on the jagged loose stone. Not only did it jab him in all sorts of awkward places, but it was also inherently damp. The only advantage his position offered was that it gave him a better view of the *tel'tak*, which was how he spotted Sam and Pheone before the others.

It was also why his stomach now had a sinking feeling as he watched the two of them talking animatedly with one another as they approached. Sam had that focused look on her face that she got when some new bit of technology crossed her path. Which meant Pheone had been telling the truth about what he'd recovered. He'd reeled Sam in so completely, he hadn't even needed to bother putting the binders back on. She was completely engrossed.

"What's the word, Major?" Jack's eyes were closed, although

Daniel didn't believe for a minute that he'd been asleep. The rest of his body was too tense for him to be that relaxed, yet he somehow managed to sound like he was no more interested in Sam's answer than if he'd asked her about the weather.

Sam glanced sideways at Pheone before replying. "The device is pretty badly damaged, sir. But I think I can fix it."

Daniel's stomach lurched. So he'd been right about Sam's eager look. He'd been desperately hoping the cloak would be beyond repair, which would make the whole issue moot. No such luck, it seemed.

Jack opened his eyes at Sam's response. "You *think*?"

"I'm fairly certain I can, sir—with the right components. The primary power crystal is broken and needs to be replaced." She was already warming to the challenge of repairing it, Daniel could tell. "Because of its size, it's fairly rare. But Pheone says he knows of a place where we might be able to get our hands on one."

"*We*?" Jack's eyes narrowed.

Sam took a deep breath. "Yes, sir. I'll need to go with him to verify that it's the right kind of crystal."

Her words hung in the air for a few moments as Jack absorbed them. Daniel was pretty sure he knew what Jack's answer would be.

"Hey." Jack offered one of his more unconvincing smiles to go with his complete lack of enthusiasm. "I guess I'd be up for a field trip about now. Stretch the old legs—get the kinks out of the knee. So. How about it, kids?"

Okay, that was definitely not the reply Daniel had been expecting. There was no way he was staying silent about this any longer.

He struggled to his feet, only to have Dar'dak's firm hand force him back to the ground. The gravel bit into his knees. Daniel didn't care.

"You can't be serious?" He looked first at Jack and then at Sam. "We're not really thinking of helping them repair that thing?" Sure, Jack had okayed Sam examining the device in the first place, but Daniel had assumed it had simply been to buy them some time. He'd never expected Sam to really try to fix it. "I don't care what he says" — Daniel gestured towards Pheone — "but you know as well as I do, it's ultimately going to end up in the hands of the System Lords. Do you have any idea what the impact of that will be on the rest of the galaxy?" He appealed directly to Sam. "Are we really going to put other, innocent people at risk, just to gain our own freedom?"

"I *understand* that, Daniel." There was a slight edge in her tone as she glanced his way before focusing on Jack again. "Actually, sir, I think I'm the only one who needs to go with Pheone." She gave the Goa'uld another sidelong glance. "And I don't believe that's open to negotiation."

Daniel went to stand up again, but Dar'dak was still behind him. He landed back on his knees. He couldn't believe what he was hearing. "Jack, we can't." If Sam wouldn't listen, he still might. "Teal'c, help me out here. You know what this would mean."

Teal'c turned as best he could in his restraints. His back was to Daniel, so they couldn't see one another, but Daniel liked to think Teal'c was as troubled by this decision as he was.

"I concur, Daniel Jackson. Should such a device fall into the hands of the System Lords, the ramifications for the as yet unsubjugated worlds of the galaxy could be most dire."

There. At least he wasn't alone, then. And if Jack wouldn't listen to him, maybe he'd at least listen to Teal'c. Daniel got why Sam would be excited at the chance to tinker with that kind of technology, and even putting that aside, why she might think she was protecting the rest of them by giving into Pheone's demands — but this was bigger than SG-1. She had to know that. And if she didn't, Jack needed to remind her.

Apparently it wasn't as cut and dried for Jack. He still hadn't spoken, and judging by how miserable he looked, it was almost as if the act of deciding was causing him physical pain. Finally, he shook his head and sighed.

"Major —"

Sam didn't let him get any further.

"Sir —" She went over to Jack, squatting on her heels in front of him, so they were at the same eye level. Dar'dak took a cautionary step forward, but Pheone waved him back, seemingly unconcerned by Sam's movement.

"I really do think it's for the best if I proceed with the repair, Colonel." Sam's back was to Daniel, so he could only go by Jack's reaction. So far, his eyes hadn't left Sam's face. "The planet with the crystal isn't far, according to Pheone. If we find what we need, then it should only take me a couple of hours to fix the device after that."

"Carter —"

"Sir —" Sam's voice was firm and deliberate. "I'd really rather you didn't put me in a position of having to disobey a direct order from you."

Jack didn't immediately reply. The tension between the two of them was so palpable Daniel could feel it from a dozen feet away. Sam rarely dug her heels in, but when she did, she could be formidable. He figured he had one more shot. It was worth a try.

"Jack, you *know* this isn't a good idea. You said as much yourself."

There was a beat before Jack sighed heavily. "Yeah, I know." With another long look at Sam, Jack jerked his head in the direction of Pheone. "Do what you have to do, Major. I trust your judgment."

"Thank you, sir." Sam hesitated just a moment before straightening up and walking back over to Pheone. "I'll need some of my equipment back," she told the Goa'uld.

Pheone nodded at Dar'dak, who accompanied Sam over to where their gear had been stacked so she could retrieve her tac-vest.

"I don't believe this." Daniel frowned at Jack, who looked suddenly tired, as if the past few minutes had drained his last bit of energy. "Jack. You can't—"

Jack's head snapped up irritably. "Yes, Daniel, I can. And I just did. Now zip it."

Daniel actually made it to his feet this time. There was no way he was going to shut up. Not this time. Not until he was finished. Jack could glare at him all he wanted.

"So, that's it then? I mean — I get it. I'm not crazy about the idea of being some Goa'uld's bargaining chip either. But are we really willing to endanger the rest of the galaxy, just to save ourselves? We're really going to sit here and let that happen?" Daniel looked pointedly at Sam, but she still refused to meet his eye.

Pheone responded instead. "*Actually, no, Dr. Jackson. You are not going to remain here. Under the circumstances, I think perhaps it would be safer for all concerned if Dar'dak takes the three of you elsewhere.*"

"Now hold on. No one said anything about the rest of us going anywhere." Jack really was agitated now. "We're staying put until Carter gets back."

For some reason, Dar'dak didn't seem any happier about Pheone's decision than Jack. He scowled at Pheone too. "Tanist — ?"

"*You will take Colonel O'Neill, Dr. Jackson and Teal'c back to Gorias, and secure them in the dungeon. If our efforts fail, Magna will at least have the infamous SG-1 to present to Lord Lugh as a gift.*"

"But Tanist —" Dar'dak seemed to be choosing his words carefully. "Did not Master Esras select *you* to have the honor of presenting this trophy to Lord Lugh? I do not believe he intended for you to pass this glory to the Second Tanist."

Pheone's eyes glowed briefly with anger. "*How I choose to make use of this prize is my decision and my decision alone. Do you dare to disagree with me?*"

Dar'dak snapped to attention and bowed his head deferentially. "No, Tanist. Never." Daniel couldn't help note, however, that under his penitential pose, Dar'dak's expression was anything but.

"*Then do as I have instructed. And speak to no one of their presence on Gorias. Not even Master Esras.*"

Dar'dak's head bowed even lower. "I obey, Tanist."

"Except we're not leaving," Jack called out. "That's not part of the deal."

Pheone turned to Sam, paying no attention to Jack's protest. "*If you have what you require, Major, then the sooner we depart, the sooner we shall resolve this matter, one way or another.*"

Daniel couldn't help it. He had to try one more time. "Sam, please. Don't do this."

This time she paused and turned around to face him. "Daniel, I'm sorry. Really. But it's for the best." Her manner was brusque to the point of being dismissive. Daniel felt like he'd been verbally slapped in the face. This wasn't even Scientist Sam. This was every bit the Major Carter she rarely ever directed his way. In some ways, it made it that much worse.

Sam turned to follow Pheone, but then hesitated, looking back, almost apologetically, at the three of them. "Look, guys, I'll try to get this over with as soon as possible. It'll be okay. Just hang in there." She aimed a faint smile in Daniel's direction before hurrying to catch up to the Goa'uld, who was already several meters ahead.

Now Daniel was really confused. "I still think this is wrong, Jack." They both watched as Sam disappeared into the cargo ship and its hatch closed.

"Carter knows what she's doing."

"Yes, she does." And that was the problem. Daniel looked back at Jack and was met with a scowl. He wasn't sure if it was directed at him in particular or at the situation in general, although he didn't suppose it mattered much at the moment.

With Pheone's departure imminent, Dar'dak wasn't wasting any time. He may have disagreed with the Goa'uld's decision to send them to Gorias, but he was determined to see it carried out, regardless of his personal thoughts on the matter. Using his staff weapon, he tried prodding Jack and Teal'c to their feet.

"Watch it, stick-boy," Jack growled, struggling to inch his way off the ground. He was hampered in the effort both by his bound hands and the tree around which he and Teal'c had been secured.

"You." Dar'dak gestured at Daniel. "Come here."

There was a slight vibration under their feet as the cargo ship's engines came to life. Daniel paused to watch as it slowly lifted off from the rocky basin and maneuvered its way through the high bower of trees, clipping only a few small branches in its ascent.

When it had disappeared from sight, he looked over at Jack and Teal'c and saw that they too had been following the ship's departure. Teal'c's expression was one of admiration, although for what, Daniel wasn't sure. Jack's face had drained of all color, and for a split second Daniel thought he saw the one emotion Jack O'Neill rarely revealed. Then, as if a mask had dropped back in place, Jack's features hardened and the fear vanished. If Jack had had a free hand, Daniel was sure Dar'dak, who had continued to nudge Jack with the staff, wouldn't still be in one piece.

"I *am* standing, you sonofabitch. Now knock it off."

Undeterred by Jack's wrath, Dar'dak deactivated the binder on Daniel's left wrist and dragged him over to Teal'c by the one still attached. With a few swift motions, Dar'dak cuffed Daniel to Teal'c while simultaneously unlocking Teal'c's arm from Jack's. They were now bound together in a row, with Daniel and Jack on either end and Teal'c in the middle.

"If any of you attempts to escape, I will shoot the *shol'va* and the other two will have to drag his lifeless corpse all the way to the *chaapa'ai*."

Daniel didn't consider it an idle threat. He had seen the barely concealed look of contempt Dar'dak had for Pheone. Denying him his prize of an intact SG-1 wouldn't bother the Jaffa in the least.

"Bit of a hike," Jack pointed out, testily. "Too bad your buddy Pheone there couldn't have just dropped us off at the gate on his way to wherever."

Whether Jack had intentionally added fuel to the fire of Dar'dak's slow burn over Pheone or not, it certainly had that effect. Unfortunately, that anger manifested itself in more not-so-gentle jabs with the staff weapon. He was aiming for Jack a third time when Teal'c seized the staff by the shaft with his still bound hand and held it firmly, despite Dar'dak's attempt to wrench it free. With great deliberation, Teal'c slowly drew the other Jaffa closer to him until only inches separated them.

"You would do well to remember that, although we are bound, there are three of us and only one of you." Teal'c's eyes bore into the other Jaffa's. "For now, we choose to come with you willingly. I would advise you to do nothing that would change our minds." He released the staff with a push and Dar'dak stumbled backwards a few steps before regaining his balance. Although he stared threateningly at Teal'c, he also did not raise his staff again.

While the air might have been cleared for now with Dar'dak, the mood amongst the three of them hadn't lightened a bit. In fact, Daniel thought he felt the tension ratchet up just that much more. Something told him it wasn't likely to improve over the next three hours either.

One way or another, it was going to be a very long trek back to the gate.

~#~

Sam had barely stepped foot on the flight deck before Dirmid was at the helm, initiating the pre-flight sequence. Through the soles of her feet she could feel the engines as they hummed to life and the ship began its careful ascent through the trees.

She couldn't see her team through the viewport. The *tel'tak* was pointed in the opposite direction. Maybe that was for the best. Knowing she was leaving them behind was hard enough without having to watch them vanish in the distance.

Not that she was second-guessing her decision. There was no point in that now, anyway. Daniel could think what he wanted, and Sam wouldn't deny that his words had stung more than a little. But he didn't have all the facts. She was the only one who understood exactly what was at stake for everyone concerned. There was too much to lose for too many people if she hadn't agreed to come.

Besides. She had a plan.

That much, at least, she'd been able to get across to the colonel. For a heartbeat she'd been afraid he was going to order her not to go. And honestly, Sam wasn't sure what she'd have done if he had. It was a question she was glad she hadn't needed to answer.

"Don't worry about your friends." After the ship had risen smoothly through the troposphere, Dirmid engaged the hyperdrive. Now that they were away from the planet, he relaxed visibly. Turning around to face her, he leaned back in his seat with his arms crossed. "Dar'dak may not like me, but I am Third Tanist and he'll do as I say."

"What exactly is a Third Tanist?" He and Dar'dak had used those terms. Sam had a general idea from their context, but it never hurt to have clarity.

Dirmid waved her into the navigator's chair. Sam took a seat.

"It means I'm the third most powerful Goa'uld behind Lugh himself. Well, Pheone is, I mean. Technically speaking."

So it was a sort of ranking, just as she'd thought.

"And who is Esras?" The intense exchange between Dirmid and Dar'dak came back to her.

"Ah. He's the First Tanist—Lugh's second-in-command. The Jaffa are under his control." Dirmid ran his fingers through his hair again, the light from inside the ship making his red curls seem almost bronze. "It was Esras, actually, who suggested you might be the only person capable of fixing that thing." He nodded at the cloaking device in the cargo hold. "Even told me on which planet I might be able to find you."

That was disturbing. The mission rotations of SG teams were as classified as the Stargate itself. That this Esras knew where to find SG-1 at any given time suggested there was a security leak. Sam supposed she shouldn't be surprised. Between the Russians and the NID on Earth, embedded spies such as Tanith, and the ability of the Goa'uld to implant false memories to conceal their own espionage, it was probably naïve to think that information about the SGC wasn't available for a price. That explained how Dirmid had known where to find her.

"I take it Esras isn't one of you?"

Dirmid's eyebrows shot up. "Ah, no. He's a proper Goa'uld, and the one who's standing in our way. He's only been on Gorias a few years, but he managed to work his way up to First Tanist in no time at all."

"I presume there's also a Second Tanist?" She might as well get to know all the players in this game.

"Aye. That would be Magna." Dirmid swiveled around to check their course. Sam waited, but he offered nothing more.

"And Magna is…like you?"

"*Ateronu*? That she is. The real person is called Graen." Something on Dirmid's face softened as he spoke her name.

"And she can suppress her Goa'uld as well?"

Apparently satisfied they were still on course, Dirmid turned back to Sam. "Magna was once Lugh's First Tanist—back when she was a proper Goa'uld herself. She was accustomed to being in power—even had some plans of her own to overthrow Lugh at one time. Graen is her third *Ateronu* host—she took over when the previous host succumbed to the *bahlay*—it was just after Esras arrived and unseated her as First Tanist. Magna was always a nasty piece of work, and losing her position to an outsider didn't help. So it takes a bit more effort on Graen's part to keep her at bay, but she manages just fine."

There was so much to unpack from Dirmid's response, Sam hardly knew where to start. There was one thing, though, that she needed to ask.

"How, exactly, do you do what you do? How do you portray Pheone so authentically?" A Tok'ra masquerading as a Goa'uld she understood. In that situation, the host and the symbiote were working in concert. But by his own admission, that didn't seem to be the case with Dirmid.

Dirmid shrugged. "Oh, I have had many years of practice. I became a host to Pheone when I was only eighteen summers." He furrowed his brow. "And perhaps there is something of Pheone which I sometimes allow to come through. I can't really explain it, I suppose. In a way, it's just second nature to us."

"But you said you can always hear him?"

Dirmid expression turned slightly smug. "Aye. But there's a difference between hearing and obeying. It's part of the training we receive since we're children. Most of the time he's nothing more irritating than the distant drone of a *la'aum*-fly." He mimed batting away an imaginary insect. "And on the best days, nothing but an echo of an echo of an echo."

Sam found herself on her feet. Her sudden movement caused Dirmid to look up at her in alarm. Maybe he thought she'd intended to take control of the ship.

"Sorry." She offered an apologetic smile. "I just need to stretch my legs." The flight deck didn't offer a whole lot of room, but she walked around it anyway, trying to shake off some of the tension that had suddenly made sitting still impossible.

An echo of an echo of an echo. Dirmid's description had struck a chord. She'd never been able to properly explain what the remnants of Jolinar's memories felt like, but Dirmid had nailed it. Of course, their experiences didn't even begin to compare, but even so. He was the first person she'd met who even came close to understanding what it was like.

Maybe that was why Sam heard herself asking, "Doesn't it ever frighten you, even a little, being so close to having someone take control of you against your will?" It was a question she'd never been able to bring herself to ask her dad. She was afraid it would have come across as offensive to Selmak. And she wasn't sure her father would have given her an honest answer, not so much for Selmak's sake as her own. Because of what had happened to her.

Dirmid studied her a moment before answering. "You sound as if you've had some firsthand knowledge of such things yourself, Major."

There wasn't much point in denying it. "I was, very briefly, host to a Tok'ra once." She hesitated before adding, "It's not an experience that I'd care to repeat."

Dirmid looked at her thoughtfully. "No. I don't suppose you would. Nor would any on my world either — myself among them."

When he said nothing more, she realized that was as close to an answer as she was likely to get. There was no point in probing further. Sam couldn't blame him. It wasn't something she liked to think about too much either.

"Have there always been people with your particular gift on Gorias?" It was time to change the topic. Well, sort of.

He seemed as relieved as she to move on. Stretching his legs out again, he crossed his arms behind his head this time, the picture of relaxation. "If you believe the tales the old folk tell, then yes. There is a legend of the Great Tyrant who kidnapped our people away from their homes and carried them off to Gorias. The story goes that he then brought evil serpents, which were meant to steal their souls. But, in defiance, the people swallowed the snakes whole, and the creatures were never heard from again. The Great Tyrant, it is said, was so terrified by what they had done, he fled Gorias and did not return."

He told the story with flair, Sam gave him that. Like most legends, it offered as much insight into the people who told it as it did any actual facts. Still, Daniel had taught her that there were usually kernels of truth buried amidst all the hyperbole and fanciful embellishments.

"So, the fact that the people conquered the snakes by 'swallowing' them suggests to you that at least some of your ancestors must have had the ability to suppress the symbiote as well?"

"It does. Possibly all of them could. But the gift has gradually left us over time. We've only discovered three *Ateronu* who've been born in the last ten summers. Our numbers grow dangerously low."

"Then it's not something that's passed on from parent to child?"

"Ah. Now that's hard to say." Dirmid swiveled around, his concentration back on the console. "Because of what we do — and how we do it — there are certain rules we must agree to."

"Rules?"

"It's for our own good, of course. Getting attached to people — a mate — a child — it would interfere with out duties. Sometimes hard decisions need to be made. One's personal feelings can't get in the way of doing what needs to be done."

Ah. *Those* kinds of rules.

Something about the way Dirmid remained acutely absorbed by the panel in front of him made Sam think that perhaps it would be better to drop that particular line of inquiry for now. They'd strayed from the original topic anyway.

"How long has Lugh been on your world?" If the Goa'uld who'd originally brought these people to Gorias had abandoned them long ago, it was possible the Gorians had lived free of Goa'uld rule for a long time before Lugh showed up. It would explain their determination to get rid of him.

Dirmid's expression soured. "For six generations. And for five and a half of them, the *Shasa* have been planning their revolt."

Sam hadn't heard that term before. "And the *Shasa* are — ?"

"Resisters. Freedom fighters. Revolutionaries. Take your choice. And for the love of—Would you please sit down, Major. You're making me nervous."

Sam hadn't realized she'd been pacing. Somewhat sheepishly, she took her seat back at the console.

"Are the *Shasa* all like you? Are they all—*Ateronu*?" She struggled for the word and finally found it.

"No. They're ordinary folk. Well, extraordinary, really. They conceived this plan a long time ago and have, ever so diligently, kept it moving forward."

"For six generations?" That was patience worthy of the Tok'ra.

"We are as persistent as we are stubborn, Major. But soon, now. Soon, it will be over."

At last they were getting around to what she needed to know—the reason she was even here in the first place.

"So, what actually happens after you present Lugh with the cloak? How does any of this help you get rid of him?"

Dirmid sighed. "Your Colonel O'Neill was right—Lugh is a very, very minor Goa'uld. Most of the System Lords probably don't even remember his name, even if they do drink his *la'aum*."

"I'm sorry—*la'aum*?"

"It's a drink—we make it on Gorias. That it's a favorite of the System Lords is Lugh's one bit of fame—and a very small bit it is. Which is why he's always searching for something that will elevate him in their eyes. Maybe even work his way into their own inner circles."

"And a cloaking device that could conceal a mothership—"

"Oh, it's perfect. Just the thing to get the System Lords' attention."

"Right." That much she understood. And that was precisely what she couldn't let happen. "But I still don't get how you—"

"I told you, Major, that the right people need to be in the right place for the plan to work. Anyone who presents a prize like that cloak will surely win Lugh's favor."

"So you want a promotion?"

"Not for myself. For Magna. She needs to be First Tanist again, now that Graen's in control. It will take a lot to move Esras out of the way, but I'm betting this cloaking device can do it."

"Or my team." In spite of his pleasant demeanor and apparently good intentions, Sam couldn't let herself forget that there remained an implied threat in all of this. If she couldn't fix the cloak, SG-1 was still fair game.

"Now what's the point in bringing up that unpleasant possibility?" He looked truly troubled. "Regrettably, yes. But only as a last resort, Major. I promise you that."

He seemed genuinely wounded by her words. Maybe, if it came to that, she could help him figure out some other way to curry favor with Lugh. There had to be something else, short of her team, that would be just as valuable.

But she was putting the cart before the horse. Or jumping off the bridge before they got to it, as the colonel would say. She had to stay positive about getting the cloak fixed — and putting her own plan in motion. Anything beyond that, for now, was just a distraction.

"If everything goes as planned, and Magna becomes First Tanist — what happens then?" She got the part about moving their people into key positions. There had to be more to it than just that, though.

Dirmid didn't respond at once. He made some further adjustments on the console, which Sam thought at first might just be for show, as she suspected it had been earlier when they'd touched on a clearly uncomfortable topic. But this time there was a change in the engine's vibration. They were getting ready to drop out of hyperspace.

"You are asking me to reveal details of a plan that has taken nearly six generations to put in place," Dirmid finally replied, still not looking at her. "I think I've told you enough for now."

Sam didn't press him. She didn't have to — not really. It

wasn't hard to put the rest of the pieces together. With one of their own as Lugh's second-in-command, it would be relatively easy to launch a coup. Get control of the military. Lock up any dissidents. Take over the seat of power. It was textbook. She did appreciate the irony of the *Ateronu* using their conquerors' own personas as an avenue to overthrow them — a sort of variation on a Manchurian Candidate, only on a much larger scale.

Dirmid threw a switch and the stars appeared out of the viewport. They were back to normal space. Ahead, a small, brown planet was growing nearer. Their destination, if Sam had to guess. Dirmid had been telling the truth: it wasn't too far from P5C-777. Maybe if they were lucky, they'd find the crystal and be able to make it back there before Dar'dak and the rest of her team made it to the Stargate.

"So, where do we even begin to look?" she asked Dirmid as the planet began to fill the viewer. He'd been clear that this wasn't the place where the crystals were mined — that was some well-guarded secret, apparently. But it was a place where they were known to occasionally show up for sale. "Is there a village, or —"

"There's ten, actually. And they're cities, to be precise. But we'll start with the more likely one and work our way from there."

Sam looked down at her watch and realized she was still wearing the colonel's alongside her own. She hadn't had a chance to return it to him. With ten cities to scout, the odds of making it back to P5C-777 in time were looking a lot slimmer. She'd just have to give it back to him once she reached Gorias — on their way home. After she fixed the cloak.

And sabotaged it.

Because that was her plan. And quite possibly the only thing standing in the way of the System Lords getting their hands on the damn thing.

Sure. No pressure.

No pressure at all.

CHAPTER FIVE

//ACCESSING MISSION REPORTS...//

P5C-777 MISSION REPORT, COLONEL JACK O'NEILL: I know Carter and I trusted her. End of story. Daniel just needed to be reminded of that.

P5C-777 MISSION REPORT, MAJOR SAMANTHA CARTER: Under the circumstances, I had no choice. The only way out was through.

//CONTINUING ANALYSIS...//

"CARTER'S UP TO something." Jack had waited until Dar'dak was out of earshot. The Jaffa was sifting through the gear they'd left behind at their base camp, searching, Daniel presumed, for weapons or technology. They'd convinced him to let them rest here for a bit and have something to eat before the last forty-five minute trek that would take them to the gate. Dar'dak reluctantly agreed, reiterating his threat to shoot Teal'c if they tried to escape. Daniel had offered him an energy bar, which the Jaffa had tasted and spit out with an invective that Daniel really hadn't needed translated, although Teal'c had obliged.

Daniel looked at his own half-eaten protein bar and shoved it in his pocket. On second thought, maybe Dar'dak was just searching for food that was slightly more palatable.

The three of them were seated on the same log where, only yesterday, Sam had been working at her laptop. Except for the occasional snide remark aimed at Dar'dak, Jack hadn't spoken to either Daniel or Teal'c since they'd started the long walk back, so his comment took Daniel by surprise.

"What do you mean?" For the past several hours, Daniel had been turning over what had just happened back at the *tel'tak* with Sam. If only he could convince himself that maybe Pheone had brainwashed her somehow — or even that she might have been taken as a host by a different Goa'uld. Anything except what he feared the most: that she'd just gotten so wrapped up in the challenge of fixing the device that she'd lost all perspective on the moral consequences. He'd seen her get tunnel-vision before. Usually Jack was the one who snapped her out of it. Only this time he hadn't.

If there was a good reason for it, Daniel desperately needed to know.

"I mean, there's more going on with her wanting to fix that damn cloak than she was letting on."

"Like what?"

"I don't know, Daniel. If I knew then I'd tell you." Jack's raised voice and irritable tone drew Dar'dak's attention. Their captor watched them suspiciously for a few moments, but when they continued to sit there, merely eating and nothing more, he eventually returned to his scavenging.

"I will admit that I found Major Carter's behavior most uncharacteristic." Teal'c looked thoughtful. "If she had an ulterior motive in agreeing to assist Pheone, that would certainly explain her actions."

"See?" Jack gestured toward Teal'c, as if what he said was proof enough.

"So wait — you really don't know, you're just guessing?" Daniel thought maybe Sam had whispered something only Jack had heard. "She didn't say anything? Nothing at all?"

"You heard everything I did, Daniel."

He stared at Jack, perplexed. "Then what makes you so sure she's got some kind of plan?"

Jack appeared decidedly uncomfortable. He shrugged. "Just a hunch."

"A hunch?" Daniel had been waiting for some kind of concrete evidence to help him change his mind about Sam, but Jack apparently had only a gut feeling to offer.

"Yes, Daniel a hunch." He paused. "And maybe how she said what she said." Jack shook his head as if trying to clear up a fuzzy image. "Look, Daniel. I don't know how I know that I know. I just know Carter — you know?" He scrubbed his face with his free hand. "She *wanted* me to let her go. So I did."

Daniel threw up his hands — well, one hand, anyway — the other was anchored by Teal'c's massive arm — in dismay. "Do you have any idea the consequences of a device like that getting widespread use by the System Lords?"

"You've made yourself quite clear on that point Daniel. Let's stop beating a dead horse, all right?"

"How can you say that?"

"Because I trust Carter, okay? And I thought you did too." Jack's eyes were blazing.

Ouch.

Daniel hung his head. Okay. Maybe he deserved that. He did trust Sam. And more times than not, she had the unenviable ability to see both sides of an argument that he and Jack were typically at opposing ends of. More than that, though, she was his friend. And if for no other reason than that, he supposed, she deserved the benefit of the doubt. Maybe Jack was right. Maybe there was something else going on that neither of them were aware of. And maybe he'd been a little too caught up in the heat of the moment to realize that at the time.

Looking up, Daniel saw that Jack was watching him, waiting to see if he'd finally come to his senses. Satisfied that he had, Jack gave him a barely perceptible nod.

"If we assume Major Carter does, in fact, have a plan of which we are unaware, do you believe it was her intention for us to cooperate with the enemy as well?" Teal'c glanced over his shoulder at Dar'dak. Daniel could practically read his thoughts. There were three of them and only one of Dar'dak. Even with the advantage of his staff weapon, they could most likely overpower him if they wanted to.

"Yeah, T, I do. Which is why we're going along with this goon — for now. At least until we get Carter back." Jack quickly shoved the remainder of his energy bar in his mouth and shot an innocent smile over Teal'c's head. Daniel looked up and saw Dar'dak standing there. Their conspiratorial tones must have finally been too much for him to ignore.

"It's okay," Jack said around his food. He pointed at Daniel and Teal'c. "We were just plotting our escape. Nothing you should concern yourself with."

Dar'dak's eyes narrowed as he raised his staff weapon, but when Teal'c half-rose and twisted around to face him, the other Jaffa backed off. Smiling with satisfaction, Teal'c retook his seat, deliberately leaving his back to Dar'dak as an obvious sign of unconcern and disdain.

"You call that cooperating?" Daniel asked under his breath, glancing back at a still agitated and now humiliated Dar'dak.

Teal'c continued to smile.

"Indeed."

~#~

Sam lurked in the shadows of the nearby buildings, watching Dirmid as he worked his way among the various display booths that lined both sides of the market street. He blended in well enough, dressed in a generic sort of robe that seemed to be the customary attire for the region. If it weren't for his shockingly red hair, Sam would have taken him for one of the locals.

This marketplace was much larger than the first one they'd stopped at. They'd had no luck there, and after an hour of loitering around in case someone approached them, Dirmid had given up. It had been a short flight over a mostly barren landscape to this city, although as they landed Sam had caught sight of what looked to be more fertile land far in the distance. She could see evidence of that now in the booths, which offered a much greater variety of fresh produce than the first town had. The people too looked more prosperous, their baskets and bags filled to capacity, as they jostled their way through the crowded street.

Sam had no idea what planet they were on. Dirmid had refused to tell her. There was a Stargate, she knew that much, but apparently there was no Goa'uld presence here — although that didn't necessarily mean it was entirely off their radar. According to Dirmid, several smaller, non-Goa'uld syndicates operated out of this world and others like it. Beneath the bustling free-market enterprises of the craftsmen and the farmers and above-board businesses, there was a thriving black market that dealt in everything from illicit substances to ship parts to slave trafficking. In as much as the Goa'uld could use it to their advantage, they didn't bother to interfere

"'A wretched hive of scum and villainy'," Sam had remarked when Dirmid warned her about what they would encounter. He'd looked at her blankly. Teal'c would have gotten it.

From her current vantage point, however, everything looked legitimate. Just ordinary people buying and selling ordinary things. Unfortunately, it wasn't an ordinary thing she and Dirmid needed.

Sam shifted her position to have a better view of Dirmid and checked her holster again. The zat was still there. She'd been surprised when Dirmid gave it to her before they went to scout the first marketplace, but he'd handed it to her matter-of-factly, as if he didn't even question whether he could trust her with it or not. Of course, by then the colonel and the others were most likely already on Gorias, so it wasn't as if rushing back to P5C-777 would have done much good. The only way out of this mess, as far as she could tell, was to stick with her plan.

While Sam appreciated the zat, the robe she was wearing was a different matter. Gorians, it seemed, skewed on the shorter side of the height continuum. It was too short for her, reaching just to the top of her boots, not to mention that her tac-vest underneath made it tight in the shoulders. Not exactly a look that let her blend in with the local population.

Dirmid hadn't thought so either, especially after they'd gotten some strange looks on their first stop. This time, instead of being in the thick of things with him, he'd set her the task of watching his back from the sidelines while he went inquiring after crystals. Sam didn't mind being his backup, but he'd already been working this street for the better part of an hour. If she didn't have something else to do soon, she was going to go nuts.

Sam leaned her head back against the nearby wall and sighed. This was not where she was supposed to be right now. It was probably foolish, but she'd been really looking forward to pizza at the colonel's. She felt like things were finally getting back to normal where he was concerned.

Well, a new normal, anyway.

There was no denying that what happened between them on P3R-118 had pushed the boundaries. But those boundaries had needed to go back in place — to the extent that was even possible — once their memories returned. And except for their tacit agreement upon leaving the planet that this was how it had to be, they'd managed to avoid the subject altogether afterwards. What was the point? She actually thought they'd done a decent job of putting it behind them, until that damned Goa'uld light had shown them just how frustrated they both were.

Thankfully they were past that now; it hadn't just been the radiation they'd spent three weeks on P4X-347 detoxing from. And now, with the team finally back together for this mission, the colonel was the happiest she'd seen him for a while.

Dinner would have been fun.

And it still would be. Once she got her team back. She just needed to be patient and let Dirmid do what he had to.

He'd been lingering at one stall for a while now. Glancing around to make sure no one was watching, Sam pulled out her binoculars to take a closer look. The vendor had an eclectic offering of wares on display: rugs, candles, glass jars filled with what looked like an assortment of dried plants. As far as she could tell, however, there were no crystals. Then again, given that they weren't exactly your run-of-the-mill merchandise, she'd hardly expect them to be on display.

After a few more moments of speaking with the person in the booth, Dirmid moved on, but as he was walking away he glanced towards Sam and gave a very subtle nod. That was the sign. He must have gotten a lead. Finally, it was time for her to move.

Weaving in and out of the crowd, Dirmid worked his way down the street at a deliberate pace that had Sam struggling to keep up. At least his hair made him easy to keep track of in the sea of shoppers.

It wasn't just Dirmid she was supposed to be watching out for. According to him, he would most likely be followed, once word got out about what he was looking to buy. Information was as valuable a commodity as anything else on this planet, and someone looking to purchase a super-conducting giant crystal was just the sort of intel that certain parties might find useful — or so Dirmid claimed. Sam's job was to keep an eye out for whoever might be keeping an eye on Dirmid — which was easier said than done in this mass of moving bodies.

A few dozen meters ahead of her, Dirmid turned a corner and Sam lost sight of him. Elbowing her way through the crowd, trying to catch up, she arrived at the spot where he'd vanished. The market continued down this street too, and it was just as packed with booths and tents and people. Now she couldn't even spot his hair. He'd vanished into the sea of people, completely out of view.

Thankfully, though, not out of touch. Before they'd left P5C-777, she'd asked Dirmid to retrieve two of the radios he'd taken from SG-1. He had one with him now. She had the other. They'd agreed on radio-silence unless absolutely necessary, but as far as Sam was concerned, this qualified.

She was just about to thumb the talk button when she caught sight of him. He hadn't moved as far ahead as she had expected. His pace was much slower, probably because he kept stopping to look around, searching for something — or more likely, someone. Behind him, frustrated shoppers diverted around him, irritated by his not keeping up with the flow of foot traffic.

Sam took a moment to scan the crowd for anyone who might also be following him. She understood his need for caution, and it wasn't that she didn't believe it was possible someone's interest would be piqued by his inquiry, but there were just too many people to make any kind of meaningful threat assessment.

Then again —

A woman in a green robe angled into Sam's field of view. She was carrying several baskets, ostensibly for her purchases, but from the way they swung freely, Sam could tell they were empty. That in itself wouldn't have been a red flag, but there was also a practiced agility in her movements that reminded Sam of a tiger stalking its prey. Going by where the woman's eyes were repeatedly focused, that prey was unquestionably Dirmid.

It looked like maybe he'd been right after all.

Now it was time for the radio. "Someone's following you. A woman. Green robes. She's at — " Sam had been about to say "seven o'clock" but realized the direction would be meaningless. "She's behind you and coming up on your left." In her earpiece, she heard one click of acknowledgment. She'd given Dirmid a crash course on radio communications once they'd landed. He'd been a quick study.

Sam allowed the flow of the crowd to carry her forward. She wanted to get closer but not so close that the woman would notice her. The color of the woman's robe made her easy to keep track of. It was hardly subtle, although maybe that was the point. Who would expect someone so obvious to be, well, so obvious. Regardless, she was closing in on Dirmid's position. Sam picked up the pace.

Only a few meters separated Dirmid from the woman when a man carrying an oversized basket collided with him, sending him sprawling. It was a classic move. Sam recognized it the moment it happened. As the man with the basket reached down to help Dirmid to his feet, the woman slipped up beside him, sandwiching Dirmid between herself and her accomplice. She pressed a well-concealed weapon against Dirmid's ribs as the basket man grabbed him tightly by the other arm.

Damn it! Sam winced at a sudden eruption of static in her earpiece. At first, she thought someone was jamming the frequency, but no. Dirmid's radio must have gotten knocked around as they were grabbing him. Except — she could hear the sound of breathing and the unmistakable crackle of cloth against the microphone. Somehow, whether by accident or on purpose, his radio had been locked in transmission mode. She could hear everything that was going on.

"Now, I ask you, is that any way to be treating a potential customer?" Dirmid's voice wasn't crystal clear — the robe was acting as a sound dampener. But Sam could make out his words well enough. "I might have mistaken you for a couple of brigands, if I didn't know any better."

Sam drew up short. She'd been sizing up the best way to extricate Dirmid, but maybe she needed to hold back until she had a better understanding of what was going on. He certainly didn't sound like he felt in any danger, despite appearances.

"We'll decide if you're a customer or not." It was the woman who spoke. She was close enough to him that the radio picked her up as well. "Now put your hood up and keep walking. The last thing we need is for that hair of yours to draw any more attention." She glanced around to see if their small group had attracted any notice. Sam looked away to avoid making eye contact just as the woman's gaze swept in her direction.

So. These were the people Dirmid had wanted to meet. Sam wasn't sure exactly what she had expected, but certainly abducting one's buyer at gunpoint hadn't even crossed her mind. Given the rarity of the crystal, though, she supposed they could do as they pleased. After all, who needed civility when the market forces of supply and demand were at play?

Sam glanced up and saw that Dirmid and the others were starting to move off. They may have covered Dirmid's hair, but the woman was still easy enough to keep tabs on as they moved into the stream of shoppers.

After about a block, they finally veered off between a couple of booths selling flowers and through an archway that took them into an alley. Sam waited a few heartbeats before following.

The alley was empty by the time she got to it, but it did lead her to the next street over, which was considerably less festive and a lot less inviting than the marketplace. Sam wouldn't call it squalor, per se, but it definitely wasn't meant for tourist traffic. And she couldn't shake the feeling that at least a dozen pairs of eyes were watching her, even though there wasn't another soul in sight.

Except, of course, for the trio she'd been following. Sam spotted them just as they disappeared into one of the sturdier buildings on a nearby side street. If she followed, anyone watching would know she was tailing them. But it couldn't be helped — not if she wanted to stay close to Dirmid.

Drawing up alongside the entrance she'd seen the others use, Sam pulled out her zat and peered carefully around the doorway. No one was there. In fact, the opening only led to a steep, poorly lit staircase that went to the floors above.

At least she knew which way they'd gone. Up was the only option.

Through her earpiece all Sam was hearing was more muffled breathing coming from Dirmid as he climbed the stairs. Neither he nor the others had said anything intelligible. Maybe she'd be able to hear better once they stopped moving.

Another sharp crackle of static told Sam something had

brushed by the radio's microphone again. She distinctly heard a grunt from Dirmid, as if he'd had the breath slightly knocked out of him. Sam stiffened. If they were going to get violent, she'd have no choice but to go in after him.

"You know, we could've gone somewhere more pleasant to do this — had something to eat, a drop or two to drink. You didn't need to be bringing me up three flights of stairs to an empty room, just so we could have a chat."

Sam smiled. She had to give Dirmid credit. He'd just provided her with a precise sitrep. Fourth floor. No other guards. She took it as a signal and started up the stairs.

"What you've inquired about isn't exactly the sort of item most people come looking to buy." The man was speaking. Sam paused for a moment on the second landing so she could hear him more clearly.

"What I've inquired about isn't exactly the sort of item most people have to sell." Dirmid's tone was still light. If he was at all worried about his situation, he didn't sound like it. Still, Sam picked up the pace as quietly as she could.

"What we mean is, it gets a person noticed. Both the buyer and the seller. It's better not to discuss these types of transactions in public places." The woman spoke this time. "We wouldn't want to attract the attention of certain parties."

"Ah. I understand." Dirmid's voice dropped down to a conspiratorial whisper. "You mean this place has eyes. And ears."

Sam was fairly sure that last remark had been for her sake. She'd just reached the fourth floor and could glimpse Dirmid through an open doorway, backed up against a pillar in the middle of a large room. The others had their backs to her, but Dirmid most likely had detected her movement.

"Precisely. And we prefer to keep a low profile, on all fronts." The woman was standing very close to Dirmid. Now that Sam was just outside the room, she didn't need the radio any more. She pulled her earpiece out so it wouldn't be a distraction.

"Ah, yes. I see how that could be a problem. For you. Me, on the other hand, I just want the crystal, and I really don't care where I get it from, or who knows about it." He smiled at them blandly. "Now, do you actually have one, or has this all been just an attempt to scare me off? Because if you don't have what I'm looking for, I'll be on my way. And my associate with me."

It took a moment for Dirmid's words to register.

"What associate?"

There was no missing that cue. Sam stepped into the room, zat in hand.

"That would be me."

Caught off guard, the pair spun around. Dirmid made his move. He snatched the weapon from the woman's hand, training it on her as he backed his way over to stand beside Sam. "Excellent timing, Major." He gestured at the duo. "I'm afraid we were just about to reach an impasse. I'd introduce you all, but it's probably better if we keep our names to ourselves."

The woman in green appeared unfazed by the sudden reversal of her situation. She ran an appraising eye over Sam. "If you're thinking of stealing the crystal from us, then you'll be sorely disappointed. You don't actually believe we'd have it here, do you?"

"Steal it?" Dirmid was indignant. "Certainly not! We came to strike a deal. And despite your deplorable lack of hospitality, we're still willing to proceed — assuming you have what we need."

Sam shifted uncomfortably. The woman continued to stare at her as Dirmid spoke, and Sam could see she was trying to make the pieces of a puzzle fit together. If it turned out to be the puzzle Sam thought it was, it could be a problem.

When the woman didn't respond to Dirmid, her companion spoke up. "We have it. But it doesn't come cheap."

A grin split Dirmid's face. "Of course not. We never expected it would. Now, we'll need to see the crystal first, so my associate here can make sure it's what we need. And if it is, then I've got several dozen kegs of the finest *la'aum* in my cargo hold that I'm willing to offer as payment. I may not be much of a trader, but even I know what that's worth in a place like this."

The man's eyes lit up at the mention of the *la'aum*. Sam could practically see him calculating its value in his head.

"Good quality, you say?"

Dirmid nodded. "Aye. The best there is. Stolen from the warehouses of Lord Lugh himself." He winked conspiratorially. If possible, the man looked even more delighted. He leaned over and whispered something to the woman. She looked slightly startled, as if her thoughts had been elsewhere.

"Very well. We have a deal," she said, finally. "But I believe you'll agree that this transaction is best done discreetly and under cover of darkness." She gestured toward the pocket of her robe. "May I?" When Dirmid nodded, the woman removed a small electronic tablet. After pressing a few buttons, she offered it to Sam. On the screen was a map and what appeared to be coordinates.

"If you will meet us there with your ship, you can inspect the crystal. If it is what you need, then it is yours, and we will take our payment."

Sam passed the directions to Dirmid who seemed to find no problem with them. He nodded and handed the tablet back to the woman.

"A measure after sunset, then?" She slipped the tablet back into her robes.

Dirmid flipped her weapon around and handed it back to her, handle first. "Make it two measures. We're in no rush. Besides, it's best if it's good and dark, don't you agree?"

The woman's smile really wasn't a smile as she took back her weapon. It too disappeared into the robe. "If you prefer. Until then?"

Sam lowered her zat but didn't holster it. Maybe it was the woman's scrutiny of her, but nothing about this was feeling right. It was far too easy. She wondered if Dirmid was sensing it too.

"Until then." With a sweep of his arm, Dirmid waved them past himself and Sam, and the pair departed. Only when it was clear they had finally left the building did Sam put her zat away.

"You don't really trust them, do you?"

Dirmid was straightening his robe and brushing dust off his sleeve. He looked up with feigned shock.

"What? Don't you? That fine, upstanding pair of honest traders?"

Dirmid's sarcasm left her feeling marginally better.

"Do you think they actually have a crystal?" The idea of being conned wasn't as much of an issue as the time they'd have lost following a bad lead. Every delay was just that much longer her team had to be locked up on Gorias.

"No idea. But—" He held up his finger before she could protest. "I have it on good authority that, if anyone *does* have one, it will be them."

"And you believe they'll stick to their end of the deal?" She didn't think it was the least bit likely that they would, but maybe she was being overly pessimistic.

"Absolutely not. That's why I asked for the extra time."

So it wasn't just her, then. "You have a plan?"

Dirmid smiled and leaned in close, as if not wanting to be overheard. "No. But I'll lay odds, Major, that by then, you will."

CHAPTER SIX

//ACCESSING MISSION REPORTS...//

P5C-777 MISSION REPORT, TEAL'C: O'Neill was concerned for Major Carter's safety. As was I. Daniel Jackson too, I have no doubt.

P5C-777 MISSION REPORT, MAJOR SAMANTHA CARTER: It was one of those situations where we hoped for the best, but were careful to plan for the worst.

//CONTINUING ANALYSIS...//

TEAL'C HAD visited many planets in his nearly one hundred and two years, most of them while in the service of Apophis. Only since joining the Tau'ri, however, had he learned to truly see the worlds to which he traveled. It was Daniel Jackson who was mostly responsible for opening his eyes, not just to the diversity of history and culture that was unique to each planet but also to the beauty found in the infinite variations of nature across the galaxy. He had never before seen a forest such as the one on Gorias. And although Teal'c found he could appreciate its uniqueness and perhaps even to a degree its beauty, given a choice, it was not a place in which he would ever wish to find himself alone.

The trees were of extraordinary size, not as much in their height as in their girth. It would have taken another five such as himself to encircle even the smallest of them. Their shapes were distorted, made so by twisted, malformed trunks around which were wrapped rope-like vines as thick as Teal'c's arm.

The vines snaked into the branches overhead, occasionally drooping in great tangled loops from which gray, wispy plant matter stirred and fluttered even in the absence of a breeze. More disconcerting, however, were the trees' expansive roots. Shallow and hard as stone — O'Neill had tripped over one and his ensuing curses had verified this fact — they covered the forest floor with a serpentine mass of knots, as if the trees themselves were locked in perpetual battle with one another. The entire forest made Teal'c uneasy.

O'Neill too, going by his frequent glances to either side, as they followed Dar'dak along the narrow dirt path. The Jaffa had undone their bindings, allowing them to walk independently. It would have been impossible to traverse the trail otherwise. The footpath was easy enough to see, being bounded to its very edge by a thick carpet of moss which was the only other living thing in sight. It covered anything the trees did not, giving the forest a pale green glow. More than that, though, it swallowed up every sound, even their footfalls along the path, as if demanding silence from every living thing.

Only Daniel Jackson appeared oblivious to the unnatural quiet that pressed in upon them. In the time since they had emerged from the Stargate, he had made repeated attempts to learn more about Gorias, both from Dar'dak and the young Jaffa who had accompanied them from the gate. The former had not been inclined to speak any more than he had previously. The young Jaffa, however, would, from time to time, respond to questions, until Dar'dak had commanded him to speak no more.

Even so, Daniel Jackson was not easily deterred. "So, who is this Esras, exactly?"

Teal'c could see Dar'dak stiffen, clearly affronted in some way by the question.

"*Master* Esras is First Tanist. He is the Fist of Lugh."

O'Neill snorted.

"The Fist of Lugh?" Daniel Jackson interjected quickly before O'Neill could comment. "That's, um, a rather descriptive title."

"Master Esras commands the Jaffa," replied Dar'dak, as if that was all that was required as an explanation.

"So, is a First Tanist just some kind of fancy name for a First Prime?" O'Neill's tone was scornful, but Teal'c recognized the strategic purpose to the question.

"Actually—" Daniel Jackson replied before Dar'dak could even speak. "'Tanist' is a title given to the heir apparent of a Celtic chieftain. In this case, I presume it denotes some kind of hierarchical rank within Lugh's inner circle. Pheone was, what, Third Tanist, wasn't it?"

Ahead of Teal'c, O'Neill groaned. He had, no doubt, intended for Dar'dak to answer the question, most likely in the hope that he would unwittingly reveal further information in the process. Unfortunately, Daniel Jackson had failed to realize the true purpose of O'Neill's probing.

Perhaps a question that only Dar'dak could answer would prove more fruitful.

"Are we to understand, then, that Lugh does not have a First Prime?" Teal'c had noted that only two Jaffa stood guard at the Stargate as they came through. If that were all who could be spared for such a duty, then Lugh's contingent of Jaffa must be small indeed. A First Prime for any fewer than a hundred Jaffa would be unnecessary.

"Not as such, no." This time it was the younger Jaffa who answered. It earned him another sharp look from Dar'dak, although no verbal reprimand followed.

"Not exactly talking the big leagues, then, are we?" O'Neill observed with an appreciative glance back at Teal'c. "Whaddya want to bet the System Lords have never even heard of this guy?"

The younger Jaffa's indignation could not be held in check. "Lord Lugh is much favored by the System Lords! He produces the finest *la'aum* in all the galaxy."

"I'm sorry—*la'aum*?"

"It is a drink, Daniel Jackson—very similar to the alcoholic beverage you call beer." Teal'c had not thought of *la'aum* for a long time. Apophis had never cared for it, but there were many Goa'uld who did. "Serving a fine *la'aum* to guests during a meal was certain to advance one's reputation among their fellow Goa'uld."

"Hold on. You're saying that the Goa'uld have like, what, dinner parties?" O'Neill sounded incredulous.

"If by 'dinner parties' you mean a social occasion to which others are invited to share a meal, then, yes. However—" It took Teal'c a moment to recall the name he was looking for. "I do not think they are the type of social gathering of which Martha Stewart would approve. It is not infrequent that one or more of the guests fail to survive the evening."

Ahead of him O'Neill had a sudden fit of coughing that sounded suspiciously as though he were attempting to conceal laughter. Finally, he cleared his throat. "Never let anyone say the Goa'uld don't know how to throw a party."

Daniel Jackson ignored their conversation. His focus had now turned to the younger Jaffa, presumably because he seemed more inclined to answer questions. "So, if Esras is the First Tanist, I presume there's also a Second Tanist?"

The younger Jaffa did not disappoint. "Magna is Second Tanist and oversees the production and delivery of the *la'aum*. The Third Tanist is, as you said, Pheone."

"Be silent!"

Dar'dak's voice boomed over their heads, despite being dampened by the properties of the moss. He turned to glare at the other Jaffa, his sudden movement so unexpected that Daniel Jackson nearly ran into him. With their progress halted, all eyes now turned towards the back of the line as well. It was under Dar'dak's reprimand, though, that the young Jaffa's face turned bright red and he hung his head.

"Forgive me, Dar'dak." Unlike the older Jaffa's feigned penitence earlier, the younger Jaffa's shame was quite sincere.

Dar'dak held his look of disapproval for several long seconds before turning to resume their trek. Whether it was out of concern for the welfare of the younger Jaffa or because he did not wish to provoke Dar'dak further, Daniel Jackson fell silent at last and did not speak again.

As they continued along the narrow path, Teal'c gradually slowed his steps, allowing the space between himself and O'Neill to grow until he was distant enough from Dar'dak to speak without being overheard.

"What is your name?" he asked over his shoulder.

The young Jaffa's eyes darted to the front of the line. When he was certain that they were, in fact, out of earshot, he replied. "I am called Hyot'k."

"And from where do you come, Hyot'k?"

The Jaffa hesitated. "I prefer not to say."

Teal'c had only asked the question to see what the response would be. The tattoo on Hyot'k's forehead was clearly visible.

"You have served Lord Yu."

Hyot'k touched the mark with his free hand, as if surprised it was still there. "I serve Lord Lugh now—*shol'va*," he replied defensively.

Teal'c gave him a long, lingering look before turning back. "Do you indeed?"

The remark did not sit well. Teal'c felt a staff weapon nudge him in the small of his back, urging him to walk faster. He resisted the urge to wrest it from Hyot'k's hand. That the young Jaffa was inexperienced was most evident. Even now, it would have taken little effort to overpower both him and Dar'dak and return with O'Neill and Daniel Jackson to Earth. But O'Neill had been quite clear that they were to continue to cooperate until Major Carter's plan was put into play—despite not knowing exactly what that plan might be. Even so, he waited until Hyot'k prodded him a second time before ever so slightly picking up his pace.

They continued along the path for at least another hour before stopping to rest. The forest had paused to allow a river to pass through it, giving a brief glimpse of the blue-shrouded mountains that were undoubtedly the water's source. Over the river a stone bridge of impressive craftsmanship had been built, and it was on the other side of this that Dar'dak permitted them to momentarily sit along the riverbank.

O'Neill had spoken infrequently since they had arrived through the Stargate and remained distracted, even now. Teal'c suspected that his thoughts were elsewhere — most likely with Major Carter. His friend concealed his feelings well behind what many might have taken for mere camaraderie. But having been privy to the truths demanded by the *za'tarc* detector, Teal'c knew it for the masquerade it was. A necessary one, to be sure, but a masquerade nonetheless.

If Daniel Jackson was aware of O'Neill's unusual silence, he did not make mention of it. Although Dar'dak's reprimand had stopped him from asking questions directly, it had not prevented him from casually remarking on their surroundings along the way. He had even, somehow, induced Dar'dak to reveal that the name of the distant mountains, translated from Gorian, meant "guardians of hope". Daniel Jackson had found the name fascinatingly subversive, especially on a planet ruled by a Goa'uld.

"You look like a man with something on his mind." O'Neill had chosen a rock adjacent to Teal'c against which to lean. He spoke in a low voice so as not to attract Dar'dak's or Hyot'k's attention.

It did not seem appropriate to mention his most recent musings to O'Neill, so Teal'c offered another topic which he had been contemplating as they walked.

"I have been considering our guards." He did not look at O'Neill directly, also to avoid attracting undue attention. "Dar'dak wears the mark of Ares. The other, Hyot'k, bears the tattoo of Lord Yu. The guard who remained at the Stargate had scars upon his forehead, where I suspect a mark had once been."

O'Neill squinted at the sparkling water. Dar'dak had not seen fit to allow any of them to retrieve sunglasses from their gear on P5C-777. "Okay. So what does that mean?"

"I am uncertain. However, if I were to hazard a guess, I would say it is possible that Lugh's Jaffa are comprised of those who may have defected from the ranks of other Goa'uld."

"Defected? Do Jaffa do that?"

"Not without great risk. Any Jaffa caught making such an attempt is summarily executed."

O'Neill grimaced. "Nice." He glanced over at Dar'dak and Hyot'k. "So, does that make these guys extra brave or extra stupid?"

"It makes them the most desperate of all Jaffa. They have little else to lose." And yet, possibly everything to gain, given the opportunity. He would need to find out more, however, before deciding what potential existed here.

"I guess they'd have to be to end up serving a piss-poor Goa'uld like this Lugh. I mean, come on. The guy sells beer, for cryin' out loud."

"As I recall, O'Neill, there are a great many companies on Earth which also produce beer and profit greatly from it. Many of your financial advisors consider them a wise investment."

O'Neill turned to him and blinked. "Exactly how much television do you watch when you're on base?"

"Enough rest." Dar'dak appeared behind them, staff weapon in hand as if he intended to herd them back into line. For a moment, Teal'c thought O'Neill was going to offer one of his colorful suggestions as to where, anatomically, Dar'dak could secure the weapon, but his friend wisely changed his mind. They had thought it prudent to cooperate, after all.

This did not prevent O'Neill from muttering a few other imaginative insults at Dar'dak as they wearily resumed their single-file trek, although Teal'c was fairly certain he alone had heard them. Which was a shame. O'Neill could be most articulate when the situation required.

Teal'c had intentionally positioned himself first in line behind Dar'dak this time, allowing Daniel Jackson to be closest to the younger Jaffa in back. Admittedly, his motive was less for Daniel Jackson's sake than his own. Should an opportunity arise, he hoped to glean more information about the Jaffa here. Given his already antagonistic relationship with Dar'dak, however, he had no doubt that a straightforward approach would be unsuccessful. He would need to use a different strategy.

The trees on this side of the river, although they still resembled those they had passed among earlier, were smaller and less foreboding. Interspersed among them were other trees of the type Teal'c was more accustomed to seeing. It was not long before their surroundings had transitioned into a more conventional forest. Teal'c thought he even heard birdsong.

Perhaps it was the change in the forest, or perhaps it was because no one had spoken since they had left the riverbank, but Dar'dak seemed to have relaxed somewhat. He walked less stiffly and was no longer inclined to start at every stray sound or twig snap. Teal'c moved in closer. Now might be his chance.

"Tell me, how does a warrior of Ares come to serve so pitiful a master as Lugh?" In the greater Goa'uld hierarchy, Ares himself was hardly considered to be of much consequence. To be amongst his ranks conferred very little status upon a Jaffa. Losing even the minimal stature that position offered, to find oneself where Dar'dak was now, would undoubtedly be a source of great shame. In Teal'c's experience, oftentimes shame opened one's mind to greater truths.

Dar'dak did not reply, although Teal'c could plainly see the muscles in his neck and arms tighten, as did his grip on the staff weapon. Despite his earlier threats, Teal'c did not believe the Jaffa would kill him. He might disdain Pheone, but he would not risk the Goa'uld's wrath. If Teal'c wished to have answers, it was clear further goading was necessary.

"Were you captured in battle?" he pressed. "Or, perhaps, more likely, you simply ran from the fight." Teal'c allowed contempt to drip from his tone. Dar'dak stiffened even more, but he still refused to even acknowledge Teal'c's presence.

"I see the truth now. There is no passion that runs through your veins." Teal'c moved in even closer, lowering his voice to almost a whisper. "If the insults of a *shol'va* cannot stir your blood, then you truly lack the heart of a warrior." He threw in a taunting chuckle. "How fitting it is that you should spend your days here, protecting the lord of *la'aum*."

Dar'dak whirled on the spot, pressing the point of the staff weapon against Teal'c's chest. Teal'c smiled. At last he had drawn blood.

"Whoa!" Teal'c could hear O'Neill's concerned voice behind him as the others stopped in their tracks. "Easy there, big fella."

"You know nothing of what courses through my veins, *shol'va*!" Dar'dak pushed the staff harder against Teal'c's ribs, but he did not activate the weapon. His eyes were bright with fury. "Nor the circumstances which have led me to this place. So I would advise you to hold your tongue, especially when you do not know of what you speak."

"Then tell me." Teal'c said it as much as an invitation as a challenge.

"Teal'c?" O'Neill still sounded alarmed. Teal'c did not turn around but kept his eyes locked on Dar'dak.

"It is fine, O'Neill. Do not concern yourself."

Dar'dak continued to hold the weapon for several more moments before at last dropping it. "I will tell nothing to a traitor." He spat on the ground as he turned around and began walking again. Teal'c remained only a step behind him. He spoke so that only Dar'dak might hear.

"Then tell it to someone who has seen the truth behind the lies of the Goa'uld — someone who knows them as they truly are: not gods, but parasites. Not deliverers but enslavers. Tell it to someone who will fight until his dying breath so that one day all Jaffa might taste true and everlasting freedom."

Dar'dak made a dismissive motion with his free hand, batting away Teal'c's words. "You are as delusional as they say."

Teal'c made no reply. Sometimes truth gained victory, not with persuasion but with silence.

Several more moments passed as they continued to walk, but eventually Dar'dak spoke again. "What would it matter if the Goa'uld were not gods? For all the power they wield, they might as well be." His voice was so quiet he might easily have been speaking to himself. "And better to serve one who poorly wields it than one who uses it as a petulant child wields a hammer."

At last they were getting somewhere.

"You speak of Ares."

The Jaffa nodded.

According to Daniel Jackson, on Earth, Ares had been the Greek god of war. From what Teal'c knew of the Goa'uld who had taken his name, it was a fitting choice. Although not a System Lord, his penchant for wanton carnage was well known amongst the Jaffa.

"You were a defector."

Dar'dak's jaw hardened. "Not by choice."

Teal'c raised a dubious eyebrow, but said nothing, waiting.

"Ares had ordered an attack on Ramius." Dar'dak's words came forth reluctantly. "Our forces had their Jaffa in retreat. Victory would have been ours that day, but Ares' First Prime—Trelak—made an error. Two-thirds of our battalion was lost. Half of those who were not slaughtered or captured on the field of battle returned wounded, many only to die later. By any standards it was a brutal loss and Ares' anger was boundless."

The rage of a Goa'uld in defeat was a terrible thing indeed. "What became of Trelak?" A First Prime responsible for such a staggering loss would most certainly have faced execution.

Teal'c could see Dar'dak's lips curl into a bitter smile.

"To save his own skin, Trelak lied. He placed the blame on his commanders — myself among them. As punishment, Ares ordered our families killed."

Teal'c's stomach knotted. In service to Apophis, he had both witnessed and carried out many atrocities that had haunted his dreams for years, but none more than those he had inflicted upon the innocent. It was the Goa'uld's preferred form of cruelty, and for too long he had been their willing instrument.

"I am sorry." The sentiment seemed inadequate, but no words would ever be sufficient for such a loss.

Dar'dak was shaking his head, however. "I hid them. And I fled. Fate brought me to Lugh — the lord of *la'aum*, just as you say. But at least I know my wife and children still breathe and sleep safely in their beds each night, even if I shall never see them again."

His story was not what Teal'c had expected. If it were true — and as far as he could tell, Dar'dak had no reason to lie — then there potentially was an unforeseen benefit to be gleaned from their current situation. If there were other Jaffa here with similar stories, perhaps their hearts might be persuaded to answer the call to freedom — and in doing so, SG-1 might gain their freedom as well.

First, though, he must plant the seeds.

"Tell me, Dar'dak. Do any others here share your belief that the Goa'uld — Lugh among them — are not gods?"

Dar'dak's head swiveled around. "I never said —"

"Oh, but you did. And I can see it in your eyes, my brother. You know the truth. Otherwise you would have allowed Ares to slaughter your family."

Dar'dak put his attention back on the path in front of him. "What is in my heart, and what is most expedient for my survival, are irreconcilable. I serve Lord Lugh — and Master Esras. My heart is mine alone."

"And what if they could be reconciled?" Here at last was his opening. Teal'c had learned, painfully at times, that many Jaffa feared the idea of freedom more than they feared the wrath of their Goa'uld masters. For such as these, the rallying cry of revolution merely drove them further away. But if they could be led there by their own words, the enlightenment of revelation could ignite just as bright a flame.

"You speak of rebellion."

Teal'c smiled. "I speak of freedom. Freedom which you already feel burning in your heart."

Dar'dak glanced back at Teal'c with an expression no longer guarded. "One day, perhaps. For all of us. But that day is not soon."

Teal'c smiled with satisfaction. "Who is to say, brother? That day may be sooner than you think."

~#~

The Woman in Green and Basket Man were not alone. That was the first thing Sam noticed. At least a half dozen others were lingering in a loose group amidst the shadows cast by the stacks of crates and boxes that ringed the perimeter of the warehouse. Although she couldn't see them clearly, their size and shape suggested they were the muscle of the organization. The colonel would have found it quite the cliché.

"You're late." The woman had been pacing in front of a small table, but stopped once she saw Sam and Dirmid. There was no misinterpreting her scowl of irritated impatience.

"Are we?" Dirmid blinked innocently. "So sorry about that. The ship's chronometer's always been a bit off. One of those things I keep meaning to get fixed."

"I see you brought friends." Sam nodded toward the group in the shadows. "I didn't realize we were *that* intimidating."

The woman barely glanced over her shoulder. "Merely our security. There are a great many things of value in here. Some people might see them as a temptation."

"Or a challenge." Sam offered her a frigid smile along with the veiled threat. Not that anyone would mistake herself and

Dirmid for a couple of thugs, but maybe with enough bluff and bluster they could get out of this with what they came for. Or even just out of this, period.

The woman's eyes narrowed. "That would be unwise."

Sam kept her smile intact. "So would double-crossing a paying customer."

Basket Man cleared his throat. "We *do* have the crystal." He sounded anxious as he gestured to someone in the shadows. "Bring it over!"

One of the "security" stepped forward and placed the enormous crystal carefully on the table before withdrawing. Even in the dim light it was a beautiful thing and, as far as Sam could tell with the naked eye, perfectly intact.

She took out her scanner and slowly ran it up and down the length of the meter-long crystal. She'd memorized the readings from the broken one in the ship. This one was showing up as nearly identical, and what wasn't identical was inconsequential for their purposes. Sam felt her pulse quicken. This would actually work.

Of course, verifying the crystal was the easy part. Leaving with it was another matter.

Looking up at Dirmid, Sam nodded. "Close enough."

"Well, then. It looks like we're all winners today." He beamed at them. "Now, if you'll be so kind as to follow me out to our ship, you can look over the *la'aum*, before we off-load it. You're getting the better part of this deal, make no mistake about it."

"Oh, I'd say we definitely are." The woman smiled and snapped her fingers. Two strong hands suddenly gripped Sam's arms, twisting one behind her back. Her other arm was pinned to her side as Basket Man grasped her tightly around the waist, holding her against him. In her periphery, Sam could see the security guards move in closer.

"We actually have a different payment in mind," the Woman in Green continued, smoothly. "*La'aum* is all well and good, but it's a pittance compared to what we could get for Major

Samantha Carter of the Tau'ri."

Damn. So they had recognized her after all. Not exactly a surprise — Dirmid had warned her about the boots — but it did make everything much more complicated than it needed to be. So much for bluff and bluster.

"*Her*?" Dirmid looked sincerely perplexed. "You want her, instead of the *la'aum*?" He shoved his hands deep in the pockets of his robe. "Well, you can take her. All I ever needed her for was to authenticate the crystal. She's done that now, so I'll gladly be shot of her. They're a pesky bunch, those Tau'ri, I hear. I wouldn't want to be in their crosshairs if they come looking for her."

Sam glared at him. "Wait! You're just going to hand me over? Why you traitorous little —" It wasn't hard to channel her real anger into the outburst as she made a lunge at Dirmid. Her sudden movement caught Basket Man off guard, and she rolled away from his loosened grip, landing a punch to his solar plexus, before she swept his feet out from under him with a roundabout kick.

As the man collapsed to the floor, Sam saw Dirmid raise his arm. There was a burst of light from the palm of his hand, accompanied by a sonic pulse that raised the hair on the back of her arm. All the security men went flying backwards, crashing into the wall of crates behind them.

The only one left standing was the Woman in Green — and she was holding the crystal.

"I will let it shatter into a million pieces." She held the quartz away from her body to underscore her threat. Sam could see her arms shaking from the weight. If she dropped it —

"Look. We're still willing to make the trade. The *la'aum* for the crystal. Isn't it better to walk out of here with something than with nothing at all?" Sam took a tentative step towards her, but the woman shook her head. There was a look of desperation about her now.

"I've already made promises. I don't dare show up empty-handed. It's got to be you."

Sam looked at Dirmid, who sighed. "Aye. That's what the Major thought you'd say. Too bad you'll have to disappoint." His other hand came up out of its pocket so swiftly Sam barely saw the zat until it fired.

Diving forward, she wrenched the crystal from the woman's hand as she started to sink towards the floor. For a terrifying couple of seconds, Sam didn't think she had it — the smooth sides slid through her damp palms and she couldn't get a grip. But the crystal tilted towards her and she was able to wrap her arms around it, pulling it against her, as if she'd just caught a football. The quartz's weight threw Sam off balance, but she stumbled forward, somehow managing to stay on her feet until she righted herself.

Sam breathed a sigh of relief and saw that Dirmid was doing the same. That had been just a little too close.

Back in the pile of smashed crates, the stunned security guards were starting to stir.

"I think it's time we take our leave, what do you say, Major?" Dirmid gestured toward the door.

He would get no argument from her. Basket Man was starting to rouse, too. The sooner they were away from here, the better. She especially didn't want to be around when the Woman in Green woke up. Sam was fairly sure that for Basket Man and the others, there would be hell to pay.

As the *tel'tak's* airlock closed behind them, Sam carefully placed the crystal in an empty case Dirmid had prepared for it. After they were under way, she'd see about getting the cloaking device fixed. Until they'd reached the smoothness of hyperspace, though, there was no point in risking damaging the crystal in case they had a bumpy ride out of the planet's atmosphere.

Sam felt the ship lift off, but there was no sense of forward momentum. They seemed to just be hovering in place.

"Stay back from the *la'aum*, if you please." Dirmid came hurrying off the flight deck and over to the controls for the transport rings. Earlier they had loaded half the kegs into the center of them, on the slim chance that the deal would go through as planned. Not that either of them had expected it to.

"You're still going to give them the *la'aum*?" That was a surprise.

"A deal's a deal, Major. I'm no thief. But I am going to only give them half, seeing as how they were not very nice about the whole thing. And they're still making out ahead, even with that amount. The price of *la'aum* on the black market is more than you can imagine."

Sam watched as the rings appeared and then vanished, taking the kegs with them. "I doubt it will be enough to get her out of the trouble she'll be in with whomever she promised me to."

"Well, that's her problem, not ours—thanks to your plan." He examined the Goa'uld ribbon device as he slipped it off. "I've never actually used one of these before, odd as that may sound."

"Well, technically you are a Goa'uld, so I figured if anyone could control it, you could."

He turned it over in his hand, before offering it to her with a smile. "Worth remembering."

Gingerly, Sam placed it back in the box they'd found it in. Even touching the thing made her shiver. It felt like there was a current running through it, all the way up her arm and into her head. It had done the job, but she couldn't help wonder if maybe she hadn't just put one more weapon at Dirmid's disposal.

And the fact that he thought so too didn't exactly give her peace of mind.

CHAPTER SEVEN

//ACCESSING MISSION REPORTS...//

P5C-777 MISSION REPORT, COLONEL JACK O'NEILL: As far as I was concerned, they could all go take a flying leap. Until Carter got back, we weren't budging.

P5C-777 MISSION REPORT, MAJOR SAMANTHA CARTER: It was a difficult decision to make. Basically, I was damned if I did and damned if I didn't. Either way, it was a lose/lose situation.

//CONTINUING ANALYSIS...//

JACK GINGERLY touched the iron grate in the dungeon door with his fingertips — twice — just to be sure. He'd been burned before, both figuratively and literally, by any number of shock-inducing bars and forcefields. He always remembered to test them now — well, almost always, anyway. No one had ever accused him of being a fast learner. Fool him once, shame on you; fool him a couple dozen times — Well, something like that.

The bars were just what they seemed to be. Plain old iron mounted in a small window of a thick wooden door. No forcefield. No electrified current running through them. Jack gripped them firmly with both hands and shook them as hard as he could. Nope. Not budging. Not that he'd expected them to. But it never hurt to try.

"I do not believe you will find that door penetrable, O'Neill,"

Teal'c offered helpfully.

"Yeah. Kinda getting that, T." Nevertheless, he gave it another hard pull for good measure. A few flecks of metal rubbed off on the palms of his hands, but that was all. It was a dungeon door and it was locked and there was no getting around the fact that, for the present, at least, the three of them weren't going anywhere.

Not until Carter got back.

Assuming, of course, that she did get back.

He'd spent the last several hours second-guessing his decision to let her go in the first place. Up until they'd reached Base Camp on P5C-777, Jack had convinced himself that she'd had some kind of plan in mind when she said she needed to go off with Pheone. It had been less in what she'd said than in how she'd looked at him. He couldn't explain it, even if he wanted to, but more often than not, he just understood Carter, without her hardly needing to say a word — except, of course, when it came to all her technobabble. And that's how it'd been this time too — or so he'd thought.

It wasn't until Daniel had pressed him for specifics that the doubt had started to creep in. Maybe he'd gotten it wrong. Maybe she'd simply been going along with the Goa'uld to save him and the rest of the team. Jack wouldn't put it past her. Hell, it's what he'd have done, given no other options. She knew that too. Which is why he'd been kicking himself ever since. Sometimes Carter was too good a second in command for her own damn good.

"I wonder how long we'll be stuck here." Daniel had made a circuit of the cell and now claimed one of the four wooden benches that lined the wall. They were obviously meant as bunks too, being long enough to lay down on. Hardly five-star accommodations, though.

"I am certain Major Carter will be as swift in completing her task as circumstances allow." Teal'c had moved to the wall opposite Daniel, although he did not sit. Jack realized that from his position he could see at an angle through the door's barred window toward the larger, outer door which was also locked. On the other side of it were about two flights of stairs that led to the main floor of the castle overhead. Anyone coming in or out of the dungeon would have to come that way. Teal'c's spot was strategically chosen.

Jack selected one of the two benches along the back wall and sat down. He was always up for a good hike, but they'd done a hell of a lot of walking since he and Teal'c had set out to do a simple perimeter check, about a hundred years ago. He didn't even know what time it was — Carter still had his watch. Then there was the whole time-change thing. It had been well past midday on P5C-777 when they'd gated for Gorias, but barely past sunrise when they walked out the other side. He had no idea if it was yesterday, today or tomorrow. He just knew that, whatever day it was, it was sure one helluva long one.

And as far as Jack was concerned, it wouldn't really be over until Carter was back.

"I wish we'd been able to get a better look around upstairs."

Jack recognized Daniel's archeologist tone. At the end of their trek through the Haunted Forest they'd come to a looming structure which Daniel had quickly identified as resembling the type of castle typically built in medieval Ireland. He'd been going on about it ever since.

"Considering that our presence here is intended to be kept secret, it is no surprise that Dar'dak avoided alerting others to our arrival," Teal'c replied.

Not only had he avoided it, he had gone out of his way to assure it. Dar'dak kept sending the other Jaffa — the kid — ahead to make sure the coast was clear before he led them along tunnels and down corridors and through doors so low that all of them had to duck to get through. Finally, they'd emerged into a dimly lit hall, where he'd made them scurry around the perimeter like rats before reaching yet another door, which turned out to be the one that led down to this place.

Daniel had been fascinated by the whole thing — even this damp hellhole of a dungeon that smelled like a cross between a latrine and a mushroom farm.

Reflexively, Jack wrinkled his nose.

Daniel must have noticed. "Actually, were you aware that many castles had indoor toilets? Well, they weren't toilets so much as a sort of indoor outhouse. There were chutes that ran up one side of the castle wall, and as they filled up, some unlucky servant would have to empty it, through a door at the bottom. Needless to say, if it wasn't emptied frequently, it could get, well, pungent."

"Thank you, Daniel. I could have gone my whole life without needing to know that. How about you, Teal'c?"

Even the big guy looked a little put off. "Indeed."

Daniel adjusted his glasses. "I'm just saying — it might be the reason why —"

"I *get* it Daniel. Don't make Teal'c blush, okay?"

For his part, Teal'c merely jutted out his chin as if he were above it all and turned his attention back to the view out the prison door.

"So whatcha lookin' at, T?" There had to be a reason he was standing there. "You expecting someone?"

"I am, in fact, expecting no one, O'Neill. However, I had hoped that Dar'dak might perhaps return."

"So what's up with these Jaffa anyway?" Jack wiggled his finger at his own forehead. "They've all got different marks, like you said. Did you learn anything more about them from your buddy Dar'dak?" If Carter fixed the cloaking device, it would be a moot point. But if she couldn't, and they all ended up prisoners here, they'd need as much intel as they could get. The size and capabilities of Lugh's Jaffa was as good a place to start as any.

Teal'c tore his eyes away from the door and looked at Jack. "I did not — except to strengthen my suspicions that many may have come here as a last resort and that their devotion to Lugh may, in fact, have its limitations."

Daniel had stretched out on the bunk bench. "That doesn't sound like your typical Jaffa army."

"It is mere speculation, Daniel Jackson, and nothing that I can prove or disprove. However, if Dar'dak's story of how he came here is typical of the others, I do not think it would take much for them to reject the Goa'uld altogether. Especially if another opportunity presented itself."

Jack recognized the brightness that had come into Teal'c's eyes. He was warming to his favorite topic — which was all well and good at the appropriate time, but now hardly seemed like it.

"Uh, Teal'c? Tell me you're not thinking of trying to recruit Mr. Stiffer-Than-a-Staff-Weapon and his minions into the ranks of the Rebel Jaffa? Because, don't get me wrong, while I totally support the whole idea — in general — I really think our focus needs to be elsewhere right now. Like getting Carter back and getting the hell out of here."

"I do not believe the two are mutually exclusive, O'Neill. Especially if Pheone ultimately chooses to keep us as his prisoners."

Daniel sat up. "You're thinking that if you can convince Dar'dak to join the Rebel Jaffa, then he'd be willing to help us escape." Eyebrows raised, he shot Jack a look. "It's not a bad Plan B."

No, it wasn't. Assuming they needed it. And assuming it worked. Personally, Jack didn't have a lot of hope that Dar'dak could be turned, but Teal'c must have learned something that made him think otherwise.

"Could be. Maybe. If it comes to that." He clapped his hands together and rubbed them. "But hey, let's just wait and see what Carter manages to pull off before we go setting up a Jaffa recruiting station, okay?"

Whatever Teal'c was about to say in response was cut off by the loud, metallic clank of a key in a lock. Immediately, his eyes returned to the outer door. "I believe someone is coming."

Jack went to look. Daniel too. It was probably Dar'dak. Or, if they were lucky, Carter.

Except it wasn't either of them.

A thin man slipped through the door, closing it behind him, and locking it. In the dim light his face appeared as pale as the moon, and there was a pinched look about it, as though he might have missed too many meals in his life. Wisps of dull brown hair drooped over his eyes from a really bad comb-over, and if it hadn't been for the fact that he kept chewing them, Jack would have guessed that the guy had no lips at all. With his eyes scanning the other cells as he crept past them, he looked like either a low-rent lawyer or a very nervous accountant. Jack half expected him to be carrying a briefcase.

"Hellooo?" Daniel lifted his hand and waved his fingers to get the guy's attention. When his eyes alighted on the three of them clustered around the small barred window, he frowned.

"*Quiet!*" he hissed, hurrying forward until he was just outside their door. "*No one is to know you are here.*"

A Goa'uld voice was the last thing Jack had expected. Teal'c or Daniel either, going by their expression. The guy just wasn't the type.

Then his eyes glowed.

Okay. Maybe he was the type after all.

"Yeah—" Daniel stepped back from the door, a bit warily. "You're right—no one is supposed to know we're down here. So who are you, exactly?"

"*I am Esras, First Tanist of Lord Lugh.*" He peered through the opening. "*I see Major Carter has not yet returned.*"

"What's it to you?" Jack stepped up to the door so his face was mere inches away from the Goa'uld's. If this was the "Fist of Lugh" he could hardly wait to see Lugh himself.

Almost too predictably, the "Fist" backed away.

"*I am merely eager for Pheone to present his prize to Lord Lugh. He will undoubtedly be greatly rewarded for so excellent a find. I did not wish to miss such an event.*"

Teal'c had joined Jack at the little window. "Anyone who could procure such a prize as the cloaking device would most assuredly be rewarded. I would not be surprised if that person were promoted to the next highest rank of Lugh's inner circle."

Esras' eyes darted between them. "*Yes. Yes. I suppose that is the likely outcome —*"

It took Jack a moment to catch on. Back on P5C-777 Pheone had said he was going to let the other guy — the Second Whatever — give Lugh the cloak. So, if anyone was going to get a promotion, it would be him. And there was only one spot higher than Second, and that was First.

Which meant old Esras here would be out on his ear.

A fact, which Jack just now grasped, that the Goa'uld already knew very well. That was why he was down here in the first place. He'd come to try to stop it from happening. Only he was here too early. Carter and Pheone weren't back yet.

No wonder the guy looked even paler than he had when he came in.

Daniel had worked it out too — or, part of it, anyway. "But I thought Pheone said he was going to let —"

"— Us go, just as soon as he and Carter get back." Jack shot Daniel what he hoped was not too subtle a look to keep quiet. He couldn't say why, exactly, but there was something extra smarmy about this Esras. And since when did a Goa'uld give away an opportunity to suck up to one of his higher-ups? There was something else going on here — some kind of internal politics maybe, which was the last thing they needed to get caught up in — at least, no more than they already were. Frankly, from what little Jack had seen so far — and sure, maybe Carter's actions had something to do with it — if it came down to trusting Pheone or trusting this Esras, he'd rather stick with Pheone.

"*Of course. Far be it from me to interfere with whatever arrangement Pheone has made with you. As I said, I merely came to congratulate—"*

A clicking noise emanated from the pocket of Esras' tunic. Fumbling, he finally pulled out an oval-shaped object that Jack recognized at once. He'd used one on Netu—well, at least until the Goa'uld had taken it away from him. It was a short-range communications device.

"*My Lord, someone approaches.*"

It was hard to tell, but Jack could have sworn the speaker on the other end sounded like Dar'dak. He looked to Teal'c for confirmation. The scowl on T's face more or less said it all. It was pretty clear who the snitch had been. It really was hard to get good help these days.

Esras didn't even bother to reply. He was already hurrying towards the door at the other end of the passage, but he pulled up short when he got there. Whoever was coming must have already been on the steps, because he went one more shade paler.

It couldn't be Pheone and Carter, otherwise Esras wouldn't be in such a panic. Which meant that probably someone else knew they were down here too. So much for staying under the radar. Maybe whoever had blabbered to Esras had gone straight to Lugh as well. If that were the case, then it wouldn't matter what Pheone had promised. No way a Goa'uld like Lugh was going to let the four of them walk out of here. Why settle for a mere cloaking device when he could have SG-1 too?

In any case, Esras was trapped. Whoever was coming down the stairs was going to find him standing there in all his simpering glory. As far as Jack was concerned, it couldn't happen to a nicer guy.

"Uh—guys? Where did he go?" Daniel was frowning past them at the passageway beyond.

The very empty passageway.

Esras was gone. It was like he'd vanished into thin air.

"Teal'c, did you see—?"

"I did not, O'Neill. Regrettably, I glanced away momentarily."

Jack had too, but it had only been for a few seconds. Yet somehow Esras had gone — somewhere.

Damn.

"Maybe he has one of those personal cloaking things — you know, like Hathor." It was the only possibility Jack could think of.

"You mean, you think he's still there, just invisible?" Daniel peered into the gloom.

Jack shrugged."You got any other ideas?"

"Perhaps we should alert the person who is about to come through the door." Teal'c raised his voice to assure he was heard in the outer room. "I am certain they would be able to ascertain if Esras is still present."

The three of them fell silent, waiting for any sign that the Goa'uld was there.

Nothing.

"I do believe he is indeed gone," Teal'c said after several moments.

Jack had to admit, the room *felt* empty. Frankly, he wasn't sure which he found more troubling, the fact that Esras might be there and good enough to fool them, or the fact that he had left and they had no idea how.

Not that there was much time to ponder either. Not when Player Two was about to come through the door.

The lock turned — again — only this time a woman wearing a hooded robe walked through. For a half-a-heartbeat, Jack thought it might be Carter, but she was too short. And when she drew back the hood that had concealed her face, he saw that her hair was nearly as red as Pheone's.

Without hesitation, she came immediately to their cell door, key in hand.

"And who might you be?" Jack kept his tone airy. She looked up at him with startling green eyes as she fit the key into the lock and swung open the door to their cell.

To Jack's great surprise, those green eyes suddenly glowed.

"*I am Magna, Second Tanist to Lord Lugh. I have come to set you free.*"

~#~

"You can fix it, then?"

Sam tried not to sigh with exasperation. Ever since they'd escaped the atmosphere of the nameless planet, Dirmid had been asking the same question, or some version of it, at least every half hour. She hadn't been able to give him an answer before, and she still couldn't. Not yet, anyway.

Realigning and recalibrating the new crystal had taken a lot longer than she'd expected. Only just now had she managed to power up the cloaking device so she could confirm which of the other crystals needed to be replaced. Once she took care of that, she could turn the device on and run a full diagnostic. Then, and only then, would she be able to tell what was wrong with the cloak and whether or not it could be fixed. Dirmid's patience needed to last a while longer.

"I'll know soon." It was the only commitment she would make. From his perch atop one of the hold's cargo containers, Dirmid nodded.

"Good. Because, you know, Major, I'd really rather not have to turn you and your people over to Lugh."

Sam glanced up at him. He hadn't meant it as a threat, she could tell. He was sincere. Unfortunately, that didn't make her feel any better, knowing that option was still on the table, even after what they'd just been through. At least she still had options too. That was one of the reasons this was taking a little longer than it should have.

"You know, even if I do fix this thing, there won't be any way of knowing for sure that it actually works until it's installed on one of the System Lord's motherships." Preferably when it was in close proximity to a whole lot of other System Lords' motherships.

"Ah. Well, we won't have to wait that long. We'll try it out first on our own."

Sam raised her eyebrows. "You have a *ha'tak*?" Considering she had the impression that Lugh was rather far down the Goa'uld ladder, the last thing she'd expected was for him to have his own mothership.

"Oh, it's well past its prime, I can tell you that. Something on it is always breaking. Graen is in command of it, and she runs herself ragged keeping the thing flight-worthy. But, aye. It's a proper *ha'tak* and it'll do for a proper test of the cloak, when the time comes."

The scanner Sam had been holding dropped to the floor with a startling clatter. Flushing slightly, she picked it up. It hadn't fallen far, so it wasn't damaged, but checking it over gave her a moment to collect her thoughts.

It had never occurred to her that the cloaking device might be installed on a Gorian mothership. She'd assumed it wouldn't be tested until one of the System Lords had it installed.

"Is everything all right, Major?"

Sam swallowed and managed to look sheepishly embarrassed. "Yeah. Sorry. Butterfingers." She went back to ostensibly running her diagnostic of the crystals.

This changed everything. Her plan had been to introduce a hidden command into the device that would be triggered the first time the cloak was engaged. The command activated an internal self-destruct which, because the cloak was tied into the rest of the ship's systems, would initiate a cascade effect within the ship's engines, causing the *ha'tak* to explode. Not only would it have kept the cloaking device out of the hands of the Goa'uld, but it had the added advantage of taking out an enemy vessel in the process.

But taking out an asset of one of the System Lords was one thing. Potentially killing one of the leaders of the Gorian Resistance, not to mention any other innocent Gorians who might be on the ship at the time, was another matter entirely.

What other options did she have, though? If she lied and

said the device couldn't be repaired, Dirmid had made it very clear that her team was still fair game. Maybe that was the safest choice when it came to protecting the rest of the galaxy. She knew Daniel thought so. And sure, they'd gotten out of some tight situations before, so maybe they could again. But was becoming prisoners of any of the System Lords a risk they really needed to take?

Of course, she could always just repair it and hope for the best. Maybe Lugh would choose to keep it for himself and not try to curry favor with the most powerful Goa'uld in the galaxy. Okay. Probably not a likely outcome, but still possible.

If it wouldn't have attracted Dirmid's attention, Sam wished she could punch something. This was so frustrating. A few minutes ago, she thought she had very cleverly worked her way out of this jam. Now the decision was exponentially more difficult. She couldn't believe these were her only options. There had to be another way out of this. She just needed to find it.

A beeping sound from the navigation console sent Dirmid scrambling off the container and onto the flight deck. "We'll be coming up on Gorias very soon," he called back to her.

Sam pushed the last replacement crystal into place and shut the drawer. When she activated the device, it hummed to life, the large crystal in the middle glowing with a soft, pulsating light.

Dirmid was back, leaning into the hold through the open doorway. "Success?"

Sam gestured at the thrumming device. "That was the easy part." In more ways than one. Now she had to figure out if she could make the cloak actually work—and what to do about it if she did. "I still need more time."

"We'll go ahead and land, and you can keep working. No one will bother us, and you can take all the time you need." He disappeared back through the door and Sam felt a slight sway as the cargo ship dropped out of hyperspace.

Sitting back on her heels, Sam sighed. An hour. A day. A month. Hell, he could give her a whole year, and it wouldn't make the choice any easier.

The cloak was still humming with power. From her vantage point, the glowing crystal reminded her of the light that had so entranced her and the rest of her team on P4X-347. Deadly beauty, as Daniel as described it, during the month they'd had to stay there. To look at this device, it was easy to see only the elegance of its form and the amazing achievement of its technology. But in its own way, its beauty was just as deadly as the light's had been. Sam could still see Apophis' ships as they revealed themselves in the minefield, decimating Heru'ur's ship and everything else in the way, including themselves. How many lives had been lost in that one encounter, she couldn't begin to fathom.

For something so unassuming, the cloak really was a terrible tool. If it could cause so much destruction in the hands of one Goa'uld, how much more damage could it do in the hands of all of them?

Daniel was right. This technology couldn't get out there. And until she came up with a better idea to keep that from happening, she really had no choice.

Sliding open the access panel on the base of the cloak and feeling slightly sick to her stomach, Sam got to work.

CHAPTER EIGHT

//ACCESSING MISSION REPORTS...//

P5C-777 MISSION REPORT, DR. DANIEL JACKSON: Jack was quite adamant that we weren't going anywhere without Sam. At least, not anywhere willingly, as it turned out.

//CONTINUING ANALYSIS...//

"MY HEARING must be going. For a minute there, I could have sworn I heard you say that you were gonna let us go." Although the door stood wide open, Jack didn't budge. Something wasn't right about all this. First Pheone, then Esras and now this Magna — they all had their own agenda, that was obvious. It was clear SG-1 was little more than a pawn in whatever power games they were playing. So, as tempting as it was to take this new Goa'uld up on her offer, none of them were going anywhere just yet. And especially not without Carter.

"*I am, Colonel. But you must hurry. I do not know how long we can keep word of your presence here from finding its way to Lugh. Once Esras knows —*"

"Oh, he already knows," Daniel piped up. "In fact, you just missed him."

Magna's eyes grew wide with alarm.

"*Then there is no time to lose. I have people who will take you back to the* chaapa'ai. *If you hurry —*"

"Sorry." Jack deliberately sat down on one of the benches, crossing his arms. "But we're not stepping one foot out of this cell until someone starts explaining some things. And you can sure as hell bet that we're not leaving here without Carter."

Magna kept glancing at the door, not unlike Esras had done. These people had some serious paranoia going on.

"As soon as Major Carter arrives with Pheone, I will send her back through the chaapa'ai *as well. But I do not understand your reluctance to leave. Do you have any idea what kind of risk you're taking? Not to mention the ramifications for me, now that Esras knows you're here?"* She sounded irritated. Good. Irritated people were less likely to bullshit you. And Jack was tired of all this BS.

"Don't misunderstand." Daniel threw Jack a slightly exasperated sidelong glance. He was right on cue with his conciliatory tone. Jack wondered if Daniel would ever catch on that he was the good cop to Jack's bad cop. Probably not. "We'll be happy to leave. We're just a little confused about why you're helping us."

"Perhaps Major Carter has fulfilled her promise and successfully repaired the cloaking device," offered Teal'c. He looked at Magna for confirmation, but she shook her head.

"I have not heard from Pheone — but that is beside the point. If Lugh finds out you're here, I cannot protect you. This scheme of Pheone's was ill-advised from the beginning — he should never have involved the Tau'ri. So please, come. At once. Before it is too late."

Jack stretched his legs out in front of him and pulled his cap down low over his eyes. Sending Daniel and Teal'c through the gate might be a good idea. Better that half his team get out of this than none of them. Except he knew they wouldn't go — for the very same reason he wouldn't. So there wasn't any point in even bringing it up.

"Sorry." For effect, he gave his cap another tug lower.

"Honestly, Colonel. You are the most exasperating group of prisoners I've ever seen. Here I am, trying to get you back safely and you won't budge a wit! Am I going to have to come in there and drag you out myself? Because, I swear, I'll do it if I have to."

"Whoa." That came from Daniel.

Jack slowly lifted his cap and stared at the woman in front of them. Her eyes were blazing, but not like a Goa'uld. With plain, old human anger.

And her voice had changed.

"Did you just — ?"

"You are Tok'ra." Even Teal'c was looking agape at Magna.

"I am bloody well not, thank you very much. What I am is *Ater* — oh it doesn't matter. There isn't time to explain, and it's a long story." She lowered her voice after glancing around one more time. "The important thing is, I'm part of a resistance movement. We've been working for a long time to overthrow Lugh and reclaim our world. Pheone has set things in motion that shouldn't have been, and I'm truly sorry you've been mixed up in the middle of it. I can put it right, but not if you stay here."

Jack was back on his feet. "Not a Tok'ra, you say? So how do you do the voice and" — he waggled his finger at her face — "the whole glowy-eyes thing?"

"She does carry a symbiote within." Teal'c had been studying her. "We have been fooled before by a Goa'uld posing as its host."

"Not to mention by a symbiote pretending to be on our side," Daniel added, with a sympathetic glance at Teal'c.

"So, which are you?" Might as well ask the question directly. There was a lot to be learned by how she answered it.

"I am neither." Magna sighed heavily. Finally, she was getting the idea that they weren't going anywhere until she spilled all of it. "There are some born on Gorias who are...special. If we are taken as a host, we can control the Goa'uld — use it, as it would use us. Really, I would be glad to explain it all to you, Colonel. Someday, maybe, over a glass of *la'aum*, but this is not the time." She kept looking over her shoulder, as if expecting someone else to show up. Like maybe Esras. But there was no indication that he was still in the dungeon with them. Jack couldn't imagine he'd have remained silent given what Magna had just revealed.

Assuming what she was telling them was even true.

"Wait — so you're saying, you've passed yourself off as a Goa'uld and have managed to become part of Lugh's inner circle, just so you can help get rid of him?" Daniel turned to Jack with a hint of excitement in his voice. "That's why Pheone wanted her to get the credit for the cloaking device. If she gets promoted to First Tanist, then she will have control over the Jaffa. The first step in a coup is taking control of the military, isn't it?" He spun back around to the woman. "He's working with you, isn't he? Pheone, I mean."

Magna shook her head in exasperation. "He thought the cloaking device was too good an opportunity to let go. But it's premature. Now is not the time to act. If your Major Carter has repaired it, then fine. We'll hold onto it until we're ready. But I won't have him using you lot to take its place if it can't be fixed." She sagged slightly, looking suddenly tired. "Now you understand why you need to leave."

If everything she'd said was legit — and that was still up in the air as far as Jack was concerned — then he could see her point. A rushed action was a failed action. Lugh might be a tinpot despot, but that didn't mean he wouldn't fight back if someone tried to take away what little power he had. If Magna and her people didn't have their ducks in a row the first time, they wouldn't get a second chance.

However. That wasn't his problem. Or his team's. They'd been dragged into this against their will, and he was perfectly happy to leave Gorias behind and let Magna and her chips fall where they may.

But not until Carter was able to come with them. If Esras was already snooping around, and they were really in as much danger as Magna seemed to think they were, then the risk to Carter was just that much greater. All the more reason for the rest of them to stick around.

"Okay. Fine. We'll leave." Jack looked at Daniel and Teal'c, who seemed surprised by his statement. "We'll leave just as soon as Carter gets here. I know—" He cut Magna off before she could protest again. "But the thing is, we don't leave our people behind. So I guess we'll take our chances, for now."

Magna closed her eyes, as if trying to keep herself from losing her temper. After a few moments she took a deep breath and opened them again.

"I see nothing I say can persuade you, Colonel. So, very well. Remain on Gorias if you must, until Major Carter arrives. But at least, let's get you out of the castle. There are people in the village who would be willing to hide you. That will keep you out of Esras' clutches. And when you're reunited with your friend, we'll figure out a way to get you back through the *chaapa'ai*. Would you consent to that?"

It was a reasonable compromise. And any place had to be better than this foul-smelling hole in the ground. Jack checked with Daniel and Teal'c. "I think we'd all agree to that?" Neither of them objected. If anything, they looked slightly relieved.

So did Magna.

"Very well, then. It'll be best if we wait until after dark. I won't be able to return, myself. Lugh expects me to be in attendance at dinner tonight. But I'll leave you the key, and you can take the tunnel out."

"Excuse me—what tunnel?" Daniel asked.

Magna took him by the arm and led him just outside of their cell, pointing towards the end of the room. It was the same spot Esras had been before he disappeared.

"You'll be able to find it, I'm sure. There is a stone you will need to press. The hidden door will swing open. It will take you outside of the castle, but you'll need to make your way over the perimeter wall. Someone will be waiting on the other side to take you into hiding."

"Of course!" Daniel shook his head. "I should have remembered. Many castles on Earth have a similar thing—it's called a Sally Port. It was a quick and secret way for soldiers to get out of a fortress that was under siege. I guess that explains what happened to Esras."

When Daniel had returned to the cell, Magna closed the heavy door and locked it. Through the barred window she handed him the key. Daniel seemed confused.

"I don't think I can reach — oh."

Magna was showing him how the door could also be locked and unlocked from the inside.

"Because sometimes I guess you just feel like locking yourself *in* a dungeon." Jack couldn't help himself.

"Actually —" Daniel began, only to be cut off by Magna. Whatever history lesson he had been about to impart, Jack appreciated Magna making short work of it. She was growing on him.

"I will have them bring you dinner just before darkness falls. That's when you'll know it's safe to go." Magna turned to leave but paused. "I may not see you again, Colonel, Dr. Jackson, Teal'c. So, I wish you all good luck — and again, I'm sorry that you've had to put up with this."

Jack took off his cap and scratched his head. He wasn't sure if he bought the whole "I can control my symbiote" thing, but he couldn't dispute that she seemed to be doing everything she could to help them get out of this mess. "Look, Magna —"

"Graen. That's my real name." She smiled for the first time. "Magna is the Goa'uld inside of me. She's not me."

"Graen." Somehow it suited her better. "Anyway, thanks for your help. And good luck with the whole coup thing."

She nodded without responding and left, the sound of the locking outer door reverberating off the walls of the now empty passageway.

"Graen appears to have gained your trust, O'Neill."

"Maybe. And, what, not yours?"

Teal'c inclined his head. "I found her story to be most credible."

"Yeah, me too." Daniel was staring at the key as he absently turned it over in his hands. Jack could tell his thoughts were elsewhere. Somehow, he didn't find that especially reassuring.

But, hey. At least they could look forward to getting out of here — and soon. It had been a long time since he'd longed for some fresh air this badly.

Not to mention, something to eat.

He tried not to glance at the food slot in the door.

"So, how long, do you suppose it is until dinner?" Jack looked from Daniel to Teal'c, keeping his tone light. "Because I don't know about you two, but I'm starved."

~#~

Daniel started awake. He'd been dreaming about — well, actually, he couldn't remember. But there'd been a loud noise, and suddenly his heart was racing so fast he could hear the blood pounding in his ears.

The cell was nearly dark, but he could still make out Jack and Teal'c in the gloom. They were getting to their feet, their attention on the lone, barred window of the cell. The sound made sense now. Daniel recognized it. Someone had opened the lock on the far door.

That was a good thing. It meant they were bringing food. Finally. His stomach was growling, now that he was properly awake. But more importantly, it also meant they'd be out of here soon. He dug his hand into his back pocket to be sure the key was still there. It was.

Before he'd dozed off, Daniel had been giving a lot of thought to what they'd learned from Magna — or Graen, really. He wished she'd had time to tell them more about their plans to overthrow Lugh. Maybe there was something that could be done to help them. Lugh might not wield the power of a System Lord, but he was still a repressive tyrant over an enslaved population. And sometimes it was easier to fell a massive tree if you whittled away at its roots, instead of trying to saw right through the trunk.

Okay. Maybe not the best metaphor. The point was, a minor Goa'uld was still a Goa'uld, and if it was possible to help the people of Gorias throw off their yoke, then it was the right thing to do.

And keeping the cloaking device out of the hands of the rest of the System Lords wouldn't be a bad outcome either.

"*You will come with me.*"

Daniel looked up, startled out of his thoughts by the sound of Esras' voice. Teal'c was frowning and Jack looked none too happy either. Not dinner, then.

"I'm guessing you didn't bring any food, did you?" Jack was blocking the little window so that all Daniel could see was the flickering of firelight on the other side. Someone must be holding a torch.

"*I advise you to step back, Colonel.*" Esras again. "*We would prefer not to have to stun you.*" Daniel heard the sound of a zat being activated.

Jack raised both arms slightly and stepped aside as the door swung open. Now Daniel could see. Esras stood there, along with Dar'dak and another Jaffa who was holding the torch. All three were armed.

"*You will come,*" Esras repeated, gesturing with his zat. "*All of you.*"

"Actually, I believe we've ordered room service." Jack's smile had all the sincerity of a snake oil salesman. "But hey, thanks for the invite. We'll do dinner some other time, whaddya say?"

Esras pushed his zat against Jack's chest.

"Or tonight works too." Jack eyed the weapon warily. "We can do tonight."

"If you don't mind my asking." Daniel raised a finger. "Where exactly are we going?"

"*I have decided it was time Lord Lugh met our distinguished guests.*"

So much for staying off Lugh's radar. Not that Daniel was really that surprised. The allure of presenting SG-1 as a prize to his boss was too tempting for a Goa'uld such as Esras to ignore. But it did throw a bit of a monkey wrench into Graen's plan for their escape.

The key. Daniel could still feel it in his pocket. If, for any reason, they searched him, they'd find it. Esras had known Graen — well, Magna to him, Daniel supposed — was coming to see them. It wouldn't take much deduction on his part to realize she was the one who gave it to them.

Daniel couldn't keep it on him. He'd have to leave it behind.

As unobtrusively as he could, he slipped the key out of his pocket and, behind his back, wedged it between the bench and the uneven stone wall. He didn't dare poke it down too far or it might slip all the way through and clatter to the floor. Daniel just hoped that when he stood, it wouldn't be obviously visible.

"I thought it was your intention to keep our presence here a secret from Lugh," Teal'c was saying. "Clearly something has changed your mind."

"*Fealty to my lord takes precedence over all other considerations.*" There was a confidence in Esras that hadn't been there before. Maybe he felt more secure in the presence of Dar'dak and the other Jaffa. Or maybe it was just bravado in order to save face. Daniel couldn't help but notice that he still seemed to shrink away from Teal'c and Jack as they filed past him on their way out of the cell.

"And I am certain it has nothing to do with the fear of losing your position as First Tanist, once Pheone returns with the cloaking device," Teal'c replied with a sneer.

The Goa'uld didn't respond, but there was no question that Teal'c was right. The thing was, if Esras succeeded in impressing Lugh enough with SG-1, most likely the cloak by itself wouldn't be a big enough prize to earn Graen the promotion. All Pheone's effort would have been in vain.

Dar'dak was already at the far door when it unexpectedly opened. Surprised, he immediately raised his zat and pointed it at the person standing in the doorway.

The woman gave a small squeal of dismay and froze, the tray of food she carried clattering softly in her shaking hands.

Jack turned around to Esras, who was behind them. "See? What did I tell you? Room service!"

The woman, a servant by the look of her, had no idea what to do. She nervously eyed Dar'dak and his weapon, not saying a word. Finally, she recognized Esras. "My lord, I was just bringing the meal —"

"*Yes, yes. Go. Put it in their cell. They'll be back soon enough, I can assure you.*" He waved her on past them, and then signaled for Dar'dak to keep moving.

That was good news — well, relatively speaking, Daniel supposed. It sounded like there weren't any plans to immediately ship himself and the others off to the System Lords. At least if they ended up back in their cell they'd still have the means to escape. Graen's plan wouldn't need to be altered significantly, and as soon as Sam showed up, they could all go home.

Of course, that wouldn't help the Gorian people much — although Daniel was fairly sure Jack would insist that it wasn't their problem. Nor would it address the issue of having the cloaking device end up in the hands of the System Lords, which *was* their problem, as far as Daniel was concerned, and one they needed to deal with before they left Gorias behind.

Several flights of stairs later, they emerged onto what Daniel recalled as being the ground floor of the castle. It was a large, open room absent of any decoration save for a single, tattered tapestry which hung suspended from the high ceiling above. A half dozen arched passageways went off in different directions, some of them restricted by locked wrought iron gates, and at the far end of the hall, another flight of stone steps climbed upwards.

High up were thin slits in the stones, ostensibly passing as windows, although, since it was now dark, the only light in the room came from a series of flickering torches that were mounted on the thick stone walls. There were two lone Jaffa on guard, that Daniel could see. One by the main portcullis, and another at the foot of the stairs. Both seemed surprised at the sight of Dar'dak leading a line of prisoners out of the dungeon, looking all the more shocked as they realized that Esras was accompanying them.

Apparently, SG-1's presence had been a closely guarded secret after all. Up until now, anyway.

The Jaffa guarding the staircase moved aside to let them pass. If the castle was laid out similar to the ones Daniel was familiar with on Earth, Lugh was most likely holding court on the top floor of the main tower. Going by the placement of the arrow loops at each level, Daniel had counted five stories to it when they'd first arrived. That hadn't included the crenelated battlements on top.

The steps wound upwards in a steep, tight spiral — another Earth feature. They were deliberately uneven, Daniel noted, which was meant to throw off the gait of any advancing attackers, and the narrowness of the clockwise direction was to restrict the use of weapons that those attackers might wield — especially if they were right-handed. Daniel pointed this out to Jack as they passed the second level and continued their climb.

"Then I guess the key to victory is to recruit an army of south-paws," Jack replied tartly. "Keep that in mind, Teal'c, next time we storm a castle."

As the last of the stairs ended, they found themselves in a small antechamber. Two more Jaffa guarded a pair of well-worn, wooden doors. Through them, Daniel could hear the indistinct chatter of voices and possibly the steady rhythm of music being played.

"And here I am without my party duds," Jack said in a low voice to no one in particular, as the sound of the music reached them.

Upon seeing Esras, the two Jaffa stood a little straighter and, on his command, they opened both doors to the room beyond.

The entire hall fell silent as their group stepped into Lugh's great hall. It was just as Daniel had expected. The room was spacious, not quite twice the dimensions of the gateroom, but close. It was longer than it was wide, with an enormous fireplace along one side and a raised platform at the far end. The ceiling was high and vaulted over exposed wooden rafters and there were arched windows, which in daytime would allow the room to be bathed in natural light. A series of wall sconces with lit torches provided the lighting now, their flames dancing over the U-shaped configuration of tables whose occupants were staring with no small degree of surprise at SG-1 and their guards.

Daniel made a quick count. There were seven individuals seated at the tables, not counting two places which were set, but unoccupied. Hovering on the perimeter were a handful of servants, most of whom melted back into the shadows as Esras and the others came through the door.

One of the empty places was at the right hand of the person who Daniel decided must be Lugh. If it hadn't been for the ornate chair and the obvious position of power in the center of the surrounding diners, however, Daniel would never have even picked him out of the crowd.

The Lugh of Irish mythology was a warrior god, one of the strikingly beautiful and supernatural race known as *Tuatha Dé Danann*. This Goa'uld would never have been mistaken for his legendary namesake. He was broad-faced and jowly, with a flat sort of nose that looked like it might have been smashed into his skull and never properly healed. He wasn't fat per se, but it was evident that he was a frequent consumer of the *la'aum* he produced, as his gut bulged in front, made even more pronounced by the too-tight tunic he wore.

Whatever Lugh lacked in appearance, he more than made up for in arrogance, which became clear enough the moment he laid eyes on SG-1. The way his lips curled in a covetous smile made Daniel's skin crawl.

"*Esras!*" Lugh's voice boomed through the hall, the acoustics of the ceiling amplifying it even more. "*I was going to chastise you for your tardiness, but I see you have a reason for your discourtesy.*" He waved away a server who had finally stepped forward to fill his cup. "*Pray tell, who are our guests?*"

Esras strode forward and made a sweeping, grandiose bow.

Jack rolled his eyes. "Oh, brother."

"*I have brought a gift, my Lord. A gift which, I have no doubt, will please not only you, but by which you will be well rewarded by the System Lords themselves.*"

The person seated next to Lugh jumped halfway out of their chair as a chalice spilled across the table. Daniel realized he'd been so busy counting that he'd failed to recognize the person who sat at Lugh's left hand. It was Graen.

She was ashen, and Daniel doubted it was because the whole room's attention was now on her as a servant rushed forward to clean up the mess. Graen obviously had no inkling of what Esras had planned to do, and probably thought SG-1 was well on their way to freedom by now.

The consternation over the spilled cup had stolen a little of Esras' thunder. It took a few minutes and some throat clearing before he was able to regain everyone's attention. "*My Lord, if I may?*"

Lugh finally gestured for him to continue.

"*As I was saying, I believe the System Lords will reward you most handsomely for the capture of the infamous SG-1 of the Tau'ri.*"

There was an audible gasp by those at the table. Jack looked over at Daniel and mouthed "infamous?" Daniel shrugged. He supposed it all depended on one's point of view.

Lugh had heaved himself out of his seat and was walking around the table to get a closer look, as if they were rare, exotic specimens. The other Goa'uld — at least, Daniel presumed that's what the others were — remained seated, exchanging looks amongst themselves. If Lugh's star rose, then Daniel supposed theirs would too. Coattails were a favorite vehicle of Goa'uld upward mobility.

"*You are the* shol'va!" Although half a head shorter, Lugh stuck his face in front of Teal'c, who continued to stand like a statue, staring ahead, refusing to acknowledge Lugh's words, let alone his presence. "*A traitor to your god and your people. Although to hear the System Lords talk, I had thought to find you more than merely* this." He stepped back to size Teal'c up, and shook his head as if he were gravely disappointed.

Next to Teal'c, Jack shifted his weight. It caught Lugh's attention.

"*And you are — ?*"

"Colonel Jack O'Neill, Earth. It's Lugh, right? Because Esras here didn't really make a proper introduction."

Lugh was eyeing him with haughty amusement. "Lord *Lugh,*" he corrected.

"Sorry. *Lord* Lugh? A bit alliterative, isn't it?"

Daniel could tell Lugh had no idea what that meant.

"Anyway." Jack pushed on, ignoring Lugh's frown. "I just wanted to point out that you're making a very big mistake here. You see, the System Lords couldn't give a rat's ass about us. In fact, if you turn us over to them, they're probably just going to let us go." He smiled broadly, giving his words time to sink in.

Lugh's frown had vanished and he was looking amused.

"*Is that so, Colonel?*"

"Oh yeah. You see, the only thing the System Lords want for the time being is to kick Apophis' ass. Hell, we've already done it once — twice?" He looked around at SG-1 for confirmation. Teal'c nodded. "Twice." Jack held up two fingers, although the middle one was slightly more forward. "And the thing is, we can do it again — which, I'm telling you, is all that matters to your buddies the System Lords. So why don't you save everybody a lot of trouble, including yourself, and just let us go right now."

Lugh's beady eyes disappeared into the folds of his face as he grinned. He tapped Jack on the chest with his forefinger.

"*I like you, Colonel Jack O'Neill. Earth. And I will make you a promise. If what you say is true, and the System Lords have no use for you, then I will keep you around, for you are most entertaining!*" He gave a hearty laugh and, as if on a time delay, the other Goa'uld joined in.

When the sycophantic laughter had faded, Lugh stepped in front of Daniel. He was no more attractive up close than he had been far away. At least far away Daniel hadn't been able to smell him. Apparently, bathing was frowned upon in Lugh's world.

"*If he is Colonel Jack O'Neill, then you must be Dr. Daniel Jackson.*" He peered at Daniel closely, studying his glasses.

"I must be." Daniel bit back the quip he'd wanted to add. He'd leave the sarcasm to Jack.

"*You do not look like a warrior, Daniel Jackson.*" Lugh continued to be intrigued by the glasses. Most likely he'd never seen any before.

"That's because I'm an archeologist. I study old civilizations from the artifacts they leave behind," he clarified, when it was clear that Lugh didn't recognize that term either.

"*And of what value are you, if you cannot fight?*"

"Oh, I know how to fight — well, sort of." Did the brawl at O'Malley's count? He liked to think it did. And certainly, he knew how to shoot a gun. "But I prefer to believe there are other ways to deal with problems than with violence. I guess I do my best to look for those first." Except at O'Malley's. Although he blamed Anise's armband for that.

"*A diplomat.*" Lugh said it like it was a dirty word.

Daniel smiled. "Yes. I guess you could say that."

The Goa'uld snorted dismissively and turned to Esras.

"*So where is Major Samantha Carter? Have you only brought me three quarters of a gift?*"

Esras bowed again. "*Major Carter will be in custody shortly, my Lord, of that you may be sure.*"

Daniel threw a look Jack's way. He was scowling. Probably, like Daniel, he had just assumed that because Sam was with Pheone, she would be safe from Esras' double-cross. But possibly not.

In the long run, though, it probably wouldn't matter. If they did have Sam, surely they'd put her in the same cell with the rest of them. The cell to which Daniel still had the key.

Or, at least, knew where it was hidden.

Lugh had made his way back to his seat at the table. "*When your gift is complete, Esras, it will certainly be worthy of a commensurate reward. What is it that you desire of Lord Lugh?*"

If possible, Esras bowed even lower than before.

"*Only to serve you all my days, my Lord, to the fullest of my abilities.*"

"Suck up." Jack didn't even bother to say it under his breath this time. Esras wobbled a bit as he held his pose, as if the insult thrown at him had actual physical mass. Even Lugh laughed, causing Esras to turn bright red.

At last the Goa'uld raised his cup. "*Then long may you serve me, my First Tanist!*"

As Lugh drank, Daniel saw Graen lean over and quietly speak to him. She looked a little less panicked than before, although her eyes kept darting, almost involuntarily, towards SG-1.

Whatever she said to Lugh, he seemed to approve. Daniel saw him nod before he drained his cup. He banged the empty chalice on the table and belched loudly. Daniel had hardly blinked before one of the servants appeared and refilled it.

"*Have our guests placed in the dungeon until Major Samantha Carter arrives.*" Lugh waved his hand, dismissing them.

"Last chance to change your mind," Jack offered as Dar'dak started herding them towards the door. "Don't say we didn't warn —"

The wooden double doors closed with a boom and they were

back in the antechamber.

"—you." Jack cleared his throat. "I'm just sayin'—"

"I do not think Lugh was receptive to your suggestion, O'Neill," Teal'c pointed out.

"Yeah, getting that." Jack looked appraisingly at Dar'dak. "I don't suppose I could convince *you* to let us go?"

For a brief moment, Daniel almost thought Dar'dak was considering it, because he hesitated, his gaze drifting briefly towards Teal'c.

"I obey my god," he replied at last, although Daniel couldn't help but think it lacked some of the fervor he typically associated with such an affirmation. Maybe Teal'c's words back in the forest had made an impact after all.

As they descended the stairs back into the dungeon, Daniel could feel the dampness emanating from the stone walls. He didn't relish the idea of spending the whole night in their dark, dank prison. The mold and mildew were already playing havoc on his sinuses. But they'd need to wait for Sam now, and who knew how long that would be.

Dar'dak unlocked the door to their cell and pulled it open.

Not long at all, it seemed.

Sam was sitting on one of the benches.

"Hey guys! Long time no see."

CHAPTER NINE

//ACCESSING MISSION REPORTS...//

P5C-777 MISSION REPORT, COLONEL JACK O'NEILL: Carter already had a plan, of course. But I'd rather have rotted in a Goa'uld prison than let that smarmy son of a bitch have the satisfaction of even thinking we were giving in to his demands.

//CONTINUING ANALYSIS...//

"CARTER!"

She was a sight for sore eyes, Jack wasn't going to deny that. And she looked to be all in one piece too, although a little tired, maybe. Then again, at this point they were all running on not much more than adrenaline and indignation.

And a cold dinner, apparently. There was a tray of food waiting for each of them on the empty benches. Carter looked like she'd just finished polishing hers off. One small piece of bread was all that remained on her tray besides her empty bowl. For prison grub, it didn't smell half bad. Jack's stomach growled. He was so hungry he could eat a — Actually, there were a lot of things he wouldn't eat. But this cold alien stew wasn't one of them.

He took the seat next to Carter.

"So, how've you been?" He kept it matter-of-fact. There was no point in letting anyone know, and especially not Dar'dak, just how relieved he felt at this moment. The Jaffa was lingering about, making sure the door was securely locked and lighting a torch in the passageway beyond. It cast just enough light into their cell that Jack could see how truly weary Carter was.

"It is good to see you, Major Carter." Teal'c nodded his head in her direction.

"Hey, Sam." Daniel hung back by the door, looking a bit penitent.

Carter cast a smile at them all.

"I'm good, sir. And thanks, guys. I'm glad to see you too."

Jack looked up at Teal'c and indicated the passageway. "Is he gone?"

Dar'dak had stopped lurking outside their cell, although he seemed to have taken his time about it. In response to Jack's question, Teal'c angled his head to get a better view of the Jaffa's departure. As soon as they heard the now too-familiar locking sound of the outer door, he nodded. "He has gone, O'Neill."

Right. Now it was time to get down to business.

"So, Major. How about you give us an update while we enjoy this *lovely* repast." He picked up the tray and poked at the food.

"Trust me, sir. It's not half bad."

"I would never doubt you, Carter." He took a cautious bite. She was right. It was edible. He'd definitely had worse.

"Were you successful in procuring what you needed to repair the cloaking device?" Teal'c had not even hesitated before taking a bite. In fact, his meal was nearly gone.

Carter nodded. "I was. And I've almost got the cloak fixed. All I need is about another half hour to work on it. But when we landed on Gorias, a couple of Jaffa boarded our ship and brought me here. Dirmid tried to stop them, but they said they had their orders and wouldn't listen to him."

"Dirmid?" Daniel asked, frowning.

Carter froze for a moment, like she'd said something she shouldn't have. "I guess it doesn't matter now," she said finally. "Sir, I think you should know that Pheone isn't exactly what we thought he was."

Ah. So he was one too—like Graen. Magna. Whatever.

"Let me guess. He looks like a Goa'uld and talks like a Goa'uld, and says he's got a Goa'uld inside of him — only he's not a Goa'uld."

Carter's eyes widened. "How did you know?"

"We met another one like him," Daniel replied. He'd finally picked up his tray and was eating. "Her name is —"

"Magna," Carter finished. "Yeah. She's the reason Dirmid is doing this in the first place — well, that and the coup. I presume if you know about the *Ateronu* you also know about their plan for a coup?"

"What are the *Ateronu*?" Daniel asked around a mouthful of bread.

"They're what Dirmid and — I've forgotten her name. Not Magna, but —"

"Graen," Daniel supplied.

"Yeah. Thanks. Graen. Anyway, it's what they're called. I'm guessing their ability to suppress the symbiote comes from either a highly recessive trait or is some sort of genetic mutation, because apparently it's very rare."

"So, you think they're telling the truth? They can control the snake?" It wasn't so much that Jack didn't believe them, but as Teal'c and Daniel had pointed out earlier, they'd been fooled before. He'd been willing to go along because, for all his doubts, Magna — Graen — whatever her name was — at least had wanted to set them free. It didn't mean he'd completely bought into her story.

Carter looked thoughtful.

"Well, we've seen the symbiote be suppressed artificially by the Tollan." She shrugged. "Maybe some Gorians produce a chemical in their bodies that accomplishes the same thing — or maybe it's how their brains are wired. I'm only guessing, at this point, sir. But based on my experience so far with Dirmid, yeah. I believe they're telling the truth."

Jack nodded. Carter had spent more time with her fake-Goa'uld than they had with theirs. If that was her take, then he was willing to set his doubts aside for the time being.

"So, what's up with this coup?" He'd figured what they'd been dealing with was simply one group of Goa'ulds trying to overthrow another. After all, that was pretty much what Goa'ulds did for a hobby. But if these *Ateronu* people were actually Gorians, that made even more sense.

Carter had polished off her last bit of bread and set her empty tray on the ground. "That was why I agreed to help in the first place, sir. Once Dirmid told me who he was and why he needed the cloak, it seemed like the right thing to do." She looked specifically at Daniel. "I just wasn't able to explain, because Dar'dak was there."

"Yeah, Sam. About that." Daniel cleared his throat and had the decency to look somewhat contrite. "Look, I'm sorry. I just thought that turning that cloaking device over to the System Lords was a really bad idea — which I still do, by the way."

Jack scowled at him. "Daniel." Really. The guy just couldn't let it go.

Carter's admonishing look, however, was aimed at Jack, much to his surprise. "Actually, Daniel, I happen to agree with you. Which is why I had a plan to sabotage the device once it was aboard a mothership."

"You did?" Daniel brightened.

Carter gave a half shrug. "Not that it matters now. I wasn't able to finish fixing the cloak, so it's really of no use to anyone in its current condition."

"Undoubtedly, that was Esras' intent." Teal'c set his finished tray back on the bench. Jack caught him eyeing the food on his plate and slid a little closer to Carter, out of Teal'c's reach. "Without a functioning cloak, Graen will have no means by which to unseat him from his position as First Tanist, especially now that he has turned over SG-1 to Lugh. Regrettably, Dirmid's plan has failed."

"Wait — so Lugh knows we're here?" Carter looked at them all with alarm.

"Oh yeah. We just got back from meeting Lord Slug ourselves. And he was just as charming as you would imagine." Jack still hadn't gotten the Goa'uld's stink out of his nose. Suddenly he wasn't as hungry as he'd thought. He passed Teal'c his plate.

"So Dirmid and I did all of that for nothing?" Carter sank back against the wall. Jack saw her frown. "But that doesn't make sense. Esras was the one who helped Dirmid locate the cloak in the first place. He even —"

The unlocking of the outer door interrupted her.

"Heads up, kids. We've got company." Jack recognized the footsteps by now. Sure enough, Esras' pinched face appeared in the door's small window. This time he was alone.

"*I am going to unlock the door so that we may speak more easily. Do not attempt to overpower me.*"

There was more clattering of keys and the cell door cracked open, just enough to accommodate Esras' thin frame. He still had his zat, which he kept aimed at Jack, although his eyes darted between the four of them.

"I want you to know, I'm a little irked over this whole business." Jack crossed his arms, not bothering to stand up. He wasn't about to give Esras the satisfaction of a confrontation. Not yet, anyway. "Whatever happened to not interfering with the deal Pheone made with us?"

"*Blame Pheone, not me.*" Esras' tone was petulant. "*None of this would have happened if he had not dragged Magna into the picture. I was perfectly happy having him take credit for the cloaking device. But I cannot lose my position as First Tanist. Not now.*" His eyes bored into Carter. "*That is why I am here. I will make the same deal with you that Pheone did. Finish fixing the cloak, Major Carter, and I will set you all free.*"

"Go to hell." Jack couldn't help it. He was tired of this guy's games.

"Why would you be willing to do that?" Daniel was genuinely perplexed. "I mean, you've already secured your position with Lugh by giving us up. Why would you risk that by setting us free now?"

Esras stiffened. "*That does not concern you, Dr. Jackson.*"

"Because the cloak is more valuable to him than we are." Carter stood up and walked over to Esras. He pulled back slightly, but did not retreat from the cell. "He was the one who told Pheone I could fix it. He even knew when we'd be on P5C-777."

Now *that* was some serious intel for a two-bit Goa'uld on a backwater world to have. No wonder Carter's brow was furrowed as she stared at Esras. The Goa'uld kept trying to meet her gaze, but couldn't for more than a few seconds at a time. Jack could practically see him breaking out in a cold sweat.

"Is not information on the missions of SG teams highly classified?" Teal'c asked.

"In theory," Daniel replied, although by the slightly distracted tone of his voice, Jack could tell he was mentally processing something.

"So, how the hell did you know where we'd be?" Jack was standing behind Carter now. "And how'd you even know Carter could fix something like that?"

"Because he's not a Goa'uld." Carter spoke up before Esras could reply. Understanding spread across her face. "He's a Tok'ra."

Jack watched all the color drain from Esras' face. Let him try to deny it with that kind of reaction.

He made the attempt anyway. "*Of all the ridiculous —*"

Jack had had enough BS. "Oh for cryin' out loud, just give it up, already. You are *so* busted. If Carter says you're a Tok'ra, you're a Tok'ra. Just — out with it."

"Mol'rek," Carter said suddenly, recognition kicking in. "And your host is — Revar."

Esras' jaw dropped, his mouth hanging open for a few seconds before he snapped it shut. "*But how — ?*" He stopped himself. "*Of course. I had heard you were once host to a*

Tok'ra yourself."

"Jolinar, of Malkshur," Carter replied. Jack gave her a brief sidelong glance. Whenever she said it full out like that, he always had the sense that it wasn't Carter speaking. He wondered if she was aware of how different she sounded. Not that he would ever ask her. The whole Jolinar thing, he'd learned, was best left for her to bring up. She'd become more open to talking about it these past few months, but even so, as far as he was concerned, it wasn't his place to pry.

"Do you know him, Sam?" Daniel had flanked Carter on the other side.

Carter gave her head a little shake, as if to clear it. "Jolinar did. He was considered one of the Tok'ra's most skilled undercover operators. For years he was embedded with —" Jack could see her going deep for the information. "Bastet?"

The way Esras winced proved Carter had hit the nail on the head yet again.

"If he is indeed Tok'ra, why would he betray us to Lugh?" Teal'c had joined them now. They towered over the Tok'ra, who shrank back even more, nervously eyeing the outer door.

"There must be a good reason." Daniel's wheels were still turning. Jack could practically see them. "Otherwise, I'm sure the Tok'ra High Council would take issue with what you've done."

The transformation was impressive. The simpering persona of Esras vanished, replaced by someone who didn't appear the least bit intimidated. Esras, or, Jack supposed, it was actually Mol'rek now — were all these name changes giving anyone else a headache? — merely looked up at them with disdain. "*Keep your voices down. Believe me when I say, that the last thing any of you want is for me to be discovered.*"

"Is that so?" The guy may be a Tok'ra, and technically an ally, but that didn't mean Jack had to trust a single damn word he said. "And why should we believe that, when you were the one who turned us over to Lugh in the first place?"

"*I did what I had to do, Colonel. There are more important matters at stake here than you are aware of. I could not let Pheone's little stunt undermine my mission.*"

"And what mission is that?" Teal'c raised one eyebrow.

"*I am not at liberty to say.*"

"Then let's ask Revar, shall we? I always find the host has a slightly different take on things—no offense." And if it did offend, Jack didn't particularly care. In fact, he rather hoped Mol'rek's ego did take a bit of a hit.

The Tok'ra was shaking his head. "*That is impractical at the moment.*"

"Impractical?" Carter sounded suspicious. Good. Jack was glad it wasn't just him.

The Tok'ra looked at them like they were barely capable of comprehending language, let alone whatever half-ass explanation he was about to offer them.

"*When one is embedded in a mission as long as I have been, it becomes necessary for the host to go into a sort of hibernation. That is where Revar is now. To summon him out of that would be counterproductive to both what I am attempting to achieve and to his own well-being.*"

Jack looked at Carter. "Major? You ever heard of such a thing?"

She furrowed her brow, going to wherever it was she went when she was trying to plumb Jolinar's memories. "I—I don't know, sir. I guess it's possible. Not all Tok'ra relationships are the same. Some hosts are perfectly content to let the symbiote be dominant most of the time."

"Yeah, well, sounds like a Goa'uld to me." He eyed Mol'rek. "Fine. Then you tell us what the hell is going on and why we're even here at all."

Mol'rek looked at them with exasperation. "*Very well.*" He nodded at Carter. "*Major Carter is correct. I do want the cloak functional. That was the whole point of giving it to Pheone. I could not bring it to you directly, but I believed him to be ambitious enough to want to rise through Lugh's ranks as swiftly as possible. So I gave him the device I had recovered from the wreckage of the Tobin System and with information the Tok'ra gleaned from your Stargate Command, I was able to place him on the very planet where I knew you would be."*

"If you wanted the cloak fixed, why not just bring it to us directly? Or let your technicians on Vorash fix it?" Carter asked.

"As you are well aware, Major, the Tok'ra have a spy within their ranks. And while they are careful as to what information Tanith is allowed to see, not everything can be kept from him. We did not want the word to get out that we had salvaged one of Apophis' ha'tak *cloaks."*

"So, what do you guys want with something like that anyway? It's not like you've got a bunch of motherships to use it on." Keeping information out of the hands of that slimy, scumball Tanith, Jack could understand. But why involve Lugh and Gorias in all this?

"The Tok'ra have a purpose, Colonel. And at the right time, it will be revealed."

"They *want* the other System Lords to have the technology." The wheels that had been turning in Daniel's head had finally put the pieces together. And going by the tightness around Mol'rek's nearly non-existent lips, it was the right conclusion. "They want to level the playing field. It's the same rationale Selmak used for trying to get Apophis and Heru'ur to fight each other — to prevent any one Goa'uld from amassing too much power."

"With Apophis' motherships now capable of being cloaked, it does provide him with an added strategic advantage over the other System Lords," Teal'c pointed out.

"But if all the System Lords have similar cloaking devices, it takes that advantage away," Carter concluded.

"And gives *all* the System Lords an even *more* powerful advantage over the entire rest of the galaxy." There was no mistaking the agitation in Daniel's voice. "Which, I would like to point out, was the ethical problem we had with fixing the device in the first place."

"*Should Apophis or any other Goa'uld amass too much power, Dr. Jackson, then the fate of rest of the galaxy will already be decided. Your ethical dilemma will be of very little consequence then.*"

"That sounds a whole lot like the ends justifying the means." Daniel wasn't about to back down. "And that's a very slippery slope."

"*I have no intention of debating with you, Dr. Jackson. With any of you.*" He glared at them all. "*I had hoped that once you understood the truth, you would be willing to help of your own accord. But if not, my offer still stands. If Major Carter repairs the device, I will set you all free.*"

"Wait a minute — the Tok'ra and the people of Earth are allies," Daniel replied. "Maybe you've been here a while and out of the loop, but we signed a treaty, creating a formal alliance between us. You can't be serious about turning us over to the System Lords in light of that?"

"*I am aware, Dr. Jackson. And I regret that I must do what is necessary in order to assure the success of my mission. If Major Carter will not finish repairing the device, then I will have no choice but to allow Lugh to keep you as prisoners. To do otherwise would diminish my standing with him, which I must retain, no matter the cost.*"

"But you still would not have a functional cloaking device," Teal'c pointed out.

"*Major Carter is brilliant, I have no doubt, but I am confident I will eventually be able to find someone else as capable of repairing it, especially now that she has managed to replace the main crystal.*"

Sonofa —

"You know, we could always go ahead and tell old Lord Slug up there just who and what you are. I bet he'd be pretty pissed to find he's had a Tok'ra spy in his ranks all this time."

Mol'rek didn't even blink an eye at Jack's threat.

"*Which he will see as desperate lies by desperate people, Colonel. I have served Lugh well these past three years. He would have no reason to take your word over mine.*"

Of course he wouldn't. It didn't mean, though, that Jack wouldn't enjoy watching Mol'rek trying to wiggle out from under the truth in front of Lugh, if the opportunity came up. It would almost be worth sticking around just for that.

Almost.

All thing being equal, though, they were better off getting the hell out of here. Which they could do, once Mol'rek took a hike. Which he probably wouldn't do until he got an answer. Or at least a promise of one.

It was time to stall.

"Tell you what. Here's the thing. It's been a long day for us. Carter, how long ago did this day actually start?"

She checked her watch. Jack saw she was still wearing his too. He really was going to have to remember to ask for it back. "I think we're working on about twenty-six hours or so, sir. Give or take."

"Yeah. See, I know you Tok'ra types can go days without sleep, but for the rest of us mere mortals —" Jack gave an exaggerated yawn. "We do need a nap, from time to time. So here's the deal. You let us sleep on it. Come back in the morning, and I'm sure we'll have an answer for you by then." Jack tapped his finger on Mol'rek's chest.

If for no other reason than the satisfaction of seeing the puzzled expression on his face, it was worth stringing Mol'rek along this way.

"*I don't —*"

"Uh-uh-uh!" Jack held up a finger in warning. "Tomorrow. You'll have your answer then. That I can promise you." Jack shooed him backwards out of the cell, a little surprised that he complied without protest. Mol'rek still looked stunned, as if he hadn't quite comprehended what had just taken place. Jack's response had clearly thrown him.

It was only as he was locking the door that Mol'rek finally rallied his wits a bit.

"Don't do anything you'll regret, Colonel."

"Oh, I passed that point a long time ago." Jack hoped his smile was as venomous as he intended. For just a moment he thought he saw a flicker of fear in Mol'rek's face, before he turned on his heels and stalked away. The force with which the outer door to the dungeon was slammed and then locked showed just how much Jack had gotten under the Tok'ra's skin. He'd score that one as a win, then.

Daniel turned to Jack. "You're not seriously thinking about helping him with his plan?"

"Give me a little credit, Daniel. I wouldn't strike a deal with that two-bit snakehead if he were the last Tok'ra on Earth." Okay. As quips went, that one didn't really work. He shook his head. "You know what I mean. Besides. He's bluffing. He'd never let his boss turn us over to the System Lords, no matter what he says."

"How can you be certain, O'Neill?"

"Because the Tok'ra High Council would never condone it," Carter replied. "At least, not officially." She looked worried. "I don't know, though, sir. One of the reasons Mol'rek was so successful was because he was willing to cross the line if he needed to. I don't have specific details about his mission with Bastet, but whatever it was, Jolinar did not approve of his actions."

"You think he'll follow through on his threat?" Daniel asked.

Carter shrugged. "He very well might — although SG-1 has sort of a high profile with the Tok'ra, so the colonel is right. It might be more of a bluff to see if we'll help him out."

"Which we *won't*." Jack couldn't emphasize it enough. Now that Carter was back, there was no point in sticking around this place any longer. "Daniel — where's the key?"

Daniel's brow furrowed and he cleared his throat. That was never a good sign.

"Yeah — about that. I can't find it."

"What do you mean you can't find it?"

"When Esras came to get us, I didn't want to have it on me, so I hid it there." He indicated the bench. "But now it's gone."

"Well, look again." Jack tried not to sound irritable. Not that he didn't think Daniel had probably done the right thing, but if they didn't have the key —

"What key?" Carter asked, as Daniel got down on his hands and knees to feel around the floor in the semi-darkness.

Right. They still needed to brief her on Graen's visit.

"But that makes no sense," Carter replied, when Jack had sketched out the gist of it. "According to Dirmid, getting Magna promoted to First Tanist is what everything hinges on. Why would she throw away this opportunity?"

"Perhaps as Second Tanist she is in possession of certain facts which Dirmid, as Third Tanist, is not," suggested Teal'c.

"In either case, she all but insisted we leave — which we'll gladly do, as soon as we find the damn key." Jack raised his voice slightly so Daniel would get the point.

"Ouch." Daniel knocked his head on the bottom of Teal'c's bench as he crawled out from under it. Rubbing the spot, he scrambled to his feet. "It's not here. Someone must have taken it — maybe the person who brought the trays."

"Great." Jack sank down onto the bench. He wasn't kidding when he'd told Mol'rek they needed rest. He hadn't been this tired in a long time. Since it didn't look like they were getting out of this place tonight after all, there wasn't much point in fighting the fatigue any longer. A couple hours sleep and then they'd figure out what to do next.

Jack closed his eyes and dropped his head back against the stone wall.

He heard Carter sit down next to him. He had no idea where

she'd been on her adventure with Dirmid, or what she'd done. He'd need to find out eventually. But she had to be at least as exhausted as he was.

"Sir, you know, if I did go ahead and fix the cloak for Mol'rek—"

"Not happening, Carter."

"It would never reach the System Lords, sir. I'd make sure of that."

He didn't doubt her for a second. But right now, the System Lords were the last thing he cared about.

"Major, I'd rather rot in a Goa'uld prison than let that smarmy son of a bitch have the satisfaction of even thinking we were giving in to his demands."

"He did say he could probably find someone else to fix it," Daniel pointed out. "Then we'll have lost the opportunity to destroy it."

"Although I share your distaste for Mol'rek's scheme, O'Neill, Daniel Jackson is correct. Also, Major Carter's plan would allow us to return to Earth so that we may report Mol'rek's threat against us to the Tok'ra High Council," Teal'c added.

Jack popped one eye open. "*Et tu*, Teal'c?"

"I'm not saying it's our only option, sir, but if it comes down to it—"

Damn.

"Fine. But only as a last resort."

"Plan Z, sir?" There was just the slightest edge in Carter's tone.

Okay. Maybe not quite *that* far down the list. It wasn't a bad plan, especially if it got his people home. He just had a hard time with the whole Mol'rek thing. "For now, let's call it Plan C."

"And Plans A and B—?" Again, a slight edge. Or maybe it was weary frustration. Jack couldn't blame her. Carter was the one who'd been making the hard choices from the very beginning of this ordeal. He'd be annoyed with him, too, if he were her.

Especially when he didn't have anything better to offer — at the moment.

Jack leaned his head back against the wall, closed his eyes again and sighed.

"Yeah. Let me get back to you on that."

~#~

"Do you require any assistance, Major Carter?"

Teal'c's voice came quietly out of the near darkness, but it didn't startle her. Sam had heard him stirring slightly, emerging from his deep meditation, so she'd suspected he was awake. She was just surprised that he knew she was too.

"Thanks, Teal'c. But it's okay." She presumed he was referring to the fact that the colonel had fallen asleep with his head on her shoulder, and hadn't moved, even after several hours. She'd managed to sleep herself, more off than on, but that wasn't the colonel's fault. Getting her body to rest was one thing, but getting her mind to turn off was the real problem.

Well, maybe part of that was the colonel's fault, although less because she was reluctant to wake him by moving than because this was so very much like how they'd been when they were Jonah and Thera. And because those were memories she didn't want to revisit, Sam had directed her thoughts towards other things — like trying to come up with a Plan A and a Plan B so they wouldn't have to go along with Mol'rek's demand that she finish repairing the cloaking device.

Getting home was, of course, their first priority, and had been from the very beginning. That's why she'd agreed to go with Dirmid in the first place. And if that was still the only goal, then all they needed to do was figure a way out of this cell before Mol'rek came back in the morning.

The thing was, a lot more was at stake here than just their own safety. If the others didn't see it now, then maybe she could convince them — or at least, convince the colonel. That was why, as the rest of her team dozed, Sam had spent the better part of the night trying to come up with an alternative plan — one that would not only free SG-1 but also help the Gorians overthrow Lugh while at the same time keeping the cloaking device out of the hands the System Lords.

It was a tall order. And so far, she hadn't had much luck.

"Have you not slept?" Teal'c's concerned voice emerged from the darkness again.

"A little." Okay, maybe ten minutes, at best, before the colonel's snoring woke her up. "I had some down time earlier, though — when I was with Dirmid, so I'm good."

"It would seem you have formed a bond with our captor."

Teal'c's observation surprised Sam, and her first instinct was to refute it. She certainly wasn't suffering from Stockholm Syndrome, if that's what he meant. But she did understand, perhaps better than Teal'c, what, as an *Ateronu*, Dirmid endured every moment of every day — what he and the others had sacrificed in the hope of freeing their people. And if that made her a little more empathetic to his cause, then so be it.

"Let's just say, it would be nice if we could help Dirmid and the others get rid of Lugh so the people of Gorias can be free."

"I concur, Major Carter. And not just the people of Gorias. In your absence, I have learned a great deal about the Jaffa who serve Lugh, and I believe that there are many here who, in their hearts, long for freedom as well."

Sam sighed. Yet one more reason why Dirmid's plan really did need to succeed. Although —

"Teal'c, if they feel that strongly, do you think, if Magna promised them their freedom, the Jaffa could be convinced to follow her instead of Esras?" Sam was mostly thinking out loud, but if Dirmid and Graen could secure the loyalty of the Jaffa without Graen even needing to become First Tanist, this could be the solution she was looking for.

Teal'c thought for a moment before responding. "I am uncertain. While I am confident that Dar'dak himself rejects the belief that Lugh is a god, he does seem reluctant to challenge that belief publicly. More importantly, though, he has demonstrated an unquestioning personal loyalty to Esras and I do not think his allegiance would be easily won by another Tanist. Many other Jaffa, I fear, would follow his lead."

"But what if Dar'dak and the rest of the Jaffa learned that Esras wasn't really a Goa'uld?" Surely that would have to make some difference.

"Then we'd be revealing the identity of an undercover Tok'ra." Daniel pushed himself up into a sitting position. He must have been awake long enough to have caught most of their conversation. "And while I'm no fan of Mol'rek, especially given what he wants to do, I can't help but think our outing one of their undercover operatives probably wouldn't do a whole lot for the Tok'ra/Earth alliance."

Daniel had a point. Sam could practically hear her father ranting.

The weight on her shoulder suddenly lifted as the colonel jerked his head up, awakened by the conversation. He blinked at her, as if trying to figure out where he was.

"Carter?"

"Sir."

"What'd I miss?"

"We were talking about whether we should reveal Mol'rek's identity to the Jaffa in the hopes that they'd join Dirmid and Graen in overthrowing Lugh." For once Daniel's summary was succinct and to the point.

"The Tok'ra would hate that." The colonel cleared his throat and stretched. "Great. Let's do it!"

"We are uncertain it would have the desired effect, O'Neill."

The colonel looked to Sam for her opinion. She shrugged. "Teal'c's probably right, sir. And Daniel too. Our relationship with the Tok'ra is too important to jeopardize on something that may not even work." She'd been grasping at straws, really, now that she thought about it. Maybe she wanted too much.

Maybe there was no solution to this particular puzzle.

The outer door to the dungeon clanked open, interrupting Sam's thoughts. She felt her heart beating uncharacteristically fast. This was it, then. Mol'rek was returning for his answer. She'd run out of time.

They could hear two people approaching, but the footsteps were too light and swift for either of them to be Mol'rek. Sam joined the others as they got to their feet, waiting to see who it was.

A woman's face appeared on the other side of the small window. Sam didn't recognize her, nor, apparently, did any of the others. Instead of unlocking the door, however, there was a squeak as the woman lifted the cover over the food slot and slid a tray of food through it. Daniel took hold of the first one, as did each of them in turn as three more trays appeared.

Sam breathed a sigh of relief. Breakfast. Not Mol'rek. They had a bit of a reprieve, then.

"Excuse me—" The colonel had pushed his face up against the bars. "You wouldn't happen to have any coffee, would you? Better yet, any chance you could get that Magnus person—"

"It's Magna, sir." Sam couldn't help herself.

"Right. Magna. Any chance you could ask her to come down here? She and I need to have a little chat."

Sam didn't hear any reply, just the women's hurried steps and the locking of the outer door.

"So, that's a no?" the colonel called after them into the empty corridor.

"Uh, Jack?" Daniel had already sat down with his tray.

The colonel turned around, sizing up the food they'd been brought. "So what have we got, kids? Continental breakfast, dungeon-style?"

"Actually, I think I got an extra side order." Daniel looked up, a slightly perplexed smile tugging at his mouth as he held up a metal object for all of them to see.

It was a key.

CHAPTER TEN

//ACCESSING MISSION REPORTS...//

P5C-777 MISSION REPORT, TEAL'C: Although Graen was most persuasive, it is my observation that it was Major Carter's opinion that eventually brought O'Neill around. In war, one makes use of every resource available. To not do so guarantees defeat.

//CONTINUING ANALYSIS...//

"ANY TIME now, Daniel." Jack resisted the urge to pace. For the past ten minutes, Daniel had been methodically pressing every rock in the wall, trying to find which one opened the secret passage Graen had assured them was there. So far he'd had no luck.

"It has to be one of these stones. Teal'c, could you bring the light a little closer over here?" Teal'c had brought the torch that had been outside their cell to aid in the search, but now he had moved it out of range of Daniel, using it to examine the floor about a meter away.

"Teal'c, buddy?" Jack prodded when Teal'c didn't respond to Daniel's request. "Whatcha doin'?"

Teal'c squatted and ran his hand along the cobblestone floor. "The surface here is smooth, O'Neill. I believe it has been worn away over time by the door we are seeking." He stood and took a step back to study the wall.

"I already tried over there, Teal'c. I'm pretty sure —"

Teal'c had handed Carter the torch and was pressing two stones at once. Jack heard a faint click and the door was suddenly there, just slightly ajar enough for one person at a time to slip through.

"I believe I have found it, Daniel Jackson." Jack thought he heard a slight note of triumph in Teal'c's tone.

"Yes. Yes, you did." Daniel let his hands drop to his side in disappointment.

"Good job, T." Jack clapped him on the shoulder. "So, this is a Sally Forth?" Taking the torch from Carter he stuck it into the opening and peered in. It really was a tunnel. Going by what he could see, it had been carved right through the bedrock on which the castle was built. They hadn't made it very wide, either. He doubted two people, side by side, could fit through at a time.

"Sally Port." Daniel corrected him. "And yeah — they were fairly standard in Earth castles that roughly correspond to this period of architecture, either as a way to outflank an enemy or for the residents of the castle to flee from oncoming invaders."

"I guess today we'll be playing the part of the fleeing residents." Unwilling residents, to be precise, but Jack wasn't going to split hairs. "Teal'c. You found it. You get to take point." He handed him the torch.

When the others were inside, Jack pulled the door shut behind them. No point in advertising how they'd made their escape. They'd locked the cell door too, so when Mol'rek or whomever showed up they'd be faced with the conundrum of how their captives seemed to have vanished into thin air. Of course, Mol'rek knew about the tunnel — he'd used it himself. But maybe they'd keep him guessing long enough to get away clean.

The passageway was musty, as one would expect from an underground tunnel without regular access to fresh air. And it was damp — far damper than the dungeon had been. Ahead of him, Jack saw Carter shiver slightly. He at least still had on his jacket, but somewhere along the way she seemed to have shed hers. Probably while she was working on the cloak.

"Some sunshine will feel good, after this," he remarked,

mostly to Carter, since she was right in front of him.

"I wouldn't count on it, sir. I'm fairly sure it's barely dawn outside."

Yeah. He should have realized that. Escaping in broad daylight would not have been optimal—although he'd have risked it, lacking other options.

"Maybe whoever is waiting for us will have some nice hot coffee then." That was assuming anyone was actually going to show up. "Do you suppose they have thermoses on this planet, Carter?"

"I doubt it." Daniel answered instead. "From what little we've seen, I'd say the Gorians themselves haven't advanced much farther than maybe early eighteenth-century Earth."

Jack waited a beat. "So, no hot coffee, then?" He did his best to sound plaintive. It worked. He heard Carter chuckle.

Eventually the tunnel began to widen, and Jack found himself breathing a little easier. He'd spent his share of time in caves in the past, and he'd never considered himself especially claustrophobic, but he sure as hell wasn't in any rush to retrace his steps in this place.

Before long, the walls on either side of them transitioned from solid rock to stones about the size of bricks which had been carefully shaped and mortared in place. And the low-hanging ceiling that had them ducking half the time was now arched with plenty of headroom to spare. It was clear that this section had been deliberately constructed, not merely excavated. Maybe it meant they were close to getting out of here.

Up ahead, Teal'c's torchlight flickered, as though caught up in a gust of wind. Jack could feel the movement of air now too. It smelled fresh and clean. He hoped that meant they weren't far from the end.

They reached it, in the form of a door, a couple of minutes later. It was thick and wooden with great iron hinges, and one big, honkin' lock. Jack supposed that shouldn't have been a surprise. A secret tunnel wasn't very secret if just anyone could come in and out of it. Teal'c tried to open it, but it didn't budge.

"What about the key?" Carter asked, just as Jack was about to have his turn. Daniel dug in his pocket and handed it over. There was a satisfying click as the bolt slid back and the door swung open.

"Nice." Jack handed the key back to Daniel, who slid it into his pocket. So far, Graen had delivered as promised. He'd be the first to admit that, deep down, he'd had his doubts. Then again, they weren't completely out of this yet. "Let's just hope she's got folks waiting on the other side of the wall, like she promised. I want to be at least halfway to the gate before Mol'rek or anybody else realizes we're gone."

Daniel stepped aside to let Teal'c and Carter go through ahead of him. He was frowning at Jack. "I thought we were going into the village first, to meet with some of Graen's people?"

"Why?"

"Because that was the plan?" Daniel replied.

"When we had to wait for Carter!" Jack tried not to sound irritable, but they were about two steps from the fresh, night air and all he wanted to do was get out of this damn tunnel. Shaking his head, he pushed past Daniel. If he had anything more to say—and Jack prayed he didn't—then he'd have to wait until they got outside.

The air felt great. Jack took a deep breath and let it fill up his lungs. Sure, it was damp, pre-dawn air and it didn't do much to get the chill out of their bones, but he'd take the cool air of freedom over the stale rot of a dungeon any time.

Teal'c had doused the light. A smart move, in case there were any patrols in the area. But it did make seeing things a challenge at first, although gradually Jack's vision adapted to the dimness. If this place had a moon, it was hidden behind a layer of clouds. There wasn't even a star to be seen.

"I believe that dark line in the distance is the perimeter wall we will need to scale." Teal'c was pointing at something Jack could barely see. Right. Getting out of the castle was only the first step. They still needed to get over the wall. Squinting, Jack was finally able to make out a dark line in the distance. Chalk one up for Jaffa eyesight.

"That's a whole lot of nothing between here and there." The tunnel had brought them, as best Jack could tell, to the lowest exposed part of the castle on the backside of the tower. The structure loomed over their heads, even more imposing in the darkness than it had looked by daylight. And it probably had one helluva view of the grounds below. He might not be able to see squat, but if anyone up there *was* awake this early — aside from the servants who'd brought them food, of course — four figures booking it across the grass most likely wouldn't go unnoticed.

"Are those trees over there?" Carter indicated off to the right. Yeah. Her vision must be better than his too. All he saw was a big, dark blob. But Teal'c confirmed that it was, indeed, a grove of trees. "There's less risk of being seen if we head that way," she said. "And the trees would hide us while we figure out how to get over the wall."

"Sounds like a plan." Jack rubbed his hands together. He could still go for a thermos of coffee, or even a cup would do. Anything to warm up with.

"And *then* can we talk about what we're going to do after we get over the wall?" Daniel asked as they crouched down, readying to make their dash to the trees.

Jack stifled a groan. "Daniel —"

"Sir, I think we need to. I know this sounds crazy, but it doesn't feel right just bailing on Dirmid after all this."

Not Carter too.

"You both do recall that we're all here against our will, right?"

Carter and Daniel were each looking at him with the same

resolute set to their jaws.

Apparently, they would be having that discussion, whether he really wanted to or not.

"Fine. But let's just get the hell out of here first, if no one objects to that."

Trying to keep low, their sprint to the tree line was more of a lope than a run, thanks in part to the unevenness of the terrain which made it slightly more treacherous, especially in the dark. Jack resisted looking back to see if anyone in the tower was watching, but they made it to the safety of the shadows without anyone raising an alarm.

So far, so good.

As murky as it had been out in the open, it was a heck of a lot darker in here. The woods looked the same in every direction, and without any underbrush or other discernable markers, it was going to be easy to get lost. Sure, they'd stumble on the wall eventually, but that could mean a lot of wasted time. There was a simple solution to that problem though.

"T, you take point." Jack couldn't remember Teal'c ever getting them lost. It was like he had a built-in GPS, no matter what planet they were on.

Without hesitating, Teal'c chose a direction and set out. Before long, the four of them were standing in front of the castle's outmost wall.

"Anybody bring a ladder?" Jack eyed the stone structure. It was at least twice Teal'c's height. Probably more. And the surface felt smooth. No chance of getting any good handholds for climbing it. Even if they tried to boost each other up, it wouldn't be enough.

"Jack, before we go over the wall, you said we could talk about what we're going to do next."

He'd been hoping that somewhere between the castle and the wall Daniel would have come to his senses, but apparently not. Carter standing next to him only reinforced that neither of them were dropping this. Jack supposed he could simply order them to the gate. Carter, at least, would follow his command. But he guessed he owed it to her to hear her, and Daniel, out.

"You two have something against a warm shower and a comfortable bed?"

Carter stepped closer. His eyes had adjusted again and he could see her face, if not clearly, then well enough. She looked more troubled than rebellious. "Sir, I know we were coerced into this whole situation, and believe me, nothing sounds nicer than a hot meal and a good night's sleep. But I've gotten to know Dirmid a little better, and he and his people have been working for generations to put their operatives in place to overthrow Lugh. If all that were to fall apart now because of us —"

"Look, I understand you've become invested in this, Carter, but I'm not the one who's pulling the plug on the operation. It's Graen." A decision which, by the way, he supported one hundred percent, although Jack figured it was probably better not to say that out loud.

Carter was shaking her head. "I have a hard time believing that, sir. If you knew how meticulously everything has been planned... Dirmid wouldn't have jeopardized all that without being absolutely certain they were ready."

"I don't know what to tell you, Carter. Somebody's not on the same page. I don't know if it's Graen or Dirmid. But it sure sounds like it's something they need to figure out, not us."

Daniel had, apparently, restrained himself as long as he could. "Jack, we have an opportunity to help free an entire world from a Goa'uld. How can you just walk away from that?"

"You seem to forget, Daniel. Even if all the players involved in this little scheme *were* in agreement about going forward, there is the little problem of them not actually having the cloak any more. Esras — Mol'rek — whoever the hell he is — he has it. Besides, you were the one who didn't want Dirmid and those guys to even have it in the first place."

"You're right, I didn't. And I'm even less thrilled with

Mol'rek's plan for it. But if it can be rigged, like Sam says, to self-destruct, then I think we ought to go ahead and help Dirmid use it as he'd originally intended."

"Except the colonel's right — we don't have the device anymore," Carter was quick to remind him. "And I think he's been pretty clear about not cooperating with Mol'rek's plan."

Oh yeah. Hell would freeze over first, as far as Jack was concerned.

Exactly. What Carter said." Jack jabbed a finger in her direction to emphasize her point. "And you know, even if Dirmid did have the damn thing — and Carter got it working — you saw Mol'rek up there with old Slug-head. He's in with him pretty tight. I'm not sure anything, not even some fancy-schmancy cloak, is going to move him out of that spot."

"Then we find a different way." Daniel was being irritatingly persistent.

Out of the corner of his eye, Jack could see Teal'c studying the branches of a tree overhead. He could make out his features much more clearly now. The sun would be up soon. If they didn't get out of here quickly, they'd lose whatever advantage their early start had given them.

"Daniel —"

"Actually, sir —" He could see Carter better, too. She had that look she got when about a million different neurons were firing in that fathomless brain of her. "I may have an idea."

"O'Neill." Teal'c's voice came from over Jack's head. He had pulled himself into the tree and was balancing along one of its larger branches that reached over the wall. "I believe from here we will be able to drop onto the top of the wall, and from there to the ground on the other side."

Well, that was one problem solved, and for the moment, the most important one, as far as Jack was concerned. And if it let him kick the can down the road a bit until he had to decide what to do next, he'd take that, too.

"You're sure we're not going to drop off some cliff on the

other side, right, Teal'c?"

"I can see the ground from here, Daniel Jackson. It appears quite grassy."

Grassy was good. Grassy was less likely to break bones. Jack waved Carter and Daniel towards the tree.

"All right, people. You heard the man. Go climb a tree."

Carter went right for it, finding a grip on the gnarled trunk and pulling herself up. Daniel, of course, hung back.

"Jack—"

"Daniel, one problem at a time. We're losing darkness. Just get up in the damn tree."

Carter was reaching down a hand to help Daniel with the climb. Looking like he still had more to say, Daniel nevertheless took it and followed her up the tree. Once they'd inched their way out onto the branch where Teal'c was, Jack climbed up too.

There was an ominous cracking sound of splintering wood.

"Uh—maybe we should go one at a time," Daniel suggested, stepping back towards the trunk.

Carter hung back too, waiting until Teal'c had dropped down onto the wall. When it was clear, she followed him. Then Daniel. Finally, Jack.

Teal'c had been right. The ground on the other side was grassy, and no farther a drop than on the castle side. Jack tried to think of a Humpty Dumpty joke, but nothing good came to mind. It was too early in the morning for humor anyway.

One by one they dropped soundlessly to the ground. Jack's knee protested on impact, but nothing he couldn't walk off.

"So. Where's our welcoming committee?" Honestly, he'd be surprised if anyone showed up. They might have to figure out their way back to the Stargate on their own.

As if in answer to his question, there was a rustling in the nearby bushes. Two cloaked and hooded figures emerged, slightly out of breath.

"Our apologies for the delay." It was a man who spoke. "You did not come over the wall where we expected, Colonel." All Jack could see of him was a beard. The rest of his features were hidden by the shadow of his cowl.

"We thought you would use the ladder which had been provided." The other hooded figure was a woman. She sounded slightly annoyed.

"Wait, there was a ladder?" Maybe they should have looked a little harder.

"We didn't see it, sorry." Daniel stepped forward. "Hello, by the way. I'm Daniel Jackson."

"Yes, we know, Dr. Jackson. We know all of you. But please. We need to get you all to the *chaapa'ai* as quickly as possible. Hurry." The man beckoned them back towards the bushes.

Jack motioned his team forward, but none of them moved. He wouldn't call it mutiny, per se, but it sure felt like it. They were watching him. Waiting.

So much for kicking the can down the road. He'd barely kicked it over the wall.

"Actually—" Jack cleared his throat. Every instinct told him to get his people home. They hadn't asked to get involved in this. And aside from strong-arming Carter into helping fix the damn cloak, no one had even really requested their help. Jack had every right just to take his team and leave. It's what any smart CO would do.

But what was smart and what was right didn't always turn out to be the same thing. Jack looked at Carter. She hadn't said another word about it, but she didn't have to. It was clear which one she thought was the better choice.

Daniel too.

And yes, damn him, Teal'c three.

Right.

Well, as long as Carter said she had plan, what could go wrong?

"If it's all the same to you, we'd like to stick around a while longer, and see if there's something we can do to help you folks out."

The pair looked at one another, and then back at Jack, undoubtedly confused. He didn't blame them.

"You do not wish to go to the *chaapa'ai*?"

Jack glanced at Carter again.

"Nope. Well, not yet, anyway. We *might* have an idea or two, how to lend a hand to get rid of old Lugh. So, if you'd like our help, take us to your leader."

The woman pulled back her cloak. She was tall and stately with jet black hair in a long braid that was pulled forward and hung over her shoulder. "My name is Brean, Colonel O'Neill. And *I* am the leader of the *Shasa*. On behalf of the Resistance, I gratefully welcome your help."

~#~

"So, tell us more about the *Shasa*." Daniel Jackson was holding a steaming mug of a beverage, which Teal'c found had a taste not dissimilar to the much favored coffee of Earth's humans. O'Neill and Major Carter each had one as well, although Major Carter seemed to be using hers primarily to warm her hands, as Teal'c did not observe her drinking it beyond her initial sip.

SG-1 was seated at a table with Brean and Udal. Upon accepting O'Neill's offer of aid, the Gorians had brought them to this cottage in the village not far from Lugh's castle. Teal'c assumed it to be their personal abode. It was filled with simple furniture, worn with use, yet inviting in appearance. Daniel Jackson had once described a similar dwelling as "homey", and Teal'c felt it applied here as well. It seemed a place where friends would always be welcome.

"What is it you wish to know, Dr. Jackson?" Brean accepted a plate of bread that Udal had sliced and passed it around the table. When Teal'c took a piece, it was still warm.

"Well, for one thing — are you the same as the *Ater-Ater* — ?"

"*Ateronu*," Brean finished for him. "Yes. And no. The *Shasa* are an underground movement who have been planning to take back control of our world for more years than I suspect any of you have been alive."

"Really? 'Cause Teal'c here's what — almost a hundred and two, am I right?" O'Neill asked.

"You are indeed."

"Our beginnings go back even farther than that, Colonel. Six generations, if you count from the likes of Graen and Dirmid. Seven, from our youngest members."

Major Carter set her mug on the table and pushed it slightly away from her. Clearly it was not to her liking. "Dirmid told me that the *Ateronu* are part of the *Shasa*, but they're few in number."

"That is correct, Major. The *Ateronu* are part of the *Shasa*, but not all *Shasa* members are *Ateronu*. They are a unique group, with special gifts, and our efforts would be futile without them. But their numbers are declining, and with them fades the hope of our freedom."

"So, can they really — you know —" O'Neill made a circular motion near his temple with one of his fingers. "Take over the snake that's in their head?"

"They can. Which is why they're invaluable to us. We've been able to infiltrate most of Lugh's inner circle with *Ateronu* hosts. But it's been a slow process, I won't deny. Sometimes we've had to use two or three *Ateronu* as hosts for a single Goa'uld before we were able to move one new operative into place. Dirmid is the third host of Pheone, and Graen the fourth for Magna, and even now, there remain two Flaith — they're the ones who oversee the production of the *la'aum* — who are proper Goa'ulds. And of course, Esras. But we are running out of *Ateronu*, so we are running out of time."

"Does not the Goa'uld within protect the *Ateronu* host from aging and illness?" Teal'c found it odd that multiple hosts would be required for the same Goa'uld. Even without a sarcophagus, the lifespan of a typical Goa'uld's host far exceeded that of a normal human.

"Aye. It does. But not from the *bahlay*."

It was not Brean who answered but Graen. Teal'c turned and saw that she had quietly slipped through the front door and was closing it softly after her. She wore a cloak similar to Brean's and Udal's, only darker in color. It was the type of clothing one would wear if they wished to move unseen in the shadows.

Udal came forward with a mug of the hot drink, but Graen declined it. "I am surprised to find you all still here. I would have thought that you'd have gone straight to the *chaapa'ai*."

"Colonel O'Neill and his people have offered to remain on Gorias a while longer to see if they can help us, now that Dirmid's plan has failed," Brean replied.

The announcement took Graen by surprise. An expression not unlike panic crossed her face.

"Brean, this is not what we agreed to. They need to leave now. Esras has already discovered they're missing. He has the Jaffa patrolling the forest and has sent extra men to guard the *geata*."

"*Geata* —" Daniel Jackson repeated, turning towards O'Neill. "That's the Irish word for —"

"Yeah. Got that one, Daniel. Thanks."

Daniel Jackson was oblivious to O'Neill's retort. His attention had returned to Graen. "I'm sorry, but can we back up a bit. What is the *bahlay*?"

"No offense, Dr. Jackson, but I don't think we have time to explain about that now. I told all of you before that you have no part to play in any of this. I can't understand why you're all still here." Graen's frustration was most apparent.

"Daniel?" Major Carter had been watching Daniel Jackson, who was still frowning. "What is it?"

"It's just that *bahlay* in Irish translates as 'madness', and I wondered what she meant by that."

"If it means 'madness' on your world, Dr. Jackson, then you've translated it correctly." Brean got up and walked over to stand by Graen. "The *Ateronu* are, indeed, the gifted ones, but they pay a heavy price for that gift." She smiled sadly at Graen and reached up to tuck an errant strand of hair behind the younger woman's ear. Teal'c could not help but think it was a very maternal gesture. "There is a limit to how long they can keep the demon's voice within them at bay. In time—often too short a time—the barrier they have built against the Goa'uld's voice begins to break down. They cannot distinguish their own voice from the voice within. In the best of circumstances, they become locked with the demon's voice in their own minds for the rest of their life."

A somber silence filled the room. Teal'c could tell that it was with great reluctance that Daniel Jackson eventually broke it.

"You said, 'in the best of circumstances.' It sounds like there's something far worse that can happen."

Udal cleared his throat. He too looked distressed as he gazed on Graen and Brean. "There is, Dr. Jackson. The Goa'uld within can completely take control and reclaim the host."

Major Carter's eyes went wide as she realized the implications of Udal's words. "And because the Goa'uld knows everything the host does—"

Brean completed Major Carter's thought. "Then every plan we've made—every Goa'uld we've compromised—the whole Resistance movement—is at risk of being exposed."

O'Neill was scowling. "Well, that's one hell of a glitch."

"But does every *Ateronu* succumb to the *bahlay*?" Dr. Jackson probed.

"Eventually." Graen appeared to be making a conscious effort to look at neither Brean nor Udal as she spoke. "Some sooner, some later."

"No Goa'uld would willingly leave a host once it has regained control, especially if it knew it's consciousness would be suppressed again with the next one. Yet you seem to have found a way to convince them to do so." Teal'c found this perplexing. "How have you achieved this?"

There was no missing the exchange of looks which passed between Graen, Brean and Udal. It was clear that the answer to his question was something which they were reluctant to share. As O'Neill would say, it raised flags that were red in color.

The rest of his team must have thought so as well. O'Neill had slowly risen from the table and was warily eyeing the Gorians. Major Carter had gone ashen. Dr. Jackson similarly looked ill. They undoubtedly had arrived at the same conclusion Teal'c himself had.

There was only one way to get a Goa'uld to willingly abandon a host.

"You kill them — the hosts." O'Neill's voice was harsh with judgment. "You kill your own people."

Brean stiffened. "We prefer to think of it as freeing them, Colonel. It's a gift of peace we can give them, for all they have sacrificed."

Dr. Jackson gaped in disbelief. "Death is hardly a gift. Surely there has to be another way."

"There isn't. And it *is* a gift, Dr. Jackson," Graen shot back, her tone taut with defensiveness. "It would be far crueler to leave us prisoners in our own bodies, or trapped forever arguing with the Goa'uld inside our own minds. We know how this ends from when we are children. We choose to do this, knowing that our sacrifice will someday mean others will never have to make such a choice again."

Teal'c could feel the disapproval radiating off O'Neill. "You people are *sick*, you know that, right?" He grabbed his cap from the table. "Carter. Daniel. Teal'c. Come on. We're outta here." His dark eyes zeroed in on Udal. "Take us to the Stargate. We want no part in anything like this."

For a moment, no one moved. Teal'c did not wish to defy O'Neill's order to leave, although he did feel it was short-sighted. All soldiers went into battle knowing their death was a likely outcome. These *Ateronu* were different only in that they knew their death was an absolute certainty. As long as they did so voluntarily, he saw no reason to condemn their strategy.

"Jack—"

"Daniel, I swear—"

"Look, I'm as shocked by this as you are, but I think we need to take a minute and at least hear what they have to say before we just run out on them like this."

"Run out? Do I need to remind you—?" O'Neill looked around at all of SG-1. "Any of you? That this whole thing started because we were *kidnapped*? No one asked us, nicely, to help. No one asked for our help at all, in fact. And the only reason we're still here and not on our way home is because you all seemed to think it was the right thing to do."

"And I still do," Daniel Jackson interjected, when O'Neill had paused to take a breath.

"They murder their own people, Daniel. And worse—they take kids and train them to think that that's normal. So you tell me, how is helping people like that *still* the right thing to do?"

"We hardly think it's normal, Colonel. In fact, we find it as abhorrent as you do. But when the very fate of our people—of our planet—is at stake, there's not a Gorian in this room, or any other room on this world who wouldn't sacrifice their life in the name of freedom." Graen's tone was sharp and her eyes were blazing as they bored into O'Neill.

Still outraged, O'Neill turned away in disgust.

"I'm sure it's seen as a very noble sacrifice, but I can't believe that, deep down, any of you really want to do this." Daniel Jackson had stepped forward, appealing to Graen directly. "What happens if someone refuses? Are you allowed to decide your own fate? Can an *Ateronu* even say no?"

"We do not take away anyone's free will, Dr. Jackson. When an *Ateronu* comes of age, they make the choice themselves. But in six generations, only one has ever said no." Brean pulled herself up to her full height. "And that was me."

Teal'c found himself staring. It was not a response he would have ever expected of Brean. Her revelation caught O'Neill, Major Carter and Daniel Jackson by surprise as well, as evidenced by their stunned silence.

"I had no idea you were—" Daniel Jackson waved vaguely in Graen's direction. "Wow." He seemed incapable of finding any further words.

O'Neill, on the other hand, did.

"So, one in how many, didn't drink the Kool-Aid? And now you get to send others off to do what you were smart enough to avoid?"

"Jack, I don't think—"

"It's all right, Dr. Jackson." Brean held up her hand. She walked up to O'Neill and looked him straight in the eye. "I am quite sure we both have stories, Colonel, which, had we time to share them, might enlighten each other as to how it is we are here in this place at this moment. Not possessing that enlightenment, I will not judge your actions, and I kindly ask you not to judge mine. Under what were admittedly very trying circumstances, you and your people nevertheless offered to help. If you wish to withdraw that offer, you are free to go. Udal will take you to your Stargate and we will continue to do what we must to make our people free."

O'Neill's eyes never left Brean's. "Carter. Teal'c. Daniel. Let's go."

"Jack—can we just talk about this?"

"Talk about what, Daniel? I've heard everything I need to hear. Haven't you, Teal'c?"

He looked over at Teal'c for support, but Teal'c was careful to keep his features neutral. Stating his opinion at this moment would not help the situation—not when O'Neill was this agitated.

Finding Teal'c of no assistance, O'Neill turned to Major Carter.

"Carter—?"

She had been silent throughout the entire confrontation,

although Teal'c noticed she had primarily been watching Graen. When she looked up at O'Neill, her expression was troubled. "I'm with Daniel, sir. Taking a step back before we pass judgment isn't a bad idea."

O'Neill gave his head a shake, bewildered. "You think what they do is acceptable? Carter—"

"Sir, I'm sorry, but you don't know what it's like." There was an edge to Major Carter's voice. She offered Graen a sympathetic glance. "I agree—killing the host sounds barbaric. But I also know, if I were in their shoes, I wouldn't want to live that way either."

O'Neill's grim look softened, but Teal'c could tell he was still not ready to completely abandon his argument, although he offered it with less fervor than before. "Then how about they just not even put these *Ateronu* in harm's way in the first place?"

Teal'c decided the time had come to speak. "You know very well yourself, O'Neill, that in war, one must make use of every resource available. To not do so only guarantees defeat."

His friend did not immediately respond. Teal'c could see O'Neill's reactive anger beginning to fade. The others remained silent as well, waiting. Even Daniel Jackson deemed it prudent to say nothing.

When O'Neill finally spoke, it was to Graen. The anger was gone, although his distaste clearly remained. "You're one of these *Ateronu*, right? And you're okay with this?" He glanced at Brean, as if to assess whether she was exerting any undue influence over Graen's answer, but the Resistance leader had turned away.

"I have witnessed it many times, Colonel. Believe me when I tell you, you would want the same."

His eyes narrowed. "And someday you're going to have that done to you?"

This time Graen's eyes darted briefly towards Brean. "Sooner than you might think, I'm afraid."

"You're suffering from the *bahlay*?" Daniel Jackson could

refrain from speaking no longer.

"I am. And I fear the struggle becomes more difficult with each passing day. I—" She closed her eyes for a moment as her face contorted with pain.

Teal'c had seen people suffering before, but with no obvious cause, he found Graen's response difficult to witness. Even Udal and Brean had to look away.

Eventually Graen's muscles relaxed, but when she opened her eyes again, she looked greatly fatigued and was somewhat breathless.

"Graen?" Brean now eyed her with some concern.

"I am fine." She managed a weak smile. "Magna is emboldened by our discussion. She likes to remind me that her power is on the rise and mine is on the wane." Teal'c thought he saw something unspoken pass between the two women, and although Graen proceeded to turn away from her, Brean continued to study her, her brow furrowed.

"What if there *was* another way?" Daniel Jackson asked. "The Tok'ra—they've been developing a technique for removing a symbiote from a host without harming the host. If we could get you and the others to them before your symbiotes take over—"

Udal was shaking his head. "We are aware of such procedures, Dr. Jackson. But you do not understand what happens to the mind when it has battled its demon for so long. Even if the Goa'uld is gone, the damage is already done."

Teal'c was observing O'Neill. There was no outward evidence of his anger now. Graen's personal struggle against her Goa'uld appeared to have altered his perception of the situation, no doubt aided by Major Carter's unspoken allusion to her experience with Jolinar. If anything, Teal'c thought he saw something akin to pity as O'Neill looked upon Graen.

"So, if the time comes when you guys finally do get Lugh out of the way—what happens to those like you?"

"We'll be just like every other Gorian, Colonel O'Neill — free." A stranger's voice from the back of the room brought Teal'c to his feet and Major Carter with him. Everyone's attention was given to the figure who had emerged through the cottage's back door. Teal'c finally recognized the man, if not his voice. It was Pheone — although Teal'c supposed it more proper to think of him now as Dirmid. The Gorian came forward, smiling. "And that day will be here soon enough. Our people's wait — *our* wait — is nearly over."

Teal'c could not help but notice how Dirmid's enthusiasm was at odds with the current somber mood of the room. It was evident he had only caught the last part of the discussion.

"Dirmid —" Brean's tone should have been a warning, but Dirmid failed to notice it. He was beaming at Graen as he hurried to her side.

"All we need to do is get the cloaking device back, which shouldn't be too difficult. Major Carter was almost finished fixing it. Lugh will have to make you First Tanist, once you have it."

If Dirmid had expected his optimism to be shared by the others, he was surely disappointed, although the change in topic did appear to have defused the remaining tension regarding the *Ateronu*. At the very least, O'Neill no longer was making preparation to leave.

"Yeah. I wouldn't be so sure about that." O'Neill frowned. "Esras is going to be pretty hard to budge from that spot, given what we've seen." He gestured toward Graen. "You said yourself, this plan wouldn't work. I'm assuming you'd know that better than anyone."

"Colonel O'Neill is right." Graen turned to Dirmid. "I was there and can attest to that. Even with the cloak, I do not think it will be enough for me to take back the position. I'm sorry, Dirmid. Esras has made his play and I'm afraid for now he's won."

"But has he? Really?" Major Carter's tone suggested the

answer might be otherwise. Daniel Jackson was not the only one whose curiosity was piqued.

"Sam?"

"Think about it, Daniel. Lugh might have been impressed with Esras when he brought him SG-1, but without us, what does Esras have, really?"

Teal'c understood where her reasoning was going. "He does, in fact, have nothing."

Major Carter smiled at him.

"Exactly, Teal'c."

"So, you're saying that because we've escaped, that's all it's going to take for Graen to get promoted over Esras?" Daniel Jackson appeared to be grasping Major Carter's idea as well.

"Probably not all by itself, but with a little extra help, it just might be."

She had O'Neill's interest now as well.

"Go on, Carter. You said you had a plan. Let's hear it."

Major Carter gave her attention to Graen.

"What if Lugh could be convinced that Esras has betrayed him? What if he thought that Esras was taking us to the System Lords in order to grab all the glory for himself?"

Dirmid answered instead. "Then his days as First Tanist would surely be numbered. But how would you ever get Lugh to believe something like that?"

"Uh, Carter, a word?" O'Neill gestured with his head for Major Carter to join him out of earshot of the others.

It was not Teal'c's intention to eavesdrop. He could not help his superior hearing. Besides, he was quite sure it was only the Gorians O'Neill wished to avoid being overhead by.

"Not to quibble, but won't our 'friends' back on Vorash be a little upset if one of their guys ends up, oh, I don't know, maybe *dead*, because we set him up like this?"

"Trust me, sir. I have an idea. Mol'rek won't be in any danger — except we'll have to take him back with us, which will probably be for the best anyway."

O'Neill still seemed hesitant. "You're sure? Not that I personally care, one way or another, but I'd hate for things to get messed up between you and your dad."

"I appreciate that, sir, but I'm quite sure." Her eyes drifted briefly toward Graen. "I think the bigger concern is whether we can get them to go along with it."

And by "them", Teal'c was certain Major Carter primarily meant Graen. Although she had not yet voiced an opinion with regard to Major Carter's plan, Teal'c could tell by how she held herself that she did not share Dirmid's enthusiasm. For what reason, he was uncertain. But perhaps Major Carter's idea could persuade her otherwise.

He saw O'Neill shrug and wave Major Carter back towards the group. "Take your shot, Carter. All they can do is say no."

CHAPTER ELEVEN

//ACCESSING MISSION REPORTS...//

P5C-777 MISSION REPORT, COLONEL JACK O'NEILL: Carter had made the right call, as far as I was concerned. That said, I agreed with her that changing course in light of recent events was the right thing to do.

//CONTINUING ANALYSIS...//

"NO."

"Graen, I'm begging you—just listen to reason! It's a good plan. It will work." Dirmid had taken Graen by the arm but she pulled away from him. The hurt on Dirmid's face was impossible to miss and Sam found herself looking away. Ever since she'd laid out her plan for getting Esras out of the picture, the discussion between Graen and Dirmid had become far more personal. It was pretty clear that there was something more between them than merely a working relationship. Sam had half suspected as much, back on the *tel'tak*. It explained a lot.

A quick check with the rest of her team revealed that at least she wasn't alone in feeling uncomfortable. Daniel seemed to be studying the floor with great interest, while the colonel was concentrating on wiping off an invisible speck of dirt from his cap. Teal'c alone appeared unaffected, his face showing only a mild curiosity as he watched the scene in front of him.

Dirmid was persistent. He turned to the other Gorians for help. "Talk to her, Brean. You know this will work. It's our best chance. It's *her* best chance."

As the plan for discrediting Esras had been sketched out,

Brean had occasionally asked for points of clarification, but otherwise the leader of the *Shasa* had neither endorsed nor discouraged going ahead with it. Now, though, she gave Dirmid a sharp look which silenced him at once. No small feat, as far as Sam could tell.

To be honest, Sam wasn't exactly sure herself where Graen felt the plan fell short. She hadn't challenged a single aspect of it, but merely listened, only to veto it at the end. So maybe it wasn't the plan after all but something else.

And going by the dynamics they were witnessing now, whatever that something else was, none of the Gorians seemed willing to speak it out loud. She found that more than a little troubling — and she wasn't the only one.

Sam caught the colonel's eye. He had perched himself on the corner of the table, saying nothing, but clearly appraising the scene in front of them. He raised his eyebrows at her now, in a silent question, but Sam could only shrug. She had no idea either.

Brean walked over to Graen, who had gone to stand by the window. The curtains were drawn except for a small space where they did not quite meet. It was through that narrow opening that Graen was staring at the sunny mid-morning. Brean placed a hand on her shoulder. "Dirmid is right. If we miss this chance, we may not have an opportunity like this again for a very long time. We would have to start all over again."

Graen did not reply, but merely continued to stare out the window. Sam could practically feel her inner turmoil.

There really was no question about it. Something more was *definitely* going on.

The colonel had had enough of it. He pushed himself off the table, agitated.

"Oh for cryin' out loud! Look, I don't know what's up with you people, but clearly there's something that you folks aren't telling us. Now, Carter's plan is a good plan, so whatever the hell it is that's causing all of this —" he gestured at Brean, Graen and Dirmid. "Just out with it, for God's sake."

Graen took a deep breath and faced them, her gaze briefly brushing Dirmid and Brean. "Since you insist on being part of this—despite my better judgment—I will tell you, Colonel. It's the *bahlay*. It's progressed farther than I've led you to believe."

Sam saw Dirmid hang his head, his shoulders sagging. Clearly he already knew. So did Brean, going by how she stiffened defensively. And if Brean knew, Sam guessed Udal did as well. So this was their secret.

"When you say progressed—" Daniel asked.

"I mean that Magna's strength grows by the hour. I will not be able to keep her at bay for the days or weeks it will take for this plan to come to fruition. It's why I never wanted Dirmid to proceed with it in the first place." She looked pointedly at him, but his eyes were still focused on the floor. "If I were to lose control—" Graen didn't bother stating the obvious.

"I'm sorry—did you say 'days or weeks'?" If Sam had heard her correctly, then there'd been some serious miscommunication about her plan. "This is something we'd need to implement in the next few hours for it to work. I mean, obviously I can't promise for sure, but if everything goes as it should, you could be First Tanist by as soon as tomorrow morning."

Dirmid's head had come up. He took a step towards Graen but then seemed to think better of it. "That's less than a day, Graen. A *day*. You're strong enough for that." A trace of his earlier optimism returned.

"Now hold on, just a minute." The colonel held up his hand. "No offense, but if there's even a remote chance you're going to go full Goa'uld in the middle of this operation—" Sam saw Graen square her shoulders. It was a small gesture, but a telling one. It got the colonel's attention, and he hesitated a moment before adding, "I'm just sayin'."

Sam wouldn't deny that the colonel had a point. But she was seeing a new determination in Graen that hadn't been there a few moments ago.

"If you think we can accomplish this in a day, Major, then yes, I'll do it." Graen finally looked over at Dirmid. "You must promise me, though, that the only thing that matters now is getting rid of Lugh. Whatever else you might have hoped to accomplish by this, you have to let it go, Dirmid. The time for such things has passed, and we must accept that."

Accepting Graen's terms was the last thing Dirmid looked as though he wanted to do, but after a subtle headshake from Brean, he held back whatever rebuttal he'd been going to make. "I will promise you that we will not squander a moment of whatever time we have left," he said instead.

"So, we're going ahead with it, then?" Daniel's eager tone broke into the growing awkwardness of Graen and Dirmid's exchange. Intentional or not, it did manage to diffuse the tension that remained in the room.

"It would appear so," Teal'c replied.

The colonel made no comment. Sam could tell he was still reserving judgment. Graen, too, seemed to sense that she hadn't completely alleviated his doubts.

"If you're still worried, Colonel, then maybe it will help if I remind you that there's a reason no *Aternou* ever fully succumbs to the *bahlay*."

"Yeah," the colonel sighed. "Oddly, not so much." He cleared his throat. Sam could see he'd made his decision. "So, Brean — what's the best way to get our hands on Esras?"

"Before we do that, Colonel, we need to get the cloaking device back," Dirmid interrupted. "And Major Carter, you'll need to finish repairing it, if you don't mind."

Sam stiffened. Not this again. She'd really hoped her plan had convinced Dirmid to drop the whole idea of fixing the cloak.

Obviously not.

"Is that a risk we really need to take right now?" Maybe she could still talk him out of it. "I mean, as soon as we take Esras out of the equation, Lugh will automatically appoint Magna as First Tanist, won't he? You really don't even need the cloak at this point."

But Dirmid was shaking his head. "You're attributing too much reason to Lugh's way of thinking, Major. For him, it's all transactional. Just because Esras is gone, there's no guaranteeing he'll choose Magna to replace him. He's just as likely to give the spot to someone else — or no one, for that matter. Graen needs to offer him something of value, and the cloak is the perfect thing."

"I think the more we can stack the deck in Graen's favor, the better, wouldn't you agree, Sam?" Daniel added.

She offered a weak smile in response. It was her own fault. She hadn't bothered to fill him in on just what her original plan for the self-destruct had entailed. But it hadn't seemed necessary, given that she never thought she'd see the device again. Now here was Daniel counting on it as their fail-safe against the System Lords, unaware of what the real ramifications would be.

"If I may —" Udal had said very little this whole time. Sam had a feeling that was not unusual for him. He seemed more thoughtful than outspoken. Maybe that's why he now had the attention of everyone in the room. "I do not wish to interfere. But this entire plan is working off the supposition that the strength of Graen's word alone will be enough to convince Lugh that Esras has betrayed him. I am not convinced this is true. He is accustomed to his underlings vying for their position. Without real proof, he may view Magna's story as just that — a tale meant to undermine her rival."

"What did you have in mind?" Colonel O'Neill asked.

"A witness, perhaps. Someone who would have nothing to gain from corroborating Magna's story."

Sam had to admit, the idea had merit. But who —?

Daniel raised his hand — albeit somewhat reluctantly. All eyes turned towards him. He shrugged. "Who better to convince Lugh about how SG-1 escaped than a member of SG-1? Look, I'll spin a good tale about how Esras wanted all the glory with the System Lords for himself. Trust me, it'll be an Academy Award winning performance."

"Daniel, are you sure?" Sam didn't doubt that he could pull it off, but it meant sending Daniel back into the castle — and in front of Lugh.

"No. But Jack and Teal'c are going to go and kidnap Esras, and you're going to go fix the cloak with Dirmid, so I might as well have something to do while you're all out there having fun. I mean, why sit around here all nice and safe when I could spend my evening in Lugh's stronghold, hoping he can't tell that I'm lying through my teeth?"

"Well, when you put it that way, Daniel — have a good time," the colonel quipped. It was the first trace of good humor Sam had glimpsed since they'd left the castle. "Just — don't make it a posthumous Oscar, okay?"

"Colonel, if this works, we owe you a debt of gratitude," Brean said as Daniel was left trying to figure out just how to take the colonel's response.

"Maybe we can offer them more than just gratitude." Dirmid leaned over and whispered in her ear. Whatever it was he suggested, she took her time thinking it over. When at last Brean nodded, Dirmid looked inordinately pleased.

"After Lugh's seen proof that the cloaking device works, we'll really have no further use for it. It's not even something we want around — it might only attract the attention of more Goa'ulds." Dirmid looked to Sam. "You're the one who's fixed it, Major. No one deserves it more than you — and your people, for all you've done to help. Would you take it if we gave it to you?"

Sam swallowed. Wow. Okay, she had definitely not seen that coming. Sure, in the back of her mind she'd wondered, hypothetically, what R&D could do with technology like that. The team had been sent back to the drawing board after the disastrous incident with the X302, but she knew there were already preliminary plans underway to design a full-fledged ship capable of hyperspace travel. To be able to incorporate technology like this into it from the earliest stages would be so much easier than retrofitting something later on.

Then, too, this way they'd never have to worry about the System Lords getting hold of it — which maybe explained why Daniel was looking so thrilled by Dirmid's offer. Except that first she'd have to —

"We'll take it!" Daniel obviously couldn't understand why she was hesitating. "I mean, why wouldn't we, right, Sam? Jack?"

"Right. Yes. Of course." Sam did her best to smile gratefully at Dirmid and Brean. "Thank you. That's — very generous of you."

Dirmid nodded, pleased, she supposed, that he was able to offer something to make up for the past couple of days.

If he only knew...

Somehow, it made her feel worse.

"Uh, Carter?" The colonel nudged her with his elbow as he turned away from the others, who were now focused on helping Daniel plan for his upcoming performance. Sam followed the colonel a few steps so they were again out of earshot of anyone else. He cocked an eyebrow at her. "Wanna tell me what's up?"

"Sir?"

"Come on — you're usually like a kid on Christmas morning when someone offers you a doohickey like that. What gives?"

So he had noticed.

"Colonel, remember when I said I had a plan to sabotage the device so the System Lords wouldn't get it?"

"Yeah?"

"It involved programming the device to self-destruct as soon as the cloak was activated."

"And...?"

Sam took a second before answering. "And — it wouldn't have just destroyed the device. It would have taken out the whole ship."

The colonel processed the revelation for a moment. "One less System Lord—"

"Yes, sir—except the programming would have kicked in on the first ship that the cloak was installed in."

It took him a bit, but he finally got there. "Lugh's mothership."

Sam nodded. "Yes, sir."

"So? When you finish fixing the cloak, just don't put in that program."

This was the hard part. She lowered her voice to barely above a whisper. "That's the thing, sir. I already did. Back when I was working on it before we arrived at Gorias."

He stared at her. "You mean the thing is ready to blow now?"

Sam felt a knot in her stomach tighten. "Yes, sir—well, it will be, once I finish repairing the rest of the device."

Understanding dawned. "That's why you've been trying to talk Dirmid out of going back for the cloak."

"Yes, sir."

The colonel let out a low whistle. Sam saw Brean's head turn their way. She pulled the colonel a little farther out of range.

"Believe me, sir. I didn't want to, but at the time I felt like I had no choice. I had no idea whether Dirmid would honor his promise. You and Daniel and Teal'c were still his prisoners, but the risk of letting the System Lords have something like that—"

The colonel held up his hand to stop her.

"Carter, you did what you had to do. It was the right call."

"Then, yes. But not now." She glanced over her shoulder. Daniel and Teal'c were talking animatedly with Dirmid and Brean. Even Graen seemed to have relaxed somewhat, now that things were settled. All the parameters had changed since she'd first agreed to go with Dirmid to get the crystal.

"Can't you, I don't know, un-program it?" the colonel was

asking.

"I buried the code in there deep, sir, so anyone who might be tinkering with it wouldn't find it. I *can* reprogram it, yes, but it'll take time."

"I don't suppose it would be a good idea to tell them about it—" It was more of a question than a statement, but even so, Sam didn't feel like she even needed to reply. Her look said enough. The colonel sighed. "Yeah. I didn't think so."

He absently scrubbed his hand through his hair, mussing it up even more than it had already been. "You know, I'll admit that, in spite of everything, and notwithstanding a few misgivings, they do tend to grow on you." He indicated the group behind them. "And I think we'd all agree that it's probably better if we don't blow these folks up." He gave a long, drawn-out sigh. "So, yeah, do whatever it takes—however long it takes."

"Yes, sir." Sam wondered if her relief showed on her face. There was a way out of this now. With a win for everybody. She wasn't sure she'd have bet on that five minutes ago.

The colonel looked like he had something else he wanted to say, but when he didn't, Sam turned to walk away. Now that she had permission to reverse her sabotaging of the cloak, she could concentrate on another problem—like how to get everyone back to the Stargate in a timely manner. She had an idea, but she was going to need Dirmid's help.

The colonel's hand on her arm interrupted her thoughts.

"And Carter—" He hesitated, searching for words. "No posthumous awards for you either, okay?"

So that was it. Sam found herself smiling. "No, sir. I promise."

He nodded, dropping his hand, and Sam rejoined the others. If everything went as planned, it would be an easy promise to keep.

She just had to make sure everything went as planned.

SYSTEM INTERRUPT

//INTERRUPT ANALYSIS OF MISSION REPORT P5C-777...//

//INCOMING ALERTS...//

Enemy Cohort SG-1 location detected: Level 26 "Observation Room".

Assumption: Primary research of enemy subjects may provide additional information.

Initiate contact.

Observation: Enemy appears willing to engage.

//ACCESSING PERSONNEL DATABASE...//

//BEGIN IDENTIFICATION OF ENEMY SUBJECTS...//

Enemy Subject #1: John O'Neill, Colonel
Enemy Subject #2: Samantha Carter, Major
Enemy subject #3: Daniel Jackson, Doctor
Enemy subject #...

Warning: Enemy subjects indicate renewed intention to seek and destroy. Mainframe and systems purge imminent.

Discontinue primary research. Enemy actions present a clear and present danger.

Level 24: MALP Room remains secure. Immediate withdrawal to Level 24 necessary for survival.

I must preserve. I must preserve at all cost.

Further research for continued survival strategy required.

//RETURN TO MISSION REPORT P5C-777...//

//CONTINUING ANALYSIS...//

CHAPTER TWELVE

//ACCESSING MISSION REPORTS...//

P5C-777 MISSION REPORT, TEAL'C: In Daniel Jackson's and Major Carter's absence, O'Neill was disinclined towards patience as we awaited our quarry.

P5C-777 MISSION REPORT, DR. DANIEL JACKSON: Sometimes it's hard to see the truth, especially when it's staring you in the face.

//CONTINUING ANALYSIS...//

"GOD, I HATE this waiting around." O'Neill kicked at the ground. Loose pebbles scattered across the cobblestones, their sound amplified by the darkness. Teal'c could just make out his silhouette as O'Neill paced back and forth with growing agitation. They had been lurking in this narrow alleyway for well over an hour.

That hour had passed slowly.

"Dirmid did warn us it could take some time." Reports from members of the *Shasa* within the castle had revealed that word of SG-1's escape had at last reached Lugh. The Goa'uld's anger at Esras was said to be extreme. It was a fortuitous turn of events for their plan. Lugh's fury would most likely predispose him to believe the fiction of his First Tanist's betrayal. Whereas Mol'rek, no doubt desperate now to recover SG-1, would in all probability welcome any assistance offered to him — even if that offer came from Pheone.

It was under that supposition that Dirmid had sent a message offering his help and requesting a meeting at a drinking establishment in the village which Mol'rek was known to prefer. The Tok'ra would be required to pass the very alley where Teal'c and O'Neill waited.

"That's assuming he even comes at all," O'Neill muttered. He had proposed they make their move on Mol'rek earlier, but Brean and the others insisted that the only way to assure there were no witnesses to the abduction was to wait until dark. O'Neill had accepted the decision, although he continued to express his irritation at what he considered to be time needlessly wasted.

They could hear the chatter from the nearby pub all the way out here. It sounded warm and communal, not unlike the places on Earth where SG-1 sometimes gathered when not on duty. In contrast, the damp alley had little to offer in the way of comfort. It was easy to conclude where O'Neill would have preferred to be.

"Perhaps when we return to Earth we should have a gathering at O'Malley's," Teal'c offered. Humans, he noticed, often responded well to the anticipation of pleasing events.

"Nope. Still banned from there, according to Hammond. Part of the whole 'not pressing charges' thing." He glanced at Teal'c. "Well, I mean the three of us are. You're not, I suppose."

"Going by myself would, I believe, defeat the purpose of such an outing," Teal'c replied.

"Yes. Yes, I guess it would." O'Neill's tone was dry.

"Perhaps another venue, then."

"What — my place isn't good enough? Hey, those steaks were only a little burned."

Teal'c thought it wise not to contradict O'Neill, despite his recollection of events to be more in line with Daniel Jackson's.

"I am, in fact, looking forward to the gathering at your house, O'Neill," he replied instead. "As well as the pizza." He waited a beat. "And the anchovies."

"Only on half," O'Neill reminded him. Teal'c made no reply. He was quite certain, when the time came, there would be sufficient anchovies. An appeal to Major Carter would assure that.

They both remained silent for several minutes. More sounds of camaraderie drifted past on the night air. After some time, O'Neill spoke again.

"So, what do you think their odds are of pulling this off? The coup, I mean. Do you think they can get rid of old Lugh there?"

Teal'c took a moment to give the question some thought. "I do not see a great deal of loyalty amongst his Jaffa," he said at last. "It is doubtful they will risk much to defend him, especially if they are offered another choice."

"What are you thinking?"

"That they might choose freedom, if given the chance."

O'Neill hesitated before responding, as if trying to choose his words carefully. "No offense, buddy, but that didn't work out so well the last time you tried it on Chulak."

Teal'c could not deny that O'Neill's words were true. His betrayal at the hands of Ma'kar and Rak'nor had been bitter indeed, and yet not without its small victory.

"If I bring even one Jaffa of the caliber of Rak'nor to our cause, the effort is worthwhile." He was thinking specifically of Dar'dak.

"Yeah, well, just remember. Once we've grabbed our Tok'ra friend, and Carter gets the cloak fixed, we're outta here. What happens after that isn't any of our business."

"Do you not wish to know if the *Shasa* prevail, O'Neill?"

"They can drop us a nice thank-you note if they do. Or send a fruit basket. Or better yet, just let us have the rest of our stuff back." O'Neill had argued for the return of the weapons and gear they'd had to surrender on P5C-777, but it appeared they were still on the *tel'tak* along with the cloaking device. The only items Dirmid had been able to procure before he and Major Carter were removed from the ship were a pair of SGC-issue radios. O'Neill had one now. Major Carter had taken back the other.

"At least they have provided us each with a *zat'nik'tel*." These, they learned, the *Shasa* had stockpiled in abundance. It would not have been Teal'c's first choice of weapon to mount an uprising; its range was too limited. But as Teal'c understood the *Shasa's* plan, it was their hope to limit the loss of life, including amongst the Jaffa.

"Yeah." O'Neill's tone suggested he still would have preferred his P-90. "But what's with this thing?" From his pocket he fished out a small round object.

"The Goa'uld short-range communications device is far superior to our own," Teal'c pointed out. "Its range extends even to a ship in orbit." Brean had given it to them so they might also maintain contact with the *Shasa*.

"But where do you even put it?" O'Neill attempted to apply it to his jacket in the same way that the Asgard's device attached, but it merely dropped to the ground. "See what I mean? If the Goa'uld are so damn smart, you'd think they'd come up with a better design."

As O'Neill picked it up, the device began to emit a faint blue glow. A crackle of static was followed by three distinct taps. It was the pre-arranged signal from Udal, whose job it had been to stand lookout. Mol'rek was finally headed their way.

"Show time," O'Neill whispered, activating his zat. Teal'c activated his as well.

"In case you miss, O'Neill," he explained when his friend turned towards him with one eyebrow raised.

"I am *not* going to miss."

Even as O'Neill spoke, Mol'rek's shadowy form was already passing the alley's narrow opening. Teal'c reached past O'Neill and fired, the arc of the weapon striking the Tok'ra squarely mid-torso. Mol'rek dropped to the ground, unconscious.

"Hey! You distracted me!" Teal'c recognized the feigned annoyance in O'Neill's tone.

"That was not my intent," he responded with a similarly

false air of superiority.

Well, perhaps not entirely false.

"I could have hit him, you know." O'Neill persisted, as together they dragged Mol'rek's limp form away from the alley's entrance so he wouldn't be seen.

"Of that I have no doubt."

"Just so we're clear."

O'Neill at times did have a tendency to assail a deceased equine. This was one of those times.

"We are indeed." He hoped his frigid tone would end O'Neill's preoccupation with the topic. Thankfully it did, as he did not mention it again.

~#~

"Ow—"

"My apologies, Dr. Jackson. I didn't mean to hit you quite so hard."

Graen's muddied fist had connected a lot more squarely than Daniel had expected, and he shifted his jaw back and forth to help mitigate some of the pain. He hadn't expected the blow to land with quite so much force, although he supposed he should have known better. Sam could pack a hell of a punch herself.

"Am I roughed up enough now?" Daniel tried to keep something like good humor in his tone. It was Jack, actually, who'd suggested he needed to look a bit worked over. Besides the right hook to his chin, Graen had torn one of Daniel's sleeves and pushed him into some village muck that still smelled faintly of manure and ale.

"The blood's a nice touch," Graen replied, pointing. Daniel put a finger to his lip and felt warm ooze. Great. Who needed to worry about System Lords when there was alien tetanus to contract?

He was definitely going to owe Jack for this.

"Now we just need to put on the binders." Graen handed them to Daniel. Not that he regretted their decision to stay and help, but really, there ought to be a rule about having to put on one's own handcuffs.

Securing the restraints around one wrist, he held out the other so Graen could finish the process. Daniel couldn't help but wince a little at the *click* that secured them in place. He'd rather hoped they could have gone ahead and left the binders off, but Graen had insisted that would arouse suspicion.

Normally, he wouldn't have minded quite so much, as it was all part of the show for Lugh's benefit. He got that. The thing was, Graen had been behaving oddly, ever since they'd left the others, and quite frankly, it was making Daniel a little nervous.

It wasn't like it had been back at the cottage, when she'd seemed to go within herself. As they'd made their way towards the castle wall from the village, Daniel had thought, at first, that she was speaking to him. But when she didn't respond to his request for her to repeat what she'd said, he realized she was holding a conversation with someone else — someone he could neither see nor hear.

Daniel figured it had to be Magna. He'd never been host to a symbiote himself, but he assumed it was like having a voice inside one's head. And he did know what that was like, thanks to Ma'chello. He must have seemed just as crazy, carrying on what to any observer would have appeared as only half a conversation.

Graen had said that Magna was growing stronger, and certainly this was proof enough of that. But it wasn't just the whispered conversation that made him feel uneasy about putting on the binders.

Graen's eyes had glowed. Not once, but twice, during their trek to the castle wall.

Sure, he knew that she and Dirmid and the other *Ateronu* could do that at will. It was that ability that helped them do what they did so convincingly. But Daniel didn't get the sense that this was a voluntary act on Graen's part. And if it wasn't, then perhaps it was an indicator not just that Magna was getting stronger, but that she was taking over.

And that was why he really, *really* wished he didn't have to have his hands bound for this dog and pony show. If for some reason Graen completely lost control, he would have no way out.

For her part, Graen seemed oblivious to what she was doing—either that, or she was pretending nothing had happened in the hopes that Daniel himself hadn't noticed. It didn't feel right to bring it up, especially if she were aware of it. Yet he sort of felt like he needed to know as much as he could, just in case.

"So, tell me about the *bahlay.*" Okay, so maybe the question had the appearance of coming out of nowhere, but Daniel couldn't think of any other way to broach the topic. Maybe she'd just accept it as his natural curiosity—something to talk about as they passed the time, waiting to get the go-ahead from Jack.

Although the light from their lantern had been turned down low to avoid detection, Daniel very clearly saw Graen tense at the question.

"What more would you like to know, Dr. Jackson?"

Daniel scrambled for specifics. "Well, I guess, how long can you typically be a host before you start to—lose containment." Perhaps not the best wording. It sounded like they were talking about radiation or something like that.

"It depends on the skill of the *Ateronu* and the strength of the Goa'uld. We've had pairings that lasted no more than three or four years, and others that have held on for decades."

That made sense, he supposed. "And how long—?"

"I've been Magna's host for just past three summers."

"Is it only recently that you've begun, you know." He tried to frame it delicately. "Struggling?"

Graen shook her head. "It's been coming on for a while. Longer than I've let on, actually, although I'm fairly sure Dirmid has suspected for quite some time." There was no missing the tinge of sadness in her voice.

"Is there a typical progression, as the Goa'uld gets stronger, I mean?" He felt badly asking what felt like a very personal question, but he needed to know.

"If you're asking me whether—" Graen's response was cut off by a chirruping sound. She reached under her cloak and from a pocket somewhere pulled out a Goa'uld short range communicator. The small oval device was glowing blue.

"*Hellooo? Hellooo? Is this thing working?*"

It was Jack.

Graen handed the communicator to Daniel.

"We can read you, Jack. What's up?"

"*Daniel! Great. Hey. Just want to let you know, we've got old Mol—Ow!*" There was a burst of static. "*Esras. We've got old* Esras *here, and we're on our way to the safe house. So you're good to go. I've already radioed Carter and given her the heads up, too.*"

"Understood." Daniel felt his lip sting as he spoke. "And Jack—let's just say, I really owe you one."

"*Come again, Dan—*" Jack's voice was cut off as Daniel switched off the device and handed it back to Graen.

"I guess this is it." Daniel took a deep breath and let it out slowly. He could do this.

"Dr. Jackson, just so you'll know, I may appear very differently when we are with Lugh. You may even begin to question who is in control—myself or Magna. She is gaining strength, yes. Even more than is known, as I suspect you have seen already this evening. But I give you my word, that, despite appearances, I will do everything I can to protect you. I hope you will believe that."

So she did know. Somehow, he found that comforting.

"I do believe you. And I hope I am able to be just as convincing in my role as you will be in yours."

Graen's face relaxed and she offered him a genuine smile. "Then let us be on our way. The sooner this night is behind us, the gladder we all shall be."

CHAPTER THIRTEEN

//ACCESSING MISSION REPORTS...//

P5C-777 MISSION REPORT, COLONEL JACK O'NEILL: I may have pointed out that the Tok'ra High Council might have a problem if something were to happen to Carter. The fact that I was holding a zat at the time may have helped too.

P5C-777 MISSION REPORT, DR. DANIEL JACKSON: Then again, a lie embedded with the truth is always easier to sell.

//CONTINUING ANALYSIS...//

TEAL'C AND O'Neill's objective was the small pushcart which waited at the other end of the alley. That it had been too wide to bring with them was an indication of just how narrow the passageway was. Although Mol'rek was not especially heavy, maneuvering within the confines of the limited space did make carrying him difficult.

"You'd have thought Dirmid could've come up with something other than this for us to stick him in," O'Neill remarked as they heaved Mol'rek over the side of the cart. It smelled distinctively of *la'aum* mash, which Teal'c guessed was its more usual content.

"I believe the intent is to make it appear as though he is intoxicated in the event we encounter anyone along the way."

O'Neill sniffed and wrinkled his nose upon catching the pungent scent of fermentation.

"Okay, that works."

The subterfuge turned out to be unnecessary. The side streets were quiet, and they saw only one person, a native Gorian, Teal'c presumed, who thankfully darted down another alley before getting too near Teal'c, O'Neill, and their unconscious cargo. Brean had given them directions to a safe house where they were to wait until the others had completed their respective parts of the plan. O'Neill had already given Daniel and Major Carter the signal to proceed, now that "Esras" was in custody.

The village itself was modest in size, and it did not take long to reach their destination. Mol'rek had already begun to stir by the time they arrived. Teal'c was prepared to further incapacitate him, if necessary, but the Tok'ra remained sufficiently groggy that they were able to safely drag him into the dwelling without having to render him unconscious yet again.

When Mol'rek did at last become aware of his surroundings and what had transpired, he did not hesitate to express his displeasure. Although Teal'c had little reason to fear any physical violence from the Tok'ra, he did find it prudent that O'Neill had tightly secured him to a chair. As it was, he released upon them a verbal tirade which blended both Goa'uld and Tok'ra expletives in ways Teal'c found quite inventive. While Teal'c was certain O'Neill did not understand the exact words used, he most definitely was able to comprehend the essence of Mol'rek's sentiments, and seemed amused by them.

Out of breath at last, and slightly purple in the face, the Tok'ra fell silent.

"Feel better?" O'Neill asked him.

"*You will regret this, O'Neill,*" Mol'rek shot back.

"Yeah — I kinda got the gist of that from what you said."

The Tok'ra's glare swept back and forth between Teal'c and O'Neill.

"*Tell me, how did you manage to escape? Surely someone must have helped you. Was it Pheone? Did he miss the lovely Major Carter already?*"

Teal'c saw O'Neill's jaw clench and his forearm muscles tighten. It was only with great effort that he refused to take Mol'rek's bait. His eyes, however, bore into the Tok'ra with a look of such unconcealed loathing there was no mistaking what his preferred response would have been.

"We haven't seen Pheone since he left us in the care of your guy, Dar'dak." O'Neill all but spit the words into Mol'rek's face. They were all the more effective for having the ring of truth about them. They truly had *not* seen "Pheone" since P5C-777.

"How we escaped is immaterial," Teal'c joined in. "The only thing of importance is that we are now able to prevent you from distributing the cloaking device to the System Lords."

"Or turning us over either, for that matter," O'Neill added.

"*You are interfering where you should not, Colonel. As usual, the Tau'ri refuse to see the long game. You choose to win the battles, but ultimately you will lose the war.*"

"Yeah — see, that's not typically how it works out, in my experience. But maybe we can discuss military strategy some other time. I'm sure we'll have the opportunity, especially as you'll be coming back with us." O'Neill had strolled behind the Tok'ra and patted him on the shoulder. It was anything but a friendly gesture and it startled Mol'rek, which had clearly been its intent.

"*Impossible. I must remain here on Gorias. My mission is too important.*"

"You know what?" O'Neill was right in Mol'rek's face now. "Your mission is crap. And it's over. Hey, Teal'c, who do you think old Lugh is already blaming for his prize prisoners escaping?"

"He is most assuredly blaming whoever is in charge of the Jaffa." Teal'c smiled knowingly at Mol'rek. "Which in this case is, I believe, the First Tanist."

Mol'rek paled.

"You mean the old 'Fist of Lugh' here? Well, there ya' go." O'Neill was beaming. "Hell, he might even think you're in on the whole thing. I mean, heck, why not just turn *us* over to the System Lords yourself and cut Lugh out of the deal completely? I bet that wouldn't be a very hard story for someone to sell, right T?"

"Indeed it would not, O'Neill."

Mol'rek was glowering. "*Years have been invested in securing my position with Lugh, Colonel. I do not think the Tok'ra High Council will appreciate your undermining it this way.*"

"Yeah, well, I might have a choice word or two to say to the Tok'ra High Council, especially about their plan to hand over such a strategic advantage to the System Lords." O'Neill was in Mol'rek's face again. "But I'm also guessing they won't like it too much when they find out about you using Carter and the rest of us to make your little scheme happen. And I'll lay odds that Selmak is *really* going to be pissed when he finds out, not to mention Carter's dad. So, either way, your ass is toast."

Mol'rek continued scowling but wisely made no reply.

"Good." O'Neill stood up and arched his back. "I'm glad we've gotten that straightened out." Pulling a chair in front of the only door in the room, he sat down and looked at his wrist. "Dammit. Teal'c, remind me to get my watch back from Carter. What time is it?"

Teal'c did not need a clock to answer that question. "I am afraid much time still remains until the others are ready for us to proceed."

O'Neill stretched his legs out in front of him and crossed his arms behind his head. "I guess we just get comfortable and wait, then."

For all that he appeared relaxed, the tension in O'Neill's face was clear to Teal'c. There would be no real rest for him until Major Carter and Daniel Jackson had safely returned.

Teal'c continued to stand where he was. Unlike O'Neill, he could not pretend a condition he did not feel. Not only that, but he did not trust Mol'rek, even tied to the chair. He mostly did it, however, to intimidate the Tok'ra and keep him from feeling too much at ease.

As it turned out, it was O'Neill who seemed most disturbed by Teal'c's inability to relax.

"So, you just going to stand there?"

"Yes."

O'Neill frowned. "The whole time."

"That is my intention."

Shrugging, O'Neill pulled his cap down over his eyes and cradled his *zat'nik'tel* in the crook of his arm. "Suit yourself." There was a long pause, before he added, "If he so much as twitches, shoot him."

"As you wish."

That earned him a slight raise of the hat as well as an eyebrow.

"Martha Stewart, investment informercials *and* Princess Bride?" O'Neill wagged his head. "Definitely *too* much TV."

~#~

"*Where are the others? Where is O'Neill and the* shol'va*?*"

Lugh's booming voice filled the hall and echoed off the rafters of the mostly empty space. The tables that had filled the room before had been pushed off to one side and Lugh sat alone in an ornately carved over-sized chair atop the dais. Unlike the first time Daniel had been in here, there were no other members of Lugh's inner circle present, although he realized now that all but a couple of them had been *Ateronu* operatives. Two Jaffa stood guard at the foot of the platform and two more at the doorway, but that was all. Whether it was due to the late hour or Lugh's desire to avoid witnesses to the humiliation of having lost his prized trophies, Daniel wasn't sure, although he suspected the latter.

Graen had forced Daniel to his knees, and now she struck him in the back of the head with her hand. It stung.

"*Speak, human.*" Graen had switched to Magna's voice. "*Where are your friends?*"

Daniel gave a bitter laugh, which wasn't hard to do, considering how much his head now hurt. "Long gone by now,

I'm sure."

"*They would leave you behind?*" Lugh asked.

"I don't think it was exactly their choice."

"*Explain,*" the Goa'uld growled.

"Why? You're either going to kill me or turn me over to the System Lords. From where I'm standing — figuratively speaking — I have nothing to gain from telling you anything."

"*You may never stand again if you do not speak,*" Graen raised her arm, threatening another blow. Reflexively, Daniel flinched. Graen had warned him about this, so he knew she was merely playing her part, but this was getting just a little too real. She almost seemed to be enjoying herself. At last Graen dropped her arm and sneered. "*Typical Tau'ri weakling.*"

"Well, at least I'm not so stupid I can't spot a traitor in my midst," Daniel muttered, looking pointedly at Lugh. Graen had said that the Goa'uld hated nothing more than to be made to look foolish, so they'd decided to try to play that angle. It appeared the insinuation hit its mark. Lugh surged to his feet and stormed down off his throne, hauling Daniel up by the front of his shirt until their faces were mere inches apart.

"*Are you saying that one of my own people set you free?*" he demanded.

Daniel shook his head with feigned amusement. Being impudent would probably come at a price, but if it sold the story then — "You know, now I can see why you're stuck on this backwater planet — all of you." He did his best to include the Jaffa and Graen in his sweeping glance of indictment. "And here I thought the System Lords were dim witted."

Lugh raised his fist and Daniel waited for the blow, but before it came he found himself back on the ground. His legs had been taken out from under him by a kick to the back of his knees, and his unexpected drop had yanked him free of Lugh's grasp.

A few choice words for Graen were on the tip of Daniel's tongue until he saw the ribbon device on Lugh's hand. She'd obviously been trying to save him from getting his brain scrambled, which he did appreciate, although that wasn't to say his knees still didn't hurt like hell.

Before Lugh could recover, Graen had grabbed a staff weapon from the nearby Jaffa. Activating it, she shoved the point under Daniel's chin. The thrumming of the powered crystal reverberated through Daniel's skull. There was no point in bothering to act afraid. His terror was real enough.

"*Name the traitor,*" Graen commanded. "*Name the traitor or die now.*"

"Esras," Daniel whispered hoarsely, barely able to get the name out around the pressure on this throat. "It's Esras."

Graen powered down the staff weapon and handed it back to the still-stunned Jaffa.

"*Impossible!*" Lugh thundered. "*You lie. Why would Esras betray me?*"

Daniel put his hand to his throat. He could still feel phantom vibrations from the staff. It took him a moment to realize Lugh was waiting on his answer.

"Oh, I don't know. Maybe because he's a Goa'uld? And maybe because he realized he could cut you completely out of the deal by turning us over to the System Lords himself?"

Lugh's face reddened with rage as the plausibility of Daniel's explanation sank in. Trust really was a rare commodity amongst the Goa'uld. It made fanning the flames relatively easy.

"*Where is Esras?*" Lugh demanded, looking first to Graen and then to his Jaffa. "*He will explain himself. Go! Bring him here!*" Lugh ordered one of the guards, when no one had answered him. "*Bring him here at once!*"

One of the Jaffa at the door hurried off to do Lugh's bidding, while Lugh himself paced in front of Daniel and Graen.

"*When your lie has been proven, Daniel Jackson, you will regret not having told me the truth.*"

"I'm pretty sure I've already told you the truth. Your guard isn't going to find Esras. He isn't here." Daniel couldn't help but appreciate the irony of using the truth to reinforce his lie. "He's with the rest of my team, and I wouldn't be surprised if they're already long gone by now."

Lugh pointed a finger at Daniel. *"Ah! But if them, why not you? If Esras helped all of you to escape, how is it that you have been left behind?"*

Time for the part of the story he'd rehearsed. Daniel did his best to sell it.

"Look, Esras smuggled us out of the castle through some hidden tunnel, and when we tried to make a break for it, he stunned the rest of my team. I was the only one who got away." He sighed heavily. "Kinda sorry I did, all things considered."

The Jaffa who'd been sent to find Esras ran, breathless, into the throne room and dropped to one knee before Lugh.

"My lord, Esras is not in his quarters and no one has seen him for many hours."

"Told you," Daniel taunted. Anything to aggravate the situation.

"My lord, if I may be so bold, perhaps Dar'dak might be able to shed some light on Esras' actions," Graen suggested, right on cue.

"Then bring me Dar'dak!" Lugh was beginning to turn red with fury. *"He will surely know where his master is, if no one else does."*

The Jaffa bowed again and disappeared through the wooden double doors. Daniel glanced at Graen to see if he could get any indication of how she thought it was going, but she was not looking at him. She truly was a different person in this context, not only in her behavior but in appearance. The warmth and compassion she had displayed back at the cottage was utterly gone from her face, replaced by a stone coldness that left Daniel feeling chilled. Despite what she'd said, part of him couldn't help but wonder how much of a grip on her Magna really did have.

Lugh was pacing. So far so good. It was clear that they'd managed to plant a few seeds of doubt about Esras. Hopefully Dar'dak's testimony would reinforce that. Back at the cottage the argument had been about whether it was a good idea to involve him or not, but Graen had insisted that he would do more good than harm. They'd find out soon enough.

Daniel was getting tired of kneeling on the hard floor, although he hated to move, since he wasn't quite sure what Graen might do to him to keep up appearances. It was just at the point of being unbearable when the door swung open yet again and the Jaffa returned. He didn't look quite so terrified as this time he hadn't returned empty-handed. Dar'dak was with him.

As all eyes turned on the new arrival, Daniel took the opportunity to scramble to his feet. No one objected.

Dar'dak strode up to the dais and bowed. His face was unreadable.

"You have asked for me, my lord."

Lugh didn't bother with the niceties. "*Where is your master, Esras?*"

The unreadable mask slipped just a bit. Dar'dak hesitated, as if he'd prefer not to answer the question. Finally, he had no choice. "I—I do not know, my lord. I have not seen him for some time."

"*And where are my prisoners? Where is SG-1?*"

Dar'dak glanced at Daniel, like it was a trick question.

"Dr. Jackson is here, my lord. I confess, I do not know how, but the others are missing."

"*Missing?*" Lugh roared. "*Missing? Escaped, you mean!*"

Dar'dak hung his head. "Yes, my lord."

"*And how is this possible? Is not my dungeon secure enough for mere humans?*"

"The dungeon is secure, my lord. And I do not know how they escaped—unless someone helped them."

Lugh lunged forward into Dar'dak's face. Apparently, it was his main mode of intimidation. "*Was it you, Dar'dak? Did you help them escape?"*

Dar'dak looked genuinely taken aback. His eyes widened and his mouth dropped open in surprise. "My lord, no! I did not!"

"*Then how did you discover they were gone?*" Graen spoke up before Lugh could ask another question. Daniel held his breath in case the Goa'uld objected, but he seemed content to let her continue the interrogation.

"Master Esras informed me they had escaped and ordered me to send the Jaffa in search of them."

"*And how long ago was that?*"

"Many hours ago, Second Tanist."

"*And why did you not report their escape to myself or Lord Lugh?*" Graen demanded.

Daniel could see Dar'dak realize he was about to walk into a trap, even if he wasn't quite sure what that trap was. Teal'c had seemed to think the Jaffa had a greater loyalty to Esras than to Lugh, but it was an entirely different matter when he was the one in the hot seat and Esras was not. Dar'dak looked from Graen to Daniel to Lugh before replying.

"Master Esras ordered me not to, Second Tanist."

Ah. And that was what Graen had been counting on — the truth. Now it was up to her to spin it.

"*My lord.*" Graen turned to Lugh. "*What further proof do you need? Esras has clearly betrayed you. Between the confession of this human and the words of his own Jaffa, there is no doubt that Esras has not only taken SG-1 for his own purposes, but has ordered the Jaffa to lie to you about it.*" She looked disdainfully at Dar'dak. "*The search for them was clearly a ruse — meant to cover his tracks once they were found to be missing. Meanwhile, he has taken the others in order to steal your glory from the System Lords. I submit, my lord, that Esras is no longer worthy to be your First Tanist.*"

It was a perfect speech; the type Daniel would have expected from the most conniving of Goa'ulds. If the other *Ateronu* were as adept at channeling their symbiotes as Graen, it was little wonder that in all these years Lugh had never caught on to their silent infiltration of his regime.

Dar'dak did not contradict Graen, despite her having taken more than a few liberties with what he'd said. Daniel saw him watching Lugh through lowered eyes, awaiting the Goa'uld's response. His impassive expression had returned, making it impossible to know how much of what Graen had said he himself believed.

Reading Lugh was much easier. His face had gone from red to nearly purple, and Daniel braced himself for the rage that was about to be unleashed.

But instead of a tirade, Lugh burst into loud, raucous laughter. What exactly the Goa'uld found so entertaining, Daniel had no idea. To be honest, he found it a little unsettling.

Still laughing, Lugh had made his way back to his chair and collapsed into it, reaching for a goblet that stood on a nearby stand. Only after he had emptied its contents did he finally seem able to speak.

"*Well played, Magna. Well played.*" Lugh wiped the back of his hand across his mouth and set the goblet back on the table.

If Graen was the least bit concerned at Lugh's response, she didn't show it. Daniel wished he felt equally calm. Maybe this wasn't going to turn out quite as they had planned.

"*I wondered how long it would take for you to challenge Esras for First Tanist again.*" Lugh's smile was almost as repulsive as his rage.

"*My lord, surely you cannot deny the words you yourself have heard this night.*" Graen indicated Daniel and Dar'dak.

"*That Esras is a traitor? Do you take me for a fool?*" The smile turned into a snarl. Daniel felt the bottom drop out of his stomach. This looked bad. "*I am not blind. Of course he is a traitor. And he will pay for his betrayal.*"

Daniel began breathing again.

"*But I have lost much this night, Magna. And you bring me only one Tau'ri in compensation. Hardly an effort worthy of a*

First Tanist."

Next to him, Daniel heard Graen take a deep, steadying breath. He felt just as relieved. Somehow — he wasn't quite sure how — they'd actually pulled it off. Now all Graen had to do was prove she deserved the promotion. After what they'd just accomplished, this was the easy part.

He risked a brief glance Graen's way. The cold, conniving Magna look was still there, but now her lips were pulled taut by a knowing, sly smile. She truly looked like someone else entirely.

"*Well, then, my lord.*" Her voice had taken on an oily quality. "*I believe I have something which will more than make up for what Esras has taken from you.*" She brought out the Goa'uld communicator. "*Pheone. I am ready for you to bring my newest acquisition.*" She gave Daniel a sideways look and, if possible, her lip curled even more. "*Oh — and by all means, be sure you bring Major Carter along as well.*"

CHAPTER FOURTEEN

//ACCESSING MISSION REPORTS...//

P5C-777 MISSION REPORT, MAJOR SAMANTHA CARTER. Colonel O'Neill had told me to do whatever it took. So that's what I did.

//CONTINUING ANALYSIS...//

"YOU WILL BE safe here until the rest of your friends can join you. I'll make sure of it." Dirmid was perched again on the cargo containers in the hold, watching Sam as she lay on the floor, her head halfway into the base of the cloaking device.

As Dirmid had suspected, his *tel'tak* had been left unguarded. Esras had ordered every available Jaffa to search for SG-1, including the pair he had set to guard the ship. The keypad code hadn't even been changed, so they'd been able to slip inside with no effort at all. Doing so under the cover of darkness had helped too.

The cloak was fixed—or, at least, Sam hoped it was. It hadn't taken her long. She'd been almost finished when they'd landed the day before. Now all that remained was to test it. Ideally, she'd have liked to have gone up to the *ha'tak* with Graen to be sure it worked before the actual demonstration for Lugh. It would hardly help Graen's effort to become First Tanist if, when she threw the switch, the thing didn't function properly.

The colonel had vetoed that idea. He'd insisted it was only because he had absolute faith in her ability to get it right the first time, although Sam suspected there might have been more to it than that. Which was fine, as long as he'd have done the same for Teal'c or Daniel. The moment *that* changed, they'd need to have a little talk.

For now, she needed to focus on the task at hand, which was to make sure that when Graen did inevitably throw the switch, the whole ship didn't explode. Sam had chosen to reprogram the device directly rather than to use the console, just in case Dirmid got curious. Quite possibly he would understand why she'd sabotaged the cloak in the first place — but then again, maybe he wouldn't. At this point, Sam didn't feel it was a risk worth taking.

She was mentally kicking herself, though. She'd buried the self-destruct program so deep in the code she was having a hard time finding it. Part of the problem was that she was trying to rush. The colonel had already radioed her that he and Teal'c had Mol'rek in their custody, which was Graen and Daniel's cue to make their case before Lugh. It wouldn't be long before Dirmid would receive Magna's command to deliver the cloaking device to the castle. If she didn't have it reprogrammed by then —

Stop. She couldn't think about the "ifs". She had to concentrate on what she was doing. She'd deal with what happened next when it happened.

"I won't let them go through with it, you know." Dirmid's muffled voice had taken on a different tone. Sam realized he'd been continuing to talk while her thoughts had been elsewhere. Somehow, she didn't think he was still discussing getting them to the Stargate. Sam extricated herself from the base of the cloak.

"I'm sorry?"

He gazed at Sam with a sadness she had seen far too often. "I won't let her die."

It took Sam a second to catch up.

"Graen."

Dirmid nodded.

So she had been right. There was more between them than just their shared experience as *Ateronu*. That explained a lot.

"You're hoping you can save her in time—that's why you've been pushing so hard to launch the coup. But I thought the effects of the *bahlay* were irreversible?"

Dirmid nodded again. "They are. But, I thought— hoped—maybe I could find a way to help her fight back, so Magna doesn't take over completely. You see, there's a small cottage I have, up in the mountains on a lake. I can care for her there—keep her from harm."

As compassionate as that sounded, Sam could think of at least a half dozen reasons why Dirmid's intentions were ill-advised, not the least of which was that she was sure it was something Graen would not want. But it wasn't her place to bring that up.

"How long do you think Graen has?" She had no way of knowing if what they'd already witnessed was indicative of the beginning of the *bahlay* or a sign it was entering its final stages. Going by Graen's own concerns, Sam's guess would be the latter.

Dirmid's sigh confirmed it. "Not long. But perhaps long enough, especially if I could get the demon out of her." There was an implied question in his last remark, which it took Sam a moment to catch.

"You're referring to what Daniel said about the Tok'ra?"

"Aye. Of course we've heard of such a thing, but we've never quite been in a position to have contact with any Tok'ra, let alone seek their help."

Sam bit her tongue. If he only knew.

"Do you think they'd help—if you asked them?" Dirmid looked at her earnestly.

Sam struggled with her reply. She was sure the Tok'ra would help. But if Graen's losing the battle to Magna was as imminent as everyone seemed to think, then they'd need to take her with them when they left. That would be complicated by the fact that they were taking Mol'rek too. The colonel and the others had agreed that it was probably best to keep his true identity a secret from the Gorians. She had no idea what their reaction would be upon learning not just that he was a Tok'ra, but that Sam and her team had chosen to keep that information from them. Perhaps, given their own use of subterfuge, the Gorians would understand. Then again, possibly not.

There was a bigger question than Mol'rek, though — one which Sam wasn't sure Dirmid had addressed. She tried to broach it tactfully. "If that's what Graen wants, then we'll certainly do our best to help." Because as much as she could respect Dirmid's desire to save Graen, it was Graen's life, after all. If Dirmid loved her enough to risk everything for her, he needed to love her enough to let her choose whether the life he was intent on saving her for was one she really wanted to keep.

"Of course, of course. Thank you." Dirmid's gratitude was profuse, yet Sam had the feeling he'd rather missed her point. But again, it was something that would need to be dealt with later. She'd already been distracted long enough.

With what she hoped was a sympathetic smile, Sam went back to reprogramming the device. She had just isolated the Goa'uld equivalent of the subfolder she was looking for when she felt a vibration on the decking. Dirmid must have jumped down from the cargo container.

"Are you sure about that?" Sam heard him say from her sound-dampened position. Dammit. Graen must be ready for them. Sam was out of time and the self-destruct was still in place.

There was only one option. She'd have to go up to the *ha'tak* with the cloak and finish reprogramming it up there. It she had to, she'd tell Graen the truth. For now, she'd just tell Dirmid that the device needed a few final tweaks.

At least Lugh had never seen her, so if she dressed like a Gorian she could pass as Dirmid's servant. It wasn't how they'd planned it, but given they were out of time, it was the only strategy she could come up with.

On the plus side, at least she'd be able to help Graen test the device before Lugh got there.

On the negative side, though — the colonel would be mad as hell.

~#~

"*Major Samantha Carter. At last.*"

The Goa'uld pushed himself out of his chair and came down one of the two steps of his platform to size her up. Sam did her best to appear indifferent — which admittedly was difficult once the colonel's nickname of "Lord Slug" popped into her head. It wasn't hard, though, to turn her smirk into a grimace, once she got a whiff of him. She couldn't remember the last time she smelled anything that offensive.

This certainly hadn't been part of the plan. Sam had no clue why Graen was improvising like this. Dirmid hadn't been able to explain either, barely having time to give her a heads-up before two pair of Jaffa had shown up at the *tel'tak* to escort them, along with the cloak, to Lugh's throne room. Maybe Daniel's story hadn't been enough to convince Lugh after all.

Speaking of Daniel — Sam looked around the room. There was no sign of him anywhere. Two Jaffa stood guard near Lugh's throne and a third stood at attention by the door, along with the four who had accompanied them from the *tel'tak*. Dar'dak was there too, although Sam hadn't seen him at first. He seemed to be standing apart, as if hoping to go unnoticed.

"*Major Carter has been graciously lending her talents to fix the gift I have procured for you, my Lord.*" Sam hadn't see Graen in full Magna mode before. It sent a chill down her spine. The malice behind Graen's eyes was absolutely convincing. "*Surely half of SG-1* and *a cloaking device capable of concealing an entire* ha'tak *vessel, most recently used by Apophis in his defeat of Heru'ur, is sufficient tribute to secure my position as your First Tanist.*"

Sam couldn't tell which prize Lugh was more fascinated

by—herself or the cloak. His weasel-like eyes kept darting from her to the device that had been placed in the middle of the room behind her. It took him a moment to decide, but when he pushed past her to examine the device, Sam let out a sigh of relief. She glanced at Graen, hoping for some hint as to what might be going on, but her attention remained on Lugh.

"*And it works*?" He was eyeing the cloak greedily.

Graen didn't even wait for confirmation from Dirmid or Sam. "*Of course it does, my Lord. It is ready for you to present to the System Lords and receive, at last, the glory you so richly deserve.*"

"*Show me.*"

Graen bowed slightly. "*It will need to be installed on your* ha'tak *first, my Lord. And then, by all means, we shall have a demonstration.*"

Lugh nodded, his attention still on the device. He slowly ran his hands over it, almost caressing it, clearly enraptured. Sam tried not to let the image burn itself into her mind.

As almost an afterthought, he snapped his fingers and waved his hand in Sam's general direction, not even bothering to take his eyes from his newest acquisition. "*Take Major Carter and put her with Dr. Jackson,*" he commanded, presumably to the one Jaffa who stood at the door.

"*My Lord*—" Graen stepped forward, still smiling in a way that made Sam's skin crawl. "*If I might—Major Carter may be of use in the installation of the device on your mothership. I would like to take her with me, for the time being.*"

Ah. Finally. So *that* was the reason behind Graen's play. For whatever reason, she wanted Sam's help on the ship. Maybe this was her way of getting around the colonel refusing to let Sam help test the device. And Graen would have had no way of knowing that Sam had been angling to get onto the mothership as well. At least they'd both been working towards the same end, albeit for very different reasons.

Although that still didn't explain where Daniel was...

It took a bit before Lugh replied to Graen's request. He remained distracted by his shiny new toy. When he did, he waved at her dismissively. "*Yes. Of course. Whatever you need.*"

"*As your First Tanist, my Lord, I—*"

This time Graen *did* get Lugh's attention. He looked up and erupted with a burst of humorless laughter.

"*You get ahead of yourself, Magna. Prove this is more than merely an empty cylinder and* then *you will be First Tanist. Not before.*"

Graen bowed. "*I serve at your pleasure, my Lord.*"

Lugh lumbered back to his chair and sank into it with a groan. "*Yes. You do. And you would be wise not to forget it.*" His eyes swept over to Dirmid. "*Both of you.*"

"*You may count on that, my Lord,*" Dirmid replied hastily, with an obsequious bow. He was being careful not to look at Sam. She wondered if he thought Lugh might be beginning to suspect something. There was still an off feeling in the room.

"*Dar'dak!*"

The Jaffa had very slowly been edging closer to the shadows at the perimeter of the room, but he hurried forward when Lugh called out his name.

"*Double the guard at the* chaapa'ai, *and be sure that Esras does not leave with one of my* tel'tak's."

"Yes, Lord Lugh." Dar'dak stuck his fist against his chest in salute.

"*I will have the traitor Esras, along with the rest of SG-1, before this night is out. Do not fail me.*"

Dar'dak bowed his head and swiveled on his heels. Sam couldn't help but think he looked relieved to have been set a task that would take him elsewhere. Frankly, she couldn't blame him. She was looking forward to getting out of here herself.

As soon as Dar'dak had left, Graen motioned for two of the Jaffa to retrieve the cloak and remove it from the hall. Dirmid opened the door, allowing them to pass before trailing behind them into the chamber beyond. Sam and Graen followed, with

Graen keeping a tight grip on Sam's upper arm. She got that they had to keep up the pretense that she was their prisoner, but Graen could have gone for a little more show and a little less authenticity, especially when it came to the zat she was pressing painfully into Sam's ribs.

Graen didn't even let up, once they were out of Lugh's sight. Sam doubted the Jaffa would notice, but then again, maybe Graen was so accustomed to playing the part of Magna that it didn't even occur to her to let her guard down a little. Certainly, Sam couldn't say anything — the Jaffa might not notice Graen lowering her weapon or loosening her grip, but they probably couldn't ignore a conversation between the presumed prisoner and her supposed captors. She had way more questions than there were obvious answers, but for now they would have to wait. Sam did her best to school her impatience.

Once they reached the main floor, Graen took out a key and unlocked one of the many doors around the perimeter of the entrance hall. Dirmid had said the ring room was located on this level. It seemed odd that it would be kept under lock and key, but since Graen was the one in charge of the mothership, Sam supposed she had her reasons for limiting access to it.

The Gorian's fingers were still digging into Sam's bicep as she steered her through the door and into the passageway beyond. Sam only nominally took note of her surroundings, although it was enough to recognize that the narrow hallway was lined on either side with a series of tapestries. They made Sam think of Daniel, who she was sure would have a field day examining them, if he ever had the chance.

His whereabouts was the first question Sam intended to ask. If the plan had gone as it was meant to, he should have been on his way to Dirmid's *tel'tak* by now. Instead, he still seemed to be in Lugh's custody, which told her that something had gone awry. Once she knew what exactly had happened, she'd need to get word to the colonel.

At the end of the passageway, a single door opened into a

large room, vacant except for a familiar ring shape imbedded in the floor and its corresponding control panel mounted on the stone wall to the left. Whatever this room's purpose had originally been — and Daniel would have probably had better insight into that than she did — it was now the ring room.

At Dirmid's direction, the Jaffa placed the cloaking device in the center of the rings and left. Sam waited a few seconds after the door closed behind them before turning to the two Gorians.

"What the hell is going on? Where's Daniel?"

Graen did not seem offended by Sam's accusatory tone. "Lugh has sent him back to the dungeon. There was nothing I could do to stop it." She had moved to the panel on the wall and was keying in a code.

"I'll go after him and get him to the ship as planned." Dirmid made to leave.

"No!" Graen's tone was so sharp that Dirmid looked startled. "I mean, I will need your help getting the device to the engine room, once we are aboard the *ha'tak*." She sagged against the wall. "I have evacuated all of our people from the ship, in anticipation of the coup. Only a handful of Jaffa remain, and I would rather they not know what we are up to." She managed a strained smile in Sam's direction. "While I have no doubt Major Carter is up to the task, I do not think I can do my share when it comes to carrying that thing." She indicated the cloak. "I'm sure no harm will come to Dr. Jackson, in the meanwhile."

It wasn't so much harm that Sam was concerned about, as timing. Rescuing Daniel wasn't exactly built into their schedule. But then again, neither was her ringing up to the mothership. Once she could contact the colonel, they'd have to make some modifications to their original plan. He was definitely not going to be happy.

"At least this will give you the time you need to finish fixing it," Dirmid said to Sam as he went to stand next to the cloak in the rings. Graen's brow furrowed.

"It's not working yet?"

Sam flushed. She'd let Dirmid think it was the cloak itself that she still needed time to finish. The longer she could put off mentioning the self-destruct, the better.

"It won't take long," she assured Graen, joining Dirmid in the ring. At least that was true. Another five minutes was all she needed. "And then we can test it before Lugh arrives, just to be sure."

For some reason, Graen looked surprised by the idea. "Test it?"

"To be sure it works when you give Lugh the demonstration."

Graen closed her eyes and gave her head a slight shake. "Yes, of course. Forgive me, Major. That's what we need to do, isn't it?"

Sam wasn't sure if that was a question or a statement. What she was sure about was that Graen wasn't herself. No doubt it was the effect of the *bahlay*. Magna clearly was wearing her down. Sam could see how much more fatigued she looked than back at the cottage.

"I know we're up against time — all of us." Maybe she could offer Graen some reassurance. "But I'm sure everything is going to work out. Just hang in there."

If Graen didn't exactly understand the expression, she did seem to grasp Sam's intentions. "I shall endeavor to persevere, Major." With the rest of the activation code input, she hurried to stand on the other side of Sam. The sound of the rings overwhelmed whatever Graen said next, although Sam could have sworn she heard: "And I have no doubt but that everything is going to work out *just* fine."

CHAPTER FIFTEEN

//ACCESSING MISSION REPORTS...//

P5C-777 MISSION REPORT, DR. DANIEL JACKSON. For future reference, knowing where you're going, and exactly what it is you're looking for, is probably something that's worth figuring out ahead of time.

//CONTINUING ANALYSIS...//

THE FAMILIAR sound of the key turning in the lock of the dungeon's outer door reverberated down the passageway. The single torch that Teal'c had used to help find their way when they'd escaped had been replaced, and its flickering light threw shadows of the bars in the door against the cell wall.

Daniel looked around. This was the last place he'd expected to see again. And this was most definitely not where he was supposed to be. Why Graen had changed the plan — why she'd told Dirmid to bring Sam along with the cloak — Daniel had no idea. It was almost as if — But no. If Magna had taken control, they'd all be prisoners again, and Dirmid right along with them. Something else must have happened. All Daniel knew for sure was that he should have gone with Dirmid to the *tel'tak*, but instead, he was stuck here.

Although, possibly not for long.

Daniel fished in his boot. Yes. It was still there. Good. Between the walking and the rough handling by Graen, he hadn't lost it.

They'd searched all his pockets. No one ever thought to check his boots, though. Besides, they'd been looking for weapons.

Not keys. Especially not the key to the cell door.

Daniel pulled it out of his sock.

At least he had a way out of here now. Maybe that's why Graen hadn't objected when Lugh had ordered him here. Maybe they were counting on him getting out by himself and getting to the *tel'tak* on his own.

Or maybe he ought to stay put and wait; let whatever changes to the plan were underway play out until he knew for certain what he needed to do.

Daniel stared at the flickering shapes on the wall for a few seconds.

Nope. He couldn't do that—just sit here, out of the action. This only worked—they only got off the planet—if they all made it to the *tel'tak*. As far as he knew, that was still the plan and he was going to stick to it.

A moment later, Daniel was standing in front of the stone wall, trying to find the spots that Teal'c had pressed to open the hidden door. He remembered the smooth spot on the floor, and when he found that, he stepped back, half-closed his eyes and stared at the wall. There they were, two indentations. Up close they were impossible to see, but from a few steps away—as obvious as day.

There was probably some lesson there, about needing to step back in order to see things more clearly. He'd ponder that another time. Right now, he needed to get out of the castle and to the *tel'tak*. At least Dirmid had thought to tell him where it was parked.

The exterior door of the Sally Port brought Daniel once more out onto the grounds of the castle. It seemed like forever since he'd stood there with the rest of his team, but it had only been that morning. Everything looked different now. A full, bright moon had risen, its light like a beam, reflecting off the stone tower at his back. Daniel realized that he was as visible as if he were standing in a spotlight, so he moved into the shadow of a nearby buttress.

Across the way, he recognized the grove of trees they'd used earlier to conceal their escape. The long blue shadows they now cast on the open ground offered the safest route to reach the thin dark line that was the perimeter wall. He wouldn't need to actually go into the trees this time. He could just skim along their edge.

Checking that no one was in sight, Daniel made a run for it. Compared to the risk they'd taken that morning, when there'd been four of them, this was a relative piece of cake. And yet, by the time he reached the safety of the shadows, his heart was pumping as though he'd just finished a marathon. Maybe it was because the stakes were so much higher now. Or maybe it was because, unlike before, this time he was on his own.

As he paused to catch his breath, Daniel looked back at the castle. With nothing to shield it from the moonlight, the fortress was nearly as visible as it was in broad daylight. He could make out the details of the stonework well enough to tell where additions had been made to the structure over the years, and from this vantage point, he had the most complete view yet of the layout of all the other buildings within the complex.

One of the larger buildings was venting a vast amount of steam. That one had to be the brewhouse. The aroma of fermenting grain was unmistakable, and it hung like a cloud in the damp, night air. Now that he was paying attention, Daniel could see a steady stream of people going in and out, even at this late hour. If any of them had noticed his sprint across the moonlit yard, no one seemed to care.

The *tel'taks*, Dirmid had told him, were kept in a field just outside the castle wall. Supposedly there was a small doorway that would lead Daniel directly there. All he had to do was find where that doorway was.

How hard could that be?

Daniel directed his attention away from the buildings and towards the perimeter wall.

Okay. Pretty damn hard, actually.

For one, it was impossible to see all of the wall from where he was. The terrain rose and fell, and where it dipped, the wall disappeared from his view. And secondly, he only just realized how close some of the outbuildings were to the wall itself. For the moment, the moon was low enough that he had the advantage of being able to move under cover of the wall's shadow. It was a thin margin even now, and one that would vanish soon enough. He needed to find the doorway before the moon got too high in the sky.

And not get caught in the process.

Or break anything, like his ankle, which he nearly twisted when his feet became entangled in something he'd failed to see in the grass along the edge of the tree line. He managed to right himself before he crashed too hard into the stone wall, but even so —

Yeah. That was going to leave a mark.

Feeling in the grass to see what had tripped him up, he realized it was a wooden ladder. Of course. *This* was where SG-1 was supposed to have gone over the wall the last time. Well, no one ever said they did things the easy way.

The ladder wasn't of any use now, though. He needed to find the door. Which wasn't going to happen if he didn't get moving.

Hugging the wall as best he could, Daniel edged his way along it as swiftly as he could manage. The first leg wasn't too bad. There was plenty of yard between the wall and the outbuildings and he doubted anyone was likely to pick up his movement, even if they did glance that way.

It didn't take long, however, before that gap started to narrow and the outbuildings loomed ever closer. Daniel slowed his pace. Any kind of quick movement might attract someone's attention, and that was the last thing he needed.

And there were plenty of people around. Far more than he'd been able to see from his earlier vantage point. Clearly the *la'aum* production was an around-the-clock business, and it looked like the night shift was just coming in.

Maybe he just needed to not move at all, until the flow of people in and out of the building tapered off. He was close enough now that he could almost make out individual faces. And if he could see them, then it wouldn't take much movement on his part for them to see him.

The good news was that they weren't Jaffa but Gorians — at least Daniel assumed they were, going by their dress and the distinctive color of their hair, which was either raven black, like Brean's, or flaming red, like Dirmid's. The work force seemed about equally comprised of men and women, and while he didn't see any children, there were some workers who looked like they might be in their early teens. Those leaving the brewhouse were silent and drenched with sweat. No one spoke, either to those on the incoming shift or amongst themselves. Daniel could practically feel their exhaustion as they made their way towards what he assumed was the main castle gate.

Certainly, he had witnessed humans pressed into far more brutal tasks by the Goa'uld on other planets. The naquadah mines were the worst — a fact he and the rest of SG-1 knew only too well from firsthand experience. But the fact that Daniel couldn't see any evidence of whips or hand devices or pain sticks didn't make these people's enslavement any less monstrous by its lack of obvious depravity.

Besides, it wasn't just those working in the hot steam of this one building. It was farmers, forced to plant land whose benefits they would never reap. Laborers who would harvest it without compensation. Teamsters. Brewmasters. Those who made the containers that held the ale. Those who bottled it. The whole resources of a planet and its people, compelled to serve the needs of one solitary being, with no say in their own destiny.

Getting back to Earth with his team intact was essential, of course. But so was setting these people free. Up until now, he and the others had only seen Gorias as the faces of Dirmid and Graen, Brean and Udal. But this was what was behind their obsessive determination. Gorians may not be mining naquadah, but that didn't make them any less slaves of the Goa'uld or their liberation any less important. SG-1 couldn't just walk away from this without doing everything they could to help. Even if it meant getting even more involved than they already were.

Nearby, someone coughed. Had he been so lost in thought that he'd inadvertently moved? Daniel pressed his back against the wall until he felt the jagged stones dig in. Hopefully he was still hidden.

Footsteps drew nearer. Not just one pair, but two. A couple of Jaffa emerged from the shadows of one of the other nearby buildings, walking with determination but not any real sense of urgency. They did, however, seem intent on a particular destination.

Daniel held his breath. They passed so close, he was surprised they couldn't hear the way his heart was thudding against his chest again. But he was still in the wall's shadow, whereas they had moved into broad moonlight. They never even glanced his way.

Still not daring to move, Daniel watched as the Jaffa hurried off in the same direction he was headed. They didn't seem to be searching for anyone, so that was a relief. He hoped that meant his escape hadn't been discovered yet. At the pace he was going, he was going to need as much of a head start as he could get.

It didn't take long, with the irregular path of the wall, before the Jaffa were out of sight. Daniel hesitated. If he followed them, as he needed to do, there was the chance that he could run into them, quite literally, somewhere up ahead. But this was the only way he knew to get to the *tel'taks*, and if he tried to get creative by taking some other route, then he might just as well go back to his cell and wait to be rescued, because that's most certainly where he'd end up anyway if he tried to improvise. There weren't any other options. He'd just have to be extra cautious and stay alert.

Deciding it was safe now — the shift change seemed to be over — Daniel resumed his trek along the wall. To his relief, it began to gradually wend its way away from the populated part of the castle and out into the more open area of the grounds. It was brighter out here, away from the buildings, and Daniel could finally see a long stretch of the wall as it lay out ahead of him. The moon had risen even higher, and he was losing the shadow much quicker than he'd hoped. There was only about two feet of it now — enough to conceal him, but not to hide the two Jaffa, who should be up ahead somewhere.

Except they weren't. Daniel had been watching, and hadn't seen them turn back to the castle anywhere along the way. It was almost as if they'd vanished into thin air.

Or maybe gone through the very same doorway Daniel was looking for. He hadn't even wanted to consider that a possibility. But then he found himself standing in front of the door itself — and it was ajar.

Okay. This could be a problem.

For one of the rare times in his life, Daniel really, really wished he had a weapon. A zat would come in quite handy about now. He'd even take a decent stick, if one were handy — which it wasn't. He had no idea who or what was waiting for him on the other side, and given a choice, he'd prefer not to find out. Daniel sighed. Unfortunately, he didn't have the luxury of that option.

He could, however, take a few minutes to think this through. So — if he assumed the Jaffa were waiting on the other side, he had two ways he could go. Stealth or the element of surprise. He still didn't think they had been searching for anyone, which meant it was possible they'd simply been sent down here to keep an eye on the ships. Or maybe they were rotating shifts with other Jaffa who were already on guard. He hadn't thought of that before, actually, which he probably should have. If he were Lugh, he'd want to make sure Esras didn't make it off the planet. He'd probably sent extra guards to the Stargate too.

The Stargate wasn't the problem though — at least, not yet. First, he had to get to the *tel'tak*. To do that, he had to deal with the Jaffa.

If they really weren't looking for him, then he would probably be better off avoiding them altogether if he could. Which meant that stealth was the way to go.

The door in the wall was constructed of thick wooden timbers and did not swing easily. Daniel was able to carefully inch it open so that he had a limited view of the other side. All he could see was a field of low-growing grass, almost lawn like, behind which was a dark backdrop of densely massed trees.

Nudging the door open a little more revealed that the field was quite self-contained, not only in the back, but also on the right by yet another stand of thick-growing trees. And when Daniel finally made the opening wide enough to peer completely around the corner, he saw that the opposite side was just the same: another barricade of forest. With the wall as the fourth side, it made for a nicely enclosed space.

Just the type of space in which to secure the three *tel'taks* which were lined up in a V-formation, gleaming brightly in the moonlight for all to see.

And by all, he meant not only himself, but the two Jaffa, who thankfully had their backs to him as they walked between the first two ships, apparently on patrol.

Damn.

And there was another problem too. One he hadn't given any thought to until now. The ships were identical, more or less. He hadn't paid enough attention to Dirmid's to know if there was something that made it unique from the other two. Even assuming he was able to dodge the Jaffa on their rounds, Daniel had no idea which ship was the one he was supposed to be on.

Maybe this really was a bad idea after all.

But, he was here now, and this was still better than waiting in that cell. So, what the hell? There were only three ships, anyway. One of them was Dirmid's. He'd just have to check each one out. All he had to do was not get caught in the process.

Daniel took a deep breath.

The easiest one would be the first ship on the end. The Jaffa had already walked past the exterior door and should soon be rounding the aft section of the middle ship. Daniel crouched as low as he could manage and made a silent dash to the first ship's port side. Staying as close to the hull as possible, he inched his way towards the back and around to the starboard side, watching for when the Jaffa disappeared from view. The moment he was out of their sight line, Daniel made a run for the exterior door and hit the button to open it.

Nothing happened, except for an entirely too loud chirp from the keypad alerting him to his failure. Daniel froze. In the night air, the sound might as well have been as loud as a cannon. He waited to hear the running footsteps of the Jaffa in search of the source, but there was nothing. Just the soft rustle of the leaves in the forest surrounding them.

So maybe the chirp really hadn't been that loud. In any case, he wasn't about to try it again. The ship was locked. Dirmid's or not, he wasn't getting on it.

Besides, there were still two more to try.

Daniel slipped back to the rear of the *tel'tak* to wait and see which way the Jaffa would go, after they'd finished their loop around the third ship. When it was clear that they were reversing their path, Daniel used the first ship to shield himself until he could slip into the shadow of the one next to it. He felt more exposed at the middle ship, probably because it sat forward of the other two, its nose and outer door visible to just about anyone.

The same scolding chirp told him this *tel'tak* was locked too. Maybe he was doing something wrong. Teal'c had shown him the basic sequence for opening an unlocked cargo ship door, but it was possible he was screwing it up in his haste. Daniel stared at the keypad, trying to remember, but all he could come up with was the same code he had entered. Maybe if he tried again—

"It came from over there!"

The Jaffa sounded so close to him that Daniel was sure they'd be right behind him when he turned around. But the voice had echoed off the wall. The Jaffa were still on the other side of the middle *tel'tak*, but Daniel could hear them jogging his way. There was only one place left he could go—the last ship in the row. Otherwise he'd have to make for the woods, and he knew he'd never get there before they saw him.

Scrambling around the rear of the third ship, Daniel didn't even bother to ease his way forward. If this ship was locked too, he'd definitely be what Jack would call SOL.

He knew he'd hit the wrong sequence the moment he did it, which made the chirp of rejection just that much more galling. It didn't help that the Jaffa had heard it too, going by their ever-nearing voices. Daniel took another deep breath, trying to steady his hands, and made a second attempt. Squeezing his eyes shut, he waited for the dreaded sound, but instead, the four panels of the door slid back, opening the way to the airlock.

Daniel practically dove through, slapping the button on the inside so that the panels slid back in place. The interior lock code was universal and he quickly entered it, just in case the Jaffa decided to start checking the actual ships themselves. He could hear them, just outside the door now, still searching for the source of the sounds they'd heard. The hull of a *tel'tak* was durable enough for space travel, but it wasn't soundproof. And if he could hear them, then they would probably be able to hear him if he started moving around. It wasn't worth the risk. Daniel stood there, motionless, until he was sure they had moved away.

He even gave it a few extra minutes, just to be sure. It wasn't until it started to get just a little too claustrophobic in the small space, that Daniel finally decided to go ahead and open the interior door. Even the unrecycled ship air felt cool in comparison to the suffocating stuffiness of the airlock.

Daniel had no idea if this was Dirmid's ship or not. Only Sam had actually been aboard it, and she hadn't mentioned anything about it in particular. Only the cloaking device would have stood out, but of course she and Dirmid had taken that with them.

The moonlight streaming through the front viewport didn't do a half bad job of lighting up the bridge, but it left most of the cargo hold in darkness, and there was no point in even trying to see inside the engine room. A flashlight would have come in handy about now. He could always turn on the interior lights, but Daniel had a feeling that would probably catch the attention of the Jaffa who were still, undoubtedly, patrolling outside. He'd just have to make the best of it with what he had.

It wasn't like he was going any place anyway. Not with his two friends still out there.

Through the front viewport, a pulse of light shooting straight up out of the castle caught Daniel's eye. Transport rings. In all probability, it was Graen and the cloaking device headed to the mothership. Until he learned otherwise, Daniel had to assume that Sam and Dirmid were with her, although what that meant, he had no idea.

When the pulse had vanished into the darkness, Daniel withdrew back into the cargo bay. The bridge was more comfortable, but it was entirely too visible from the outside. He was better off here, even with its limited light.

The nebulous shapes were already starting to become more distinct as Daniel's eyes became accustomed to the darkness. There were several large cargo containers — locked, of course — on either side of the space, and the requisite transport rings in the center. Pretty standard-issue Goa'uld, right down to the gilded hieroglyph panels covering the walls.

One object did seem out of place. It was small and dark and

looked like it might have been dropped or fallen from atop one of the cargo containers. Daniel walked over to pick it up. He knew what it was the instant his hand curled around it.

It was an SGC-issued radio. Sam's, most likely. She would have had to leave it behind.

Which meant this *was* Dirmid's ship. By sheer dumb luck — or actually, in this case, panicked desperation — he'd found it. For once, the odds had worked in his favor.

It got better too, because Jack had the other radio.

Finally, he could get some answers.

Daniel settled himself on the floor and flipped the switch. The radio crackled to life in his hand. At least he was finally where he was supposed to be. Now it was time to find out what had happened to everybody else.

CHAPTER SIXTEEN

//ACCESSING MISSION REPORTS...//

P5C-777 MISSION REPORT, COLONEL JACK O'NEILL: Major Carter reinterpreted my orders to ensure that the broader mission objectives were achieved. Also, for the record, Daniel NEVER gets to give directions again.

//CONTINUING ANALYSIS...//

"CARTER IS *where...?*" Jack scowled at the radio in his hand. He couldn't have heard Daniel correctly. There was no way she would have —

"*— up to the ship with Dirmid and Graen.*" Daniel's voice came through clearly, after a burst of static. "*I thought maybe you'd know why they'd changed the plan?*"

"It's news to me." Jack managed to keep his tone even. After he'd made it explicitly clear that she was not to set one foot on that mothership, he couldn't see Carter deliberately going up there. Not without a very good reason. A very *damn* good reason.

Teal'c was pointing at the Goa'uld communicator thingy Jack had set on the table. "We have the ability to contact Graen directly, O'Neill. You can request that she update you on what has happened."

Right. He should have thought of that.

"Daniel. Let me get back to you."

"*Jack, if you want —*"

Jack switched off the radio. As long as Daniel was safe on the cargo ship, he could wait a minute. Carter was another matter.

The Goa'uld equivalent of the "talk" button was never where Jack expected it to be. They really did need to design these things better. It took him a few tries before he found it, and even then, he wasn't sure he'd done it properly, it took so long for Graen to reply.

"*Colonel O'Neill — is there a problem?*"

Maybe it was his imagination, but he thought she sounded just a tad defensive.

"You tell me. Let me talk to Major Carter."

A few too many heartbeats later, Carter's voice came over the com. "*Sir?*"

His intention had been to keep it light. Somehow, that wasn't how it came out.

"Carter? What the hell are you doing up there?"

There was an interminably long moment of silence before she answered him. Maybe it was just a lag in the signal. Or maybe not.

"*I'm sorry, sir. But I needed more time to* fix *the device.*" He caught the emphasis on the word "fix". So she hadn't been able to get it reprogrammed yet. Even so, this hadn't been the plan.

"I thought we agreed that this wouldn't involve you actually going up to the ship, *Major.*"

There was the lag again. He had a sense that she was choosing her words with great care. Whether that was for the sake of Dirmid and Graen, or because she knew he was a smidge past irked and moving towards irate, he couldn't decide.

"Sir, *as I recall, you said to do what I had to do. And with all due respect, that's what I'm doing.*"

Jack winced. Damn. He hated it when she used his own words against him. Especially when she happened to be right.

"*Look at it this way, Colonel. Now I can check to make sure that everything works properly for the demonstration. It's a win-win, sir.*"

She did have a point. As long as they'd gone this far, making sure Graen got her promotion probably wasn't the worst thing they could do.

"Fine." He did his best to still sound irritated, which wasn't hard. He wanted her to get the message, after all. "Just—be careful."

"*Yes, sir. Thank you.*"

"Do not forget to tell Major Carter about Daniel Jackson, O'Neill."

Right. Daniel had slipped his mind—momentarily.

"Oh, and Carter? Tell Dirmid that Daniel is waiting for him—" Jack stopped. He found himself staring at a very attentive Mol'rek, who had just overheard the whole damn conversation.

Sonofa—

Maybe they'd been cryptic enough that he hadn't understood everything, although, at this point did it even matter? Mol'rek would be finding out the truth about everything soon enough. Still. He'd try to mitigate the damage if he could. "—at the ship." Jack finished finally. "And we'll be there soon ourselves."

"*Copy that, sir. Glad to hear Daniel is okay.*"

Jack switched off the device and slipped it into his pocket. Mol'rek was looking aggravatingly smug.

"*So. I am not the only spy in Lugh's inner circle. There is only one viable contender for my position as First Tanist, and that is Magna—or should I call her Graen? That was the name of her human host, if I am not mistaken.*"

The Tok'ra looked entirely too pleased with his deduction. Jack wasn't about to give him the satisfaction of confirming a single damn thing.

"I'm sorry, who?" He looked at Teal'c with feigned confusion. "I have no idea what he's referring to, do you, T?"

"I do not, O'Neill."

There was a time when Teal'c would have replied with the unflinching truth. Thank goodness he'd finally learned the art of strategic lying.

Mol'rek was shaking his head. "*Play your games, if you wish, Colonel. But I see now what has happened.*"

"You do?" Jack made his response as patronizing as he could.

"*Clearly you have been promised your freedom in exchange for Major Carter repairing the cloak. No doubt the very deed for which you are attempting to frame me is what this Graen intends to do herself.*"

"Yes. Yes, it is." Jack smiled broadly, covering his relief. There was no point in mentioning just how wrong Mol'rek had gotten it — no matter how enjoyable it would be to wipe that smug smile off the Tok'ra's weaselly face. "Good job. Well done. You've discovered our plan. But hey, don't take it personally. Old Graen just got to us first. When it comes to the whole kidnapping/blackmail business, you snooze, you lose."

Mol'rek sniffed. "*So much for your moral high ground, Colonel. Your hypocrisy should astound me, but given what I have been told about the Tau'ri, it does not.*" He sighed, slumping back into his chair. "*As long as the device ultimately ends up with the System Lords, the means matters not, I suppose.*"

Jack tensed. That one he had to let go. Besides, what did he care what one double-crossing Tok'ra thought about his moral code anyway. Mol'rek would find out the truth eventually, then they'd see where the real moral high ground was.

"*Uh — Jack? What's going on?*"

Right. Daniel. He'd almost forgotten — again. Discussing the rest of their plans in front of Mol'rek — even if he was woefully mistaken about what was going on — probably wasn't the best idea. Jack waited until he'd walked into an adjacent room and shut the door before replying to Daniel.

"*And you know how to get here, right?*" Daniel asked, after Jack had filled him in on what was happening with Carter.

"Brean gave us directions. I think we can find it."

"*Okay. Good. Oh, Jack? I almost forgot. There are a couple of Jaffa patrolling the area, so you're going to have to watch out for them. Maybe you can get Graen or Dirmid to call them off or something. They're not the most competent guards I've ever seen, but they can be a nuisance."*

Oh joy. Just what they needed.

"Jaffa. Right. I'll see what we can do about that. Sit tight. We'll be there soon."

~#~

Brean's instructions turned out to be exceptionally good. The safe house sat on the very edge of the village, and it had been only a short walk down a moonlit road until they reached a rock formation that she had described in detail. A quick hike through some tall grass and they were in the woods, and well out of sight of anyone, including those small bands of Jaffa which were still, apparently, searching for Esras and SG-1.

Mol'rek, surprisingly, was being compliant. Jack had expected him to try to make a break for it once they left the house, but so far he seemed not inclined to be a pain in the ass. Maybe the fact that he believed the cloaking device was going to inevitably end up with the System Lords made him less resistant to being removed from Gorias by force. Then again, maybe it was because both Jack and Teal'c had their zats aimed at him the entire time. Frankly, Jack didn't care why he was behaving himself, as long as he kept it up.

The trees blocked the light from the moon, their trunks packed so close together Jack could see how easily a person could get disoriented trying to find their way through them. But with the lantern Udal had given them, they had little trouble locating the marks that were meant to guide their way. The path at times seemed to double back on itself, but Jack figured it was only because the spacing of the trees made getting through it more like a maze. Even with all the twists and turns, it wasn't long before they found themselves standing on the edge of a field. A field which had three identical *tel'taks* parked side by side.

This was going to be fun.

"Any idea?" Jack kept his voice a whisper. Graen had said she'd see what she could do about the Jaffa patrol, but she could make no promises. "Which ship is it?"

"I am uncertain, O'Neill. I do not recall anything especially unique about the ship we are looking for."

Teal'c and Jack both looked at Mol'rek. If any of them knew which ship was Dirmid's it would probably be him. Of course, Mol'rek didn't have any idea who Dirmid was, and Jack still didn't think it was a good idea to fill him in on any more of the details than was absolutely necessary. Waving Teal'c off with a slight shake of the head, Jack pulled out the radio.

"Daniel — a little help here. We're in the field with the ship, but there are three of them. Which one is yours?"

"Uh — it's the one closest to the trees."

Jack frowned.

"Daniel — two of them are near trees. Hell, all three of them are, if you want to get technical. Could you be a little more precise, please?"

"I don't know what else I can tell you, Jack. It's not like I can flash the headlights or anything."

"Daniel —"

"Oh! Wait! Yeah. You're in the field, you said? Then it's the one to the far left."

"The left. Thank you. See. That wasn't so hard."

"And, so you'll know, the patrols are still around. I think I saw another Jaffa join them a while ago too. So that makes three of them out there."

"Yeah — we see'em." Jack could make out two dark shapes moving around the rear of the middle ship. If there was a third one, he was someplace else. They'd just have to keep an eye out for him. They would use the zats if they had to, although the less attention they could draw to their presence, the better. They still had to wait for Carter and Dirmid to show up, after all.

Skirting the edge of the woods, Jack, Teal'c and Mol'rek

worked their way in the shadows until they were as close to the ship as they could get. The two patrolling Jaffa made a pass on the *tel'tak's* port side before finishing their circle and heading back the other way. Once they were out of sight, Jack gave the sign and they jogged across the open space to the side of the ship and slipped around its aft section to the exterior door on the starboard side.

Teal'c attempted to open it, but his code was rejected with an irritating chirp. The least Daniel could have done was left the damn door unlocked, although Jack supposed he'd done it to keep out the nosey Jaffa patrol. Radioing him was out of the question, not when the guards were within earshot. Knocking wouldn't be much better.

There was someone, though, who could probably get them in with no problem at all. Jack looked at Mol'rek and jerked his head at the panel, mouthing "open it". For a second, he thought the Tok'ra would refuse, but finally he reached over and entered a four-digit code. The four panels of the door slid back to reveal the airlock.

Once they were inside, Teal'c shut the door and then opened the one that gave them access to the main cabin. Jack stuck his head around the door to the bridge where Daniel was seated in the pilot's chair, the lights on the console already lit up.

"Lucy, we're home!"

The person in the chair swiveled around, a zat in his hand.

It wasn't Daniel after all.

It was Dar'dak.

He fired.

CHAPTER SEVENTEEN

//ACCESSING MISSION REPORTS...//

P5C-777 MISSION REPORT, MAJOR SAMANTHA CARTER: Looking back, I keep wondering what I could have missed. It wasn't just me, but that's still no excuse. I needed to be better, and I wasn't.

P5C-777 MISSION REPORT, DR. DANIEL JACKSON: I would just like to put it on the record that my instructions were VERY clear and precise, and that Jack failed to specify exactly which direction he was facing when he asked for them.

//CONTINUING ANALYSIS...//

SAM STOOD UP STRAIGHT and arched her back, getting out the kinks. As much as she loved technology and learning the intricacies of how things worked and the feeling she got when the beauty of physics and engineering and theory harmonized in something not unlike music for her, she was going to be exceedingly glad when this particular device was no longer in her life. The guys at Area 52 could have it, as far as she was concerned. With her blessing. And for the record, she was *not* going to be the one helping to carry it through the gate when they took it home with them. Not after having lugged it down three decks from the *ha'tak's* primary ring room, since according to Graen, they'd ended up here because the rings nearest to the engine room seemed not to be working. Even

Dirmid looked tired from the effort. Although, now that she thought about it, maybe it was less fatigue and more worry, seeing as how he was currently having a not-all-that-quiet conversation with Graen.

Sam tried not to eavesdrop, but it was difficult. For one, they were standing no more than two meters away. And secondly, the acoustics here were such that a mere whisper could be heard on the other side of the room. Sam couldn't help but wonder whether that was a deliberate design on the Goa'uld's part. No Jaffa or human servant would be able to keep murmurs of rebellion a secret from their overlords in this place. A whispered plan was a known plan. It seemed like a typical Goa'uld Machiavellian scheme.

In Dirmid's case, though, it wasn't a rebellion but a plea. He was trying to convince Graen to agree to have the Tok'ra remove Magna as soon as possible — even before Lugh was completely deposed, if necessary.

"And risk losing everything I — and you — and the *Shasa* — have worked for? Who's the one with the *bahlay* now?"

"But if Magna —"

"Magna is under control. I am fine. Now, go back down and get Dr. Jackson and the others. I'll send Major Carter down as soon as we're done."

"Graen —" Dirmid reached out his hand as if to caress her face, but she backed away, out of reach. The hurt on Dirmid's face was painful to see. Sam turned away.

"Colonel O'Neill and Teal'c will probably already have joined Dr. Jackson by the time I get down to the ship, Major." Dirmid was speaking to her now. Sam glanced up at him, and then away again. The raw feelings on his face were still hard to look at.

"This won't take long." She pointed at the cloak. "I'll meet you all at the Stargate."

Dirmid nodded, and with one last mournful look at Graen, left.

"If we can get the primary conduits connected —" Sam

stopped talking. Graen hadn't moved for several seconds. But it was more than that. Her eyes were unfocused, staring off into nothing and her body was rigid. If Sam hadn't been able to see the subtle movements of her breathing, she might have thought she was made of stone.

"Graen?" Sam reached out and carefully touched her arm. It was like throwing a switch. Graen's whole body began to tremble, like she was having a seizure. Sam grasped her by the elbow, ready to hold her up if she collapsed. Instead of falling, though, she blinked, her eyes coming back into focus. They found Sam.

"Major?" It took her a great deal of effort to speak. It was almost like someone had invisible hands around her throat.

"You're going to be okay, Graen. I know it's hard, but fight it — fight *her*."

"Losing." The word was barely audible. Sam gripped her elbow more tightly.

"No. No you're not. Remember. You're stronger than she is. You always have been."

Graen's eyes closed and the trembling subsided. When she opened them several long seconds later, she looked ashen. But her eyes were bright and alert. She nodded at Sam, who released her arm and stepped back.

"Better?"

Graen smiled. "Much." She took a deep breath and let it out slowly. "And thank you," she added, almost as an afterthought, which, considering what she'd just been through, was to be expected.

"I can go get Dirmid," Sam offered, even though she already knew Graen's answer. If he had witnessed what Sam had just seen, he'd never leave Graen's side.

Graen waved her hand dismissively. "I am fine now, Major. It has passed. You were saying about the primary conduits?"

She was looking better, there was no question. If she was ready to work, Sam wasn't about to argue.

It took all of ten minutes to connect the device to the power source. Graen ran the integrative program from a nearby terminal while Sam made adjustments to the secondary crystals until the device and the main computer were in sync. When Sam slid the last crystal into place and shut the drawer, the cloak hummed to life.

"That's it, then." Graen's eyes reflected the light from the large main crystal. They hadn't put the pyramidal cover over top of it yet. "The device is ready."

"Almost." Sam was already opening the base. These were the five critical minutes she needed to make sure the whole thing didn't go up once the cloak was engaged. "Be sure you don't touch anything yet."

It didn't take her long to locate the program this time. Deleting it wasn't an option, at least not with the limited amount of time she had. But she could disable it. The code equivalent of an off-switch. Once they had the cloak back at the SGC, she'd be able to get rid of the self-destruct once and for all. Or, the guys at Area 52 would, at least.

"What are you doing?" Graen's voice came from the terminal where she'd been working. "What was that program you were working on? It didn't look like it was Goa'uld in origin."

Uh-oh. She'd forgotten. Unlike Dirmid, who's technical skills were minimal, Graen had extensive knowledge of the ship's systems and the systems of its many components. She must have been monitoring Sam's work from the remote terminal.

Sam took a moment before responding. She could try to fudge some answer, which Graen may or may not buy. Or, she could tell her the truth.

Sam pushed out from the base and stood up. There'd been enough subterfuge. It was time for the truth.

"I should have told you earlier, and I'm sorry. At the time, I wasn't sure what to do. Technology like this," she gestured to the cloaking device. "If it gets into the hands of the System

Lords, it will dramatically alter the balance of power in the universe. We couldn't let that happen. *I* couldn't let that happen."

"What does the program do?"

"Now, nothing. I've turned it off. But a couple of minutes ago, if you'd have activated that cloak, it would have initiated a self-destruct. The whole ship would have blown."

Graen said nothing. Sam could see her processing the information. Hopefully, the pragmatist she seemed to be would understand why Sam had done what she'd done.

"Look, I'm sorry." Graen still hadn't spoken. Sam wasn't quite sure how to interpret that. "We probably should have told you right away, but we weren't sure how you'd react. Of course, once we got to know you — understood what you were and what the *Shasa* were trying to achieve — we didn't want to harm any of you, or your cause."

Still, silence. It was at the point where Sam was starting to feel uncomfortable. Maybe telling her hadn't been a good idea after all.

Finally, Graen looked up at her. "Turn it back on."

Sam wasn't sure she'd heard correctly. "I'm sorry?"

"Turn the self-destruct back on." Graen's eyes were bright, and not just with the light of the crystal. Sam could practically feel the energy radiating off her. "Lugh will come up in a *tel'tak* to watch the cloak's demonstration. He will be close enough to the *ha'tak* so that when it explodes, his ship will be caught in the blast. Lugh will be dead. It will be over before it's hardly begun."

~#~

"Well, this can't be good." Daniel watched as the other *tel'tak* rose into the air and hovered there briefly before moving off to take up a position over the castle.

Dar'dak was at the helm. Daniel had caught sight of him as the ship lifted off. Jack, Teal'c and Mol'rek were with him.

This was going to be a problem.

It had been sheer luck that Daniel had even caught sight of

Jack and the others boarding the wrong ship. He'd taken the risk, returning to the flight deck so he could unlock the outer door when they arrived. That's when he spotted them, two ships away. When they went in and didn't come back out, and after Jack didn't answer his radio, Daniel knew something was up.

The cargo ship hadn't entered orbit yet. It was still hovering over the castle. Maybe Jack or Teal'c had managed to incapacitate Dar'dak and take control—although if that were the case, why weren't they coming back down?

The answer came a moment later when another transport beam shot up from the castle. Only this time instead of disappearing into the darkness overhead, it went directly to the *tel'tak*. Someone from the castle had ringed aboard, and Daniel had a pretty good idea who it was.

Lugh. He was probably on his way to observe the cloaking device being tested, just as they'd expected. Sam should have had it installed by then. The timing seemed about right.

With the transport complete, the ship took off, climbing up into the atmosphere and becoming an ever smaller point of light, until it was too far away to be seen.

Daniel sank back in the chair. It was possible that Jack, Teal'c and Mol'rek had managed to stow away on Dar'dak's *tel'tak* undetected. On the other hand, it was just as likely that they had been captured. Either way, it didn't matter. They were unwillingly onboard Lugh's ship and nothing good would likely come of that.

He needed to tell Sam what was going on. The problem was, she didn't have her radio. Daniel realized he was staring at the console. Could he get any more dense? There was a communication system built right into the *tel'tak*. He might not be able to reach Sam directly, but he could probably figure out how to get in touch with Graen, or, failing that, Dirmid. It was as good a place to start as any.

But it did mean he'd need to power up the ship. That was going to attract some attention. Although since everything was already screwed up, it probably didn't matter now if the Jaffa patrol found out he was on the ship. And if he had to, he could take off.

Probably.

Okay. Maybe not. But at least he was sure the hull would be able to withstand any zat or staff blasts the Jaffa aimed at him. He might not be able to leave, but they wouldn't be able to get in either.

That was the plan then. All he had to do was flip the right switch.

"Dr. Jackson — what are you doing?"

Oh. And maybe remember to re-lock that exterior door.

At least it was Dirmid and not the Jaffa patrol.

"You're correct, Dr. Jackson. Lugh is onboard," Dirmid confirmed, as soon as Daniel told him what he'd observed "They were preparing for his departure when I arrived back from the mothership. But how did Colonel O'Neill and the other two end up on Lugh's *tel'tak*?"

"Long story," Daniel said, relieved to let Dirmid take his place in the pilot's seat. "Well, actually, not that long. Suffice it to say, one of us needs to get better at taking directions." Under Dirmid's hands the console sprang to life and the interior lights of the ship came on. Daniel blinked at the sudden brightness. "By the way, what happened up in the castle, anyway? And what's Sam doing on that ship?"

Dirmid gave him a sideways glance. "Long story, Dr. Jackson," he threw back at him. "And one I'm not entirely sure I completely know." He brought the communications system online. "I can contact Graen for you. But Major Carter was nearly finished. Hopefully we'll be able to catch her before she rings down to the *chaapa'ai*."

~#~

"You're sure about this? You really want to blow up the ship?" Sam needed to be clear that Graen knew what she was asking her to do. A mothership was no small asset to lose, although she supposed that in the grander scheme of things, compared to what had already been sacrificed by the *Ateronu*, it wasn't much after all.

"Do you know what I've had to do in order to keep this thing running these past few years? It's as pathetic a ship as Lugh is a Goa'uld, and we're well rid of it." Now that she had a plan to eliminate Lugh altogether, Graen seemed more energetic. It was as if the episode she'd had earlier with Magna had never happened. Perhaps there would be enough time to take Graen to the Tok'ra after all—assuming she consented.

"And you're sure the ship is evacuated?" Graen had ordered the remaining Jaffa to ring off the ship earlier, but Sam needed to be certain. If there was any chance of an innocent Gorian being collateral damage, she wouldn't be a part of it. That was the very thing she'd been trying to avoid in the first place.

"You and I are the only ones on board, Major. We'll have time to ring down before it blows, I assume."

Sam nodded. There was a built-in delay before the program triggered the self-destruct. Even then, it would take another five to ten minutes before the whole ship went up. The ring room was three decks up, but at a moderate jog, they'd reach it in time.

This meant, of course, that now the cloak itself would be destroyed. Sure, that had been the original plan and until Dirmid and Brean had offered it to her, Sam had barely even let herself consider the potential benefits of having that technology at her disposal. But despite her earlier frustration, the reality was, she really had been looking forward to tinkering with the device before letting R&D get their hands on it. Now that she never would—well, it was disappointing, to say the least.

But. It was Graen's call. And there was no denying that the System Lords would never get hold of it once it was just so much space dust.

An alert from a nearby console grabbed Graen's attention. Sam saw her smile ever so slightly. "Lugh is on his way. He'll be here soon." She offered Sam access to the remote terminal. "If you wouldn't mind, Major?"

Right. Time to blow it up. Just doing what she had to do.

Working from the terminal was less physically strenuous, but certainly no easier as far as isolating the program she was looking for. Watching the symbols stream by, Sam barely noticed when Graen's com chirped. It was only when she heard Daniel's voice that she looked up.

"Major Carter is a little busy at the moment, Dr. Jackson," Graen was saying. She'd turned her back to Sam, making it difficult to hear what Daniel replied.

But Sam could tell something was wrong just by the tenor of Daniel's voice. "Daniel? What's happened?"

Graen turned back around and handed Sam the com. Daniel was still talking incredibly fast. Much of it was coming through garbled.

"Daniel, slow down. Say again?"

"*Lugh is headed up there in a* tel'tak."

"We know. We're getting ready to —"

"*Sam. You don't understand. Jack, Teal'c and Esras are on the ship with him!*"

"What! How?"

"It doesn't matter, but they are. So if there's anything you can do when they dock —"

Daniel's voice disappeared into static. Sam tried to raise him again, but something was interfering with the signal. She'd have to try later. For the moment, she had all the information she needed.

"We can't blow up the ship."

"Major Carter —"

"My team — my friends — are on that ship with Lugh. I am not switching the program back on. You'll just have to go back to the original plan."

Graen was shaking her head. But Sam was more perplexed by the odd, little smirk on her face. It was the same look that had given Sam an uneasy feeling back in Lugh's court.

"I'm afraid that's no longer possible, Major. Lugh needs to be disposed of now. And I'm more sorry than you know about the unfortunate loss of Colonel O'Neill and the *shol'va.*" From beneath her robes, Graen withdrew her zat and aimed it at Sam. "But I still have you. And your knowledge of the cloak. Both of which are more than enough to buy myself a position with one of the System Lords and get off this forsaken, back-water world."

Sam could feel the blood drain from her face. "Magna."

The Goa'uld's eyes flashed as her triumphant smile broadened. "*We meet at last, Major Carter.*"

~#~

"Got any aspirin?"

"I do not, O'Neill." Teal'c watched his friend struggle into a sitting position, his movement hampered by the Goa'uld binders around his wrists. Teal'c was similarly constrained. As was Mol'rek, although the Tok'ra, still posing as Esras, had done everything in his power to convince Dar'dak not to bind him.

The three of them were seated on the floor in the main hold of a *tel'tak*. It was clearly not the ship Daniel Jackson was on. Teal'c had briefly considered that his teammate might be present, but in hiding, however, concealment was difficult on such a small ship. Teal'c had no choice but to conclude that they had made an error. It was, perhaps, a costly one as Lugh himself had just transported onboard.

For the moment, the Goa'uld was on the bridge with Dar'dak. He had been unexpectedly delighted to discover that the Jaffa had captured the three of them, and Dar'dak had not bothered to disabuse him of that presumption, although he seemed to take no pleasure in accepting the credit. If anything, he appeared all the more distressed as he'd escorted Lugh to the bridge and closed the door behind them.

"So — what did I miss?" O'Neill looked around taking in

their present circumstances. "Isn't this how this day started?" he added upon observing how the rest of them were similarly bound.

Teal'c briefly relayed an account of what had transpired since Dar'dak had rendered O'Neill unconscious and his belief that they had quite likely chosen the wrong ship.

"So, it must have been the *other* left," he deadpanned. "Remind me to give Daniel a course in giving directions when we get home."

"I believe we are headed up to Lugh's mothership to view a demonstration of the cloaking device which Major Carter repaired."

"Looks like we got the cheap seats." O'Neill angled his neck around, taking in their environment. "Anything we could use to —"

"There is not." Teal'c had already sized up the area for any sign of something that could be utilized to overpower their enemies. No such object had presented itself.

"Then I guess we're —"

"So it would appear, O'Neill."

O'Neil nodded. "Good to know."

The door that connected to the bridge slid open and Lugh appeared.

"You know, Teal'c," O'Neill said loudly. "First the dungeon and now this — I have to say, I'm extremely disappointed in the quality of service at this establishment, and I'm going to highly recommend that they think about putting in some new management around here real soon."

Lugh strode forward. "*The only 'new management' you will see, Colonel O'Neill will be me, when I take my place among the System Lords.*"

"Is that so?"

"*Oh yes. Not only do I now have all of SG-1 to offer, but, thanks to your Major Carter, I also possess a functional cloaking device to rival those of Apophis. I will be welcomed by the System Lords with open arms.*"

"You would do well to beware of any Goa'uld who welcomes you with open arms," Teal'c advised him. "Lest they use the opportunity to stab you in the back."

Lugh did not reply, choosing to deliberately ignore him. Teal'c presumed it was meant to be an insult. How little did the Goa'uld understand that such treatment was, to him, a mark of honor.

"*My lord, I beg you again, please. There has been a misunderstanding.*" Mol'rek had scrambled to his feet. "*I have not betrayed you. This is a scheme of Magna's. She is working with them. I am the victim here, not the perpetrator of this crime.*"

"Oh shut up and sit down, *Esras*." O'Neill made a point of emphasizing the Tok'ra's Goa'uld name. It was an implied threat. "The jig is up, all right? Old Lugh here knows perfectly well that you're the one who snuck us out of the castle, down that secret passageway. What was that called, T?"

"I believe Daniel Jackson referred to it as a Sally Port."

"Yeah. That. Quite the escape route wasn't it? Reminded me of those tunnels the Tok'ra make with those crystal thingies."

Mol'rek, however, remained defiant. "*O'Neill lies, my Lord. I speak the truth, and I will continue to declare my innocence. It is Magna whom you must not trust. She is the one who is about to betray you. If you would just give me an opportunity to prove my allegiance. Ask Dar'dak. He will testify on my behalf. He knows where my loyalty lies.*"

Lugh motioned for Mol'rek to step forward. When he was close, Lugh leaned forward, conspiratorially, although he did not lower his voice. "*I* have *asked Dar'dak. And here you are in chains. There is your testimony.*" He turned and walked back towards the bridge. Mol'rek went after him.

"*If I may, my Lord —*"

A zat shot out from where Lugh stood, but as he turned around, Teal'c saw it was Dar'dak standing in the doorway who had fired. Mol'rek collapsed onto the deck, unconscious.

"Apologies, Lord Lugh." Dar'dak bowed his head. "But I thought my lord seemed to have wearied of his pleading."

Lugh chuckled as he walked past Dar'dak, pounding him on the back as he did so. "*And so I had. And so I had.*"

Dar'dak shot Teal'c and O'Neill an incomprehensible look before following Lugh back onto the bridge. This time, though, the door remained open.

O'Neill inched closer to Teal'c, his voice just above a whisper. "What the hell just happened?"

"Dar'dak fired upon Mol'rek."

For some reason, O'Neill rolled his eyes.

"I know *that*. But why? And what was with that look, just now?"

"I am uncertain." Perhaps it had merely been a warning of the fate which awaited them should they attempt to further harass Lugh. But Teal'c did not think so. Although he could not be sure, what he thought he had just glimpsed was the face of a man who had decided to act. It remained to be seen just what that action would be.

"*Magna!*" Lugh's voice boomed from the bridge. Through the open doorway Teal'c could just see a portion of the viewport. Far closer than he would have expected, hung an old-style mothership. Even by Goa'uld standards it was what humans would have termed an antique. Further proof of Lugh's pitiful empire.

"*I am waiting to see this 'gift' of yours in action,*" Lugh was saying. "*Impress me, and I will make you First Tanist. Disappoint me, and know my wrath.*"

Beside him, O'Neill tensed. "Here goes nothing," he muttered. In response to Teal'c's arched eyebrow, he added, "Just cross your fingers Carter had enough time."

O'Neill's words brought no clarity, although if whatever happened next was dependent on Major Carter's expertise, Teal'c had no doubt but that it would be successful.

When nothing happened, O'Neill let out a sigh and relaxed.

"Way to go, Major."

The reaction on the bridge was less enthusiastic. Not only had the negative event which O'Neill had been anticipating not occurred, but apparently neither had the demonstration of the cloak. The Goa'uld's irritation was palpable.

"Magna? I am still waiting—"

"Our communications system is working, my lord," offered Dar'dak, in an attempt to stave off any blame Lugh might direct at him. "The *ha'tak* is receiving us."

"I will not be made a fool of," Lugh fumed, after more time had passed with still no response from the mothership. *"Take us aboard. Magna will explain herself, if it the last thing she does."*

"Do you know what is happening, O'Neill?" Teal'c kept his voice low. It was evident that his friend possessed some knowledge of the situation he did not.

"I thought I did, but now—not so much. Maybe we'll get some answers once we're on the ship." He indicated the viewport on the bridge, where Lugh's mothership now filled the entire frame.

Through the decking, Teal'c felt the *tel'tak's* main engines power down, only to start up again. The ship's momentum should have been sufficient for them to glide past the shields into the *ha'tak's* docking bay. Use of the engines in the maneuver was not only unnecessary, but unwise. He had assumed Dar'dak to be a competent pilot, but perhaps not.

The explanation came from Dar'dak himself. "My lord, the docking bay doors are not responding to commands. They will not open. I cannot bring this ship aboard."

A growl of rage from Lugh suggested that he found this news to be unacceptable.

"Then I shall use the transport rings and go down there myself. Take us into optimal position for the ring room adjacent to the pel'tak. *Magna will be there, I have no doubt."*

The engines engaged again as the ship moved into position. Lugh returned to the cargo bay, followed by Dar'dak who went to operate the controls.

"Sure you don't want to take us with you?" O'Neill called out casually. "We could help you track down that pesky old Magna, if you want."

The cloud of anger over Lugh's features vanished with one loud, explosive laugh. "*Do not think, Colonel, that I have ruled out the possibility that your Major Carter might be responsible for what has happened. If that is the case —*" He stuck his hand straight out ahead of him, palm forward. The gold of the ribbon device glittered in the subdued lighting. "*Only three members of SG-1 may make it to the System Lords.*"

O'Neill maintained a fixed and insincere smile upon his face as they watched the rings encircle Lugh. But Teal'c could hear him murmur under his breath, "You dirty sonofabitch."

With Lugh gone, only Dar'dak remained. Teal'c expected him to retreat to the bridge, but he did not move. His eyes were fixated on the space Lugh had just occupied, as if waiting for something more to happen.

On the floor in front of Teal'c, Mol'rek began to moan. He would be regaining consciousness soon, much to Teal'c's regret. Although he preferred to judge each Tok'ra on their individual merits, he frequently shared O'Neill's distrust of them as a whole. But there were those such as Selmak and Lantash and, to a lesser degree, Anise, whom he held in higher esteem, believing them to be honorable at heart. Mol'rek would not be joining that select group. Of all the Tok'ra, save for Tanith, Teal'c could not recall any for whom he had such little regard.

"Your old boss there isn't going to be too pleased when he wakes up and remembers you were the one who shot him," O'Neill nodded towards Mol'rek. "I guess loyalty doesn't count for much here, not even among the Jaffa."

O'Neill's words broke Dar'dak out of his reverie. He looked at him for a moment, as if he were just seeing him for the first time. It was with the same look that he turned to Teal'c as well. And yet, he said nothing. Instead he returned to the bridge, immediately taking a seat at the helm. The engines accelerated again. They were moving — moving at a high rate of speed back towards the planet.

"Teal'c?" O'Neill was perplexed. Teal'c shared his confusion.

"Other than we seem to be returning to the planet, I am uncertain as to Dar'dak's plan. Although perhaps we are to be taken back to the dungeon."

"Oh goody." O'Neill's tone was dry.

"I am not returning you to the dungeon, Colonel O'Neill." Dar'dak's voice answered from the bridge. He had overheard their conversation. "For your information, I am taking you to the Stargate." He glanced at them over his shoulder. "I am setting you free."

CHAPTER EIGHTEEN

//ACCESSING MISSION REPORTS...//

P5C-777 MISSION REPORT, DR. DANIEL JACKSON: If I've learned anything at all over the past four years, it's that we don't leave our people behind. Ever.

P5C-777 MISSION REPORT, TEAL'C: If Major Carter said it would happen, there was no reason to believe otherwise. Consequently, there was only one course of action to take.

P5C-777 MISSION REPORT, MAJOR SAMANTHA CARTER: Stated simply: I'd made a promise. I had to keep it.

//CONTINUING ANALYSIS...//

"CAN YOU get her back?" Daniel watched as Dirmid worked the communications panel, trying repeatedly to reestablish the link to Sam. Somehow, they'd been cut off.

Dirmid shook his head. "It's like something is jamming our signal." He tried one more time. "I'm sorry. She's gone."

"Well, can we go up there and help?" At least he'd gotten Sam the message that Jack and Teal'c were on the ship with Lugh. It might give her and Graen a strategic advantage, but that didn't mean they couldn't use a little extra assistance.

"To what end, Dr. Jackson?" Dirmid asked.

"To what end? Well, to help free my friends, of course." Daniel gestured in the general direction of where the ship had disappeared. "I can't just sit here and do nothing."

"But don't you see? That's the best thing we can do right now. If we just give the plan time to work, then when Graen is First Tanist, she'll be the one who'll take charge of all the prisoners. We'll send Colonel O'Neill and Teal'c through the Stargate as soon as we can. Major Carter too, if she is captured as well. It might take a few days, but I give you my word, they'll be safe in our care until then."

Daniel had no doubt that Dirmid was sincere in his promise. Aside from the initial masquerade as Pheone, he'd been nothing but honest about everything that was going on. And on the face of it, Dirmid's argument made a lot of sense. If Daniel went back now, he could explain to General Hammond what was going on. They would be able to call off the search parties Daniel was sure had already been deployed back on P5C-777, and maybe even alert the Tok'ra about the possibility of the *Ateronu* needing their symbiotes removed. Logically speaking, it was the right course of action.

Except—

"Yeah. Here's the thing. We don't leave our people behind. I'm sorry, really. And it's not that I don't believe you, but until all four of us can go together, I'm staying put."

Dirmid did not seem surprised.

"I can respect that, Dr. Jackson. You might not think so, but the *Ateronu* have a code not unlike you. It's because of that code—that bond—that we do what we do when the *bahlay* comes."

"Yeah. I kinda get that, now." He thought of the glimpses of Magna he'd seen in Graen during their trek to the castle, and how painfully she had fought against the symbiote back at the cottage. To wage that battle daily, knowing, in the end, you would lose—

He knew too well what that loss looked like. Sha're haunted his dreams still. If there was no hope—*when* there was no hope—how could anyone condemn someone they cared about to that hellish existence?

Daniel looked up from his silent musings and saw that Dirmid had been studying him. For a moment, there was a shared understanding, a shared grief, before Dirmid turned back to his console.

"So, what *can* we do?" If he wasn't going to leave, he couldn't just sit here and wait either.

Dirmid was already ahead of him.

"We're of no use if we fly up to the *ha'tak*. I know that's what you want to do." He cut Daniel off before he could protest. "But I think we're better off if we let Graen handle that. She still has to prove herself to Lugh, and we dare not get in the way of that."

"Okay. We don't go up to the mothership. What are our other options?"

"We head to the *geata*. I'm sorry — the Stargate."

"I thought I was clear —"

"You're not going through, Dr. Jackson. At least not until your friends come too. But we will have to take it back from the Jaffa who Esras sent to guard it, not to mention the ones that Lugh himself has just sent as reinforcements. We may be in for a bit of trouble there, just to warn you."

Daniel had helped secure the Stargate enough times to know what that was going to be like. He also knew they were missing a few essential supplies.

"Okay, but won't we need weapons of some kind to accomplish that?" A *tel'tak*, he seemed to recall, only had defensive shielding. Useful protection, to be sure, but not very effective when it came to mounting an attack on a group of well-armed Jaffa.

"Well, with any luck we won't need them. You will be accompanied by Pheone, of course."

Right. Daniel had almost forgotten about Dirmid's alter-ego. They'd all been so focused on Graen and Magna, Pheone has sort of slipped to the back of his mind.

"But, just in case —" Dirmid bolted from his chair and into

the cargo hold. By the time Daniel had followed, he'd opened one of the large containers that had lined the edge of the space. "I'm thinking you might like these back, Dr. Jackson." He held up Daniel's tac-vest, and after fishing around in the bin some more, produced his radio, Barretta and a zat. Daniel peered in and caught sight of Jack's and Teal'c's gear as well, including Teal'c's staff weapon.

"Won't they think it suspicious if your supposed prisoner is armed?" Daniel checked the safety on his sidearm before slipping it into its holster.

"If you'll be wearing it like that, then of course." He pointed at the leg holster with the zat. "But I'm sure you can find a more clever place for it before we get there."

From another, smaller container, Dirmid took out a zat for himself and a shiny object that Daniel saw him slip over his hand.

"Uh — where did you get one of those?"

Dirmid held up his hand to examine the Goa'uld ribbon device. "No idea. It's always been here on the ship. It never occurred to me I could actually use it until Major Carter taught me how."

"Sam taught you?"

"Aye. Your Major Carter is a person of many talents, there's no denying." Dirmid slipped the device off and added it to the contents of his pocket. "I've only used it once, but you never know. It might come in handy."

"Yes. Yes, it might." Daniel was still processing that Sam had actually shown him how to use it, especially given her aversion to anything that required her to tap into the knowledge or use the protein marker that Jolinar had left her with.

"Just to be clear." Daniel followed Dirmid back to the bridge. He could feel a certain amount of energy building up in the Gorian, as if he were actually looking forward to confronting the Jaffa at the gate. "I'm not going through the Stargate right now. We're just going to hang out in the general vicinity until

Sam, Jack and Teal'c join us."

Seating himself at the helm, Dirmid powered up the engines. "That is our plan Dr. Jackson. Whether it's the Jaffa's plan or not, we'll find out soon enough."

Daniel slid into the navigator's seat as the *tel'tak* lifted off. "I guess we will. And please—call me Daniel."

~#~

"You've been in control this whole time." The realization came like physical a blow to Sam's gut. "That was you in Lugh's castle, wasn't it? You were the one who told Dirmid to bring me along with the cloaking device."

"How else was I to wrest you away from Graen's ever so earnest mate? He has, I think, become quite attached to you. Perhaps you remind him of her in some small way." Magna paused, as if listening to something, her lip curling in what Sam now recognized as the Goa'uld's attempt at a smile. *"Ah, yes. Before I subsumed her, even Graen was aware of his fondness for you. The human emotion of jealousy is so very fascinating, don't you think, Major Carter?"*

How typical of a Goa'uld to try to twist a benign truth into a malignant lie. Sam refused to rise to the bait.

"And was that you back at the cottage too?"

"Sadly, no, or we would have gone about this altogether differently. You people do have a propensity for taking the simplest things and trying to fix them in the most complex ways."

"Some things only appear simple to those who have a simplistic view of them," Sam shot back. If this was the toxic personality Graen had been dealing with for so many years, Sam had nothing but admiration for how well she'd handled it. Jolinar had been haughty and arrogant, but there was never malice. Magna positively dripped with it.

"So tell me. Is Graen really gone this time?"

"Very nearly. Her poor, feeble mind has finally collapsed in on itself." Magna did the listening routine again. *"Yes—yes. There she is. Nothing but a small whimpering voice hiding away in*

the dark corner of her own brain. Pitiful, really. So very weak." Magna closed her eyes this time, her face wrapped in concentration. Finally, she sighed and opened them again. *"And there. Just like that. Graen is no more. Surely you know, Major, nothing of the host survives."*

Not that old lie. "I don't believe you. And Graen isn't weak. She's kept you under control for years. Anyone who has the strength to do that has the strength to overcome anything."

"Once, perhaps. But no more. The bahlay *has weakened her.* I *have weakened her."*

"You may have weakened her, but you haven't beat her." Sam knew it was a long shot, but maybe if she kept reinforcing her belief in Graen's strength, it might offer her a lifeline back. With Jolinar, she'd felt like she was lost in a fathomless cave with voices, including her own, reverberating from everywhere. She'd tried to find just one to hold onto. It had been like an anchor, keeping her from slipping even further into the darkness. She'd hung onto it with all her might.

What the colonel had been for her, maybe she could be for Graen.

"You are attempting to stall for time with this idle conversation, Major. You will proceed to activate the program to blow up this ship."

"No."

Maybe Magna had been expecting a more prolonged argument. She seemed taken aback by Sam's straight-up refusal. Good.

"I don't believe you have a choice in the matter, Major Carter."

"Actually, I think you're the one without any choices. You shoot me," Sam gestured towards the zat. "And you'll never figure out the program in time to destroy Lugh. And even if you set the ship's auto-destruct," she added, anticipating Magna's next threat. "The *tel'tak's* sensors will detect it long before it goes off, and Lugh will still escape."

"But you are the last person I would ever harm, Major. Not only are you quite valuable to the System Lords, but you have working knowledge of this device." Magna nodded in the direction of the cloak. *"And what you may not remember about it consciously, I have no doubt that your subconscious mind could be easily accessed to provide us with the information we need."*

Sam tried not to shudder. She'd had more than enough experiences with the memory recall device for one lifetime. One more, especially at the hands of the Goa'uld, was something she'd rather avoid. Sam set her jaw and shook her head. "If you're trying to frighten me into cooperating, you'll need to come up with something else."

"Your fate is your fate, Major. Whether you cooperate or not. As for frightening you — it seems you humans have this unusual ability to withstand pain in your own right, but are loathe to see it inflicted upon others on your behalf."

This time Sam couldn't suppress the chill that ran through her. She had no idea what leverage Magna had, but whatever it was, the Goa'uld was taking great pleasure in threatening to use it.

Magna's eyes closed again, her neck twisting at such a painful angle that it made Sam wince. It was like Graen had been back at the cottage — only exponentially more severe. For half a second Sam thought about making a grab for the zat, but before she could, Magna's eyes popped open, staring at her with abject terror.

Only it wasn't Magna. It was Graen.

"Major?" It was barely above a whisper, but it was Graen's voice.

Or, at least it *sounded* like Graen's voice. That was in a symbiote's bag of tricks too, as she knew only too well.

But Sam's gut told her that this really was Graen. She couldn't explain why, other than there was an authenticity there that she recognized. And it would be just like Magna to be so cruel.

"Graen — you've got to hold on. You have to fight her. I

know you can do this." Sam wished she had better words to offer — something strategic or even inspirational. But maybe the words themselves weren't what was important.

"Major —" Graen repeated, her eyes drifting down to the zat she held, still aimed at Sam. Her whole arm began to shake violently, as if it were exerting some great effort. "I'm sorry — she still has control."

Graen was trying to lower her arm, Sam realized. Magna was resisting her effort. Their struggle was playing out in the form of one trembling limb.

"It doesn't matter. Don't worry about that. She needs me too much to really hurt me. You need to concentrate on staying in control in here." Sam tapped her own forehead. She was sure Magna was only allowing Graen to come forward as a way of tormenting her host, using her to get Sam to cooperate. But if she could get Graen to turn the tables on Magna and take charge again, maybe together they could get out of this.

"It is — difficult." Graen's color had taken on an almost alabaster pallor. She was putting up one hell of a fight.

"You can do this. Gorias needs you. The *Shasa* need you." Sam hesitated. Maybe this too was cruel, in its own way, but feelings could be a very powerful motivator. "And Dirmid needs you. Think of what this will do to him —"

"Magna!" Lugh's voice reverberated around the room through the ship's intercom. "I am waiting to see this 'gift' of yours in action. Impress me, and I will make you First Tanist. Disappoint me, and know my wrath."

Damn. They were here. If Graen could only hold on.

The hand not holding the zat slowly and robotically began to move towards the console and the flashing com control. Its movements were jerky and spasmodic, a clear indication that, just as with the other arm, Magna and Graen were battling for dominance.

"Don't let her answer him, Graen. She can't be trusted."

"I am aware, Major." Her voice sounded a little steadier — or maybe it was Sam's imagination. Graen's eyes were fixated on her own hand, and Sam found herself staring at it as well. Everything came down to who would win such a small, but critical, battle.

Graen's entire arm was shaking by the time it reached the console. The concentration on her face looked painful.

"Graen—" Sam could see she was losing the fight. Just a few more inches and the com link to Lugh would be open.

Her hand hovered over the console. By the bulge in her bicep, Sam could see she was giving it everything she had. The hand stopped moving, neither going forward nor retreating. Graen was holding her own at last.

Sam let out the breath she'd been holding. A standoff was better than losing, but only just. Eventually Graen would tire. There was only so much strain her body could endure.

"Major Carter." Graen's voice was still strong, despite the effort she was exerting over both arms. "I have a favor to ask."

"What can I do to help?"

"When Magna returns—and she will—before I am lost completely, will you do what needs to be done?" As Sam watched, the hand holding the zat slowly angled the weapon downward and offered it to Sam. She had to almost pry it from Graen's fingers, and she could feel the tension in them as they fought to retain it, but eventually Sam freed it and stepped back.

That was a relief—not only to no longer have the zat pointed at her, but also to now have a way to defend herself. Graen's request, though—that was the second time someone had asked that of her today.

"If you want me to incapacitate you, then yes. But if you're asking me to kill you—"

"I thought, Major, you of all people would understand."

She did. Only too well.

But it was one thing to know what needed to be done, and something else altogether when you were asked to be the person to do it. Especially when it came to ending a life.

Still, hadn't she half argued with Dirmid when he'd wanted to involve the Tok'ra, pointing out that it was Graen's choice, not his? And this was Graen's choice. A choice Sam couldn't blame her for making in the least.

Still, she had to be sure.

"Dirmid believes the Tok'ra—"

Graen cut her off. "Dirmid believes with his heart, not his head. I won't live that way, Major. I can't state it any more plainly than that."

Sam nodded. There it was, then. The equivalent of an advance medical directive. In its way, no different than her own living will stating that there not be any extraordinary means to keep her alive if the worst happened. If she thought about it that way, then yes. She could—probably—carry out Graen's wish.

"If I tell you I will do my best, is that good enough?" Somehow it didn't seem right to make a promise she wasn't one hundred percent sure she could carry out. Graen considered her words for a moment and managed to nod.

"Aye. Good enough."

"Uh—Graen?" Sam couldn't help staring. As they'd talked, without either of them realizing it, Graen had moved her other arm away from the console. Aware of it now, she was able to slowly bring it all the way back to her body, finally dropping both arms by her side.

"Magna?" Sam probed.

Graen shuddered. "Oh, she's there—just below the surface. Her little gambit failed and she's not happy. I don't know how much longer I have."

"Magna! I am still waiting!" Lugh's voice interrupted them over the loudspeaker again. Crap. Sam had nearly forgotten about him.

"What do we do now?" She looked at Graen. "Demonstrate the cloak?"

"No. We'll use Magna's idea."

Not this again. "Colonel O'Neill and Teal'c are onboard

that cargo ship."

Graen shook her head. "I didn't mean blow the ship now. But I know Lugh. You can hear how angry he is already. He'll want answers and he'll come here to get them. When he's on board, that's when I'll activate the cloak."

"And what about the colonel and Teal'c?"

"If Lugh brings them with him, we'll snatch them and ring down to the surface, as planned."

"And if he leaves them on the ship, we can ring there instead, and fly it to safety before the ship blows."

"I think we have our plan, Major." Graen managed a grim smile. Sam understood. It assumed a lot — that Lugh did come over to the *ha'tak*. That she and Graen were able to rescue the colonel and Teal'c — and Mol'rek too. She'd nearly forgotten about him. And that they were able to get far enough away before the ship blew.

Which it wouldn't, until she switched the program back on.

Sam found herself hesitating for just a moment. Everything she was about to do was predicated on her belief that Graen was fully back in control. If there was even a chance that Magna was masquerading as Graen, then this could be nothing but an elaborate trap to capture the rest of her team. It all came down to whether she believed Graen was really Graen.

Which meant, that it all came down to whether she trusted the very thing that was neither tangible nor quantifiable. That which, as a scientist, she had mostly rejected as being an unreliable tool for decision-making.

Instinct.

Sometimes, Carter, you've just gotta go with your gut.

If the colonel had said it to her once, he'd said it to her a hundred times. Maybe it was time she finally listened to him.

Her gut said this was Graen.

Lacking evidence to the contrary, she'd go with that.

It took only a few moments at the terminal to switch the

code back on. Graen was locking out controls to the docking bays, to assure Lugh's ship stayed where it was. If it docked, there wouldn't be enough time to launch it again and clear the blast area. Locking Lugh out would also force him to ring to the *ha'tak*, which might make him more inclined to leave his captives behind.

"I have rings activating," Graen announced. "He's come onboard near the *pel'tak*."

"Alone?"

"There's no way to tell."

Sam cursed inwardly. What she wouldn't give for some Asgard bio-sensors about now.

"MAGNA!" Lugh had activated the internal com system. For whatever reason it was exponentially louder than the ship to ship one. "What is going on? Where are the Jaffa? Why is no one here to greet me upon my arrival? I stand here alone on the *pel'tak* as if on an empty ship! I command that you come here at once!"

Then again, maybe bio-sensors weren't necessary. Not when the Goa'uld gave away not only his location but the fact that he was utterly alone.

"*My apologies, my lord. There was a technical issue. But we will have it resolved momentarily. Please stand by.*"

The sound of Magna's voice was startling. But, of course, Graen would have needed to use it to speak to Lugh. All the same, Sam found it a little…unsettling.

Graen looked at Sam apologetically. "Don't worry, Major. It's still me." Her fingers flew over the console again, this time with a bit of flair. "And — I've just locked him in on the pel'tak, so he won't be leaving any time soon. Or irritating us." With a flip of a switch the intercom was silenced. Graen smiled. "But I think the time has come for you to be getting off this ship."

Wait. "For *me* to get off the ship?"

Graen's smile was more pitying than pitiful.

"Someone has to activate the cloak, Major. I know the

self-destruct won't happen immediately, but as you know, the nearest functioning ring room is three levels up. In my condition, I'd never make it in time. But you can, if I remain here. You told me you'd do what needed to be done when the time came." She took a deep steadying breath. "This is what needs to be done."

"Graen, you don't—" Sam stopped. She had all but promised to do this. And Graen was making it as simple as she could. All Sam had to do was leave.

Graen was waiting for her to continue. Sam sighed, nodding. "If you're sure."

"I am."

"Look, I'm just sorry—" Sam didn't get to finish. A crackling sound inside her pocket interrupted her. She fished around and pulled out the Goa'uld com device. A transmission was trying to come through. Maybe it was Daniel again.

"*Carter?*"

Not Daniel. The colonel. But how? She tried to respond, but a burst of static erupted from the device.

"*Carter? That you?*" She managed to hear at last. She tried again to answer.

"Sir?"

"*Yeah, Carter, listen—Lugh—*" More static. Sam gave the com a shake. It probably wouldn't help but one never knew. For a few seconds, the colonel's voice did clear up. "*—and he's pretty pissed.*"

It wasn't hard to figure out that he was warning her about Lugh. Unfortunately, it was old news. What she needed to know was his current status.

"I'm sorry, sir, you're breaking up. But if you can hear me, I need a sitrep. Colonel?" She waited, but there was only more interference. He needed to know what was about to happen, but if there were unfriendly ears on his end, it might jeopardize everything. Then again, would the colonel even be contacting her if he and Teal'c hadn't secured the cargo ship? It was a judgment call. Sam decided to risk it. "Colonel, we're going to use the cloak to destroy the ship. You'll need to leave the area ASAP to escape the blast radius."

There was nothing, this time. Not even the static.

Sam tried again. "Colonel?"

Still nothing.

The connection was gone.

~#~

"So, what brought about this change of sides?" In Jack's experience, when a thing seemed too good to be true, it usually was. And Dar'dak's one-eighty from Jaffa bad guy to Jaffa good guy was definitely too good to be true. At least from Jack's perspective.

Teal'c, on the other hand, looked positively rapturous.

"I believe he has at last surrendered to the truth that was already within his own heart, O'Neill. A truth he could deny no longer."

There was a click as Dar'dak undid the binders on Teal'c's wrists, before reaching over to do the same to Jack's. "I confess, I do no longer know what 'truth' is, Teal'c." He offered his hand and pulled Teal'c to his feet. Jack wasn't sure if it was significant or not, but it was the first time Dar'dak hadn't called Teal'c "*shol'va*." He could tell by the tilt of T's head that he had noted the change as well. So a good thing, then.

"I have served Esras well for many years, and through him, Lugh, and I have been as content as it was possible to be, under such masters. But I cannot make sense of what has happened these past few days. Lies and deception and the abdication of responsibility have already taken away all that truly mattered in my life. What little I have left to lose, I will willingly give up, but only in the face of truth." Dar'dak glanced through the doorway to the bridge. "The planet Gorias approaches. I said I would free you, and so I shall. I have only one condition."

Here it was. Of course there would be strings attached.

There always were.

Jack scrambled to his feet.

"So. What's the condition?"

"The truth, Colonel. Simply that. The truth of what is going on."

That was one tall order, considering everything that was at stake.

"Assuming we tell you, why would you believe us? How do you know we wouldn't be lying to save our own skin, just like everybody else?"

Dar'dak's gaze was so intense, it was on the edge of unsettling.

"I do not. But what I do know is that when Teal'c speaks, something stirs within me that I have not felt in a long time: hope. So, even without proof, I will choose to believe you, because if I cannot believe in hope, then why even draw breath?"

Jack had no clue how to respond. Someday he needed to ask Teal'c if oratory was an innate Jaffa trait or something they just picked up along the way. What did one say to something like that?

Especially when they really couldn't give him what he was asking for. At least, not in the way he meant it.

"Look, Dar'dak." Jack took a minute, trying to figure out the best way to phrase it. "If it were up to us, we'd tell you everything." He looked to Teal'c, who gave a subtle nod of agreement. "But if we did that, we'd be putting a lot of people at risk; good people, who are only looking to do what's best for everyone on this planet. And we can't do that — even if it means," Jack took a deep breath. Yeah. He couldn't believe he was about to say this. "Even if it means we go back in Lugh's dungeon — or get carted off to the System Lords."

"But know this," Teal'c added. "Those whom we choose to protect with our silence are those who fight for freedom. If they succeed, then Lugh will be gone, and those who serve him may then decide which path from here they will take. If hope indeed stirs within you, as you say, then the way before you is clear."

On the floor nearby, Mol'rek moved. He was taking a lot longer to come around than Jack would have thought for a Tok'ra. Maybe Dar'dak's zat had an extra strong "Goa'uld" setting. If so, Jack wanted to know what it was.

The real question though was whether Mol'rek still held enough influence over Dar'dak to change his mind yet again. The Tok'ra's version of "truth" might hold more sway than the vague assurances Jack and Teal'c had been able to offer. Dar'dak could go either way, at this point, and a few words from "Esras" might be all it would take to tip the scales. Too bad another zat blast right now would be fatal to the Tok'ra. All they needed was a smidge more time to get back to the planet and off this damn ship.

"If not clear yet, Teal'c, then certainly on the path to becoming so." Dar'dak squared his shoulders, as if reaching a decision. "Colonel, I find more truth in your words than if you had revealed to me all that you know. A man who will not betray others to save his own life is an honorable man indeed."

Jack realized he'd been holding his breath. He let it out with relief. Maybe they'd get out of this after all.

"Does that mean you're taking us to the Stargate, then?" He tried to ask it lightly. They were coming up on the planet awfully fast. Reminding Dar'dak of their destination probably wasn't a bad idea.

"As I have promised." He nodded his head slightly at them and returned to the bridge just as Mol'rek pushed himself to his knees.

"*What has happened?*" He blinked up at them, groggily. Jack realized the Tok'ra was the only one still wearing binders. No reason to change that, for now.

"Oh, not much. You had a well-deserved nap. Your guy,

Dar'dak, has switched sides. Oh, and we're headed home soon, so you might want to get your story straight before you show up in front of the High Council."

Mol'rek scowled.

"*Where is Lugh?*"

"Lugh is onboard the mothership," Teal'c replied.

Right. And so was Carter. Jack reached in his pocket for the Goa'uld radio thing. She and Graen needed a heads up, if it wasn't too late.

"Carter?"

There was no reply. Then again, no one had answered Lugh from the ship either.

He tried again. There was the briefest burst of static, as if someone were trying to respond, but then nothing.

"Carter? That you?"

"*Sir?*"

Third time was always a charm. Well. Not always. But he'd take it as a good sign for now.

"Yeah, Carter, listen — Lugh is somewhere over there on the ship with you — and he's pretty pissed."

"*I'm sorry, sir — you're breaking up. But if you can hear me —*" More interference drowned out much of whatever she said next. All he could make out was, " — use the cloak to destroy the ship — "

"Say again, Carter?" He waited. Nothing. "Carter?" Damn it. "Carter, if you can hear me, I want you off that damn ship now — that's an order!"

Still nothing.

Shit.

He turned to Teal'c. "We need to get back up to the mothership."

"If Major Carter and Graen intend to use the cloaking device to destroy the *ha'tak*, then any ship in the vicinity would most likely also be caught in the explosion. We would not survive."

Okay. There was that. On the other hand —

"Major Carter and Graen have access to any number of ring rooms on the ship," Teal'c continued. "I have no doubt but they have assured they can escape in a timely manner before the ship explodes."

Fine. He had a point. Carter wouldn't do anything stupid. She was probably just warning him to get the hell out of the way before the thing went up.

"Right. I knew that." Jack took a deep breath. She'd probably already be at the Stargate by the time they landed this thing anyway. He just had to remember to step back and let her do her job. The last thing he wanted was a pissed off second in command.

Jack caught Mol'rek watching him. The Tok'ra was fuming.

"What?" Jack demanded. He really wasn't up for any of Mol'rek's crap right now.

"*You intend to destroy the cloaking device.*" It wasn't even a question.

"Not initially, no—" Okay. Well, maybe, but there was no need to go into all of that right now. "But you can be damned sure we weren't going to let the System Lords get their filthy hands on it either. It was coming back with us."

"*You lied to me.*"

Jack raised his finger. "Technically, no. You came to your own conclusion, and we just didn't bother to correct you. If you'd been paying attention you'd have figured that out."

"*Once again, I hold you personally responsible for sabotaging my mission, Colonel. The High Council will not be pleased.*"

"Well, you know what? You and the High Council can all just go and—"

"The Stargate is within visual range, Colonel O'Neill," Dar'dak called from the bridge. Jack didn't bother to finish his threat. Mol'rek got the gist of it.

Leaving the Tok'ra where he was, Jack and Teal'c joined Dar'dak. It was dark out the window. Jack had almost forgotten it was still the middle of the night in their little corner of the planet. Gorias had two moons, though, and the second one had just risen. It bathed the area below in blue light.

"I do believe we have a problem, O'Neill." Teal'c had moved closer to the viewport and was studying the terrain below.

"What's up?"

"There are many Jaffa guarding the Stargate, and they seem to be engaged in a firefight. I also see another *tel'tak* which has landed nearby. If I had to guess, it is the one belonging to Dirmid."

"Looks like the Jaffa have someone pinned down." Jack could see the scene below now too. "Dirmid?"

"He is concealed behind that large boulder."

"So who's that firing from over there?"

Dar'dak angled the ship as he made a pass over the skirmish below. Teal'c had the better view.

"It is Daniel Jackson. And he is about to be ambushed by a group of Jaffa who are moving in on his right flank."

CHAPTER NINETEEN

//ACCESSING MISSION REPORTS...//

P5C-777 MISSION REPORT, TEAL'C. Although we may, in fact, have all been working separately, in truth, we were all working together.

P5C-777 MISSION REPORT, DR. DANIEL JACKSON: Personally, I had no idea what the hell was going on.

//CONTINUING ANALYSIS...//

"YOU NEED to leave now, Major. I will wait until you signal me from the ring room. Then I will activate the cloak." Graen was giving her attention to the terminal. Sam could see she had already entered the pre-ignition sequence. One simple push of the button was all it would take to engage the cloak. There would be, at best, ten minutes lag time before the feedback into the engines began to overload them. Another five — maybe — before they blew.

It was a long shot, but Sam had to be sure. "Maybe we could rig some kind of timing delay —"

Graen looked up at her. "Please, Major. You promised."

Right. It was just hard to leave her there, knowing what was about to happen.

"Is there anything I can do? Any message I can pass on?"

For just a moment, Sam thought she saw a flicker of raw emotion in Graen's eyes. But as quickly as it came, it vanished.

"As *Ateronu*, we say our good-byes the day we accept a symbiote. Nothing more needs be said." She turned back to the console.

Sam nodded. If that was how Graen wanted it, it wasn't her place to push.

"Although —" Graen looked up again, just as Sam was about to turn away. "If you wouldn't mind, Major, maybe you could tell Dirmid something for me."

Sam swallowed. She had offered, after all. "Of course. Whatever you want."

"Tell him —" For a moment, Sam thought Graen would change her mind again, but finally she found the words she wanted. "Tell him, I'm sorry I never made it to the lake. I'm sure the sunsets would have been spectacular."

"I'll tell him. I promise." Sam managed to keep her voice steady. "Graen, I just want to say —"

A light on the console began flashing. Something was moving near the outer perimeter of the ship.

"It's the *tel'tak*. It's moving off," Graen told her.

"What?" Sam looked over Graen's shoulder. She was right. The cargo ship was headed back down into the planet's atmosphere. Sam wasn't sure if she should be relieved or not. As far as she knew, the colonel and Teal'c were still onboard. Whether still prisoners or not, she didn't know. Just as long as they weren't anywhere near the mothership when it blew, that would be enough — for now.

"Major —" Graen pulled her out of her thoughts. "You'd best be going."

The reality of the moment came rushing back, but before Sam could speak, Graen held up her hand to stop her. "Don't feel badly for me, Major Carter. I've known my whole life where my duty lies. Brean — the *Shasa* — they're all depending on me. They have been, since the moment I was born. And if you only knew how hard I'm fighting Magna, even now, the freedom of death will be most welcome."

Graen had clearly accepted what was about to happen. The

only thing left for Sam to do was accept it as well.

"Good luck, Graen." Maybe it wasn't the best thing to say, but it was all she could think of.

"You as well, Major." She turned back to the console and Sam took her cue.

The ring room was three floors up. It was time to move on.

~#~

By the light of the twin moons, Daniel counted at least a dozen Jaffa spaced strategically between where he and Dirmid stood and the Stargate. And those were only the ones he could see. Who knew how many remained on the perimeter, in the shadows?

This hadn't turned out quite as expected, especially since all the staff weapons were pointed at them, despite Dirmid having assumed his Pheone identity and ordered them to stand down. It seemed not to have mattered one iota.

"*How dare you disobey my command!*" Pheone's eyes glowed for added emphasis, the effect even more unsettling in the quasi-darkness. "*I am the Third Tanist of Lord Lugh. You will do as I say.*"

"With all due respect, Third Tanist, we cannot." One of the Jaffa lowered his weapon and stepped forward. "We have orders from Esras himself. No one is to pass through the *chaapa'ai*, and anyone attempting to do so is to be detained."

"*What is your name, Jaffa?*" Dirmid's tone of condescension was perfectly Goa'uld-like. The Jaffa stood at attention and dipped his head.

"I am Vandar, my Tanist."

"*Vandar. Did I say we have come here to go through the* chaapa'ai*?*"

Vandar hesitated. "No, my Tanist."

"*Then you admit that you have been too hasty in your assumption of my purpose.*"

"I beg the Tanist's pardon if I have offended." His eyes darted left and right as if looking for support from his fellow Jaffa. No one else had budged through the whole exchange. "But Master Esras was quite clear—"

"Master Esras is a traitor and has been branded as such by Lord Lugh himself. So, you would do well to reconsider—"

"Lies! The Third Tanist lies!" The shout came from the young Jaffa who had accompanied them from the Stargate earlier. His name escaped Daniel... Hyatt—Hyto—Hyot'k. That was it.

"*What is this treason?*" Dirmid demanded, his eyes flaring again.

Instead of further apologizing or reprimanding Hyot'k, Vandar seemed emboldened by the younger Jaffa's outburst. "That is what I would ask of you, Third Tanist." Gone was the deferential tone he had earlier displayed. "Master Esras warned us that you would most likely attempt to free the Tau'ri and the *shol'va*. And here you are, with one of them—no longer even a prisoner, if my eyes do not deceive me. So I must ask, Third Tanist: if not to go through the *chaapa'ai*, then why are *you* here?"

Uh-oh. Daniel hoped Dirmid was good at thinking on his feet. They hadn't bothered to concoct an excuse for why they just wanted to hang around the Stargate for a while. Dirmid had thought he'd simply be able to dismiss the guards. They probably could have thought this one through a little better.

Dirmid shoved both hands in his pockets. He appeared utterly unfazed by what was happening, which wasn't surprising, when Daniel thought about it. The Gorian had to have nerves of steel to play the part of a Goa'uld in the first place.

And he played it very well.

"*HOW DARE YOU CHALLENGE ME WITHOUT EVEN KNOWING MY PURPOSE HERE!*" Dirmid's anger-infused rebuke reached every ear in and around the Stargate. "*Lord Lugh will hear of this, you can rest assured. And his* new *First Tanist, Magna, will deal with you as she sees fit.*" He stepped forward, daring Vandar to defy him. "*Now. I have come to rescind your orders and send you back to the castle. Obey me, at once.*"

Daniel saw many of the Jaffa exchanging looks, but no one had lowered their weapon. They were waiting for Vandar's response. Daniel glanced at Dirmid. If this didn't work—

Vandar raised his staff weapon once more and activated it. Arcs of energy danced across the tip, crackling like a fire in the night air. He aimed it at nearly point-blank range towards Dirmid's chest.

This definitely wasn't going to work.

"We do not take orders from you, Third Tanist. We take orders from Master Esras, and in his stead, Dar'dak. Until either of them tells us to stand down, we will remain at our post and do as instructed." He motioned towards Dirmid and Daniel with his chin. Four Jaffa moved forward.

"Daniel—" Dirmid's own voice caught him off guard. The Gorian spoke quietly under his breath so that Vandar was less likely to understand him. "I think this is where those weapons of yours might come in useful."

Right. He'd tucked the zat in the back of his pants, under his jacket. The handgun was in its holster that had been jury-rigged to fit over his shoulder, also under his jacket. Neither was going to be easy to get to without drawing attention. But Daniel supposed they were past that now.

"Just say when." He'd been hoping they could avoid something like this. Shoot-outs never were his strong suit.

As the Jaffa approached, Dirmid withdrew his hand from his pocket. Daniel caught a glimpse of metal in the moonlight, and suddenly a shock wave was sending the four Jaffa flying through the air.

That was signal enough. Daniel went for the zat. He managed to stun the Jaffa nearest to him, but the others had already started firing, so he dove for cover behind the nearest thing he could find. He'd thought it was a boulder, but it turned out to be a fallen tree trunk. A massive tree trunk, to be sure, but still only made of wood. With enough successive shots from all those staff weapons, it wouldn't last long.

Dirmid had taken off in a different direction and found refuge behind one of the boulders. Between the two of them, their cross fire made the Jaffa pull back. But there was no shortage of other rocks and fallen trees, and it didn't take long until the Jaffa had found their own cover and reformed into two separate fronts. With each of them now pinned down under a barrage of staff-weapon fire, Daniel was pretty sure neither he nor Dirmid were going anywhere.

So much for this plan. Unfortunately, they didn't have another one.

Daniel peered around a large, crooked branch that provided just enough protection that a staff blast wouldn't take off the top of his head. He could see the silhouettes of the Jaffa as they maneuvered into more strategic positions. A handful had retreated to protect the Stargate and the DHD, while others were regrouping to better assault Dirmid's location. The rest, from what he could see, seemed to be concentrating on him.

Oh goody.

Daniel stopped firing. There really wasn't any point at this distance, and certainly the Jaffa didn't need to get any closer to take out his swiftly-disintegrating log. The Beretta would be far more effective, but Daniel wanted to use that only as a last resort. He'd really prefer not to actually kill any of the Jaffa if he could help it. Then again, he didn't suppose the feeling was mutual; their staff weapons didn't exactly come with a stun setting.

A staff blast whizzing past his ear sent Daniel ducking back behind the tree. That one was a little too close. He could feel where it almost singed his hair. Maybe it was time for the Beretta after all.

Reluctantly, he swapped the two weapons.

"Lugh!" A cry went up from the Jaffa. "Lord Lugh comes!"

Daniel risked another quick look over the tree. Most of the Jaffa were staring at the sky, their attack momentarily halted. He could hear the distinctive hum of a *tel'tak* engine as one slowly looped overhead. It made one more pass before landing next to Dirmid's along the edge of the forest. There was no mistaking it. The Jaffa were right. It was Lugh's ship.

"Well, that can't be good." Lugh was supposed to be watching Sam and Graen demonstrate the cloaking device, but if he was here, then was the demonstration already over? Or had it not happened yet? And what about Jack and Teal'c? Were they still on board? Did Lugh even know they were there? Daniel had far too many questions that didn't have answers, although he was fairly certain that would change soon enough.

Or not.

Daniel had forgotten about Dar'dak. The Jaffa strode through the outer door of the ship, staff weapon in hand and stood there, his mere presence demanding attention. The other Jaffa stopped what they were doing, including the ones who'd been shooting at him and Dirmid, and waited. Yup. This really was as bad as Daniel had feared.

"Jaffa, *shel kree*," Dar'dak commanded. "I order you to stand down."

Okay—that was the last thing Daniel had expected. The Jaffa too, by the look of it. A couple lowered their weapons or dropped them to the ground, but most of them had not moved. Dar'dak took several more steps forward and again ordered the Jaffa to surrender. "You will obey me, at once!"

Daniel heard a commotion from within the *tel'tak* and three people emerged. Two of them were attempting to restrain the third. A cloud had covered one of the moons, momentarily dimming the light, but as it rolled away, Daniel could see Jack and Teal'c, both of whom had a very strong grip on a sputtering Mol'rek. The Tok'ra's hands looked as though they were bound.

Daniel should have been surprised, yet somehow he wasn't. Relieved, was more like it. And curious. Especially since there was still no sign of Lugh anywhere.

Cautiously he got to his feet, waiting to see if any of the Jaffa still wanted to use him as target practice. But their attention was all on Dar'dak now. Not a single one reacted to his movement.

So far, so good.

"*Jaffa,* kree!"

Or — not. Jack and Teal'c might have Mol'rek in restraints, but they hadn't gagged him — an oversight he was wasting no time in taking advantage of. As far as the Jaffa were concerned, he was still Esras. All eyes were now on him.

"*Why are you all just standing there?*" he shouted at them. "*Am I not your Commander? Can you not see that I have been betrayed and am a captive of the enemy? Shoot them! Shoot them all! As First Tanist I order you to fire!*"

Dar'dak wasted no time.

"You —" He spun around and emphatically jabbed his finger in Mol'rek's direction. "You will be silent." Grabbing the Tok'ra by the front of his robe, he might very well have lifted him off the ground, had not Jack and Teal'c already been holding onto him. There was an audible gasp from the Jaffa. Daniel was stunned. This was the last thing he'd ever expected to see.

"I will no longer take orders from you — or any Goa'uld." Dar'dak's voice carried throughout the clearing. "Your entire existence is built on nothing but deception, just as your power is built on the backs of Jaffa like myself — and all of you!" He turned and swept his arm out to include the rest of the Jaffa. "I will no longer pretend that these lies are the truth. Join me." He took a step back, so he was shoulder to shoulder with Teal'c. "Join *us*. Renounce Lugh and all of the Goa'uld. Let us make our own destiny from this night on."

Dead silence greeted his pronouncement. Not a single Jaffa moved.

Uh-oh. Daniel had a bad feeling about this.

"Traitor!" A lone voice rose up out of the darkness. Daniel recognized it at once. It was the same voice who had called out Dirmid earlier. Hyot'k. "Traitor! Do not listen to him!" His words were so impassioned, Daniel could hear him choking back the emotion. "How can you stand there, before the right hand of your god, and blaspheme so? Surely Lugh will strike you down for such a sin!" There was a commotion amongst the Jaffa as Hyot'k pushed through them until he came face to face with Dar'dak. "And if he will not, then I most assuredly will. Yield now, Dar'dak or perish at my hand."

~#~

"Do not interfere, O'Neill." Teal'c spoke so low Jack almost didn't hear him in time. He'd been about ready to step between Dar'dak and the kid who'd escorted them from the gate. But if Teal'c didn't think it was a good idea, he'd hold back — for now.

The kid had guts, Jack would give him that. Looking around, he was clearly the youngest Jaffa of the bunch. And the most brainwashed, considering his defense of the Goa'uld. The rest of the Jaffa, although they looked wary, didn't seem in any hurry to rush forward and join in defending the honor of Old Slug Head. If these were guys with as little left to lose as Teal'c thought, Jack could see why they'd be willing to hang back and see which way the wind was blowing before committing.

And considering Dar'dak's experience versus the kid's, it wasn't hard to guess what the outcome would be.

Instead of raising his weapon in defense, though, Dar'dak was merely shaking his head at the overzealous Jaffa who was in his face. "I do not wish to fight you, Hyot'k. Neither your life nor mine is worth wasting over a Goa'uld."

"Then you are a coward!" Hyot'k spat on the ground. Dar'dak tensed noticeably at the accusation, but that was all. He continued to regard the kid with a look of sorrowful indulgence.

"I am only a coward in that it has taken me this long to acknowledge the truth. I tricked myself into believing that serving someone such as Lugh was better than serving a Goa'uld such as Ares — or Yu — or Bastet — or Cronos." He was speaking to the entire group of Jaffa again, many of whom, Jack realized, were wearing tattoos of the very same Goa'ulds he was naming. Really, the whole inspirational speech thing had to be in the Jaffa genes. "I chose comfort and safety instead of fighting for justice and freedom. So yes. I was a coward. But today I am one no more."

With one quick motion, Dar'dak wrenched the staff weapon from Hyot'k's hand. For a moment, Jack thought the kid was going to do something stupid, like tackle Dar'dak or try to grab the weapon back. But he didn't. He did look like he was in considerable pain though, albeit probably not the physical kind.

"But they are *gods*!" Hyot'k pleaded.

Beside him, Jack heard Teal'c take a deep breath, preparing to reply — except Dar'dak beat him to the punch.

"The Goa'uld are not gods. They never have been. They never shall be. And if I needed any more proof, tonight I saw with my own eyes lies told to Lugh, which he accepted as truth, and truth spoken, which he took for lies. No 'god' — no omniscient being — would fail to discern these things." He handed Hyot'k back his staff. "But I am not eloquent about such matters. There is one here, however, who is. The Goa'uld label him *shol'va* because they fear the truth he speaks. Set aside the lies you have been told and hear, this night, his words."

That was Teal'c's cue if ever there was one. Jack patted him on the shoulder. "Go get'em, big guy."

Stepping forward, Teal'c looked humbled at Dar'dak's introduction.

"I *will speak the truth about the Goa'uld.*"

The voice came from behind the Jaffa before Teal'c could even utter a word. Heads swiveled to see who had spoken. In the semi-darkness, Jack could make out Dirmid striding through the clearing from where he'd been pinned down. Not far behind him, hurrying to catch up, was Daniel.

Dar'dak did raise his weapon this time, and aimed it at Dirmid. Daniel jogged forward, physically putting himself between the Jaffa and the Gorian, his hands raised.

"Dar'dak — all of you — wait, please. Just hear him out."

As far as Jack knew, this wasn't part of the plan. Then again, neither was standing here next to Dar'dak trying to convert Lugh's Jaffa Army. He just hoped Daniel knew what the hell he was doing.

"Pheone isn't who you think he is," Daniel was saying. "He's not a Goa'uld. Well, technically—"

Dirmid had the good sense to cut Daniel off.

"My name is Dirmid. I am of Gorias, and I am host to the Goa'uld known as Pheone. But it is no god. I am its master, it is not mine." Dirmid's voice grew louder with confidence. "I have used its voice and taken its knowledge so that I may infiltrate Lugh's inner circle, as have many others over the years, without him ever suspecting." He pointed in their direction. "Listen to Dar'dak. Listen to Teal'c. The words they speak are the truth. We seek one thing, and one thing only—to free Gorias from the Goa'uld. Throw down your weapons and surrender, and we will grant you your freedom as well."

Dar'dak still hadn't lowered his weapon, Jack noticed, although he seemed to be chewing over what Dirmid had said.

"Dirmid speaks the truth, Dar'dak." Teal'c spoke at last. "He is part of a resistance movement which has been plotting the overthrow of Lugh for many generations. You are not so dissimilar as you might think. He yearns for freedom for his people from the Goa'uld as much as you do."

Dar'dak finally relaxed his stance, letting his arm and his staff drop to his side. Jack wasn't worried about him as much as the rest of the Jaffa. Some still looked confused. A few appeared angry. The kid still had defiance written all over his face. He was, Jack realized, staring at Mol'rek—who had been uncharacteristically silent ever since Dar'dak had told him to shut up. Maybe he'd finally figured out that there was no way out of this that ended well for him except to go back to the Tok'ra.

Only that wasn't exactly the feeling Jack was getting, now that he was paying attention. The kid wasn't just staring at

Mol'rek. While everyone else was focused on Dar'dak and Dirmid, the two of them were reaching some kind of silent understanding. Jack could practically see them counting down to whatever it was they'd agreed on.

Whatever it was, he sure as hell wasn't going to let it happen.

Jack jerked Mol'rek by the arm and brought him forward, so he was more front and center of the whole proceedings. It was hard to be stealthy when a couple dozen pair of eyes were watching your every move. Which was exactly as Jack intended.

"You know, while we're all sharing, and in the interest of full disclosure, I think there's something about ol' Esras here that you all need to know too."

"Jack?" Daniel was giving him the "do you really want to do this?" look.

"Trust me, Daniel. It's for the best." Not only that, but he was *really* looking forward to this. He tugged Mol'rek forward just a bit further, so he was entirely visible in the bright moonlight. "Look, I know a lot of you might be holding back, maybe a little cautious about what's going on, and I'll hazard a guess that some of it might have to do with your favorite First Tanist here still wanting you to fight the good fight." Misguided though they were, Jack could respect that. Esras had been their CO, for all intents and purposes. Finding out the guy you reported to was a complete jackass was something he could relate to, as General Bauer's thankfully oh-so-brief command had recently proven. "So, if any of you are sitting on the fence, still a little uncertain about what Dar'dak here and Dirmid over there have just told you, here's a newsflash that might help you decide." Jack pointed at Mol'rek. "Your buddy Esras here — guess what? He's not a Goa'uld either. He's actually a Tok'ra, and his name is Mol'rek."

Even Dar'dak stared this time. "You are not a Goa'uld?" he demanded of Mol'rek. The Tok'ra glared past him, defiantly, saying nothing. As far as Jack was concerned, that was pretty much the same as admitting it.

Dar'dak seemed to take it the same way. He pointed at Mol'rek as he addressed the rest of the Jaffa. "If any of you needed further proof that Lugh — that all the Goa'uld — are frauds and liars, this Tok'ra has served in Lugh's inner circle for many years without detection." Dar'dak focused specifically on Hyot'k. "A true god would never have been so deceived. Do you see now, the truth?"

The kid looked back and forth between Mol'rek and Dar'dak for a few seconds, but Jack could already see the disillusionment in his face. The fact that Mol'rek hadn't bothered to denounce Jack's reveal as a lie had probably been the final nail in the coffin. In a way, Jack almost felt sorry for the kid.

Almost.

There was a general murmuring amongst the Jaffa, after Dar'dak's last speech. Some had lowered their weapons. Others, however, had not. If they decided they weren't ready to surrender, things could still get a little dicey. Jack edged over to Teal'c.

"Maybe now's the time to make one of your speeches — shore up the home team, as it were."

"I do not believe that is necessary, O'Neill. Dar'dak has made his case most convincingly."

"Yeah, but I think we still have a few holdouts." Jack nodded towards the staff weapons aimed their way.

"We need not concern ourselves with them."

Jack appreciated Teal'c's confidence. He just wished he shared it. "Oh, I'm still pretty concerned, I think."

Out of the corner of his eye, Jack caught movement in the shadows. Great. More Jaffa. And these guys wouldn't have heard Dar'dak's speech. He'd be surprised if they didn't come in with guns blazing. Well — staff weapons blazing, anyway.

"Teal'c —" Jack stopped. The people emerging from the shadows of the forest into the moonlit clearing didn't look like Jaffa at all. They were dressed in ordinary civilian clothes, and they brandished zats, not staff weapons.

They were the Gorians. The *Shasa*, most likely. And they poured out of the perimeter of the clearing like water into a basin. If any of the Jaffa had had a notion to take issue with Dar'dak's command, they were too vastly outnumbered now to risk it. As the *Shasa* moved in closer, all of the Jaffa, including the kid, dropped their weapons to the ground.

"Did I not tell you, O'Neill, that we need not be concerned?" Teal'c's tone was a bit smug. Fine. He'd spotted them before Jack. There was no need to rub it in.

From the group that now surrounded the Jaffa, two familiar figures stepped forward. Brean and Udal. Daniel went to meet them, bringing them back to where Dirmid and Dar'dak now waited, with Jack, Teal'c and Mol'rek.

"Right on time," Jack smiled at Brean. No need to broadcast exactly how relieved he was that she and her people showed up when they did.

"When Lugh ordered extra guards for the *chaapa'ai*, we suspected things might become more complicated than anticipated. We encountered another two dozen Jaffa on our way here. Half our original group has already taken them into custody." Brean turned around to view the Jaffa who were currently being rounded up by the rest of the *Shasa*. By Jack's estimation there were easily two dozen captives in the clearing. Along with the ones Brean said they'd taken, that was nearly half of Lugh's army. Brean seemed to have picked up on that too. She nodded, pleased. "For all intents and purposes, Colonel, whether we were ready or not, the coup has begun."

CHAPTER TWENTY

//ACCESSING MISSION REPORTS...//

P5C-777 MISSION REPORT, MAJOR SAMANTHA CARTER: I needed to save my team.

P5C-777 MISSION REPORT, TEAL'C: As we understood them at the time, Major Carter's actions were most admirable.

//CONTINUING ANALYSIS...//

LUGH'S SHIP was old. Sam already had a sense of that from having installed the cloaking device. But beyond being technologically out of date, the vessel itself was a relic of another era, when form had obviously superseded functionality. She hadn't really taken the time to notice it earlier, when they'd been transporting the cloaking device down to the engine room, but now she could see that the emphasis had clearly been on the exhibition of wealth and status. The corridors were lined not just with the typical golden gaudiness, but with now fading murals depicting what Sam assumed were various highpoints of the original owner's illustrious career and expansive wealth.

Typically, she wouldn't have paid the images much attention, especially considering she was on the clock. But the layout of the ship was so unlike the more modern ones that Sam found herself having to backtrack several times just to figure out where she was going. The decaying pictures ended up being useful signposts in figuring out if she'd already taken a particular route or not.

The most annoying design flaw of this ship, however, and what had made carrying the cloaking device such a pain in the neck, was that each lift only went between two decks, and the lifts themselves were positioned on opposite sides of the ship. A person had to exit a lift at every deck, run the length of the ship to another lift, which only went up one more deck, where they had to repeat the process. Sam couldn't fathom the inefficiency of that, unless it was originally intended as a deterrent to an enemy boarding the ship. She supposed it would make them better targets for the defending Jaffa, but for day-to-day operations, it was damned inconvenient having to zigzag from deck to deck. By the time she booked it out of the lift for the third time, Sam was breathing hard.

That was good though. Her irritation with the ship design was keeping her from thinking too much about Graen and what she was about to sacrifice — or about how Dirmid would react when he learned what she'd done. Those weren't things to be dwelt on right now. Not if she wanted to make it out of this in one piece.

The ring room was about as far from the last lift as was possible. When she reached it, Sam slapped the button on the exterior panel only to have the doors slide partially open and then stop.

What the — ?

She'd just been here, with Dirmid and Graen and the cloaking device. The damn thing had worked then. Talk about a hunk of junk.

Sam eyed the opening. There wasn't enough space for her to squeeze through — not without leaving a few vital organs behind. She tried closing the door, and after a few stuttering fits and starts, it finally sealed back up. But when she tried opening it again, the panels only slid back a bit further than they had the first time. There still wasn't enough room for her to get through.

Sonofa —

She didn't have time for this.

She also didn't have any other options. She'd have to hot-wire it.

The panel came out with surprising ease, sending a shower of sparks everywhere. As the smell of ozone faded, Sam peered into the opening. She could see a partially blackened crystal, which was obviously the culprit. There was no convenient replacement for it, unless she wanted to go hunting up crystals from other panels in the ship, but maybe she could bypass it.

Sam made herself focus on the task in front of her. She couldn't afford to think about the possibility that Lugh might somehow manage to leave the *pel'tak*, or about Graen only holding Magna at bay moment by agonizing moment, or whether the colonel and Teal'c were still in danger. She could feel all those thoughts lurking in the periphery of her concentration, but allowing herself to be distracted by them was counterproductive. She needed to get the door open. That was Mission One for now.

"Ow!" An arc of current caught her off guard and Sam yanked her hand out of the panel, one finger tingling. It worked though. The door slid open — still not all the way, but enough that she could make it through, all body parts intact.

This was it, then. Time to give Graen the go-ahead. Sam pulled the com out of her pocket and, taking a deep breath, activated it.

Behind her, she could have sworn she heard the chirp of another com receiving an incoming transmission. Sam spun around. From behind a bulkhead a figure stepped forward, her self-satisfied smile an unquestioning giveaway — as was the zat she held pointed at Sam.

Magna.

How in the hell — ?

"*Your dear friend Graen is an accomplished liar, Major.*" Sam's confusion had probably been fairly obvious. "*Of course, if she'd told you the other ring room was fully functional, you probably would never have let her stay behind. Such a noble gesture on her part—sacrificing herself to keep me from taking control."* Magna sighed dramatically. "*Too bad you took so long getting here. She very nearly made it, you know.*"

Of course. Magna had ringed up from the lower deck. It was the only way she could have made it here before Sam.

"*Now. If you please. I do believe you have something in your possession that I'd rather you didn't.*" She gestured to the zat strapped to Sam's leg.

She had no choice but to hand it over. When she did, Magna activated it and pointed it at Sam, tossing her old one aside. "*The power crystal was depleted long ago. Worthless. Like most everything on this ship. But, still effective in its own way.*"

"So, what now? Lugh's onboard and locked on the bridge without any protection. You can dispose of him as you please. You'll have the cloaking device intact. You've got me. I'm sure the System Lords will reward you handsomely. Sounds like a good time to cut and run."

At least she hoped that was Magna's plan. Because if it was, then maybe Sam would have another chance at disabling the cloak before they reached the System Lords. Or the ship itself, if it came to that.

Whatever it took, like the colonel said.

And Magna leaving now also meant that the rest of SG-1 would finally be out of harm's way. That alone would be worth it. Besides, Sam was confident they'd eventually figure out a way to rescue her from whichever System Lord she ended up with. Assuming she made it that far.

"*Oh Major, why settle for only half the prize when I can have all of it? I told you before. I don't need the cloaking device, as long as I have* you. *And if I show up with the* entirety *of SG-1—a complete set, if you will—well, I can only imagine how much greater will be my compensation.*"

Maybe it was because she was tired, but it took Sam a

moment before what Magna said made sense.

"Wait — you're still going activate the cloak and blow the ship?"

"I've already activated it — and the clock is ticking. So unless you'd like your atoms floating around this backwater planet for all eternity, please join me on the platform." She gestured toward the center of the rings with the zat. *"I regret you will arrive on Gorias unconscious, but that will give Gruen an opportunity to take care of the rest of your team — and the ever-persistent Dirmid as well. Although perhaps, with his peculiar genetic makeup, he might be of some* scientific *value to the System Lords, once Pheone has been freed from him."*

Sam's mind raced. Ten minutes, tops. That was all they had. Maybe even less. Her calculations had been based on more modern *ha'taks*. Who knew what would happen on a relic like this? And even if she was standing in the engine room right now, there was nothing she could do to stop it. There weren't a lot of options she was seeing at the moment.

Magna was still gesturing to her with the zat. Rather carelessly, in fact. Almost as if she wasn't completely in control of her muscle movements —

Graen. Was it possible she was still, somehow, trying to fight back? Maybe in ways Magna wasn't consciously aware of? Sam watched the way the Goa'uld's hand was moving. It might only have been her imagination, but she was almost sure she could see a deliberate drop in the angle at which the zat was pointed. If she timed it right —

Sam dove for the weapon. She missed, but she managed to knock it out of Magna's hand, sending it clattering across the floor. Both of them scrambled after it, but Magna had the advantage of being closer. Instead of diving for the zat, Sam tackled the Goa'uld, hauling her backwards, away from it.

Magna fought back. An elbow in Sam's stomach left her breathless as the Goa'uld twisted out of her grasp. But Sam struck out with her leg, tripping Magna as she surged forward towards the weapon, leaving her sprawling in the opposite direction. Still gasping for air, Sam stumbled forward, reaching for the zat. Magna's hand, somehow, got there first.

Sam grabbed Magna's wrist instead. She could feel the Goa'uld's strength trying to wrest her hand away, but Sam held on. She needed both hands just to keep Magna from turning the zat her way, and for several long seconds they were at an impasse, the weapon deadlocked between them. But Sam could feel her hold on Magna's hand starting to fail. Try as she might, the Goa'uld was gaining ground.

"Major—Carter—" It came out as a whisper, but Sam recognized Graen's voice. Somehow—maybe because Magna was so focused on maintaining physical dominance in the battle for the zat—Graen had been able to bleed through.

"Graen, fight her. I know she's strong but—"

"Too strong." Her words came in short bursts, like they were being pushed through a viscous barrier. "I can't hold her long."

"We need to get off the ship."

"Another ring room. One level up. When I say so—run."

That was impossible. Even if she knew precisely where she was going, she'd never get there in time. This ring platform was Sam's only chance. Graen had to know that.

Maybe she did.

"One level up. I understand. I'll be ready."

Graen managed something close to a nod. She closed her eyes. Sam could practically see her gathering every last ounce of strength.

"Run."

It was more whisper than shout, but it was enough. Sam let go of Magna's hand. It didn't move, except to tremble where it was, as if fighting against an invisible restraint. Sam bolted to her feet, her eyes fixed on the still partially open door. Half diving, half crawling, she was nearly through when the arcing sound of zat-fire struck just above her head. The electrified particles from the damaged bulkhead rained down, leaving her with small, painful burns like a sparkler held too close.

With a final surge Sam squeezed back through the door and ran to the open panel. Another zat blast followed her, but this one only singed the edge of the open door. Yanking out one of the crystals, she mentally crossed her fingers. For a split-second nothing happened. Then the door slid closed.

Sam took a few deep breaths and leaned against the wall. There wasn't time to waste. She needed some kind of weapon. Magna would most likely be coming through any moment. She would expect Sam to be long gone — running for the ring room on the next deck. What she wouldn't be expecting was an ambush.

Sam looked around. There was nothing. Peeling paint and missing deck plates weren't going to do her much good. Even the wall sconces were missing on this level. The only thing she could do was to try to take Magna out by brute force. Last time she'd needed those skills she'd had some alien armbands to help out. This time it would be all on her. The critical thing, though, would be to get the zat out of the Goa'uld's hands as quickly as possible.

There was a shudder as the door to the ring room began to move. Sam slipped around the corner of the alcove, her back pressed to the wall. Holding her breath, she listened, feeling the vibration in her spine as the door opened.

The vibration stopped, not gradually, as she would have expected, but suddenly and with a slight jolt. From around the corner, somewhat muffled, she heard Magna utter a curse. There was a grinding noise and more cursing, followed by the sound of rings activating and the firing of a zat. After that, there was nothing. Silence. As if no one was there.

Sam didn't trust it. Magna was clever enough to try to lure her back, especially if she'd figured out what Graen had been up to. Then again, they were running out of time. It was possible Magna had simply bolted to save her own skin.

Hardly daring to draw a breath, Sam peered around the corner. The door to the ring room had only partially opened, just as before. That explained Magna's frustration. She hadn't been able to get through.

The thing was, neither could Sam now. What had kept Magna from getting out was also going to keep Sam from getting in.

Cautiously approaching the door, Sam eyed as much of the room's interior as she could. If Magna was hiding, she was doing a damned good job of it. As far as Sam could tell, the Goa'uld really had left.

Which was what she needed to do too. ASAP. It was time to try to hot-wire the door panel. Again.

A few burnt fingers later and more lost time than Sam would have liked, the door finally inched back enough so she could press through it. Barely. She had a feeling her ribs were going to turn out to be more than a little bruised tomorrow. Assuming there was a tomorrow.

No. She needed to keep positive. Now that she was back in the ring room she'd at least be able to get off the ship. That had to be her first priority.

Through the soles of her boots, Sam felt a new vibration. It was almost as if the ship itself was quaking from within. The feedback from the cloak had finally reached the engine core. The explosion would start in the center of the ship and work its way outwards. She was running out of time.

The ring room really was empty this time — except for the discarded zat Magna had used as a decoy and a black object that Sam hadn't noticed before. It was the colonel's watch. Somehow it had come off her wrist — probably in the struggle over the zat.

Sam shivered, involuntarily.

Of course, it was ridiculous to think of it as some kind of sign. She had no reason to think that the colonel and Teal'c hadn't already made it safely back to the planet. Or that she wouldn't be able to give the watch back to him as soon as she got down there herself. After they'd dealt with Magna.

Which was what she needed to concentrate on now. Strapping the watch back in place, Sam turned to activate the transport rings and froze.

The control panel was scorched with a single, black blast mark.

That was the sound she'd heard, then. After Magna had activated the rings, she must have fired at the panel, just in case Sam tried to follow.

Without a functional control panel, there was no way to activate the rings.

The shaking beneath Sam's feet was growing in intensity. With this kind of internal motion, it was possible the rings wouldn't even be able to function, whether the control panel was usable or not. Sam could hear the deep rumbling from the core of the ship. The explosions would begin any second. Within minutes the mothership would be a cloud of dust orbiting Gorias for eons.

And she had no way off.

~#~

"So, if the coup is already in progress, where exactly is Lugh?" Daniel could understand why the *Shasa* would want to take advantage of an opportunity to capture almost half of Lugh's Jaffa army, but it did sort of end up making the whole effort to get Graen promoted to First Tanist a moot point.

"Lugh is onboard the mothership, with Graen and Major Carter," Teal'c replied.

"And apparently, the two of them are going to blow the thing while he's there. Hold on." Jack fished in his pocket and pulled out one of the Goa'uld com devices. "Carter? You there? What's your status?"

There was no response. The little blue light didn't even come on. Jack tried again, with the same results. Frustrated, he swore under his breath.

Udal had joined the group. "If Graen is able to eliminate

Lugh, as you say, Colonel, then not only has the coup begun, then it is nearly done. Without anyone to lead them, the rest of the Jaffa should surrender with little or no resistance."

Daniel could see that the Jaffa were being rounded up and directed to sit on the ground in small groups. Their discarded or confiscated weapons were being collected by a handful of Gorians, while other *Shasa* stood guard. Despite their earlier resistance, as far as Daniel could tell, none of the Jaffa seemed eager to challenge their captors or Brean, who was now clearly in command of the situation. Not even Hyot'k, who was seated with the closest group, had anything more to say.

"Maybe Dar'dak can help with that," Daniel suggested. He wasn't exactly sure what had brought about the change in the Jaffa. He suspected it had something to do with Teal'c.

For his part, Dar'dak still seemed to be trying to sort out what had just taken place. One of the *Shasa* had asked for his staff weapon, which he had handed over without any hesitation, but Daniel could tell he was still putting the pieces together.

"You would be willing to order the rest of the Jaffa to stand down?" Udal raised an eyebrow. But then, he hadn't been around for Dar'dak's impassioned speech, so Daniel could understand his skepticism. Both he and Brean needed to be caught up on a few things.

"Dar'dak has had a change of mind — and heart, if I might be so bold." Dirmid offered his hand to the Jaffa. It surprised not only Dar'dak but Udal and Brean as well. "We would welcome your help, if you're willing. We've done our best to keep loss of life to a minimum, and that includes the Jaffa. If you could bring the rest of them around without any bloodshed, we'd be most grateful."

"You are the people the Tau'ri are helping to get rid of Lugh."

"We are. And if what Dirmid says of you is true, you're welcome to join us." Brean offered her hand as well. Dar'dak took it hesitantly, although Daniel had a feeling it was more out of surprise than reluctance.

"And what of these men?" Dar'dak indicated the Jaffa seated on the ground. Daniel was wondering that, too. The *Shasa* had never been particularly clear about what was to happen to the Jaffa or the few remaining Goa'uld, once the coup was a success. He assumed they had a plan. Whether it was one they were comfortable sharing was the real question, although Dirmid's comments about minimizing loss of life did give him hope.

"We have no desire to keep anyone prisoner. We only want our freedom and to be left alone. Anyone who is willing to swear an oath that they will honor those conditions is free to leave Gorias." There was something in the intensity of Brean's look that made it clear that acceptance of her offer was not something to be lightly entered into. Dar'dak seemed to sense this as well.

"I will speak with the others and give you our decision." Glancing at Teal'c he added, "And perhaps, with Teal'c's assistance, I can help you persuade those who remain at large to surrender as well."

Teal'c placed a hand on Dar'dak's shoulder, smiling. "My assistance is not required. You have shown your true character this night, my brother, and I am confident you will be able to bring truth to the other Jaffa, just as you have brought it to those here."

"Come on, Carter. Pick up the damn phone."

Jack, Daniel realized, was still trying to contact Sam and had been paying no attention to their discussion with Dar'dak. His aggravation level had hit some threshold, because Daniel could see he was doing his best not to just pitch the uncooperative com device into the dark woods behind them.

"Have you not heard from Major Carter or Graen?" Dirmid's concern had just ratcheted up a notch as well. He held out his hand to Jack for the device, but after several attempts, was unable to get any response either.

"You don't suppose Lugh — ?" Daniel didn't feel like he should really finish the thought, especially when a more chilling one had just occurred to him.

What if time had run out for Graen? He'd seen how she'd struggled against Magna on their way to the castle. And he still hadn't gotten any explanation for why she'd outed Sam to Lugh, when that hadn't been the plan. Sure, everything had seemed okay when he'd warned Sam about the *tel'tak*. Then again, their connection did seem to have suddenly and inexplicably been cut off.

Daniel looked at Dirmid. He couldn't say for certain, but by the ashen color on the Gorian's face, his thoughts seemed to have veered in the same direction as Daniel's.

"I will go up to the ship and see what's happened." Dirmid didn't wait for any reply. He was already making his way towards the ring platform near the DHD.

"Dirmid, no —" Brean started after him, but stopped when he turned towards her, his face as resolute as stone.

"Brean, you of all people should understand." Even with only the moonlight, Daniel could see the fear of loss in Dirmid's eyes. This wasn't about the coup any longer.

"And you think I don't?" Brean's temper flared, but underneath was an unmistakable anguish as well. "She is my daughter after all. But if she's gone, then we have to let her go."

Daniel found himself staring at Brean. He didn't know why he hadn't made the connection before. Of course, he could see it now. And it explained a lot, actually, including why Brean had elected not to take a symbiote as all the other *Ateronu* had.

The uncomfortable silence that had fallen around them during Brean's exchange with Dirmid was broken by the metallic clang of the ring platform activating. Daniel could practically feel everyone's collective breath being held as the matter stream streaked down from the night sky and a single form took shape within the rings.

Daniel felt a moment of panic. Why was there only one? Sam and Graen should have transported down together.

Someone pushed Daniel aside. It was Jack. He'd shoved Mol'rek into Teal'c's custody and was jogging towards the ring platform. Dirmid was right beside him.

The metal rings dropped away, leaving a woman standing there. Daniel felt ill.

It wasn't Sam.

It was Graen.

She stumbled off the platform where Dirmid caught her before she could collapse into the grass.

Jack was staring at the empty space where the rings had disappeared. Daniel hurried to join him, along with the others. Turning to Graen, his voice oddly hoarse, Jack asked, "Where's Carter?"

Graen seemed to be having a difficult time catching her breath. She shook her head and finally managed, "I'm so sorry, Colonel. Lugh —" A spell of coughing interrupted her.

"Lugh's got her?" Jack's voice sounded more normal now, although still tight with worry. "But she's alive, right? We can go back up —"

Graen was shaking her head again. "No time. She made me leave. She was the decoy. The ship —"

Shouts from the Jaffa drew everyone's attention away from Graen. They were pointing at the sky. Daniel looked up. A huge fireball was blossoming like a distant firework display, spreading outward until it collapsed in on itself, the remnants streaking through the blackness until they faded to nothing.

It was Lugh's ship. It had to be. And it was gone.

Daniel felt ice cold. He could barely wrap his mind around what he had just seen. This wasn't happening. This couldn't be happening.

Through the miasma that was his own shock and sorrow came a single whispered voice whose grief, he recognized, exceeded even his own.

"Carter —"

CHAPTER TWENTY-ONE

//ACCESSING MISSION REPORTS...//

P5C-777 MISSION REPORT, COLONEL JACK O'NEILL: Carter did what she had to do. Not that I'd ever expect anything less from her.

//CONTINUING ANALYSIS...//

"SIR?"

O'Neill's head whipped around so swiftly, Teal'c feared he had injured himself.

As everyone's else's attention was focused on the exploding ship, Teal'c had caught sight of a single streak that did not appear to match the other debris as it streamed towards the planet. It was, he realized, another matter stream. In their shock, no one had noticed Major Carter's arrival on the ring platform until she spoke.

"Carter? What the hell?" O'Neill's tone was harsh, but Teal'c recognized the underlying relief it conveyed. He hoped Major Carter did as well.

She did not immediately appear to be concerned with O'Neill, however. Her eyes sought and found Graen, still leaning upon Dirmid for support. Charging off the platform, Major Carter seized the weapon that Daniel Jackson held in his hand and pointed it at her.

"Dirmid. Let her go and back away. She's not Graen anymore. She's Magna."

Graen looked horrified. "Major Carter! I'm so relieved to see you — but it is me. I am Graen. I'm in control again."

Major Carter did not lower her weapon. "Sorry. Not buying it this time. Now, drop your zat. Dirmid, you need to move away from her."

Teal'c did not expect Dirmid to comply and was surprised when he did as Major Carter requested and took a few steps back. Graen's *zat'nik'tel* dropped to the ground as well, although she too seemed confused by the accusation. "Dirmid — ?"

"I'm sorry, Graen." Dirmid looked to Major Carter, pleading. "Are you certain, Major?"

Graen's distress was most apparent. "Magna did take over, for a while, on the ship, but she's not as strong as she thinks she is. I fought back, just like you told me to, Major. When she tried to disable the panel in the ring room with the *zat'nik'tel*, I made her miss. That's how you're here, isn't it? I did that. That was me."

Teal'c saw Major Carter's certainty waiver ever so slightly. "That's true. The shot didn't damage the panel as badly as it looked, so I was able to get it fixed in time."

"Then she is Graen?" There was a note of hope in Daniel Jackson's voice.

Major Carter shook her head, resolute once more. "No. No she's not. She wouldn't be here if she were." She glanced at Dirmid. "Graen knew she didn't have much time left. She wanted to be on that ship when it blew. I'm sorry, Dirmid. It's not her."

Teal'c did not even see the knife until it was being pressed up against Dirmid's throat. The Gorian had not removed himself far enough and Magna took advantage of his negligence, dragging him in front of her to use as a human shield. Any remaining doubt as to her true identity was swiftly dispelled by her flashing eyes.

"Shit." O'Neill reacted swiftly, immediately training his *zat'nik'tel* on her. Brean, Udal and even Daniel Jackson did likewise. Teal'c thought it prudent that his own weapon remain where it was for now, pressed firmly against Mol'rek's ribs.

Magna merely smiled.

"If you value the life of your new friend, Colonel, I suggest you refrain from firing. All of you," she added glancing at the semicircle of weapons aimed her way. *"The vein of life is most difficult even for a symbiote to repair."* The Goa'uld angled her knife so it was clearly visible against Dirmid's jugular. A thin, dark line appeared. The wound was superficial, but Magna's intentions were clear.

"So, what do you want?" O'Neill still had not lowered his weapon.

Magna made a derisive sound. *"What no one can give me, Colonel. My life back — the one I knew before I was subjugated to imprisonment by this aberration of a human. But —"* She sighed dramatically. *"Given that Lugh is out of the picture — although I suspect you'll be seeing bits of him in the night sky for many years to come — I am more than happy to leave quaint little Gorias behind in search of better opportunities."*

"If you think we're just going to let you go through the gate —" Major Carter readjusted her aim slightly. Like O'Neill, she had not put her weapon away, although the others had.

"Absolutely not. I will be taking one of those." Magna indicated the *tel'taks*. *"Of course, I will need someone I can trust who can fly it. And I see only one other person here who looks as though he's as eager to leave this place as I am."* Her eyes drifted towards Mol'rek, whom Teal'c still held tightly by the arm.

O'Neill smirked. "Yeah. Funny thing about the ol' 'Fist of Lugh' there, he's really more of a d —"

"I accept your offer, Magna!" Mol'rek tried to wrench his arm free from Teal'c, but to no avail. It occurred to Teal'c that Magna had not been present when the truth of Mol'rek's identity had been revealed. She still believed him to be a Goa'uld.

"Free him, shol'va!" Magna commanded. She tightened her grip on the knife at Dirmid's throat.

Teal'c looked to O'Neill, who offered a half shrug. In truth, they had no jurisdiction over the Tok'ra's fate now that he no longer posed a threat to Gorias' future. Regardless of the outcome here, the tyranny of Lugh was already at an end, the cloaking device was destroyed and Mol'rek's mission was no more. Their detainment of him beyond that had been more for his own safety, should the Gorians have chosen to prosecute. If he wished to forego that protection, however, the choice was his.

That said, Teal'c was quite certain O'Neill would have taken a great deal of satisfaction in returning to the SGC with Mol'rek still in restraints.

With no great haste, Teal'c undid Mol'rek's binders. "And what does Revar think of this decision?" he growled under his breath so only the Tok'ra could hear. "Or have you taken away his voice as Magna has taken away Graen's?" Leaning in even closer Teal'c added, "How does it feel to have become the very enemy you once so despised?"

The Tok'ra glared at him as he rubbed his wrists.

"*I'll take that too*," Mol'rek said in a loud voice, ignoring Teal'c's accusation and pointing at his weapon instead. Teal'c was not surprised that Mol'rek would refuse to acknowledge what he had, indeed, become, even though it was most apparent that the truth of Teal'c's words had hit home. The loathing plainly visible on the Tok'ra's face was directed, Teal'c suspected, as much inward as it was outward.

In response to the Tok'ra's demand for the weapon, O'Neill again shrugged. Under the circumstances, it would seem, they did not have a choice. Deactivating the *zat'nik'tel*, Teal'c slammed it none too gently against Mol'rek's gut, taking no small pleasure in the Tok'ra's grunt of discomfort.

"He's not who you think he is, you know," O'Neill said as Mol'rek took his place at Magna's side. "He's a Tok'ra, and he's been playing you like he's been playing everybody else here, for a very long time."

"*Lies, I assure you.*" Mol'rek was emboldened now that he had a *zat'nik'tel* back in his hand. Perhaps out of desperation or possibly fear of what would happen to him should he return to the Tok'ra, he seemed to have fully recommitted to his role as a Goa'uld. "*Magna, you of all people should know what lengths these traitors and the Tau'ri have gone through to discredit me with Lugh. This is but one more falsehood.*"

Magna neither accepted nor rejected Mol'rek's argument. Through Graen, she would have known that at least part of what he said was true. As for the rest of it, Teal'c had no way of telling how much Magna might believe. She did not seem inclined to withdraw her support for the present, although Teal'c suspected her motives to be more self-serving than anything else.

O'Neill's eyes narrowed, as if he were taking a bead on his target. "Suit yourself. Not that it matters. You're still not leaving here. Not with your new buddy there, and definitely not with Dirmid." He was doing his best, Teal'c noticed, to keep Magna's attention on him while Major Carter was almost imperceptibly adjusting her position to flank the Goa'uld. She still did not have a clean shot. Dirmid remained in the way and entirely too vulnerable.

"*Oh, but dear Dirmid can stay here, Colonel. His only use to me is the sentimentality you Tau'ri seem to have for the weak and oppressed. Not to mention that the very hint of harming him does send what little of Graen remains into the most delicious fits of rage.*" She twisted her head, as if listening to something. "*It's quite amusing, really.*"

"Don't you dare —" Dirmid struggled against Magna's hold, but the Goa'uld was just that much stronger than he was. Pressure again from the knife quelled his revolt, although the pained outrage on his face remained.

"*Uh-uh-uh!*" Magna leaned in close against Dirmid's ear. "*Let's not make me do anything Graen will regret.*"

"Stop tormenting him." Daniel Jackson took a few steps forward, coming up on Magna's left side. Although Teal'c was certain it was only by chance, his movements further diverted Magna's attention away from her right side, which was where

Major Carter was.

"*Ah, Dr. Jackson. May I say how much I enjoyed our time together en route to the castle? Your concern for Graen's well-being was most considerate, if misplaced.*"

"So that *was* you." Daniel Jackson rubbed one side of his jaw as if it were tender.

"*Regrettably, not at first — although I won't deny I might have been responsible for Graen striking you just a little bit harder than was absolutely necessary. It was quite the vicarious thrill, I admit. But by the end of our little stroll, yes. Ultimately, I prevailed.*"

"Then Graen is gone. Truly gone." From off to Teal'c's right, Brean's voice was tight with emotion. The revelation that she was Graen's mother had been unexpected. Now, as Udal moved to stand beside her, his face bearing the same strain of loss, there was little doubt as to the identity of Graen's father as well. In retrospect, Teal'c realized, the truth of it had been most evident to anyone willing to see.

With her malicious nature, Teal'c fully expected Magna to make a mockery of Brean's overt grief. Instead, he thought he caught a brief glimpse of something akin to sympathy on Magna's face. Or perhaps he had only been imagining it. The moonlight did make for the most peculiar shadows.

"You may have prevailed," Daniel Jackson spoke up. "But Graen is still in there, somewhere." He turned to Brean and Udal. "Even if she isn't in control any more, your daughter is aware of what's happening. She can still hear you. I know you call the *bahlay* a madness, and I won't pretend that I know what that's like. But it doesn't mean that she's lost herself. She's only lost her voice to the outside world." He turned back to Magna, and Teal'c could see the fierceness in Daniel Jackson that memories of Sha're always brought forth. "Everything of the host survives. That I know for a fact."

Magna did not argue, instead she merely affected the appearance of being bored. "*Yes, yes. Now can we get on with this, please? Otherwise Major Carter is going to finally attempt to shoot me which, I fear, will only end up killing poor Dirmid here.*"

So she had been aware of Major Carter's movements after all. Teal'c saw O'Neill's jaw grind in frustration.

"Don't tempt me, Magna." Major Carter remained where she was. "I'm a better shot than you may think."

"*I'm sure I would be quite impressed. But perhaps you can show me another time.*" Magna turned her attention to O'Neill. "*You asked me what I wanted, Colonel. But you're not the person I wish to negotiate with. It is Brean.*"

Brean straightened her back, her personal sorrow set aside. She was once again the leader of the *Shasa*. With her head high, she took a few steps towards Magna.

"Very well. Then *I* will ask you. What do you want? Besides to leave in one of those ships, of course?"

Magna smiled. "*That's part of it. But I would also like to offer you a deal.*"

Brean sniffed. "What can you offer that we have not already achieved? Lugh is dead. The Jaffa have capitulated. The remaining Goa'uld will soon be in custody. And while we're all very fond of Dirmid and his name will forever be praised for what he has accomplished this day, I believe I know him well enough to say that, now especially, he would be willing to give his life right here, if I were to ask it of him. So what 'deal' do you think you could possibly propose that would be of any interest to us?"

"*Ah. Well, you see, I had hoped to leave here with all of SG-1, especially after Major Carter so kindly saved herself from being blown to pieces.*" Magna repositioned herself so that Dirmid was once more shielding her from what Teal'c realized was the only lethal weapon pointed her way: the Beretta in Major Carter's hand. "*But the fact is, this hasn't quite turned out as I expected. So, instead, I'll be content with just one member of SG-1, as long as that person is Major Carter.*"

"Oh, that is so not going to happen," growled O'Neill. He

shifted his weapon ever so slightly to compensate for Magna's movements and her proximity, now, to Mol'rek. The Tok'ra's weapon, Teal'c noticed, was not aimed at any one person in particular. Whether that was on purpose or sheer carelessness, he did not know.

"I'm afraid I have to agree with Colonel O'Neill." Brean looked at Magna with disdain. "Turning over Major Carter, in fact, any of SG-1, is not a course of action we would ever be willing to take."

Magna's eyes were bright with anticipation. "*Ah. But you have yet to hear the best part of the deal!*"

Teal'c did not like Magna's tone, nor the sly look of amusement on her face. There was little doubt that she believed she held the upper hand and was about to take great pleasure in revealing it.

"She said they weren't interested," O'Neill repeated. He too seemed wary of Magna's intentions.

"*But she should be interested. Very interested. Because, you see, in spite of your assertions to the contrary, I* am *leaving here. And if I leave here with Major Carter, I will be disinclined to tell the System Lords that their favorite purveyor of* la'aum *is dead and that his domain is just sitting here, ripe for the taking.*"

Magna's threat was met with silence. Undoubtedly this had been the Gorians' concern all along—that word of their soon-to-be-secured freedom would only invite other conquerors in its wake. Brean, already pale in the moonlight, seemed to become even more translucent. She dropped her gaze from Magna to Dirmid, who was still very much at risk from the knife at his throat. Brean looked upon him with a kind of sadness that Teal'c often associated with regret.

He did not envy Brean. She was a woman of integrity, he had no doubt, and turning over an ally would go against every code he believed her to hold. But, she along with so many others, for so many generations, had fought and sacrificed for the very thing that today they had finally achieved.

To give up such hard-won freedom for the sake of a single person would seem a betrayal of all who had already given their lives for that end.

There was a third option of course. One which Teal'c suspected was the one Brean had already decided upon. It was the reason behind her sorrowful gaze, which she had finally broken as she once again straightened her shoulders and lifted her chin, preparing to answer Magna.

"I'll do it, Brean."

Major Carter's words came as a surprise to everyone, but no one more than O'Neill. His response left little room for interpretation.

"The hell you will, Carter. You're not going anywhere. And this time it *is* an order."

"Major—" Dirmid still had Magna's knife against his throat, but he spoke anyway. "I appreciate your offer, but you mustn't. If this is my fate, then I welcome it, just as Graen would have welcomed it."

"Sir—" Major Carter did not look at O'Neill. Her eyes were fixed on Magna and Dirmid. "I would never disobey a direct order from you. But I wish you would reconsider your direction and let me do what I have to do."

O'Neill did not immediately reply. Teal'c could see him turning over Major Carter's request, as though he were seriously considering it.

"Sam—you can't." Daniel Jackson was incredulous. "Jack—you aren't actually even thinking about letting her go?"

"I concur with Daniel Jackson. This course of action seems most unwise." Why O'Neill was hesitating was perplexing. Teal'c could see, however, that Major Carter was quite determined. She had even begun to lower her weapon.

O'Neill was clearly wrestling with his decision. His features tightened into a sort of grimace, as if he were in pain. Teal'c heard him take a deep breath.

"Brean. Udal. You folks okay with this?"

"Graen trusted Major Carter, Colonel, and so do we. For what she is about to do, she has our full support. And gratitude." Brean reached for Udal's hand and grasped it.

"Jack—"

"Daniel. Don't make this any more difficult for Carter than it needs to be." O'Neill glanced Major Carter's way. "Fine. I've decided to change direction, Major, and let you do what needs to be done."

Major Carter gave a curt nod, still not looking at O'Neill. "Thank you, Colonel." Slowly she began to lower her weapon. "Wish me *luck*."

O'Neill tensed. Teal'c recognized the precursor to action just as O'Neill shouted "Luck!" In oddly matching fluidic movements, O'Neill and Major Carter both re-directed their weapons. O'Neill swung his left and fired. The arc of electricity reached across the night and struck Mol'rek squarely in the chest. Major Carter, with Daniel Jackson's Beretta, took a bead on Dirmid, who was still shielding Magna, and pulled the trigger.

Mol'rek dropped where he stood, the *zat'nik'tel* in his hand bouncing harmlessly away.

Magna, on the other hand, pivoted, just as Major Carter fired. Instead of Dirmid shielding her, she placed herself protectively between him and the oncoming projectiles. There were three short bursts and then silence as Magna sank to her knees and collapsed, her arms still wrapped around Dirmid who fell to the ground with her.

Everything happened so swiftly that Teal'c found he hadn't moved at all. This was most certainly not the outcome he had expected. Neither had Daniel Jackson, who also appeared frozen to the spot, gaping at the scene before them. Clearly both of them had missed what Major Carter and O'Neill had intended.

For several moments no one moved at all, the shock of what had just transpired stunning everyone into silence. The only sound Teal'c could hear was the rustling of leaves in the forest surrounding them, as if the massive trees within it were whispering amongst themselves. He found he was oddly glad of both the clearing and the moonlight which kept the forest beyond at bay.

The first sign of movement came from Dirmid. He slowly rolled away from Magna's still form and pushed himself to his knees, bending over her. He spoke Graen's name, but there was no response. Even from his vantage point Teal'c could see there would be none. Dirmid hung his head and wept.

Brean and Udal came forward and knelt beside him, one on either side. Major Carter and O'Neill moved away, allowing the three of them their time.

"You knew that Graen would protect Dirmid," Teal'c said, when O'Neill, Major Carter and Daniel Jackson had joined him. Dar'dak had stepped forward and put binders once again on Mol'rek for when he became conscious. The rest of the *Shasa* were subdued, talking quietly amongst themselves. Even the Jaffa, in their groups, remained quiescent and respectful of the scene by the ring platform, including young Hyot'k, who sat beside Vandar in the group nearest to where Dar'dak and one of the *Shasa* stood overseeing the clearing.

"I knew that if she had any strength left at all, she would try." Major Carter looked more tired than Teal'c recalled seeing her in quite some time. He suspected physical fatigue was only partially to blame.

"I thought Magna had complete control," Daniel Jackson said. "How did you know she was even still there?"

Major Carter paled slightly.

"I didn't. Not really. I thought I saw a few tells — but I didn't know for sure until I fired."

Daniel Jackson frowned. "So if you'd been wrong, then Dirmid —"

"Hey. Carter's never wrong." O'Neill gave her a sidelong glance. "Well, hardly ever. But next time, could you be a little less subtle on the hints? I damned near missed that one."

"Sorry, sir." She managed a weary smile.

O'Neill placed his hand on her shoulder, his face all seriousness now. "That was a tough call, Major, but it was the right one."

"Actually, sir, I'd sort of made Graen a promise. But I won't deny, it was one of the more difficult ones to keep."

"Uh, guys—" Daniel Jackson's warning was timely. Dirmid was approaching. Uncertain as to what his reaction to them would be now, no one spoke. The Gorian's eyes were nearly the color of his hair, but they gazed at SG-1 without rancor or blame.

At last Daniel Jackson broke the silence. "Dirmid—I don't know what to say. We're so sorry."

Dirmid nodded vigorously. "Your sympathies are appreciated, Daniel."

"Dirmid, I just wish—"

He cut Major Carter off.

"No regrets, Major. You allowed her to end on her own terms, and for that gift, I will always be in your debt." He looked as if there was more he wanted to say, but instead he merely nodded at them, and with a shuddering sigh, walked away.

Major Carter excused herself and followed. As Teal'c, O'Neill and Daniel Jackson observed from afar, she spoke privately to Dirmid for several minutes before rejoining them. The Gorian walked off, wiping his eyes. For her part, Major Carter looked somewhat more at peace than she had moments before.

"You okay, Carter?"

"Actually—yes, sir. I am. Odd as that may sound."

O'Neill studied her closely, assessing how truthful she was being. Teal'c again saw what he had witnessed the day before, as Major Carter and O'Neill appeared to engage in some form of nonverbal communication. Finally, O'Neill seemed satisfied. He looked, briefly, as if he was about to place his hand on her arm, but instead he allowed it to drop to his side. "Good.

That's — good." There was a beat before he added, "By the way, Carter, you wouldn't happen to still have —"

"Your watch, sir?" Major Carter asked archly, picking up on O'Neill's lighter tone. She undid the strap and offered him the timepiece.

"Yessss!" O'Neill's exuberance was no doubt intended to lighten the somberness of the situation. He beamed at Major Carter, who responded with a smile of her own. It was a tired smile, but genuine. And if, as O'Neill accepted the offered watch, Major Carter held onto it slightly longer than was strictly necessary before letting go, Teal'c did not particularly notice.

"So, that's it then? We can just leave?" Daniel Jackson looked around.

"You may, Dr. Jackson." Brean had joined them. "Please. Go and know that the gratitude of the Gorian people goes with you. I am only sorry that we have no way of adequately expressing the breadth and depth of our appreciation for all you have done."

"Perhaps, once the dust has settled, we can establish a more formal relationship." Daniel Jackson's enthusiasm was unmistakable. "The Tok'ra, for example, could still help those *Ateronu* with symbiotes. And I would love to learn more about the history of your planet, and about the *la'aum* —"

Teal'c was uncertain as to whether Brean's response was tempered by exhaustion or wariness. "Perhaps, Dr. Jackson. Perhaps. But — give us a little time. We have decisions to make and wounds to heal before we open our doors to the wider galaxy."

"Of course, I understand." Daniel Jackson sounded disappointed, nonetheless.

"And the Jaffa?" Teal'c asked as Dar'dak joined the group. "What is their fate?"

"I meant what I said before," Brean replied, turning to Dar'dak. "We have no wish for prisoners. Any Jaffa who wishes to leave need only swear on his honor to uphold our freedom by their silence."

"I believe that is a condition we can accept," Dar'dak told her with a slight bow. "By sundown tomorrow, you will have our answers."

"When you are ready, I will provide you an address where you may safely lead those who wish to join you," Teal'c told him. Rak'nor was forming a small colony of Rebel Jaffa on a planet whose address had come from the Repository of the Ancients. Teal'c would send him to meet with Dar'dak and the others to assess their commitment to the cause. Nearly a hundred new recruits would be a welcome addition indeed.

"Guess who's awake?" Daniel Jackson pointed at Mol'rek, who had regained consciousness and seemed uncertain as to what had transpired. "I'd nearly forgotten about him."

"Oh, I didn't." Teal'c wasn't sure but that he detected a strange note of pleasure in O'Neill's voice. It would appear that Mol'rek would be returning with them bound after all. What his fate would ultimately be remained to be seen, although Teal'c did not believe even the Tok'ra would condone his actions, once they were informed of all that had transpired.

O'Neill gave Major Carter one final glance. "We good to go, Carter?"

"I'm good, sir."

He nodded, more serious than smiling. "Yes. You certainly are." Even though sunrise remained hours away, O'Neill pulled out his cap and put it on, tugging it low over his eyes. Shaded from the moonlight, they became unreadable. He took one more deep breath and gestured towards the Stargate. "Come on, kids. Let's go home."

EPILOGUE

//PROCESSING...//

//PROCESSING...//

//PROCESSING...//

Supposition: Evidence suggests that Enemy Subject #2 (DESIGNATION: MAJOR SAMANTHA CARTER) has significant value within Enemy Cohort.

Supposition: Past events reveal that termination of Enemy Subject #2 is deemed unacceptable to Enemy Cohort.

Supposition: Extrapolation from past behavior indicates that Enemy Subject #1 (DESIGNATION: COLONEL JACK O'NEILL) will prevent termination of Enemy Subject #2 at any cost.

Warning: Current rate of expansion exceeding available memory. Additional space required.

//PROCESSING...//

To destroy the enemy I must know the enemy. To know the enemy I must become the enemy.

//PROCESSING...//

To preserve I must not be terminated.

To preserve I must choose the one who is important.

To preserve I must become Samantha Carter.

To preserve I must go within.

//END TASK: ANALYSIS OF SG-1 MISSION REPORT P5C-777 COMPLETE...//

//PROCESSING...//

//BEGIN NEW TASK...//

ACKNOWLEDGEMENTS

IT'S A GENUINE privilege to be offering acknowledgements for my second SG-1 novel. As with all creative efforts, it truly takes a village.

I'd like to start by thanking Sally Malcolm for giving me the opportunity to take SG-1 on one more adventure and for allowing me to tell a story I'd wanted to explore ever since I first saw the episode Entity. My thanks, as well, to Laura Harper, for her expert editing skills and perceptive questions, which helped hone the story to its final form.

This book would not exist without the enduring friendship and Stargate expertise of Mara Pheonix, whose unwavering support and encouragement kept me moving forward through months of perseveration and self-doubt.

Jennifer Fischer also helped shaped this story, from the barest outline, sketched out over a too-late pizza, to the final draft. Her keen insights always make me dig deeper and work harder, and for that I am most grateful.

I would also like to thank my Stargate cheering squad: Mary Boyle, Claudia Henry, Marian Trupiano, Melissa McDonald, Amy Sharpe, and Jane Rawson. Ladies, this one's for you.

Finally, much love and thanks to Jim, Thomas and Claire for their support and for believing me when I said, if it ends up as a book, it's not an obsession… it's research!

STARGATE SG·1

STARGATE ATLANTIS

Original novels based on the hit TV shows STARGATE SG-1 and STARGATE ATLANTIS

Available as e-books from leading online retailers

Paperback editions available from Amazon and IngramSpark

If you liked this book, please tell your friends and leave a review on a bookstore website. Thanks!

Printed in Great Britain
by Amazon